THE ANDERSON FILES

Inspector Anderson Mysteries Omnibus

Published internationally by Best of Both Worlds, UK
Park Rd, Birmingham, UK

Digitally produced by Best of Both Worlds

Contents

The Eynhallow Enmity

An Inspector Anderson Mystery

Chapter One

Inspector Anderson hung his head out the Rover's window and hurled abuse at the policemen standing along the quayside. 'Oi, get that bloody van moved. Yes, you, you tit. The harbour needs to be clear, right!'

Anderson pulled his head back into the car. 'I hate the islands, Harrison.'

The sergeant, concentrating on finding a parking place, just smiled and nodded.

'Oh – what the bloody hell is he doing now?' Anderson leaned back out and bellowed again. 'Oi, you! Yes, you, with the whiskers. Get that van moved, dickhead!'

He slumped back in the seat, and his colleague gave another sympathetic smile. 'I think it's going to be a long day, sir.'

Anderson agreed with a sigh and took out a packet of tobacco. 'Go on, park it over there, will you?' He nodded to the corner of the quayside. 'Got to stretch my legs, my bloody arse is asleep.'

Harrison halted the yellow SD1, switched off the engine, and removed a packet of twenty cigarettes from his pocket. He waved them under Anderson's nose. 'Do you want a proper tab, sir?'

'Proper! You mean have a filter suck out the flavour? No chance.' He licked his roll-up together and popped it in his mouth.

Harrison shrugged and slid a filter tip into his teeth. 'So, who do you think is in charge, then?'

Anderson stared through the windscreen. 'Dunno, but I've got a funny feeling it might be the one I just called a dickhead.'

He sighed again and opened the door.

The wind welcomed him with a powerful gust, slamming the car door shut and biting into his nipples like a teething child. He tugged at his tie, pulling the taut knot a further inch below his top button, and let out a chesty hack, before spitting a mouthful of phlegm the colour of used engine oil on to the tarmac.

Anderson hated mornings, although he figured this one must be almost over. Four hours to get there, and he reckoned it would be another eight, at least, before he'd get to take his shoes off. His legs complained, so he stretched them to a protest of creaks and cracks. After reaching into his inside pocket, he removed a small bottle of pills, knocked a couple back, straightened his moustache with two stained fingers, and looked around.

The little fishing village seemed decent enough. Quaint in that way American tourists loved. Crab-pots and nets rested against the harbour master's office, two fishermen, complete with striped jerseys, sewed nets near the jetty – a scene straight out of Treasure Island – or so he imagined, he'd never read it.

Panda cars with the blue cross of Orkney on their doors dotted the perimeter road, while bobbies meandered around with their tall helmets clamped tight on their heads. The scene was a familiar one and he yawned, loosening his neck from side-to-side, before taking a lungful of sea air.

He winced.

If he couldn't get used to the smell, it would be a miserable couple of days. At least Tingwall had a pub, which they passed on the way in. Drab looking, perhaps, but it was a boozer, nonetheless.

Having found his matches, he tried unsuccessfully to light his roll-up. 'Cup your hands over this, will you, Harrison?'

The gangly sergeant, a cigarette burning in his mouth, cantered round the car. He cupped his hands over the inspector's roll-up. 'God, it's cold, sir.'

Anderson puffed out a cloud of blue smoke and nodded. He liked Harrison. A decent sort who didn't take things too seriously. Not that standing around in crowds could tell you much about a man. Harrison was new to Special Branch, promoted two weeks earlier for the Pope's visit – an event involving most of the Branch, and about the most boring two days Anderson could remember.

'Rather not be out here myself,' Anderson said, his cigarette drooping from his lips and bobbing up and down like a conductor's baton. 'But the super wanted your personal expertise out here.'

'Really?'

Anderson coughed a laugh. ''Course not – fat sod just wants to keep us busy. He's been feeling a bit jumpy this week.' He winced again, sucking hard and deep on his cigarette in a bid to mask the smell.

'How come? The Pope's back in Rome, ain't he?'

'Yes, but this conflict business ain't sitting easy with him.' He raised his voice over a screech of seagulls. 'I heard when someone told him the Argies invaded, he thought the Falklands was on our patch.'

Harrison laughed out a deep lungful of smoke, before taking a sniff of the sea air. He also winced, and dropped his half-smoked cigarette to the ground, stamping it out with a twist of the foot.

They both ducked.

A helicopter thundered overhead, its rotors chopping the air and the resulting downdraft adding to the already ferocious wind. Anderson remained stooped until it flew over the water towards a small island and finally disappeared in the mist.

He looked down at Harrison's wrist. 'What time is it?'

'It's gone eleven, why?'

'Well, go on find out who's in charge. The pub'll be open in an hour and I've got some bloody expenses to accrue.'

Detective Sergeant Tippwick certainly did not live up to the term Anderson first addressed him as. In fact, he found him a sharp man with a keen eye, rare for the islands. Although he did rather resemble an oversized garden gnome.

Below the neck he wore tweed, patched at the elbows, with trousers tucked into a pair of Wellington boots. But above the collar, a magnificent set of moustache and mutton chops covered most of his face, leaving only a weathered nose and thick bottom lip peeping out. Even his eyes lay hidden, covered by the overhanging brows, and bushy hair that resembled a mesh of copper wire.

Anderson admired the old-timer's face-furniture, almost as much as his adeptness as a copper. By sealing off the island, posting men on all ports, blocking the trunk road, and then calling in Special Branch, Tippwick proved a diligent man. It was just a shame his Orcadian shrill and lingering vowels were completely incomprehensible.

'Say again, will you?' Anderson asked, after Tippwick spat another load of trilled octaves at him. 'You were talking about this escaped lunatic?'

'There be more t'it than that, Inspector.' His voice sounded almost as high as the wind whistling around the quayside. 'Cannae say I've heard of anything like this happ'nin' around here, not since I was a wee bairn. One deid, and the patient has goon.'

Anderson looked at Harrison. 'Deid? Goon?'

'I think he said there's a body, sir.' Harrison began scribbling a few notes, using his back as a breaker to the wind.

'A body?' Anderson scratched his chin and pulled out a cigarette paper, only to lose it in the wind. 'So, did this nutter whack him then?'

The island detective turned to Harrison, his bushy eyebrows rising.

'The inspector wants to know if it was murder?'

'Cannae say, sir, isnae sign of a struggle. Should know more when the Fiscal's office been o'er, they're flying someone oot now.'

Anderson strained his ears trying to understand, but couldn't. Only ten miles north of the Scottish coast but he might as well be in another country. He looked to Harrison again.

'He doesn't know. Says they're waiting for the pathologist. That was probably him in the chopper.'

'So where is this asylum?' Anderson asked, still struggling to get a roll-up together.

The whiskered detective pointed to the small island peeping through the mist across the water. 'O'er Eynhallow.'

Anderson squinted at the island. 'Bit bloody remote, ain't it?'

'I suppose that's the idea, sir,' Harrison said, jotting another note.

'So how we meant to get over?'

'I think there's a ferry.' Harrison nodded to the quayside.

'Aye, ol' Riley will take you,' Tippwick added.

A car beeped and the three men stepped back. A black Mercedes with chrome trim pulled up with a squeal. An officer, cap tucked tightly under his arm, got out of the rear, and with military gusto, placed the cap on his head and marched over, revealing a set of all too perfect teeth.

'Are you from Special Branch?'

Anderson looked up from trying to roll his cigarette and instantly took a dislike to him. The pips on the man's sharply pressed uniform suggested he outranked them all, despite looking no older than Harrison. He knew the type, all brass and no balls. After reaching into his pocket with his free hand, he retrieved his wallet. 'Yes, sir, DI Anderson and this is DS Harrison.'

The chief constable waved away the warrant card. 'Yes, yes, I heard somebody called you in. Was it you, Tippwick?'

'Aye, sir.' The old detective twitched his whiskers. 'Thought it best in case we needed the ports closed.'

The chief's face stiffened. 'That won't be necessary will it, Inspector? It sounds like the patient has drowned, doesn't it, Tippwick?'

'Aye, mebbe, cannae say for sure though.'

'Well, it's more than likely. There was a storm last night and the local fishermen assure me the currents around Eynhallow are strong enough at the best of times – there are no boats on that the island, I've checked. He'll probably wash up on Rousay in a few days.'

Anderson turned his back to the wind, and to the chief constable, and finally managed to lick his roll-up together. The chief's accent offended him. Too English. He clipped his vowels and enunciated each word as if reading Hamlet on stage. A bit like the super's. Both men, no doubt, educated south of the border.

Anderson placed the cigarette in his mouth and turned back round. While he may have been outranked, he knew on certain matters, even chief constables couldn't overrule Special Branch's authority, and escaped lunatics were such cases.

'Well, that all depends,' Anderson said, his cigarette conducting his words again. He nodded to Tippwick. 'He says there's a body, well, that's going to complicate things. Can't have a psychopath running about. They're sending a shrink over from Inverness to assess it all; let's wait and see what he says.'

The chief bounced up and down on his heels while the wind lifted his tunic like a skirt. 'Quite right – yes, of course. So when's he due?'

'Probably coming over with the pathologist,' Harrison said.

'Well, we might as well have a look over the place while we're waiting,' Anderson said, finding enough of a lull in the wind to light his smoke. He flicked the match to the ground. 'Best to dot the *I*s and cross the *T*s, wouldn't you agree?'

He said it in an English accent and followed the words with a cloud of smoke that caused the chief constable to screw up his nose. 'Of course, of course. Well, I have a few things to attend to. But you will keep me informed, won't you?' He snapped his tunic straight, wheeled around and marched back to the car, slamming the door shut behind him.

'Who was that knob?' Anderson asked, jabbing his cigarette at the departing Mercedes.

'Chief Constable Tiernay,' Tippwick replied.

'Tit-head more like. Right, where's this ferryman?'

'They've told him to wait in the pub,' Harrison said.

'What? I don't want him pissed. You know I don't like boats. Do you think I just spent the trip from Thurso in the toilets because I was enjoying a crap? Go gee him up.'

'Nae worry, I'll git him.' Tippwick placed two fingers in his mouth and released a shrill whistle that caused both Harrison and Anderson to duck. 'Aye, Tavey!'

His voice carried right across the harbour. A constable at the other end turned around and cupped a hand to his ear.

'Go git ol' Riley. *Loupers* want o'er the island!'

Anderson narrowed his eyes and leaned over to Harrison. 'If he ever does that again, I'll bloody brain him, so help me!'

Moments later, a figure in yellow plastic ambled down the hill toward them. He looked old, like a lifer on parole – gaunt and haggard, with skin so leathery Anderson reckoned he could have lit a match on his face.

'Are you the ferryman?' he asked, staring at a bulbous nose, covered in threaded veins and glowing almost purple, like the end of something Anderson didn't want to think about.

'Aye, that I am,' the ferryman said, giving a toothless grin.

'Bloody hell, how old are you?' Anderson turned back Harrison. 'Isn't there anyone younger? He looks like he died in the night.'

Chapter Two

When he laid eyes on the dilapidated ferry, Anderson refused to step aboard.

Once painted in Orkney's red, blue and yellow, rust now covered almost every inch – the original colour only visible on rare flakes of paint. More barnacles than iron made up the hull and planks of wood made up the deck. It took some coaxing from Harrison, and the sight of the little pub opening up on the quayside, before Anderson agreed to board. They boarded the ferry on foot, Anderson, Harrison, and Tippwick, after the old ferryman assured them the hospital lay no more than a few minutes' walk off the boat.

Despite the pleasant morning and relatively still water, by the time the old ferry cleared the harbour, Anderson was on his hands and knees spewing over the gunwale. The swaying and rocking sent him giddy and made his stomach believe he'd drunk ten pints. Sea-spray soaked through his jacket, chilling his skin, and he retched up bile, his stomach having nothing else to give. Fortunately, after five minutes, the small and very flat isle cleared in the mist.

The swell looked treacherous. Waves crashed and spilled over the shallow cliffs, and the boat began rolling and pitching even more fiercely as they neared. Twice Anderson let out a yelp thinking they passed the point of no return, but both times the boat righted itself, the swell no match for the ferryman's seamanship.

A little jetty jutted from an inlet, and with his plastic hat poking from the cabin, the old ferryman pointed at it.

'Eynhallow!'

Anderson watched as the old man dashed from the cabin and hurled a mooring rope over the side. Then, with agility of someone a quarter his age, he followed it. A moment later the ramp at the bow came down, and he stood there, grinning his toothless smile.

Anderson crawled down the ramp and slumped on to the sodden timber at his feet, lying prostrate until Harrison and Tippwick helped him up.

After rolling a cigarette, taking another couple of his pills, and coughing up a mouthful of phlegm, Anderson felt the nausea begin to subside. He told the ferryman, under a hail of Glaswegian expletives, not to move the boat, and then they trampled off, over the sodden gorse and into the island.

Eynhallow Sound ran on either side with the rolling fields of Rousay and Mainland barely visible through the mist over each shoulder. No trees, rocks, or even shrubs dotted the island. Just gorse, heather and long grass, leaving them even more exposed to the harsh wind that blew unobstructed from the Arctic and straight through the flimsy polyester of Anderson's jacket. He walked briskly, hands in his pockets, cigarette poking from his mouth, like a penguin marching to the sea.

Ahead lay the jagged stonework of the asylum with the Fiscal's helicopter sitting beside it, the rotors still spinning. Anderson gave the helicopter a wide berth. He hated the things. He'd visited more than one chopper accident in the past and recognised the type too, a Puma. A large beast with an open sided-compartment and big enough to house several stretchers and crew. *Probably Shanghaied from mountain rescue,* he thought, judging by the red and grey livery.

Harrison appeared fascinated by it, peering through the compartment and waving to the pilot like a schoolboy on a field trip. Anderson shook his head, waiting for him to sate his curiosity, before the three of them trudged up the muddy field to the asylum.

Covered in cracks and crawling with vegetation, the hospital was ancient and decrepit. A monastery or abbey in a former life, parts now crumbled away with large pieces of masonry dotting the outer walls. Moss and lichen covered most of the building, while lesions of breeze-block peeped through the plasterwork.

'What a shit-hole!' Anderson said, as they approached through a thickening moat of mud and soil.

Tippwick walked ahead, having had the foresight to wear boots, while Anderson struggled behind, his shoes sinking into the thick clay. He began hopping and swearing, clutching Harrison's shoulder for support.

'Shhh, sir! There are nuns, about.'

'Nuns, what do you bloody mean, nuns?' He tried to kick mud from his sole, but only succeeded in kicking off his shoe.

'I told you,' Harrison said, propping up the inspector as he attempted to retrieve his loafer. 'The church owns the hospital and the sisters run it.'

'Sisters? I thought you meant that as in nurses. Bloody hell, Harrison, I hate nuns.'

'Sshh,' Harrison said again, releasing his shoulder and leaving Anderson to hobble the last few steps with only one shoe on.

This day just keeps getting better, Anderson thought, as he managed to make it to the modern fire door sitting under the Gothic architraves. He leaned against it, placing his shoe back over his sodden sock.

He could see footprints all through the muddy drive, and he doubted forensics would have much luck tracing the escapee. Not his problem, he wanted to get the day done, have a skin-full, and get back to civilisation. 'You got someone here, Tip-top?'

Tippwick was stamping his boots on the concrete steps. 'Aye, a constable. He'll be inside.'

'Shall we get in then, it's bloody cold,' Harrison said. He wore his thick anorak, having made a fuss about retrieving it before they boarded the ferry, but he still shivered. 'You not cold, sir?'

'Cold? It ain't cold, I was brought up on the Gorbals, man – didn't own a coat till I was twenty. Don't that wife of yours feed you properly?' He slapped Tippwick on the back. 'Right, c'mon best go find your plod before the sergeant here gets pneumonia.'

Daubed in National Health Service green and littered with public information posters a decade old, the reception proved little improvement to the exterior.

Tippwick's constable was leaning on the counter drinking tea, a china teapot and his domed helmet in front of him. He straightened to attention as the trio tumbled through the doors like rugby players entering a pub.

'At ease, Constable Rowland,' Tippwick said, shrugging the cold from his shoulders. 'These gent'men are from Special Branch, they've just come o'er for a look around.'

The constable placed his tea on the counter and smiled. Clean-shaven and acne-ridden, the boy looked to Anderson as if he should have still been in short trousers, not in a copper's uniform.

'How do you do,' Harrison said, as Anderson stood gawping at the pimples and fresh face. 'I'm DS Harrison, and this is Inspector Anderson.'

'Thanks for coming,' Rowland said, nervously. 'It's a wee bit out of our experience, this one.'

'So's the eleven plus, I bet,' Anderson said, shaking his head at the youngster.

'Would you gentlemen like a cup of tea?' added a shrill voice.

Bewildered, Anderson shot his head around the room but couldn't find its owner, until a tiny hand rose from above the counter and grabbed hold of the teapot.

He stepped forward, leaned over the counter and saw the shortest woman he'd ever laid eyes on. Not a dwarf, the long fingers and protruding chin were too elongated and nimble, but she stood not more than a yard tall, and wore what he thought was a nurse's cap and gown.

She slid from behind the counter, a cup and saucer in her hands, which she proceeded to wave at Harrison. 'Tea?'

'Er – no thank you, Sister,' Harrison said, quite reverentially.

Anderson shot a look back at her. Sure enough, sat on her head and partly hidden by her foaming blue-rinsed hair, a nun's wimple, not a nurse's cap. It wobbled like a seagull settling down on a nest as she shuffled toward him and offered the cup and saucer like a treasured gift.

'Would you like tea?'

He backed away, seeing the hem of her black habit peeping beneath what he now realised was a white towelling dressing gown. She wore slippers too, slip-ons that left her gnarled toes sticking out. He looked across at Rowland and mouthed the words: 'Who's she?'

'Sister Mary here, was just telling me about the victim,' Rowland said. 'At least we think he's a victim, cannae really tell.'

Having no luck with Anderson, the sister thrust the cup and saucer back at Harrison. 'You sure you wouldn't like tea?'

'No thank you, ma'am.'

'What do you mean, who was he?' Anderson asked, a wary eye on the little nun.

Rowland pulled out his notepad. 'A Barney McTosh, in his late forties, found at four this morning outside the patient's empty cell.'

'And the patient?'

Rowland flicked through a couple more pages. 'A Michael Skye. Been here ten years.'

'The forensic lads have been and they cannae find any signs of a tussle,' Tippwick added.

'So who found him?' Anderson asked.

'The administrator, Sister McRowen.' Rowland replied.

'And is the body still here?'

'Yes, sir. Although, I think they'll move it now the pathologist has arrived. Oh, and a psychiatrist has come with him. She's waiting with Sister McRowen.'

'She?'

'Yes, sir.'

Anderson shook his head. 'That's all I need.'

'Do you want to speak to her first?' Harrison asked, waving away Sister Mary, who still persisted in thrusting the cup of tea at him. 'Er, I said no thank you, ma'am.'

'No, let's go and take a look at this body.'

Chapter Three

When Ruth first put her name down as a consultant for the police, she thought they'd use her skills to profile serial killers and sociopaths. In reality, she spent most of her time sitting in interviews as police officers bullied information out of psychiatric patients, or prosecution lawyers tried to convince her of their sanity.

She'd decided to give up the work – it didn't pay well and few officers ever listened to her. But when Dr Barry slapped this job on her desk that morning, stressing what an exciting prospect it looked, she took it. His wife must have agreed to give them another go. Ruth might be stupid, but she was no fool, and Gerard Barry couldn't have picked anywhere more remote to be rid of her.

Not only remote, the asylum was also a disgrace. Ruth had visited all sorts of psychiatric hospitals, from former workhouses, to modern facilities like Carstairs, but even the worst of them, and she'd been in some shocking places, were like the Savoy compared to Eynhallow.

The building, while in dire need of repair, both inside and out, was only part of the problem. The hospital had no permanent psychiatric resident, just Sister McRowen, whose diploma indicated she earned some qualification, but Ruth doubted she kept abreast of modern treatments. All *thorazine* and shock therapy. That didn't surprise her. Places like Eynhallow kept the prisons free. A rug to sweep away society's embarrassments.

Ruth knew she should care, especially after what her father

went through, and a few years earlier she would have written to the local MP, made complaints to the Royal College and demanded changes. After five years in the mental health care system, she no longer had the energy. Nothing ever came of her complaints, anyway. She'd long since resigned herself to the *status quo*, spending most of her working life chasing doctors in a vain hope sleeping with the right one might just get her a decent residency somewhere. It never did. She thought taking police work would boost her CV, something to get her a job at one of the big facilities. Well, that was the plan. So far, nothing even halfway promising had cropped up.

Now, after coming all this way, it sounded as if the escaped patient had drowned, making the trip a complete waste of her time. At least she got to ride in a helicopter. Something to remember.

She stifled a yawn as the sister began explaining the situation.

'So you see, Doctor, it appears he may have tried to swim.' She spoke in the local shrill accent. 'Must have drowned in the Sound.'

Sister McRowen could have been anything from thirty-five to fifty; without make-up Ruth found it hard to tell. And while she wore a doctor's coat, which along with the clipboard made her look every bit the austere and efficient psychiatrist, a curly wimple sat perched on her head and a silver crucifix hung around her neck.

The office felt a bit more professional, though, and similar to Ruth's in Inverness. Small, cramped and littered with psychiatry books and journals. The sister even hung her diploma on the same place behind her head. Except, Ruth didn't have a large crucifix next to hers, nor a Bible on the desk. But then she doubted the sister's drawer contained a bottle of vodka or a pair of dirty knickers.

'I see, and are these his notes?' Ruth nodded to a folder on the desk, before picking it up and flicking through the contents.

They made vague reading. Normally case notes bulged, especially for long-term criminal patients, but the sparse papers consisted mostly of recent medication reports, and only a few brief snippets of the patient's case history. In fact, after reading them, all she really knew about the patient was the date of incarceration, and his name, Michael Skye.

'As you can see,' Sister McRowen said. 'We have little to work with here.'

'I'm amazed, it doesn't even mention what his condition is. What's his diagnosis?'

'A severe form of psychosis, schizophrenia related.'

'And his history, do you know about Michael's past?' She flicked through the papers but found nothing of any relevance.

'No, he came from the courts; that's all I know.'

'You must know something else?' snapped Ruth. 'He's your patient.'

'He was Dr Franchard's patient,' McRowen said, lifting up her spectacles and rubbing her nose. The impressions from the glasses looked red and deep.

'Who?'

'The previous resident, he passed away last year. Michael was his patient, and I'm afraid the doctor wisnae good at keeping records.'

She could say that again. 'Well, what was he sectioned for?

You must have some idea?'

'All I know was that he came from a care-home. Someone it seems got hurt.'

'Home, so he was an orphan?'

'Sadly a large number of our patients have had a similar start.'

Ruth noticed the court order date – July, seventy-one. He'd been there a decade, and that's all she'd bothered to learn! 'He must have been up for release soon,' she said, still flicking through the papers. 'Why would he relapse now?'

'I'm afraid I wouldn't know.'

'But did anything recently happen to upset him?'

McRowen pulled off her spectacles again and dropped them carelessly on the desk. 'He became unsettled yesterday afternoon. We had to restrain him.'

'Unsettled, why, what happened?'

'Nothing happened. He was watching television when he began getting agitated. Barney had to take him back downstairs.' She bowed her head. 'He was the orderly who sadly passed last night.'

'I still don't understand,' Ruth said, scanning the vague paperwork. 'Look, it says here he was up for a review this month, he could have been released.'

'I doubt that.'

Ruth wanted to ask what she meant, but following a brief tap on the door, a tiny woman shuffled in wearing a dressing gown and carrying two hot cups of tea on a tray. The woman could have passed for a child, Ruth thought, if not for the craggy face and blue-rinsed hair.

'Now, I have given you two sugars, Doctor,' the little nun said in a high-pitched trill. 'I hope that's all right?'

'Erm ... that's fine,' Ruth lied, taking the cup and saucer and trying not to look shocked by her size. She took a sip of the tea and winced. It tasted like syrup.

'There are more police gentlemen downstairs, Sister,' the little nun said. 'And the pathologist is here.'

McRowen smiled. 'Thank you, Sister Mary. I shall attend to them shortly; away to your duties now.'

'As you wish, Sister.' The tiny nun crossed herself and departed, one hand holding the wimple to her head, the other clutching the empty tray.

McRowen took a sip of her tea before placing it on the desk. 'I'm afraid there was never any question of Michael ever being released.'

Ruth stared straight into her cold, grey, dull eyes, which had veins in the corners like tiny cobwebs. 'I don't understand. That wouldn't be your decision, Sister. He is, I mean was, under a section order. The court would have decided.'

'He was far too dangerous to be even considered. We should look to this incident as a blessing.'

'Blessing!' Ruth placed her palms on the desk and leaned forward. 'Two people are dead, including one of your patients. You should be – ashamed of yourself.'

'How dare you!' McRowen was close enough for Ruth to smell the tea on her breath. 'We do our best here. We still haven't had a replacement resident since Dr Franchard died.' She prodded the file in Ruth's hand. 'We had no help from the Royal College, and Michael's condition required considerable attention.'

'Why, what was so special about him?'

McRowen leaned back and rubbed her eyes again. She looked like a woman who needed sleep. 'It was only a matter of time before something like this happened. I have written for assistance several times.'

'What do you mean?' Ruth eyed her suspiciously, studying her cold features. McRowen sounded relieved, even thankful he'd gone. *She couldn't have, could she?*

'How did Michael get out?' Ruth asked.

'I beg your pardon?' McRowen placed her spectacles back on.

'I said how did he get out of his room?'

'What are you insinuating? I hope you don't think –'

'I wasn't insinuating anything, but after what you've just said, you can't blame me for thinking –'

McRowen slapped her hand on the desk and pointed a bitten nail at Ruth. 'How dare you! I was merely pointing out the tremendous strain we are under. And you have the audacity to come here with accusations of –'

'I wasn't accusing anybody, I just –'

'– I'm afraid I'm going to have to ask you to leave, Doctor.' McRowen stood up and pointed to the door. 'Unless there's anything else you wish to accuse me of?'

Ruth stood, her stare still fastened on McRowen's grey eyes. Neither woman spoke nor altered their gaze for what seemed an age. Eventually, Ruth bent down, scooped up her bag, and slammed the door shut behind her.

'Bitch!'

Chapter Four

Most of the patients had been confined to their rooms, but a few still shuffled around the corridors leering at the four policemen marching through the hospital. Anderson hated the place, it stunk of piss and sick, and to him, the patients all looked stoned. They shambled around wearing the same green smocks and hang-dog look, either grimacing or dribbling as the sisters and orderlies corralled them back into their rooms.

A recreation hall ran along the corridor, where a few patients sat watching a black and white television set playing almost silently on the back wall. They sat motionless, staring at it with the same sallow skin and droop to the eyes. Except one, who rocked aimlessly back on forth on his plastic chair and glared at the detectives.

Anderson shot him a dirty look, and almost bumped into an elderly woman in the hallway supporting herself on a *Zimmer* frame. Apart from a few wisps of hair, her head was bald, and she grinned a gummy smile. She started giggling like a child, reached down and pulled up her green smock to reveal a pair of varicose thighs and greying hirsute pubis. Revolted at the sight, Anderson increased his stride, leaving the old woman cackling behind him. 'It's Bedlam, Harrison. Bloody Bedlam!'

Harrison chuckled, and they carried on to the end of the corridor where Rowland halted at an old iron elevator. A mixture of rust and green paint, it didn't look safe, and Anderson pulled at the lattice gate causing a reverberating clang. 'Are there no stairs?'

'Not to the secure ward, sir,' Rowland said, nodding to a bricked-up archway behind the iron lift. 'Stairs were blocked-up in the sixties. Unsafe because of the damp in the basement – so the sister says.' He pulled open the lift's gate.

'So our escaped lunatic would have used this too?' Anderson asked.

'Aye, sir, and there is only one-way oot,' Tippwick said.

'And nobody on night duty?' Harrison asked.

'No, the sisters don't see the need, there is no way off the island, other than the ferry,' Rowland said, stepping into the lift car. 'Sorry, will be a wee bit of a squeeze.'

Anderson baulked as the others boarded, placing just one foot inside. 'You sure it's safe?'

'Just get in, sir,' Harrison said.

He stepped in, reluctantly, feeling the car swaying as he rested his weight inside. Rowland shut the grille and they descended. After a moment's clanking of wrought iron, a jolt and a clang, they reached the basement, where Rowland reopened the gate.

The taste of damp stuck to the back of Anderson's throat as he stepped out. A gloomy place, only three or four of the florescent lights on the ceiling worked, and one of those flickered nauseatingly. Colder than the ward above, the lack of paint on the bare brickwork made it feel even more frigid.

'Bit creepy, ain't it?' Harrison said, zipping up his anorak.

'Aye, stinks too, like the toilets at the Collier's Arms,' Anderson said, between sniffs.

Police tape covered a darkened passage ahead and Rowland ducked underneath, holding the tape aloft for Tippwick and the two Special Branch officers. 'He's just down here, sir.'

Anderson began rolling a smoke before following Tippwick and Harrison under the tape, stepping carefully on the uneven flagstones as he went. Metal doors ran along both sides of the passage, all fitted with secure bolts and spy holes, but most lay ajar. 'Aren't there any other patients down here?'

'No, wisnae others down here,' Tippwick said. 'Patient kept all alone he was.'

A sheeted figure lay on the flagstones ahead and Tippwick stopped before it. Anderson saw a few chalk marks on the floor. 'You had the scene of crime lot in, then?'

'Aye, sir.' Tippwick said, crouching down to remove the sheet. 'Waiting for the pathologist t' take him now – Fiscal's been informed.'

Anderson nodded, having begun to decipher some of his accent. He lit his smoke before looking down. 'Bloody hell, he's black!'

'Aye, sir.' Tippwick held the sheet away from the man's head. The dark face and big white eyes stared up vacantly. 'Lives with his mother and father in Dounby.'

'They're black too,' Rowland added.

'Well, they bloody would be, wouldn't they?' Anderson snapped. 'Mind you, not many *jungle bunnies* in this part of the world.'

'Ahem, I think we have to call them coloured now, sir.'

'I'll call him what I bloody like, Harrison, he ain't gonna mind.' He knelt and peered at the dead man. Lifting the sheet, he scanned down the length of the body.

Barney, a thickset man with a bushy moustache and balding

head, lay face up and virtually straight across the corridor. His toes pointed toward an open cell door, but Anderson could tell his head had missed the wall, as the plaster remained unmarked, as did the man's scalp, with no lumps of lesions visible anywhere else, either. 'Don't seem to be much wrong with him?'

'No, sir. But here, look.' Tippwick carefully lifted Barney's arm and revealed a small black truncheon lying freely from its holder under the large man's forearm. He gave Anderson a knowing nod.

'Aye,' Anderson said, the baton taking him back to his beat days. 'Must have had it out. Any keys?'

Tippwick shook his head. 'No, sir, patient must have taken them – would have needed them t' get oot.'

Anderson stroked his chin and stood up, the cigarette still clenched in his lips and the ash protruding half an inch from it. His head twitched down the corridor as the iron lift began clanging again.

'Must be the pathologist,' Rowland said.

Anderson nodded and stepped over the body. 'Is this the patient's room?'

'Yes, sir.'

He walked in. The cold and sparseness reminded him of the cells at Inverness station, except for the stained and picked foam covering the lower parts of the walls. No window, no posters on the wall, just a fluorescent light rebounding off the NHS paint, bathing everything in a sickly hue.

'Don't get much do they? If the *clink* looked like this there'd be bloody riots.' A handful of books lay on the bedside table. He picked one up. A dog-eared and stained prayer book. 'And this is how it was all found?'

'Aye.'

'Was it unlocked?'

'Yes, sir. Everything's exactly how we found it.'

Anderson stubbed his cigarette out on the sole of his shoe and placed the nub in his pocket. He put the prayer book back and stepped back outside. 'Begs the question, why the door was opened in the first place?'

'He looks quite frightened to me.' Harrison said, pointing to Barney's face. 'Could've been attacked.'

The lips were pulled back in a grimace, almost comically, revealing a perfect set of white teeth. 'You're right,' Anderson said. 'Does look like someone put the frighteners on him.'

'Could be a heart attack!' The words came from down the corridor.

Anderson watched as a portly outline, drooping under the weight of a medical case, walked toward them. He recognised the silhouette long before the man stepped under the light. 'I didn't think you did the islands, Phelps?'

The man smiled as the flickering tubes in the corridor revealed his obvious toupee and oversized spectacles hanging around his neck by a gold chain. 'Inspector Anderson! How are you?' Dr Phelps thrust the arm of his tweed jacket at him. 'I'm ruddy everywhere now, since the Fiscal got that chopper.'

Anderson shook his hand and gave him a warm pat across the shoulder. 'Been a while.'

'Yes, Lomand wasn't it?' He moved his bag aside as two of his colleagues, dressed in white overalls, walked up behind. They carried a stretcher and he nodded for them to place it on the ground.

'You know Sergeant Harrison, don't you?' Anderson said.

'Ah, Inverness CID, aren't you?' Phelps shook Harrison's hand.

'Not anymore. Special Branch now,' Harrison said, with a proud grin across his face.

'Still on probation,' Anderson reminded him.

'Good, then you still have time to change your mind.' Phelps sounded a little too sincere, but Anderson let it slide.

'And this is PC Rowland and DS Tippwick,' Harrison added.

Phelps raised his eyebrows at Rowland. 'They're getting ruddy younger by the day.' He shook his head and plonked his case on the floor, before stretching his back and looking down at Barney. 'So, what we got?'

'Seems simple enough,' Anderson said, feeling confident with his conclusions. 'Nutter rushed him last night before taking a swim for it. Don't look like a mark on him, though. You could be right about his ticker.'

'Best have a look over, then.' Phelps knelt and probed around the man's neck. 'Hmmm, yep. Looks like a heart attack, all right.' He took a wooden stick from his pocket. 'Can't say for sure until I've done the postmortem, but it looks obvious to me.'

He lifted the man's top lip with the stick. 'See the way the gums are exposed?' He continued to probe around the dead man's head. 'And no obvious bashes to the *bonce*?'

Anderson shook his head.

Phelps shrugged. 'Looks like too much rice and peas, or whatever it is they ruddy eat – I'll know more when I do the postmortem.'

'Any idea when that'll be, Doctor?' Harrison was taking notes, furiously.

Phelps scratched his head. 'Be tomorrow at the earliest. We're backed-up with bikers – all this damned bad weather.'

'But you disnae reckon it's murder?' Tippwick asked.

'It'll depend on the type of heart attack I suppose, could have been triggered in a scuffle, I'll know more after the –'

'– After the postmortem, we know,' Anderson said, moving aside and allowing the medics to load Barney on to the stretcher. 'All right, we'll leave you to it. Let me know if anything turns up.'

Phelps began supervising the medics as Anderson slapped Tippwick around the shoulders. 'Right, we're going to go and talk to that shrink.' He nodded down to Barney. 'If he wakes up, let me know.'

'So what do you think?' Harrison asked, once he and Anderson were out of earshot.

'Seems open and shut, to me,' Anderson said, holding a lump of shag in his fingers and spilling most of it on the floor. 'Whether there was a scuffle or not, makes no difference to us. The *mental's* drowned. No need to close the ports or do anything stupid.' He nodded back to Tippwick. 'Let's leave it to that lot to sort out.'

'Back to Inverness, then?'

'Whoa, let's not be too hasty, we might be able to milk a couple of days out of this.' He clapped his colleague cheerily on the shoulder before pulling open the gate to the lift. 'C'mon, let's find this shrink. The pub's open.'

Chapter Five

Ruth stood in the corridor not knowing where to go next when the clanking of wrought iron and the rattle of the gate turned her head to the lift.

Two men stepped out. One balding and middle-aged, with a drooping moustache and worry lines that looked like a plough made them. The other, younger and more handsome, albeit lankier, bounced behind in a suit straight off the rack from *Burtons*.

The older man walked up and stopped. He looked Ruth up and down, lingering distastefully on her chest, and said: 'Are you the shrink?'

She stepped back. He stunk of stale cigarettes and sweat. 'Yes, Dr Ruth Duncan.' She held out her hand.

He ignored it. 'You've spoke to this administrator, then?'

'Er, yes. Are you the Special Branch detectives?'

'Yes, ma'am,' said the younger man, thrusting out his hand and smiling warmly. 'DS Harrison, this is DI Anderson.'

'Nice to meet you,' She said, taking his hand. He had a wispy attempt at a moustache on his lip, in a similar shape to the inspector's. *He would be quite handsome if he shaved it off*, Ruth thought. Bit too tall for her though, and she doubted he possessed a Diner's Club card or a Mercedes like Dr Barry. 'So, have you established how the patient got out, yet?'

'Give us chance, we've only just bloody got here,' Anderson snapped.

'Not yet,' Harrison said, still smiling at her.

She smiled back but spotted the ring on his left hand, realising he at least shared one similarity with Gerard Barry.

'Doesn't seem too complicated though,' Harrison added. 'We think the orderly had a heart attack and the patient just walked out.'

Ruth nodded back to the sister's office and lowered her voice. 'I think you need to speak to that Sister McRowen. She's hiding something.'

The two men stared at her. The inspector, licking a rolled up cigarette closed, frowned, while Harrison screwed up his eyebrows. 'What do you mean?' he asked.

'I'm not sure, but she seems pretty happy he's gone. I think she could have left his door unlocked or something.'

'And why would she do that?' Anderson said, sparking a match and blowing a cloud of smoke over Ruth.

She coughed and wafted away the fug. 'I don't know but she said it was a blessing he had gone.'

'Well, best go arrest her then. You'd better get your cuffs, Harrison.'

Ruth glowered at him. 'You're not taking me seriously!'

'Really, am I not? Listen sugar-tits, I'm pretty sure you've got all this wrapped up but perhaps you should leave the police work to those of us that are, you know, paid to bloody do it.'

'But what if she did let him out, knowing he would try to swim for it? That would be murder, wouldn't it?'

'Manslaughter probably,' Harrison suggested. 'Do you really think she did?'

Ruth shrugged and bit her lip. She couldn't be sure, and now with the arrogant, old detective sneering at her she regretted saying anything. 'Perhaps – I don't know – but it's worth looking into, surely?'

Anderson laughed. 'And how did she disable that big black sod downstairs then, spike his tea?'

What an arsehole, she thought. 'I'm just telling you what she said, Inspector.'

'It could be worth making sure Phelps runs a toxicology.'

'Shut-up, Harrison,' Anderson snapped, poking his cigarette at the sergeant. 'It's all piss in the wind. Listen, if you are so clever, Miss Marple, perhaps you can enlighten me as to what to expect if this nutcase *did* somehow manage to get off the island.'

'What do you mean?'

'I mean what's wrong with him, apart from being three stops beyond Barking? You know, the reason we called you out in the first place?'

She hated when people spoke about the mentally ill in such a way. It showed ignorance and bigotry – two things Inspector Anderson appeared to know all about. Pig. 'He suffers from a severe and enduring mental illness. Will that do, Inspector?'

'Not quite, is he the kind of mental that likes to eat his own shit, or is he the kind that likes to smash in people's skulls?' Smoke seeped from his mouth with the words.

She glared at him. 'Neither, he's a paranoid schizophrenic and vulnerable to severe mood swings.'

'Sounds like a shit-eater to me, Harrison.' Anderson sniffed down a throat-full of phlegm. 'So what was he convicted for?'

She shook her head. 'Er ... I don't know.'

'You don't know!' He jabbed his spindly cigarette at her. 'That's bloody rich. You seem to know how to do my job well enough. So, we don't even know if he's a killer or a kiddie fiddler? Please tell me, then, what's the bloody point of you being here?'

'It's not my fault, there was a lot of stuff missing from his notes, and Sister McRowen –'

'– Well, perhaps you should bloody well find it out!' He flicked his cigarette to the floor and it bounced off her feet. 'C'mon Harrison, let's go speak to this nun and get to the pub.'

He barged past her. Harrison, a sympathetic smile across his face, followed. They knocked on McRowen's door and walked in.

'Wanker!' Ruth said aloud, before wondering exactly how she was going to get off the island.

Chapter Six

'So what do you think is going on?' Tom Cairns paid little attention to the old woman. She phoned most days. Normally with just small-island tittle-tattle. A stolen fishing net the cause yesterday, and she'd been on to him twice that week moaning about the ferry service.

'Escaped you say, when did this ... I see, yes, go on ... Well, we don't go to print for a fortnight, and I'm not sure we'll need a picture ... Okay, Mrs Trout, I'll make some calls.'

He hung up the phone.

Well, might be something, he thought. Although a decent story in Orkney was like a good-looking woman. They probably existed, somewhere on the islands, but were kept well-hidden from him. Yet, an escaped mental patient. Might be worth venturing out for – might even make the nationals.

As he began contemplating pitching the story to Edinburgh, the door buzzer went. He thought about ignoring it, but it might have been Sophie.

After ambling down the narrow staircase, he opened the old door with a tug. A pretty but officious looking woman stood in the drizzle, clutching a folder. Dressed in a trouser suit, she looked like a professional, and he wondered if he'd remembered to pay his TV licence. 'Can I help you?'

A fine rain lingered in the wind, keeping the air moist, and her bobbed, mousy hair stuck to her cheeks. She scooped it over her ears. 'Hi, yes, is this The Mainland Advertiser?' She sounded confused. His thatched home, tucked away amongst the holiday houses and chalets, didn't look like a newspaper office.

'It is. May I help you?'

'My name's Ruth Duncan, I was wondering if I could speak to the editor?' Her accent sounded familiar, but not local. She was pretty, about his age, and had a sweet button nose that dripped with rain, like a tiny tap with a split washer.

'You're speaking to him,' he said. 'The editor, chief reporter, advertising manager, tea boy, and on occasion even paperboy, Tom Cairns. How can I help?' He thrust out his hand and smiled.

Shuffling the folder under her arm, she shook it. 'I was hoping to look at some back issues.'

'Look, come in out the rain.' He held open the door.

She thanked him and stepped inside, brushing her hair back again.

'This way.' He jogged up the stairs. The wooden steps creaked behind as she followed him into his office. He sat back behind his desk, gesturing for her to sit opposite. 'Sorry, it's a little cramped up here but there's only me and Sophie – our photographer.'

He'd been meaning to clean his desk, so he shifted some of the strewn newspapers to the floor, before emptying the overflowing ashtray on top of the typewriter. He saw her scan the room, looking at the bank of filing cabinets with the rolls of film and camera equipment scattered across the top. He'd meant to clean that too.

She smiled politely and plonked herself on the seat, before fiddling with her hair, in what he perceived as a coy attempt to tidy herself up.

'So, you want some information?'

'I was just hoping to look at some back issues, going back

about a decade, or so?'

He scratched his head. 'Well, there you go.' He nodded to the stack of newspapers lying piled-up across the floor behind the door. His nemesis. An inherited collection of newspapers dating back long before he arrived. They piled nearly waist-high, spilling out halfway across the room, and completely blocking two of the filing cabinets and covering the entire corner of the office.

'Help yourself,' he said. 'Sorry, they are not in much of an order – been meaning to get Sophie to tidy them up. There's a pile of Kirkwall Herald's in the front room, too, they're weekly. We only come out every fortnight – how far back did you say?'

'Ten years.' She frowned at the mess and glanced down at her watch.

'Perhaps if you tell me what it's about I may be able to help?'

She unbuttoned her jacket and he couldn't help but glance down her blouse to her chest.

She buttoned her jacket again. 'Sorry, I can't really say anything. I'm just doing some background on a patient – I'm a doctor and I have to respect confidentiality.'

'Of course. Us journalists know all about confidentiality, too.' He waved his hand over to the pile of newspapers. 'I might be able to help, though – would save you having to wade through that lot.'

'I'm sorry, but I can't say anything.'

He raised his hands. 'Understood. I tell you what – let me make you a coffee while you make a start?'

She smiled, her eyes widening at his mention of coffee. 'That would be great, I could murder one.'

'Okay, I'll pop the kettle on.' He got up from behind his desk and marched over to the door but stopped and turned around. 'Tell me, you're not from Edinburgh, by any chance?'

'Inverness, but I studied there.'

'Ha, thought so, you got the *Auld Reekie* twang.' After an awkward pause, he remembered the drinks. 'Right, coffee. Oh, and if you can't find what you're looking for in our rag, it might me in one of the satellite papers.'

'Satellite?'

'Yes, we just cover Mainland. There's the Hoy and South Ronaldsay Advertiser, they cover the south islands, then there's the Rousay News who do the Northern lot. They're all in there. Ten years is long before my time, though, but you might find what you need. I'll get the coffee. Just give me a shout if you need any help.'

He smiled, leaving his guest standing before the mound of old newspapers, shaking her head and checking the time again.

Anderson sat in the snug like Henry VIII holding court, a glass of Scotch in one hand, a cigarette in the other, and his shoes off drying by the fire. Being the only place the landlady permitted smoking, the snug had nicotine stained wallpaper and a permanent haze of blue-grey smoke floating above the tables.

Despite the drab exterior, the pub was a jewel on the inside. Log fire, dartboard, and it served real ale, much to Harrison's delight, who slopped his pint all over the table as he sat down. 'I've booked us in for the night, sir,' he said, sipping the head from his beer.

Anderson smiled and exhaled a lungful of warm smoke. He felt relaxed, content and intended giving his liver a good bashing.

'You call that wife of yours, then?'

'Yes, kids are running her ragged, though. She said hello.'

Bollocks she did, Anderson thought. He only met her once, after work at the end of Harrison's first week. Throwing up over her shoes probably didn't help the cordiality. Mind you, Harrison was no model husband, not the way he chased skirt.

'You not got kids, sir?'

'Did have once. Her bitch of a mother got her in the divorce, along with the house, and half my pension.'

Harrison's face stiffened. 'I'm sorry, sir.'

'Don't be, she took her down south. Probably talks like a *Sassenach* now.' He rubbed the glass of Scotch in his palms. 'Now, liven up, you're two drinks behind.'

Harrison, evidently taking the hint for a change of subject said: 'So what did you think of that psychiatrist?' He spoke with his moustache covered in beer foam.

'Her!' Anderson began coughing, remembering Dr Duncan. The woman had a rod up her backside. 'She's either a dyke or barren. Would get on well with my ex.'

'She ain't that bad – nice set of tits on her.'

'Frigid as they come. You can tell by the suit.'

Harrison took a large mouthful of beer. 'So you don't think there's anything in what she said about Sister McRowen?'

''Course not.' He screwed out his cigarette in the already burgeoning ashtray. 'Just another bloody amateur detective.'

He'd spoken to McRowen, and while he found her by no means affable, he doubted she had anything to do with what happened, not directly anyway. She had, however, made him feel like a boy again, and not in a good way. Reminded him of standing before his schoolmistress at Bishopbriggs again. He even found himself rubbing the palm of his hand in preparation for the ruler. It never came, of course, although he didn't doubt McRowen would enjoy dishing it out. They didn't hit it off.

Throughout the interview, she continually glared over her spectacles, never once lowering her beady eyes, as if she thought was about to swipe the contents from her desk. She was no killer, though. And while she couldn't explain why the orderly opened the patient's door, Anderson knew enough about cell protocol to understand how rules got broken. Barney probably decided to give the patient a *beasting*. Would explain the truncheon being out. Anderson understood. Stuck in the middle of nowhere, in that shit-hole, you'd need some sort of diversion. Barney wouldn't have known his heart was about to pack in.

'You don't think there's much chance the patient got off the island, then?' Harrison said, before sliding a cigarette from his packet using his teeth.

'Nah, probably jumped in the sea in panic, trying to get away from that big black orderly. He'll wash up. You saw the sea around that island. I doubt *Duncan Goodhew* would've stood a chance, let alone a nutter. '

Harrison nodded and took a deep draught of his beer, and wiped the foam from his face with his sleeve. 'Then why did you send that shrink away to get some background?'

The door to the snug swung open, allowing the chatter from the main bar to filter through.

'Any glasses in here?' The landlady shouted, standing in the doorway, her face half-hidden in the fug. Anderson raised his empty glass, and she scuttled over, wiping her hands on the front of her floral apron.

'Pop us another one in there, will you, love.'

He thrust the glass in her hand, and she walked out, muttering about having better things to do than wait hand on foot on ferry *loupers*.

Anderson turned back to Harrison. 'The last thing we need is some lesbian trick cyclist telling us how to do our job. As long as she keeps out our way, then there's no reason we can't make the most of this little assignment – perhaps stretch it out for a day or two.'

'Wouldn't have minded keeping her occupied myself.'

Anderson laughed and began rolling up another smoke as the landlady returned with his drink. The woman handed him the scotch and emptied their ashtray, tutting at its contents.

'Aye, not a bad boozer this.' Anderson said, raising his glass up to Harrison. 'Here's to expenses.'

Chapter Seven

While a chauvinist pig – and completely disinterested in Ruth's suspicions about McRowen – she knew the loathsome inspector had a point. Other than his name, Ruth knew nothing about Michael Skye. Even the poor quality picture McRowen supplied was a decade old and would bear no resemblance now.

Anderson's words stung her. She ventured into psychiatry because of her father, and now she felt guilty, and worse, ashamed. Much of the blame for her father's deterioration lay in his surroundings, and the care he received, or lack of it.

Now, after Anderson had got under her skin, she resolved to turn Michael Skye into a person, not just a name. Not for Anderson, she couldn't have cared less about that arrogant shit, or even for Michael, but for her dad.

She thought coming to the newspaper office a good place to start, but after three hours of digging, she still wasn't halfway through the mound of back issues. None went back so far as the early seventies, no matter how low down the pile she went.

She sat sprawled on the floor, newsprint covered her hands and face, and inky fingerprints peppered her blouse. A neat stack of papers, already sifted through, lay behind her, but the undiminished mound still towered above her.

She sighed as Tom returned with yet another mug of *Nescafe*. 'Any luck?'

She shook her head. 'No, but you might just end up with this lot in chronological order by the time I've finished.'

'Sorry, been meaning to get them sorted, but every time I ask

Sophie she's given me the finger.' He passed her the coffee.

The ink on her hands smeared all over the mug. 'You both live here, then?'

'No, just me.' His features were quite goofy, large teeth and high forehead, but he smiled sweetly, and had similar sad eyes to Dr Barry.

'So you and Sophie are not an item?'

'Good Lord, no.' He looked mortified. 'She's fourteen – I say fourteen but she's going on fifty. She takes good pictures though, and I don't have to pay her much. It's a win-win for us both.' He shook his head and picked up his cigarettes. 'She lives in a home over in Dounby. Hates it. Comes here to get away. It's a shame, really. She's a nice girl, bright too. Goes to the local Catholic school.'

'Is everywhere round here run by the Catholics?'

'Not quite, but it seems like it sometimes. Goes back to the Reformation, Orkney was remote enough to slip through the net.' He offered her one of his cigarettes.

She bit her lip. Dr Barry hated her smoking and she'd gone three weeks without one. But Gerard wasn't here, he was with his wife. Why shouldn't she have some fun? 'Okay, go on then.'

She stood up and wiped some of the newsprint on a pocket tissue before taking a filter tip from the packet. He lit it for her and they both sat down at his desk.

'So how did you end up here?' she asked, as the warm glow tingled across her head. 'Edinburgh get too hectic for you?'

'Something like that. I suppose I felt like getting away, and somehow found myself here.'

She liked him. A little too young for her, though. She mostly dated doctors with big cars and even bigger wallets. Judging by Tom's holey sweater and ripped jeans, she doubted he possessed either. But she liked his eyes, and he spoke softly, and politely. Quite sweet really. 'How long have you been here, then?' she asked.

He leaned back on his chair and thought. 'Got to be nearly three years now, seems longer, things tend to move at a different pace out here.'

'Tell me about it.' She looked back down at the pile of newspapers, and sighed, gulping a large mouthful of coffee. 'So you weren't around ten years ago?'

'Sorry, but if you let me know what you are looking for, I might be able to help?'

She chewed her lip again. 'I'm not sure I can say anything.' The nicotine rush sent her dizzy so she rested the cigarette on the ashtray.

'If you are worried about confidentiality I can give you my word – would never betray a source, especially not one so good-looking.'

A warmth spread across her cheeks, but she doubted it was the nicotine. She enjoyed the flirting. Sod Gerard. She gave him a smile. 'Is that a fact?'

His eyes widened. 'Of course, never reveal a source – career suicide. And who'd risk a career like this.' He waved his hands around the room.

She laughed. He was funny. She liked that. 'Well I suppose it won't hurt, I'm not sure how long I will be around. And it might not matter – I don't want to waste your time.'

'Trust me, time is something I have plenty of.'

'Okay.' She shrugged. 'I was just trying to find the reason way a patient was sectioned over at the hospital on Eynhallow.'

'Doesn't it say in their records?'

She shook her head. 'If you think you know disorganised you should see some of the notes I get given.'

'So what's the name?'

She picked up her cigarette and took a drag as she thought, but decided he sounded genuine. 'Michael Skye. He came from a care home too. Apparently there was some incident there in the early seventies.'

He took an inhale of smoke as he thought. 'Eynhallow, you say?'

'Yes.'

He leaned back, sipped his coffee and blew the smoke toward the ceiling. 'So is he the patient that has escaped?'

She scowled over her mug. Tousled hair and sad brown eyes, and she fell for them. He must have got a lot of stories that way. She slammed her mug on the desk, causing it to spill across his papers. 'Look, the police are involved and I shouldn't have said anything.'

'Calm down, I've told you I won't say anything.' He grinned, but she wanted to slap it off his face.

'I've told you enough already to get me the sack. So go ahead, I am only trying to do my job.'

His face dropped. 'Listen, I didn't mean to upset you. I was just being clever.'

'I'm not upset, I'm angry. People in this country treat the mentally ill no better than wild animals. I just want to find out a little of my patient's history, so if you want to trick me into giving you a story and lose me my job then you can just go and f–'

'– Whoa, okay, calm down. Don't worry.' He mimed zipping up his mouth before raising his hands in surrender. 'Not a word.'

His smile seemed pretty genuine, but it fooled her before. She still felt mad, despite his wide and drooping brown eyes. She said nothing.

'I won't print anything, I promise,' he said. 'And I couldn't if I wanted to – we're only a local rag and don't come out for a fortnight. Honestly, I'm only trying to help.'

His words mollified her a little, but she still didn't know whether to sit back down or walk out.

'Please, I'm sorry, I promise I won't say a word, and listen.' He touched her shoulder. 'I'll find out what I can for you. Just to help out, and I promise, not a word in the paper.'

She suddenly felt foolish. Typical her. Somebody finally shows her some genuine interest and she assumes the worst. 'I'm sorry. I've had a really long day. I didn't mean to go off on you.'

'It's okay. Listen.' He nodded to the pile of papers. 'I'll go through those for you. If you let me know where you are staying I'll bring round anything I find.'

'I'm staying in Tingwall, at the Finn Man, the little Inn at the harbour? But I hope I'll be gone by tomorrow – no offence.'

'None taken. Look, first thing in the morning, I'll bring round what I've found.'

'I don't want to put you to any bother.'

'Oh, it's no bother for me.' He beamed his infectious smile again. 'I'll make Sophie go through them.'

Chapter Eight

Ye watchers and ye holy ones, bright seraphs, cherubim, and thrones, raise the glad strain.

Alleluia!

Cry out, dominions, princedoms, powers, virtues, archangels, angels' choirs.

Alleluia!

Alleluia!

Alleluia! Alleluia! – Alleluia!

The chorus echoed up through the narrow nave and reverberated around the vaulted ceiling. The sound of the eighteen voices illuminated the gloom far more than the flickering candles. Brennan felt ecstatic.

The boys, clean sopranos not ruined by the ravages of testosterone, sung sweetly, and he drifted in and out of a dreamy fantasy gazing at them.

All under eighteen, no bristles or shadows scarred their angelic faces. He studied his favourites. Young Dennis, his full lips and coy smile, second only to Peter McCafrey. He turned his head to the blonde boy on the front row. McCafrey looked down at the choir book on his lap. Shame, such a sweet face, and with shoulders any rugby team would be proud to possess.

Brennan continued to drift in and out of his fantasy while the boy's perfect harmony drifted around him. At least it was almost perfect.

He clapped his hands, the applause bounced off the pillars and around the cathedral.

'Now then, boys.' Even his own voice sounded strong in such acoustics, almost masculine.

The boys looked up.

Brennan stood with a knee bent and his crotch thrust forward. Both hands rested on the waist of his denims. 'Somebody is coming in too soon on the third Alleluia, is it you, Aaron?'

'No, Mr Brennan,' said a small boy in the front row. A few whispered snickers filtered from the boys at the back.

'Now then, that's enough.' Brennan clapped his hands and walked over to the row of candles on the nave, relighting a couple blown out from the many drafts.

While not yet lunchtime, St Magnus remained gloomy, with only two poor examples of stained glass allowing in any light. The warden forbade the use of electric lighting, which dated back before the war, anytime before six o'clock, so Brennan had to put up with the candles. Despite this, the Normanesque cathedral with the towering sandstone pillars and narrow aisle, produced acoustics not found anywhere else on the island – the lack of utilities a sacrifice Brennan thought more than worthy.

He turned back round to the choir and smiled at McCafrey again. The boy's eyes dropped back to the floor. 'Beautiful solo, Peter.' He lingered his smile on him before clapping his hands again, silencing a couple more sniggers at the back.

'C'mon boys, it's only a fortnight until the competition, and we are nowhere near ready. You should feel privileged to be allowed out of school for the morning to practise, or would you rather be in maths class?' He looked at all their faces. None seemed that bothered. He sighed. 'Right, we have just under half an hour before lunch and you have to get back, so one more time, from the beginning, and this time I want you to sing as if your life depended on it.'

He raised his hands, and started the choir in another rendition of *Ye Watchers and Ye Holy Ones*.

Ruth awoke to see a middle-aged woman, holding a tea-tray and wearing a headscarf, stood in the doorway.

'Thought you may want a cup of tea my dear,' the woman said in an Orcadian screech. 'It's gone twelve – the day has half gone.'

She placed the tray on the bedside table, and lifted up the man's watch already lying there. Raising it to her eyes, she scrutinised it, sniffed haughtily, and then placed it next to the teacup. She then walked over to the window and opened the curtains with a flurry.

The light caused Ruth to flinch.

'You must be very hungry,' the woman said, as she clucked around the room. 'What with missing breakfast – do you like kippers dear? It's either them or oats.'

'No, I'm fine, Mrs Trout,' Ruth said, her throat dry. She looked down at the tea and realised she needed a stronger pick-me-up. 'Perhaps I could have a coffee?'

The landlady gaped as if Ruth had asked for a line of cocaine. 'Sorry, dear, only have tea.'

'Oh, that'll be just fine, then, thank you.'

'Well, it's a lovely day you are missing, that gale last night has blown in some sunshine. Oh, and before I forget, there's a young couple to see you downstairs.'

'For me, who are they?'

'There's only one way to find out, dear.' Mrs Trout said, as she lingered at the bottom of her bed.

'Er, yes, thank you – I'll be down in a minute.'

'Oh, no hurry dear, whenever you're ready.' She stared uncomfortably for a few more seconds before turning to the door. Ruth waited until she heard her descend the stairs, and then slid out of bed.

She dressed into her casuals. A pair of white jeans, striped jersey and new trainers, which cost more than the rest of her clothes put together. After tying her hair back in a white scrunchy, and washing her face in the small sink, she took a single sip of the disgustingly sweet tea – tossing the remaining contents into one of the many plants dotted around the room – picked up the watch, dropped it into her bag, and left the room.

Not having eaten anything other than cheese and onion crisps since the previous morning, her stomach growled as she walked down the stairs.

When she got back from the newspaper office, she'd met that odious Inspector Anderson staggering out from the gents and zipping up his fly. Another stroke of bad luck. He was boarding at the Finn Mann too. She intended to avoid him by having an early night. But after Gerard refused to answer his phone, and Sergeant Harrison found her moping by the bar and offered to buy her a drink, it was the early hours before she finally staggered up the stairs to her room.

She heard Harrison slide from her bed about six that morning. Probably to phone his wife. She knew he was married, and had kids. He even showed her some pictures. Didn't stop her, though.

The chattering locals, three fishermen and an elderly bus driver, stopped their discussions and studied her as she walked in the bar.

'Ahoy there!' A figure at the back waved at her.

Tom sat smiling with a pint of bitter in his hand, a couple of newspapers on the table, and a girl with strawberry-blonde hair sipping a *Britvic* next to him.

Not much taller than Sister Mary, her feet dangled over the seat. Around her neck, and looking far too large for her, hung a single lens camera, complete with flash. It hampered her movements as she sucked her juice up a curly straw. She lifted her head, showing a pair of rosy cheeks, and two big hazel eyes that flickered at Ruth as she approached.

'Hello again.' Ruth said, returning Tom's smile. His hair seemed far more unruly than before. It must have been windy.

'Not managed to escape, then?' He nodded to the seat opposite.

She sighed and sat down. 'Still trying.'

'Nice to meet you too, Ruth,' the young photographer said, impatiently. 'I'm Sophie.'

'Sorry, my manners.' Tom rolled his eyes. 'Dr Ruth Duncan, this is Sophie Gleeson, photographer and general PIA.'

Ruth frowned. 'PIA?'

'Pain in the arse. One of his, oh-so witty comments.' The girl's accent sounded local, and she examined Ruth with the subtly of judge at a best of breed show. She smiled with approval. 'Tom hasn't stopped talking about you since your visit.' A wide smile joined up her flushed cheeks.

'Hey, now wait here, Sophie.' Tom's face reddened.

Sophie giggled. 'Calm down, I'm only teasing.'

Ruth smiled, feeling a touch abashed too. Only for different reasons. She zipped up her bag, hiding the watch.

'Are you staying for a drink?' Sophie asked.

Normally, Ruth hated being around children. She found them noisy, smelly and the reason she no longer saw many of her friends. But she liked this one. The feisty and confident spirit reminded her of when she was young. She remembered what Tom said. She knew children from care homes went one of two ways. Either full of rebellion and spunk, like Sophie, or withdrawn and introverted, and prime candidates for mental health problems – like Michael Skye.

'Well, I ought to get something to eat first. I've had no breakfast.'

Tom looked at his watch. 'I know a great fish and chip shop if you can wait half an hour.'

'Sounds better than kippers.' For some reason she'd been craving fish and chips since arriving on the islands. *Must be the sea air*, she thought.

'Might as well have a drink then,' Tom said.

'Okay.' She looked at Sophie. 'I'll have one of those.'

He smiled and finished his bitter in one mouthful, before standing up. 'Oh.' He patted the newspapers on the table. 'I managed to dig out some information for you. I'll show you when I get back.' He trotted off to the bar, leaving Ruth alone with the young girl.

They sat silently for a moment. Sophie sucking her orange juice, and Ruth feeling the youngster's eyes probing her. 'So, you known each other long, then?' Ruth asked, finally.

Sophie put down her drink. 'About three years. Since he got here from Edinburgh.'

'So how did you meet?'

'He put an advert in the paper for a part-time photographer.' She pulled a small purse from her pocket and clicked it open. 'Here!' She handed Ruth an old newspaper cutting.

Ruth read it aloud: 'Wanted, the next Fleet Street photographer of the year, to start work at the Mainland Advertiser to learn everything you'll ever need to know for a glamorous future in journalism.' She handed Sophie back the paper. 'And you got the job?'

'He had no choice really.'

'Why was that?'

'I was the only one who applied.'

Ruth laughed. It said a lot that the Sophie still kept hold of the cutting. 'They don't like newcomers here much, do they? So what do you do when you are not working for Tom?'

'Not much. Not much else *to* do. I don't know if he said, but I don't have a family.' She said it in a factual way, like someone confessing to not owning a car.

'I'm sorry to hear that,' Ruth found herself using her therapy voice.

'No, it's okay. I'm quite lucky – I've got my job with Tom.'

'Well, I think he's lucky to have you.'

'Oh he is,' Sophie said, as he walked over carrying the drinks. She leaned in and whispered, 'No matter how bad my life is, at least I can always look down on him.'

Both the girls laughed as he sat down.

'Okay, what's so funny?' He handed Ruth her orange juice and sipped the head from a fresh pint of bitter.

The girls just looked at each other and sniggered.

He shook his head and passed the newspapers over to Ruth. 'Here you go. I've marked the page numbers on the front for you.'

She thanked him and looked through them. One was a copy of The Mainland Advertiser from May 1971, the other, a Kirkwall Herald dated June the following year. She opened the Advertiser to the page Tom marked, and read the headline aloud: 'Father Dies in Care Home Fracas.'

Scanning the article revealed little other than what the headline suggested. The priest, Father James Walker, 62, died following an altercation at St Mary's care home, the report said. His death was being treated as suspicious and several of the boys were helping police with enquiries.

'Then there's nothing until July the next year.' Tom pointed to the other paper.

Ruth opened it. 'Where is it?'

He pointed to a news-in-brief column on the side. 'Orphan Committed to Eynhallow.' Ruth continued to read the story. 'Kirkwall Crown Court, today committed a 16-year-old boy to indefinite detention under the 1959 Mental Health Act, after the Judge, Lord Justice Clerk George Frazer, accepted the suspect was unfit to stand trial.

'The youth, who can't be named for legal reasons, was accused of attacking Father James Walker at St Mary's Home for Boys.' She looked up. 'Is this it?'

'Yep,' Sophie said, still sipping her orange juice.

Tom took out his reporter's notebook. 'But we did call the Fiscal's office in Thurso for you.'

Sophie coughed. 'Excuse me?'

'Sorry, Sophie called them.' He leaned in to Ruth and whispered. 'Her shorthand's better than mine.'

'And?' Ruth asked.

'Seems Father Walker had a weak heart,' Sophie said, slurping the remnants of her orange juice.

'Heart?'

'Heart attack, according to the Procurator's report,' Tom said. 'The *fracas* may only have triggered it off, and there was some debate during the inquest about it, but at worst that's manslaughter, not murder. How long did you say he spent in that asylum?'

'Ten years!' Ruth shook her head.

Times were changing but not quickly enough, and these types of scandal still occurred. The previous mental health acts were a licence to witch-hunt and Ruth had heard of long-term psychiatric patients committed in the fifties for nothing worse than epilepsy. One woman spent forty years in a sanatorium for a stutter – she remembered reading about it during her PhD.

'Sorry,' Tom said, nodding to the papers. 'If it doesn't help.'

'No, you did great, I couldn't have asked for more. Thank you.' She gave him a smile and Sophie cocked her eyebrows. 'It probably doesn't matter now, anyway. Police think he's drowned.' She sighed.

Tom checked his watch again. 'Won't be long until the chip shop opens. Do you want to take a walk, it's breezy, but there's no rain?'

She smiled and nodded.

'Okay, if we have to,' Sophie said, finishing her juice.

'I wasn't talking to you,' Tom said, scowling. 'You should have been in school three hours ago – you'll have old Tippwick after me again.'

Chapter Nine

The boys filed down the nave between the rows of battered wooden benches, and Mr Brennan took their smocks as they approached the cathedral door. It lay open, revealing the start of a fairly bright afternoon. He smiled at each boy in turn and commented on his performance.

'Thank you, Michael, beautiful today,' he said taking the boy's smock. 'But make sure you don't come in too early on the chorus. Gareth, same to you, and perhaps next week you could get a haircut?'

Brennan shook his head. Gareth's hair looked *so* last decade. He wasn't a fan of long hair even during the seventies, but at least it covered the boy's big ears. He wouldn't be asking Gareth to stay for extra practice.

He smiled at the twins, identical blonde hair so fine he could see their scalps even under the dim light of St Magnus. 'Nice solos, you two.'

The boys thrust their smocks at him and darted out the door, not giving him a glance as they ran off.

Two boys remained. Peter and Dennis. Brennan stared as they walked sheepishly up the nave, their smocks in their hands, their heads bowed to the flagstones. *Decisions, decisions,* thought Brennan, studying Dennis' full lips, before casting his eyes on Peter's powerful shoulders.

Brennan bit his lip, but had decided. He took Dennis' smock and watched him dash off into the afternoon, before stopping Peter with his arm across the door.

'It sounded like you were having trouble in your solo, Peter. Have you not been doing your vocal exercises?'

Peter stared over Brennan's arm. 'I have, sir, honestly. Every night.'

'Sounds like your throat was a little dry to me, Peter. I think you should stay behind a while and do some exercises with me.'

'I can't Mr Brennan, sir. I'm going home for lunch; my mother's picking me up – she'll be here in a minute.'

Brennan smiled and closed the door. It creaked before shutting with a wooden chop that echoed ominously in the space around them.

'Nonsense, Peter, I saw you mother in town this morning. She's working until five this afternoon. She told me. We have an hour before you have to be back in school.'

He took the smock from the boy's arms and lingered his hands on the powerful arms and shoulders. The timid eyes were cast to the floor, but Brennan, smocks under his arm, led the hulking teenager by the hand down the nave. Dumping the white gowns on the floor, he pulled the boy behind the pillars that flanked the right of the transept.

A single candle flickered beneath the columns, illuminating just enough for what Brennan wanted to see.

After a tirade of protests, Sophie finally agreed to go to school. Tom drove her, with Ruth beside him looking as if she'd never sat in anything as dour as his VW Beetle. Dressed in a pullover and trainers she looked more like the girl next door than the TV licence official of yesterday. She even smiled as they watched Sophie trudge through the school gates, the camera still fastened around her neck.

'She seems a handful,' Ruth said, as the car sat rattling at the curb.

'I wouldn't have it any other way,' he replied, putting it into gear. He pulled off, leaving a cloud of white smoke on the pavement behind them.

'So what is the story with you two?' Ruth had helped herself to one of his cigarettes.

'Dunno, two lost souls, I guess. I know what it's like for her. I came from a home too.' He never liked admitting that, it always received raised brows and an, 'Oh!'

Ruth gave a thin smile. 'Sophie's very lucky to have you.'

'I'm a pushover. Tippwick does a better job of keeping her in line than I do.'

'Tippwick?'

'Detective Sergeant Tippwick. A local copper.'

'Oh, where does he fit in?' She was trying to unwind the window, but the door winder hadn't worked since he bought the car. He flipped open the ashtray for her.

'Our Sophie was not always the sensible girl she is now. Got herself into a bit of trouble a couple of years back – shoplifting that sort of thing. Tippwick took her under his wing and made me take her on. Good-hearted is old Tippwick.'

'Perhaps you should look into fostering her? You obviously get along.'

He didn't answer. He doubted they had time for *that* discussion. 'You ready for those chips?'

'Yes, I'm starving. They'd better be nice.'

'Best in all Orkney. Oh, by the way. Did I tell you that you look very nice today.'

She blushed. 'No, you didn't, but thank you.'

'A pleasure, so much better than the drowned rat outside my office, yesterday.'

'Drowned rat!' She gave him a scowl.

'Ah, no, err ... I meant.'

She laughed.

'Tell you what,' he said, slowing the car at a set of lights. 'I know it's early, but do you fancy a cheap bottle of wine, too?'

She bit her lip, and her eyes flickered across his face for a moment. 'I'm not sure, I don't know if I'll be needed by the police today.'

'Well, it's not too big an island. I'm sure they'll find you.'

He distinctly remembered Mrs Trout asking if she should tell one of the detectives where Ruth was going. A Sergeant Harrison, if he remembered correctly.

Ruth's reply had been quite curt. She now sat curling her hair around her fingers, offering occasional glances at him before finally looking up and smiling.

'Okay,' she said. 'Why not?'

'Is anybody there?'

Brennan stood in front of the candles at the altar. He could have sworn he heard the cathedral door open. Must be his nerves. Or his conscience. He shook his head and turned back to see Peter, shirtless with his bare arms exposed, peeking from the pillar. 'Get back. It's nothing.'

Peter stepped back into the gloom and Brennan smiled and walked toward him. He stopped, noticing his breathing sounded laboured. Heavy. He stood up straight and put his hand on the base of his spine. He felt a stitch.

The cathedral suddenly darkened. Before him, the shadows under the pillars lengthened. He turned back to the nave. The candles had blown out. All of them.

His eyes peered into the darkness. Was someone there? He wanted to call out, but a shooting pain shot across his chest, expelling every ounce of his breath.

He clutched at his left shoulder. A squeezing and stabbing started under his rib cage. His gasps became broken and hoarse, and a tingling shot up and down his arm.

He stumbled and landed on his knees.

'Mr Brennan, sir?'

He couldn't see Peter, but heard him. He lifted his arm toward the sound of his voice, and bit at the air to get enough breath to say: 'Help ... help me.'

Brennan slumped on to all fours, the tingling turning his arms numb. Peter's footsteps disappeared down the nave toward the cathedral door. It banged close.

The squeezing around Brennan's chest increased, as if a huge vice began tightening around his ribcage.

'Arghh!'

The scream caused the tingling up his arm to turn into another shooting pain. His mouth began snapping at the air trying to force some into his lungs. None entered.

He gulped silently and helplessly, aware he was no longer breathing. But the sound of breaths still echoed around the cathedral. Slow, panting breaths.

There.

Something shuffled under the nave. Despite the pain, he looked up. Something moved, hidden in the long shadows under the columns. Still trying to gulp in mouthfuls of air, Brennan craned his neck toward the pillars. The darkness and pain made focusing impossible. Was it Peter? No, he'd gone. Who then? So close, so very close.

He held his hand out, pleading at whoever stood there, but the stretch made his chest feel as if it would explode. He opened his mouth. One last attempt to breathe. No air entered. Instead, he pulled his lips back into a grimace before collapsing, his face slapping the flagstones.

He twitched, experiencing his final ever sensation. A warm moistness under his denims, caused by the urine now spreading over the flagstones around him.

Chapter Ten

As it turned out, the fish and chips were a real treat. Ruth and Tom ate them on the cliffs surrounding Tingwall harbour while watching the fishing boats chugging out to sea. Gulls flocked above, and the sounds, combined with the smell of sea air, only added to the flavour of the battered fish, which tasted better than any Ruth had tried in mainland Scotland.

With the sun breaking free from the clouds and the wind having eased, the early afternoon felt warm.

After they finished eating, Tom popped into the local off-licence and bought a bottle of claret, and they walked back to his office-cum-apartment across the quayside, strolling under the cacophony of gulls.

'Sorry, about going off on you, yesterday,' Ruth said, dumping the remnants of her lunch into a litterbin. 'It's just that – do you have a cigarette?'

He fumbled in his jacket and pulled out his packet. He took out two filter tips and placed them in his mouth, lighting them both. He passed one to her and she inhaled deeply.

'I just get really pissed off sometimes,' she said, savouring the glow as it warmed her chest.

'You don't say. Almost as feisty as Sophie.' He cupped his cigarette backward in his hand. Despite the sunshine, the wind still gusted strong.

'I suppose we have a lot in common,' she said. 'I wasn't an orphan, but I didn't have a father when I was younger.'

'He run off?'

She shook her head. 'He was ill. It's the reason I got into psychiatry – it's not right, Tom. We treat stray dogs better than our mentally ill, and it just makes me so mad sometimes. He was let down. By the family, the hospital, and me.'

He straightened his lips at her. 'I'm sorry.'

They walked silently for several minutes until they arrived at his cottage. He opened the door, stepping over a pile of unopened post, and invited her into the downstairs room.

The apartment was distinctly male. Other than a coffee table, littered with newspapers, a small two-seater sofa, and a TV, he owned no other furniture. A small kitchenette sat in the corner, and with only one door leading off to a tiny bathroom, Ruth presumed the sofa folded out as a bed.

She could see touches of Sophie around the room, though. A vase, containing a couple of dying daffodils, sat perched on the edge of the coffee table, while tacked on the back wall, two posters – Che Guevara and Adam Ant. Tom didn't seem the revolutionary type, nor a New Romantic.

'Must have been a bit of a culture shock when you came out here?' she said, watching him rifle about in the kitchenette. 'Not much like the city, is it?'

He returned with a corkscrew and two glass tumblers. 'Sorry, not used to entertaining.' He pulled out the cork. 'And Sophie is not much of a wine drinker.' He filled the glasses. 'The culture-shock is probably what attracted me,' he said. 'Had enough of Edinburgh. Why, do you miss it?'

She shook her head, taking one of the glasses from him. 'Not really, didn't seem to do anything other than study when I was there.'

'Not a party girl, then?'

'That came later.'

He sat next to her on the sofa and raised his glass. 'Well, here's to *Auld Reekie*.'

'To Edinburgh,' she said, clinking their glasses together.

Even after the lashings of vinegar on her lunch, the wine tasted sour and acidic. She shuddered as it trickled down her throat. 'You never answered me when I asked if you'd thought about fostering Sophie. I think you'd make a good dad.'

He took out a cigarette and gulped at his wine. 'I would jump at the chance, if I could.'

'So, what's stopping you?' She placed her glass on the table and nodded to his cigarettes. He passed her one and took a deep drag of his.

'My record.' The smoke masked his mouth.

'Oh, I see.' He didn't look the type. She wondered what his conviction was for. 'Perhaps they may still consider you?'

He shook his head.

'Why? Sorry, you don't have to tell me. It's none of my business.'

'I don't mind you knowing,' he said. 'But you'll think a lot less of me after I do.'

'I doubt that, we all make mistakes.' She turned to face him square on.

'I was banged up for drugs,' he said, as if obvious. 'I'm clean now, but I was hooked for quite a few years. That's how I ended up here.' He blew a smoke ring to the ceiling. 'It started with just a bit of pot during study sessions, then I got on to uppers at the weekend, and by my third year I was doing four or five grammes of *Charlie* a day.'

'That's quite a habit, how could you afford it on a grant?'

'I couldn't. I'd borrow a lot and I'd sell a bit myself. I didn't really care where I was getting it, or how much it was costing.' He took another swig of the wine and winced. 'God this is awful, isn't it.'

He put the glass on the table and slumped back into his seat. 'I managed to scrape through my degree, though, and get a job on one of the big dailies, The Bugle.'

'So, what happened?' Ruth looked around for an ashtray but realised what the old saucer on the coffee table was for. She flicked her cigarette into it.

'I don't think I met one snapper or hack that wasn't, or hadn't been, a *coke-head*,' he said. 'It was probably the worst place for somebody like me to end up. It just spiralled. I'd wake up, have a line, take a shower, have another line. I'd get to the newsroom find out what was what, and have another line. Like I said – everybody was doing it. It was fuel, kept you upright for an eighteen-hour day.'

She knew enough about addiction through her work, and how easy it was for people to get caught out. 'How ever did you get off it?'

'By the time I was in my second year, I was doing well, there was talk of offering me the deputy news editor's job, but I was living off cocaine and very little else – couldn't function without it.' He blew another smoke ring. 'I knew it was only a matter of time before something happened. I was lucky I got caught because I don't reckon I'd be here now if I hadn't.'

'So, what happened?'

'I owed somebody some money. Quite a bit, and to pay them back I had to shift some gear. I'd set-up a deal with a couple of blokes I knew from one of the nightclubs in town. I would have ended up making more than enough to pay everybody back, and then some.'

He stubbed his cigarette out but immediately lit another. 'The only snag was that I was living in digs so I couldn't keep it at my place. There was too much of it, and the landlady would have seen it – she was always snooping around.'

'So what did you do?'

'I took it in to work, kept it in my desk drawer.'

'And someone found it?'

'Worse than that, the person who gave it me got busted. Took me down with them. They raided my desk at The Bugle. Found half a kilo. I got six years, but did three.'

She looked at him carefully. His two thin lips curled back in shame as he spoke, and his eyes drooped at the corners.

'So how did you end up here?'

He shrugged. 'Fate, I guess. When I got out it was clear that nobody in Edinburgh or Glasgow would give me a job, they'd all heard about the raid – some *friends* even sat in the press gallery when they sentenced me. Made a decent story for a couple of the rival papers. My probation officer found out about this gig, seemed a good idea at the time.'

'Does Sophie know about all this?'

He shook his head. 'No, Tippwick does, though. I have to report to him once a month as part of my probation.'

'And that's why you can't foster her?'

He nodded. 'I just feel so guilty. My past is going to screw up her future.'

'You can't think like that,' she protested. 'We all have a past.' She leaned toward him and kissed him gently on the cheek. 'And you are wrong.'

'About what?'

'I don't think less of you now.' She kissed him again, and didn't stop, even after he finished kissing her back.

Chapter Eleven

The bright afternoon had turned into a dreary evening. Despite the clouds and the sun still visible to the west, the evening star twinkled behind the spired silhouette of St Magnus creating a scene like a cheap Christmas card. Anderson, a cigarette in his lips, slammed the car door shut and looked up at the red sandstone. It pulsed in a blue hue due to the lights from the waiting ambulance and police cars bouncing off the chequerboard masonry.

He lit his cigarette, shaking out the match and flicking it to the pavement. Tippwick had been busy again. Police tape ran across the cathedral gates, and he saw Rowland, bouncing up and down on his heels outside the entrance, his domed helmet tipped low over his eyes.

A small crowd stood across the road. Half a dozen locals braving the dampness for curiosity's sake. He pulled the cigarette from his lips and nodded to them. 'Isn't *Coronation Street* on tonight?'

Harrison took his thick coat from the rear seat. 'Doesn't this wind ever stop?'

Anderson shook his head and sniffed, feeling a lump of phlegm build up in his throat, which he spat on the pavement. 'This better not be a waste of time.'

He wanted to spend the day in the pub, but somehow Kendrick got wind of them sitting idle and sent them on a security review of Kirkwall terminal. A waste of time. The only non-nationals that ever arrived in Orkney came from Norway or

Iceland, and he figured the last time they posed a threat was when the Vikings were raping and pillaging their way across Scotland.

Kendrick agreed they should wait for the results of the postmortem – that shrink's flapping proved useful when he told him what she said about McRowen. Kendrick's paranoia made him gullible. As did his faith in shrinks. Enabling Anderson to plan another night drinking on expenses. He had just settled down to his first drink of the evening when Tippwick called, dragging him back into town.

Anderson walked over to Rowland, who stiffened at the sight of him. 'Good evening, sir.'

'Who's inside?'

'Detective Tippwick, Dr Phelps and the chief constable, sir.'

'Titt-head's here, is he?' Anderson said, holding his cigarette between forefinger and thumb. He took another drag, before throwing it like a dart on to the pavement.

Rowland lifted up the police tape covering the darkened door to the cathedral. 'They've called in that psychiatrist too. She's on her way.'

'Oh great, Vinegar Tits, that's all I bloody need.' He beckoned Harrison with a nod and they ducked underneath the cordon.

The telephone rang rudely. Ruth felt a headache and a dryness in her mouth from the red wine. She awoke for the second time that day to unfamiliar surroundings.

Cheap flock wallpaper and the smell of stale cigarettes took her back to her student days, as did the strewn clothing, soft snores beside her, and contented glow of late afternoon sex.

Although it was in stark contrast to the five-star rooms in which Dr Barry would entertain her. She checked her watch – it was nearly eight.

The phone shouted for attention again and the snores ceased. A bleary-eyed Tom awoke, and following a deep yawn, reached for the receiver.

'Hullo,' he said, his voice cracking. He listened for a moment before rolling flat on the bed, the phone still clamped to his ear. 'Mrs Trout, what can I do for you?'

Ruth took the opportunity to begin her escape. She slipped her legs from the bed and, conscious of her nakedness, grabbed her clothes and bag before flitting to the bathroom.

She shut the door, throwing her hands on the sink before staring at herself in the mirror. What was she doing? She ran the taps and opened her bag for her compact. Harrison's watch lay on top of the clutter. She cursed herself in the mirror. She blamed the wine, and stuck out her claret stained tongue. After flinging water on her face, she froze as a gentle knock sounded behind her.

'Just a minute.'

Realising her bra must still be on the floor, she pulled her sweater over her chest, grabbed a rather grubby-looking towel from the radiator, covered her lower half, and slipped her head around the door.

'That was Mrs Trout,' Tom said, standing outside and not looking too bothered about his modesty. 'She says the police have been trying to get hold of you. They want to see you at St Magnus.'

'St Magnus?'

He nodded and scratched the thin hairs on his chest. 'It's the cathedral, in Kirkwall. Hurry up, I'll drive you.'

'Oh, okay. Just two minutes.' She disappeared back behind the door, and then instantly re-opened it. 'How the bloody hell did she know I was here?'

Tom shrugged. 'I told you it was a small island.'

A musty smell of dust and old oak benches tickled Anderson's nose as he walked down the nave. In such a huge chamber, his hoarse breaths echoed about him. St Magnus was like a mausoleum. Gloomy, dark and cold, with imposing pillars casting everything in shadow. With none of the grandeur he expected from a cathedral, it lacked almost any decorative features, apart from the unimpressive stained glass windows at both ends that revealed nothing but the greyness outside, and some shabby-looking tapestries hanging on a couple of the pillars.

A couple of lamps, no doubt set-up by the police, illuminated the altar at the far end, and several figures stood about. He paced down the flagstones toward them. Harrison following behind. The clip clop of shoes announced their arrival half a minute before they emerged under the lamps.

Tippwick stood next to the chief constable, who had his cap in its customary place under his arm. Their eyes waited for Anderson to emerge from the gloom.

'Thanks for coming, Inspector,' Tiernay said, his humourless face greeting Anderson with thinned lips and a cold stare. 'Think we may have something, here.'

Despite the police lamps, the transept remained dark, but

Anderson noticed a figure stooped over in the corner. The man straightened and stepped into the light.

'Inspector!' The pathologist held a pen light, which he clicked off. 'Twice in two days. Somebody must ruddy well have it in for me.'

'Nice to see you too, Phelps. So what we got?'

Phelps stood aside and nodded at a body behind him that lay unsheeted and face down. 'Looks like another heart attack.'

'Heart attack!' Anderson turned to Tippwick and shrugged. 'What's the matter with you islanders – never heard of exercise?'

'I wisnae sure if ye'd want to see it, Inspector,' Tippwick said, his hands clasped behind him. 'Cannae see any connection, but with the po'or orderly being found only yesterday, thought ye'd rather know.'

Anderson turned to Harrison, who translated. 'He says they don't look connected, but he thought you'd want to know about it.'

'While there's no sign of anything suspicious, coincidences are always suspicious in my eyes,' Tiernay added. 'Wouldn't you agree, Inspector?'

Anderson ignored him and nodded down to the dead man. 'Who was he?'

Tippwick read from his notes. 'David Brennan, twenty-six. Organises the local boy's choir.' His reading voice sounded clear, almost BBC English.

Anderson pulled out his tobacco pouch and waved it toward the corpse. 'So what happened?'

'Must have collapsed sometime after choir practice this morning. He had rehearsals with one of the schools, preparing for some competition or other. Warden found him an hour or so ago,' Tiernay said, confidently.

'Been dead about eight hours,' Phelps confirmed, as the sound of the cathedral door opened. Anderson turned as two of Phelps' men walked down the nave carrying a stretcher.

Phelps waved them over, before looking back down at Brennan. 'Your taxi's here.'

Despite the gloom, Anderson could see the dead man was young. He couldn't remember a day when he'd have gotten into a pair of trousers that tight. 'Twenty-six seems young for a heart attack. Don't look too out of shape. You sure?'

'It happens,' admitted Phelps, as his two assistants arrived. He nodded for them to proceed and they began loading Brennan on to the stretcher. 'I won't know for sure until I've cut him open, but it has all the signs of a coronary. Probably born with a defect. They can go for years before they get noticed'

Anderson frowned at Tiernay. 'So what the bloody hell have you called me out for?'

'Well – the coincidence!' Tiernay bounced up and down on his shoes, uncomfortably. 'Could be relevant.'

'Could be? Yeah, and if my aunt had bollocks she could be my uncle.'

'We have a possible witness, sir,' Tippwick said.

'Witness?'

Tiernay clicked his fingers and Tippwick strolled to the front row of benches and produced what looked like a white rag.

'What is it?' Anderson asked.

'A school shirt,' Tiernay said smugly. 'Found it behind one of the pillars, belongs to one of the boy's from the choir. I can't imagine him leaving without it, must have seen what happened and panicked.'

'What was it doing back there?' Anderson asked, jabbing his finger at the columns.

Tiernay shrugged. 'Probably having a crafty cigarette or something.'

Anderson screwed up his face. None of it was making much sense, or demonstrating any relevance. 'So why didn't this boy call an ambulance?'

Tiernay shrugged. 'Must have got scared. I've sent somebody to his house to interview him.' Anderson turned to Phelps. 'Was there signs of an assault?'

'No, nothing visible. Oh, and that reminds me, I've finished that black fella's autopsy.'

He bent down to his bag and pulled out a folder, handing it to Anderson. He opened it, but the echo from the cathedral door swung his head back down the nave. He saw Rowland's outline, letting in a female figure, whose running shoes squeaked on the flagstones as she walked toward them.

'Oh, great! Miss Bloody Marple's here.'

Chapter Twelve

Three detectives, the pathologist, two medics and a smartly dressed uniformed officer, all stared as Ruth stepped under the spotlights. She felt conscious of not being formally dressed, and noticed Anderson looking down at her trainers.

The officer in uniform stepped toward her, holding his hand out. 'Dr Duncan? I'm Chief Constable Tiernay, we haven't met, but thanks for coming.'

Ruth shook it as two medics, carrying a stretcher, walked past her. The dead man's head flopped sideways. The eyes bulged and a swollen tongue stuck out. She locked her legs together, aware they felt like buckling. The last dead body she saw had been her father's.

The blood drained from her face, so she took deep breaths. She hadn't expected this reaction. Perhaps this consultancy work was something else she was no good at. 'Who – who was he?'

'Local choirmaster, Ian Brennan,' Tiernay replied, unaware of her palpitations. 'Collapsed and died from a heart attack sometime this afternoon. The church warden found him an hour or so ago. We were just discussing the possibility of foul play.'

'Heart attack?' She turned to Harrison and Anderson, neither spoke. Harrison shuffled uncomfortably on his feet, staring at the flagstones as if a vital clue lay amongst the cracks. 'I just found out the man Michael was originally accused of attacking had a heart attack too.'

'See, Inspector, another coincidence,' Tiernay said, triumphantly.

Anderson cocked his head to the side and shook it. 'So what – means nothing!'

'Well, you said you wanted to know some background on the patient,' Ruth said.

'That was yesterday.'

'Three heart attacks, is a bit of a coincidence, sir.' Harrison gave Ruth a smile that was neither friendly nor sincere.

'Don't talk rubbish.' Anderson waved the folder at him. 'I don't know why you are trying to impress her. You said she wasn't that great in the sack, anyway.'

'Sir!'

Ruth clenched her teeth so hard she thought one would crack.

'You can't deny that three heart attacks is coincidental,' Tiernay said. 'In my experience coincidences are always worth looking into.'

'And in my experience, if you wipe your arse too hard you end up getting shit all over your fingers.' Anderson spoke with a customary roll-up in his teeth. He waved the folder at Tiernay. 'Orderly was definitely natural causes, ain't that right, Phelps?'

The pathologist nodded as the two medics began carrying the body down the nave. 'Have to agree with the inspector. There was nothing in the bloods. Aneurysm of the aortic sinus. Can't see that being caused by foul play.' He removed his spectacles, letting them drop on their cord as the medics disappeared out the cathedral door. 'I reckon that one will be natural causes too. Bet a week's beer money on it, in fact.'

He bent down and picked up his bag. 'I'll have his postmortem done by teatime tomorrow. Will let you know if anything turns up.' He looked at Anderson and Tiernay, both men were sneering at each other. 'Now play nicely, won't you children.'

Tippwick thanked him and the doctor strolled down the nave, the weight of his medical case making him hobble.

'Right, c'mon, Harrison,' Anderson said. 'Before the chief here wants us to track down the tooth fairy.' He sniffed, turned about, and followed Phelps down the aisle.

'One minute!' Ruth said.

Harrison and Anderson turned around. Ruth took out Harrison's watch and walked over to him. His face was crimson. She slapped the watch in his hand. 'Give your wife my sympathies, won't you.' She turned to Tippwick as the footsteps of the two Special Branch detectives faded behind her. 'Has the next of kin been informed?'

'Nae yet, lassie. He has an aunt in St Mary's, was going to send young Rowland.'

'Would you like me to break the news, I've been trained for grief counselling?' St Mary's, where had she heard that name before?

Tippwick rose on his heels. 'That would be very kind, ma'am.' He took out his notepad, scribbled down the address and passed it her. She glanced at the paper, relieved his handwriting had more clarity than his accent.

'Unless there's anything else?' she asked Tiernay.

The man shook his head, his eyes now glowered at Tippwick. 'No, thank you. That will be all.'

Tom recognised most of the faces outside St Magnus. The warden to the cathedral, his overhanging belly providing an unmistakable outline, stood among the flashing lights of the police cars, shaking his head at a small crowd of locals surrounding him. Luckily for Tom, Mrs Trout, who must have caught the bus from Tingwall, had collared the news reporter from the Kirkwall Herald so failed to spot him arriving. Good.

PC Rowland stood outside the cathedral, so Tom pulled out his notepad and ducked under the police tape.

'Herwig, how's it going?'

'Oh, hi, Tom.' The young constable glanced around, before leaning forward. 'Tom, please call me PC Rowland when I'm on duty, and you're not allowed back here.'

Tom ducked back beneath the tape. 'Sorry, pal. Just wanted to know what was happening?'

'Sorry, but I'm not supposed to talk to you. Not after last time.'

Two months earlier, Chief Constable Tiernay left his keys in his car. Somebody stole it. The story made a page lead in the nationals, earning Tom enough money to buy the old VW. All thanks to a few loose words from Rowland.

Tom put away his notepad. 'No problem. I only came down to give that psychiatrist a lift.'

'The one from Scotland? She's really pretty.'

Tom always found it amusing to hear people on Orkney refer to non-islanders as from Scotland. He looked back over to the crowd outside the gates. A battered Land Rover sat idling on the curbside. He couldn't see the driver, but recognised the vehicle. He turned to Rowland. 'Isn't that Clark, the salmon man?'

Rowland squinted at the Land Rover. 'Aye, I think so.'

Tom peered back. 'Wonder what he's doing here? Not

normally the inquisitive type.'

They'd only met once, but Tom found James Clark a prickly sod. Five years earlier, Clark bought an old quarry on the small island of Lamb Holm and turned it into a salmon farm. His business boomed at the same time as the stock exchange – his smoked salmon fuelling the yuppies in the city. But despite the obvious fortune, he still drove round in that battered old jeep, and never passed the time of day with anybody. He lived like as a recluse, in an old farmhouse on the island, with nothing but his fish and a few sheep for company. When Tom first arrived on Orkney he approached Clark with plans to do a rags-to-riches feature. Miserable sod threatened Tom with a shotgun and told him where to shove his newspaper.

The cathedral door opened, diverting Tom's attention from the Land Rover. Two medics clambered out with a stretcher. Tom walked back under the police tape, holding it aloft for the stretcher. He watched them carry the body to the ambulance outside the gates. Once loaded, they slammed the doors shut and drove toward the hospital, without their siren on.

As the ambulance left, the Land Rover moved away. Tom's eyes watched it until it reached the bottom of the road. He turned to say something to Rowland, but more people began emerging from the cathedral, including Ruth, with the same expression across her face he first saw in his office. The frightening one.

They drove in silence. Ruth remained cold and distant. They'd stopped off in Tingwall, so she could get changed, but since then he'd given up on conversation, receiving nothing but aloof nods. Perhaps, he thought, the impending *death-knock* had gotten to her, but she should be used to them by now. No. He knew what it was.

Always fun for a night but not many women saw Tom as a long-term thing. Ruth probably dated men with five-figure salaries and the keys to their own home. He didn't think of her as shallow. It was not about money. Tom was content with his lot, but most women preferred a man with more ambition and he understood that.

'Do you want me to come in with you?' he asked as he pulled up outside the address Tippwick had given her.

'No.' She gave him one of those smiles, which said: *please don't speak to me.* 'I have to go in alone. The rules.'

He nodded.

She stepped from the car, holding the door open. 'I'm not sure how long I'll be. I can make my own way back, if you want?'

'No, I'll wait. Unless you'd rather I go?' He felt a big thump in his chest. His heart didn't seem to beat again until she answered.

'No, please stay.' She smiled more warmly. 'I'll try and be as quick as I can.'

She shut the door.

He watched her straighten herself up and walk up the path, knocking on the door to the unassuming cottage. He shook his head, and turned on the radio.

The announcer introduced the first of that week's top twenty hits. Tom wasn't a *Chas and Dave* fan, but for some reason, *Ain't No Pleasing You* summed up the moment. He turned up the volume.

Chapter Thirteen

The bright red lipstick appearing at the door looked as if a five-year-old applied it. Its wearer, a rather skinny middle-aged woman with bad skin and long, lank hair, held a superking menthol at the end of her fingers. She stared at Ruth distastefully, the way older women often did.

'Can I help you?' Her accent sounded local, but she wore a sarong and had pair of curled Moroccan slippers on her feet.

Ruth took out her identification. 'Miss Elizabeth Carty?'

'It's Ms,' she snapped, glaring at the card. 'Are you from the police?'

'Yes, I work as a consultant. They've asked me to come here to speak to you about Ian Brennan. There's been an incident.'

'Ian?' She prodded her extra-long cigarette towards her. 'Well, I can tell you he has done nothing wrong. There are too many bigots on this island who enjoy evil gossip –'

'You don't understand, *Ms* Carty.' Ruth's tone silenced her. 'May I come in?'

The woman frowned, but opened the door wider.

Ruth stepped into a narrow hallway with pictures of Judy Garland, Bette Davis and a select few other Hollywood actresses adorning the walls. Incense burned in phallic-looking candleholders on a little table near the doorway.

'Through here,' the Bohemian-looking woman said, her long black hair swinging behind her. She led Ruth into the parlour. 'Hope you like cats.'

The smell of stale urine hit the back of Ruth's throat long

before she saw them. Her nose contracted and she sneezed.

They were everywhere. Four sat along the dresser, their almond eyes blinking languidly as Ruth let out another sneeze. Another couple miaowed at her feet, and she released yet another sneeze as she stepped over them.

'Are you allergic?' Ms Carty asked, shooing two more cats off the parlour table.

Ruth sneezed again, but held up her hand. 'It's okay, I'll be fine.'

Ms Carty sat down at the table and lifted up one of the moggies, a fat ginger tabby, which she proceeded to stroke far too firmly. It miaowed and shook itself free. 'So what's all this about? Has something happened to Ian? Has he been arrested again?'

Ruth sat down, trying to suppress yet another sneeze. She paused until it subsided. 'No, it's nothing like that – why, has Mr Brennan been in trouble before?'

Ms Carty sucked at her cigarette like a child slurping up a milkshake. 'I suppose you'll find out, soon enough,' she said, letting out a cloud of menthol smoke. 'Ian is a gay man, and a lot of people don't like that. Last year, one of the boy's in the choir made some accusations – they were unfounded.'

Ruth shook her head. 'It's not about that. I'm afraid Mr Brennan suffered a heart attack this afternoon.'

Ms Carty slowly removed the cigarette from her mouth. 'Heart attack? He's only twenty-six, what do you mean? How is he?'

Ruth took a deep breath in preparation for the next part. The part she hated. 'I'm sorry to have to tell you – aw-choo.' Her eyes began to stream. 'I'm sorry – aw-choo. But Mr Brennan – aw-choo. I'm sorry, but Mr Brennan has passed away. Aw-choo-ee.'

Ms Carty's lower lip trembled. She took a deep drag of the cigarette and bowed her head. A croak turned into a wail, and then she began bawling in earnest.

Battling against her nasal convulsions, Ruth placed an arm around her. 'I'm so sorry, Ms Carty.'

The woman clutched Ruth's arm and sobbed for a moment. 'Can I see him?' she asked, with her mascara streaking down her face.

'I'm sure that can be arranged. In fact. I think as next of kin they may want you to identify him.'

The woman wailed again, and Ruth, still sneezing, continued to comfort her until, finally, she stopped crying and looked up. 'I'm not his next of kin,' she said, the streaked mascara now reminding Ruth of Alice Cooper.

'Ah-choo. But I thought you were his aunt?'

The woman began sobbing again, but stood up and walked over to the dresser. She shooed off the cats, and lifted up a picture and walked back, showing it to Ruth. The picture contained three fair-skinned boys, wearing choir smocks, with two priests stood behind.

'That was Ian,' Ms Carty said, prodding the photograph. 'Taken from the home. He was always a singer. Beautiful voice. Must have been about sixteen then.'

'So he came from an orphanage?' Ruth sneezed, and handed back the picture.

The woman nodded, and held the picture at arm's length, letting out a little nasal laugh. 'He used to call me aunty, but I'm only his landlady. He was so brave. Coming from the background he did, and being a homosexual, especially out here – there's so much prejudice.'

Ruth's sneezes caused tears to stream down her face too. 'So he had no other next of kin?'

Ms Carty shook her head and Ruth suddenly remembered where she heard the name St Mary's before. 'There's an orphanage around here, isn't there?'

'Used to be.' Ms Carty tapped the photograph. 'That's where Ian went. It's no longer there now.'

Ruth stood up and gripped the woman's arm, studying the picture again. 'So who are the others?'

Ms Carty looked at the photograph. 'Oh, I can't remember their names. Ian never spoke much about his experiences. Must have been horrid.'

'Was one of those boys called Michael?'

'I'm afraid I don't know.'

She sounded a little nervous and Ruth realised she was gripping the woman's arm rather too forcefully. She released it and sneezed. 'What about the priests. Did Ian ever mention a Father Walker?'

Ms Carty shook her head. 'He didn't speak about it too much. Although.' She tapped the picture. 'This boy is still on the island, somewhere. Although, there must have been some falling out because he and Ian don't speak.'

Ruth desperately tried to contain her sneezing. 'Can you remember his name?'

The woman stubbed her cigarette out as she thought. 'Sorry, I don't think – hold on.' She stared at the picture. 'He has the same name as a racing driver.'

'Racing driver?'

'Yes, you know, the Scottish one.'

'Achoo-ee. You mean Jackie Stewart?'

Ms Carty thought. 'I think so.'

Ruth thanked her, sneezed, and asked if there was anyone she should call. Ms Carty said no, and sat back down. She stared at the picture and lit another superking. Ruth said she would see herself out, and sneezed, apologized for Ms Carty's loss, before sneezing again, said sorry about her sneezing, sneezed once more, and then left.

Tom, drumming away to *Eye Of The Tiger* on the steering wheel, jumped up when Ruth opened the car door. She sat down. Her eyes streamed with tears while her nose was bright red. He turned down the radio. 'I'm sorry. I guess that must have been really difficult for you.'

She looked at him with her puffy eyes, before bursting into laughter. 'Cats,' she said, dabbing at her eyes with a tissue. 'The woman has cats. I'm allergic.'

After taking a second to catch on, Tom also burst into laughter, and they both chuckled until their sniggers turned to giggles, and eventually to silence.

They sat quietly for a moment, until Ruth said: 'Do you know anyone called Jackie Stewart?'

'You mean like the grand prix driver?'

She nodded.

He thought about it, but nothing came to mind. 'No, why?'

'Oh, it's just someone Brennan used to know.' She finished wiping her eyes before saying: 'They both went to the same home as Michael.'

'Who, your patient?'

'Yes, and I'm beginning to think it might all be connected. There's too many coincidences.'

He turned the ignition key. 'You best go and tell Tippwick, or that inspector.' The Beetle failed to start. He tried again.

'Anderson! No chance. I've already embarrassed myself in front of him already.'

The car fired and he adjusted the choke. 'What do you mean?'

She shook her head. 'Never mind, it's not important, but I need more than just another coincidence. I want to find this Jackie Stewart, see if he knows something.'

'Well, I don't know him. A name like that would kind of stick –' He sat upright, remembering whom he saw outside St Magnus. 'What exactly did she say? That his name was Jackie?'

'No, just that he had the same name as him, or that Scottish racing driver, as she put it.'

Tom placed both hands on the steering wheel and stared ahead. 'Jim Clark.'

'Sorry?'

'Jim Clark was a Scottish racing driver. Won the Formula One championship in the sixties.'

'I don't get it?'

'I know a Jim Clark, well a James Clark, anyway. I saw him outside the cathedral.'

She grabbed his arm. 'Where does he live?'

He pointed ahead, to the ocean. 'Lamb Holm, just out there. We're on the south shore of Mainland. That's Scapa Flow, where they sunk the German fleet.'

'Never mind the history lesson, is there a ferry?'

'Don't need one, the road runs along the causeway, takes you right to it.'

'Then what are we waiting for, let's go.' She pulled her seatbelt over her arm.

He shook his head. He didn't relish the prospect of facing Jim Clark, and his shotgun. 'Hold on, I just told you, I saw him by the cathedral in town, he probably won't be home. Besides, it'll be dark soon and will be too dangerous to go driving round the barriers, we'll end up ditching in the sea.'

In actuality, the cat's eyes along the causeway made navigating at night pretty easy, and with stonewalls surrounding the road, they'd be perfectly safe, but she didn't know that.

'Will you take me tomorrow morning, then?'

'First thing, I promise. We'll take Sophie. She's only got PE in the morning, which she always misses anyway. Might make him easier to talk to – he's a miserable sod.' He also wanted as many witnesses as possible. Even Clark wouldn't shoot a schoolgirl.

'Oh, okay.'

He knew by now she didn't take kindly to not getting her own way, and felt relieved to see her just shrug. He lifted up the handbrake. 'So what do you want to do now?'

She smiled at him, her top lip squeezed between her teeth. 'I want you to take me back home to bed.'

Chapter Fourteen

Chief Constable Tiernay marched into Tingwall station with his cap under his arm, a folder under the other, and his lips pursed tight. As a rare and unwelcome visitor to the parish station, Tiernay's appearance caused Constable Rowland, who was sipping tea behind the desk, to bolt to attention at the sight of him. 'Ggg ... good morning, sir.'

'It was,' snapped Tiernay. 'Where's Detective Sergeant Tippwick?'

'In his office, sir. Would you like me to fetch him?'

Tiernay didn't answer but proceeded to barge his way through the inner door. He found Tippwick, also sipping tea whilst twiddling his moustache in quiet contemplation. At the sight of Tiernay, the old detective, who seemed surprised as Rowland to see the chief in Tingwall again, placed his teacup on the desk. 'Why, good morning, sir. There be something the matter?'

'I'll tell you what's the matter,' barked Tiernay, slapping the folder on the desk. 'What is the meaning of this?'

'I disnae understand, sir.'

'Your report, man. I thought we had an understanding. Didn't I say last night that the Eynhallow and St Magnus cases are closed – haven't you embarrassed me enough in front of Special Branch as it is?'

'Nae my intention, sir, but something about 'em disnae sit right in mae goots –'

'Sit right? You are a detective man. You listen to evidence not your goots – I mean guts.'

'Aye, sir, but I thought until we heard from Dr Phelps, we ought to keep an open mind. Especially after I spoke to that wee lad.'

'The one who left the shirt behind?'

'Aye sir.'

'Well, what did he say?'

'Just as the good doctor said. Mr Brennan collapsed, clutching his chest.'

'Well, there you go. Natural causes.'

'Aye, sir, but he seems to have the impression there may have been somebody else in the cathedral at the time.'

'Who?'

'He couldnae say. Didn't actually see him.'

'Didn't see him?' Tiernay glowered at him. 'You listen here, Tippwick. I don't need that boorish inspector telling me how to do my job again. So unless Dr Phelps says otherwise – both deaths were natural causes.'

'Aye, sir, but –'

'No, buts Tippwick!' Tiernay screwed his cap on to his head. 'Close the damned case or you may find yourself back in uniform. I really do not want to keep coming down here.'

'Aye-sir.'

Tiernay glanced at his watch. 'Now you've made me late for my meeting.' He about turned and marched out of the office.

The morning sun looked as bright as the yellow Beetle Tom drove across the B-roads of Orkney. Only a few clouds threatened to float in front of the sun, and even the normally cold wind blowing through Tom's open window tickled Ruth with warmth.

He whistled as he drove, while little Sophie nattered away at the back. Ruth sat in the passenger seat, smoking Tom's cigarettes and feeling awkward.

She had woke to the sound of his soft snores, his arm across her naked body, and two cups of hot coffee by the bed – Sophie possessed enough decorum not to disturb them when she arrived at work that morning. And now, as the little girl leaned in between the seats, rattling away like an old spinster. For the first time in a long time, Ruth felt like part of a family. Yet, none of it seemed right.

Why?

Tom made her laugh, they had a lot in common, he was good-looking enough and enthusiastic in bed, he had no wife or kids – apart from Sophie, but that didn't count – nor any of the bullshit machismo of Sergeant Harrison, nor the pretentiousness of Gerard Barry. He didn't even treat her as an executive toy, unlike every other bastard she'd hooked up with since graduating. No, she knew what the problem was and it wasn't Tom.

He smiled as Sophie questioned Ruth on subjects as diverse as her favourite band, if she thought boys had any ideas on fashion, and even what age she began her period. Ruth didn't mind the interrogation, she just wished they both would stop being so bloody nice. It made what she had to do later so much harder.

The drive to St Mary's didn't take long and they soon approached the coastal village with the deep blue ribbon of Scapa Flow in front of them.

Tom pointed across the bay. 'Lamb Holm.'

Ruth's eyes followed the road as it left the village, stretched across the sea and connected to an island before snaking off into the distance to yet another isle.

They drove through the village and followed the road along the causeway, leaving Mainland behind and cutting through the crashing foam of Scapa Flow that flanked them on both sides.

The barrier road soon fed into Lamb Holm and Sophie continued prattling away as Ruth surveyed the island. Perhaps a little larger than Eynhallow, but only slightly, Lamb Holm was equally barren. Hundreds of ruminating sheep kept the grass short, which spread across the isle like a giant lawn, and only a couple of bland farm buildings bordering the road broke up the monotonous skyline.

Tom slowed, pulling the car down a cutting at the side of the road. The trail fed to a fork, one road leading to a car park, fronting a rather enchanting red and white church, the other stopping at a gate.

'Pretty,' Ruth said, looking at the ornate chapel. Little red pinnacles and a tiny bell tower decorated the frontage, although she couldn't help notice the rear of the church resembled an old air-raid shelter.

'Yes, the Italian POWs built it during the war,' Tom said, stopping the car at the gate. He yanked on the handbrake's ratchet. 'Clark's fish farm is down there,' He peered through the windscreen. 'This gate's new. Told you he didn't like visitors. I guess we'll have to walk.'

With no fence either side, the purpose of the gate seemed solely to keep unwanted vehicles out. A silver padlock and gleaming chain fastened it to two posts, but the trail continued beyond the gate and stretched to the far side of the island. It bordered the barrier road that carried on through Lamb Holm and stretched back out to sea and on to the next island.

As Ruth followed the trail with her eyes, she jumped, as a loud crack sounded. Another soon followed and the trio stared at each other. 'Shotgun,' Tom said, his eyes wide as saucers.

After another report of gunfire, a tapping on the window beside Ruth's shoulder caused her to shriek.

Staring at them and steaming up the window, a grizzled face. The man wore a woollen hat, complete with bobble and propped himself on a giant, hooked walking stick.

Ruth turned to Tom. 'Is that Jim Clark?'

Equally alarmed, he shook his head.

With the winder not working, Ruth had to open the car door to speak to him. The man stepped back and straightened up as she peered tentatively out.

He towered well above six feet. Clenched jaw, leathered skin, chiselled chin and dark stubble. Her mind turned to Bronte's Heathcliff, only in a bobble hat. He leaned on what she now realised was a shepherd's crook, an implement she thought had disappeared in the middle ages. He also had a shotgun strapped to his back, and that alarmed her.

'You here to see Clark?' he demanded, his voice deep and throaty.

'Yes –' The reports of shotgun fire continuing to crackle in the air and sounded louder now the door lay open. Much louder.

'Well, ye can tell him to fix that fence. I've lost three sheep over his quarry this week.'

'I'm afraid we don't actually know Mr Clark, we're just here to speak –'

'– I don't bloody care who ye are. Tell him to fix that fence or he'll have me t' deal with.'

Sophie poked her head through the door, and sneered at him. 'Why don't you tell him yourself?'

Ruth turned to see Tom pulling the youngster back, using the camera strap around her neck and his hand to cover her mouth.

The man glowered at them, but gave a weak grin. 'Aye, I would, but last time he threatened me with his bloody gun.' He tapped his shotgun on his shoulder, menacingly. 'If I have to go up there, I reckon only one of us will be eating supper that night. Just tell him to fix that fence.' He turned around and ambled away, using the crook as a walking stick.

'Who the hell was that?' Ruth asked.

Tom shrugged. 'Don't know, but let's hurry up and find Clark before he comes back.'

Chapter Fifteen

After leaving the car and tramping around the gate, they carried on down the trail until it led to yet another gate, this one bordered by thin wire fencing – razor wire – and signage warning off trespassers.

A stile offered a route through, and after clambering over, they followed the trail down to a ledge overlooking the quarry.

The trail continued around to a run-down farmhouse sat farther up, with Clark's old Land Rover parked outside. The source of shotgun fire, however, came from below, where a shallow incline led to the quarry floor. Peering down the slope, Ruth saw several large pools of water bubbling with fish. Netting spanned across them and a trellis walkway floated around the edges. A few out-houses and corrugated sheds surrounded the pools, as did mechanical diggers and a trailer from an articulated lorry.

Clark stood on the trellis, the shotgun tight at his shoulder and the barrel pointing at a flock of gulls flying above him.

Crack. Crack.

He reloaded, and Ruth felt uneasy about approaching a man wielding a gun, so she began waving her arms, much to the disapproval of Tom.

'You sure, that's wise? Shouldn't we wait –'

Crack, crack.

'– until he's finished.'

But Ruth continued gesturing as Clark reloaded again, letting off two more shots before spotting her.

'Who the hell are you!' he shouted, marching off the trellis and walking across the quarry floor to stand below them. He looked up, the shotgun broken across his arm. 'Well?'

'Mr Clark? I work as a consultant for the police.' She began stepping down the incline. 'I wish to talk to you about – arghh!' She regretted having changing out of her trainers, the wet grass provided little grip and she slipped, sliding on her bottom to the quarry floor, landing with a thump at his feet. He scowled at her, but reluctantly helped her up.

She thanked him. Her backside hurt, but she ignored it, trying to regain some semblance of professionalism. She began brushing herself off.

Clark stared back up the ledge, as Tom and Sophie tried clambering down. 'This is no place for children!' His eyes squinted at Tom. 'I know you, don't I? You're that reporter!'

'I just gave her a lift,' Tom said, pulling Sophie back by the camera strap.

Ruth raised her palms to Tom. 'Perhaps you two should wait in the car.'

Tom nodded and tugged Sophie farther back, to some mutterings of protest, but they soon disappeared from sight.

'You're a copper, you say?' Clark's eyes dropped to her muddied suit and he sniffed. 'If this is about that fence, tell that git Jerome I'll get round to fixing it in my time!'

'I'm not here about the fence, and I'm not a police officer. I'm a psychiatrist, working for the police.' She took out her identification but he didn't acknowledge it. 'I'm here about Ian Brennan and Michael Skye.'

His grey face froze at the names.

Old for his age, the cold wind had long ago removed any softness to his skin. Stern too, with a shaved head giving him a skinhead's appearance, not a millionaire's. His eyes flickered with memories for a moment before he clicked the breech of his shotgun closed.

'If you're not a copper, I don't have to talk to you. If you excuse me, lassie. I've got work to do.' He placed the shotgun to his shoulder, turned around, and with no warning, fired.

Crack, crack.

Ruth's eardrums would ring for days, and she found herself cowed over, holding her hands over her ears, which rang with tinnitus when he finished. She couldn't even hear her own voice when she spoke. 'I know you were at St Magnus yesterday, and I know you used to go to St Mary's with Ian.'

Still with his back to her, he broke open the breech and pulled out the two smoking shells, replaced them, locked the gun closed again, and raised it to his shoulder.

Crack. Crack.

She had prepared herself this time, and the resulting tinnitus wasn't as severe. The echo of the shots subsided, and she said: 'Michael Skye escaped from Eynhallow. But you know that, don't you?'

Clark had broken the breech, but his hand hovered over the two spent shells in the chamber.

'Michael had something to do with Ian Brennan's death, didn't he?' Ruth still couldn't hear herself properly, and wondered if she spoke in that strange way deaf people did. She hoped not.

He pulled the two shells from the gun and placed them in his pocket. He turned to face her. Tears streamed down his face.

Compared to Clark, Howard Hughes lived a life of wanton abandonment. The salmon millionaire's home humbled any Ruth had ever visited – and she'd been in some strange houses.

One psychiatric patient never threw anything away, resulting in a house stacked almost ceiling high full of rubbish, atop of which the patient ate, slept and did everything else. While another patient refused to sleep indoors, and took all his worldly possessions and positioned them in the garden. He stayed there, even during the winter. Until they sectioned him.

Clark, however, lived a life of severe frugality. Nothing sat in his parlour other than a table, a transistor radio held together with insulation tape, and two chairs. If not for his millions, she thought, he would have long ago attracted social workers and psychiatrists. He obviously suffered from a severe form of depression.

He had made her tea, sickly sweet with the tang of sterilised milk, but she thanked him, and sat at the parlour table as he sat brooding opposite, holding his head in his hands.

'Been a long time since I heard that name,' he finally said, removing his hands and revealing eyes glistening with moisture.

'Who, Ian Brennan?'

He let out a nasal laugh. 'No, I've seen him flouncing about town.' He sipped at his tea. 'Poof.'

'So you mean Michael? I take it you heard about him getting out of Eynhallow?'

He nodded at the radio. 'Heard somebody escaped. Knew it was him.'

'Why?'

He sipped his tea again, and shook his head. 'Cannae say. Just had that feeling. Same as when I saw the police outside the cathedral. Knew he'd got Brennan.'

'Why? Why would he go after Brennan?'

Clark leaned back on his chair and rubbed his temples. She could hear the roughness of his fingers across his brow. 'Been ten years since they put him away.'

'For attacking Father Walker?'

Clark sniffed another laugh but didn't look up. 'He had it coming.'

'Why?'

Clark kept his head down. 'We all knew what Walker was doing. Even McKinnion.'

'McKinnion?'

'Aye, Father McKinnion, ran the home. Walker was his junior. Michael told him what Walker was doing. Didn't believe him.'

'What was he doing?'

Clark fell silent, but Ruth had guessed. She expected scandals like these to rock the Catholic Church one day. Too common, far too common. 'He was mistreating him, wasn't he?'

Clark didn't say anything and Ruth didn't press him. She could tell the man's nerves ran close to the edge. His eyes kept darting to his shotgun propped against the wall, and he couldn't hold her gaze.

'You said Michael had told Father McKinnion about Walker.'

He raised his head, eyes still glistening. 'Aye, and he did nothing. So Walker singled him out.' He bowed his head again. 'At least it kept him from us.'

Ruth opened her mouth to speak, but found words unforthcoming. He stared intently at her, his eyes narrow, his brow creased, but said: 'We all said nothing. Nothing! Even when they locked him up.'

Ruth leaned forward, and gently touched the man's hands. He withdrew them and stood, his chair scratching the bare floorboards behind. He spun around, showing her his back.

'You must leave. It's not safe.'

'What do you mean?' Ruth asked.

Clark shook his head and turned to the shotgun lying by the door again. He walked over and picked it up, and then pulled open the door. 'He'll be coming here.'

'Who, Michael?'

He placed two shotgun shells into his gun. 'He'll be coming for me next.'

'Mr Clark, I'm sure you're just being paranoid –'

'– I said leave!' He snapped the breech shut and pointed to the door.

Ruth decided it best to go. She smiled and placed a hand on his arm as she stepped out. 'If you need to talk, I'm staying in Tingwall, at the Finn Mann.'

He didn't respond, just stood motionless, until she was clear of the door. He slammed it shut.

After clambering back over the stile and tramping down the trail, Ruth climbed back into the VW, where Sophie and Tom sat bickering over which radio station to have on. They quietened as she slumped into the seat. Ruth's first words, were: 'Have you got a cigarette?'

Tom scrambled around in the glove box and pulled one out of the packet. 'So, how did it go?'

She placed the cigarette in her mouth, and he lit it. 'Michael's behind what happened to Brennan. I'm sure of it.'

'Your patient? I thought he drowned?'

'So do the police, but it all fits. Clark never said as much, but I'm pretty sure that priest Walker was abusing them all.'

'Gives him grounds for self-defence,' Tom suggested.

Ruth nodded. She'd have to tell the police, and get somebody to call on Clark. The man was suicidal. He needed sectioning, for his own safety. Someone also needed to take that damned gun off him.

'Where to now?' Tom asked, attempting to start the VW, which fired on the third attempt.

She studied his face and felt a pang of guilt. She had some bad news to tell Tom – not that she didn't like him, she did, but he wasn't her type, not really. He just didn't fit with all the other faces, faces that flashed through her mind like the contacts in a Rollodex – doctors, consultants and administrators with houses in suburbia and time-shares in the Algarve. People like Dr Gerard Barry.

But first things first, she thought, taking a deep drag of her cigarette. 'I want to find Tippwick, see if he'll come up here. They need to know what I've found out.'

'Wouldn't you be better telling that Special Branch fella, the Glaswegian?'

'Anderson!' She spat out his name like unwanted chewing gum. She shook her head. 'Not unless I have to.'

Chapter Sixteen

'Do you want us to wait?' Tom asked, as he halted the VW outside Tingwall station.

Ruth shook her head as she unbuckled her seatbelt. 'No, I'll be fine.'

'You sure?' He gave her those hand-dog eyes, again.

'Yes, I've wasted enough of your day, already.'

'I wouldn't worry about it,' Sophie said, leaning over the seats. 'He hasn't much else to do with his time.'

Ruth smiled. She'd miss Sophie, miss them both, but she knew prolonging it would only make matters worse. 'No, it's okay, but could I see you later? I could do with a chat.'

'Sure.' Sophie said, grinning.

'Not you. You've got to get to school.' Tom pushed the youngster back on to the back seat. 'Yeah, no problem, what time?'

Ruth checked her watch. 'Not sure. Come round to the Finn Mann, after lunch, I should be free by then.'

Tom nodded eagerly and smiled. Ruth didn't.

After closing the car door, she bounded up to the steps, resisting the urge to glance back at the car and the two pairs of eyes watching her walk into the station.

PC Rowland put down his teacup and gave Ruth a diffident smile as she walked up to the desk. 'Good morning, ma'am.'

'Morning, is Sergeant Tippwick here, or Chief Constable Tiernay?'

'The chief constable's due here after his game of golf – I mean his meeting, ma'am, but the sergeant is in his office. Can I ask what it is about?'

'I need to talk to him about Michael Skye.'

'The escaped patient?'

She nodded and Rowland disappeared from behind the desk, only to reappear at the inner door. 'Best come in then, ma'am. This way.'

He led her down the corridor to an office marked CID, where he knocked, before announcing her arrival. 'Dr Duncan, to see you, sir.'

Tippwick looked up from his desk where a half-eaten chocolate éclair sat on a plate. Most of the cream was smeared around his moustache. 'Please forgive me, Doctor. I was in the middle of my elevenses.'

'Sorry to disturb you, Sergeant,' Ruth said, stepping into the cramped office. Two empty desks sat opposite Tippwick, and she realised that the whiskered sergeant accounted for the entire CID unit in Tingwall.

'Something the matter, miss?' Tippwick dismissed Rowland with a nod, leaving Ruth alone in the office with the detective.

Ruth took a deep breath and began. 'I have been over to see Ian Brennan's aunt – although she wasn't his aunt – and she told me about Jim Clark – although she didn't say his name was Jim Clark – Tom found that out – and we went to see him – and he told me about Father Walker – and Ian Brennan – and how Michael knew them both – and he thinks it was Michael that attacked Ian – because Father McKinnion – he owned the home that Father Walker ran – he's the man who Michael killed – or accused of killing – ignored Michael when he said – and it's all a coincidence – but I really think that – '

'Please.' Tippwick held his hand up and wiped the cream off his whiskers. He indicated for her to take a seat. 'Ye'll have to start again, only a little slower, I cannae understand a word yer saying.'

Ruth sighed, sat down, and started her story again.

After Ruth finished her tale, Tippwick leaned back on his chair, his éclair now gone, and licked his teeth clean as he thought.

'So you see, Sergeant, I know it's all a big coincidence, but Jim Clark is pretty convinced it's Michael. He's not very stable, though. I really think you ought to send somebody over and at least take that shotgun off him.'

Tippwick nodded. 'Aye, sounds highly strung – and all three boys were under a Father McKinnion, you say?'

'Yes, but Tom's looked in the phone book and there's no record of him on the island.'

Tippwick twitched his whiskers and leaned forward, just as the door opened behind them.

In the doorway, wearing chequered trousers, a gaudy green sweater, golfing shoes on his feet, and clutching a folder, Chief Constable Tiernay stood with a rigid face and narrowed eyes. He turned to Tippwick. 'What's going on?'

'Doctor Duncan just dropped by with some interesting information, sir.'

'Oh?'

Tippwick proceeded to tell him an abridged version of Ruth's tale. The chief remained motionless in the doorway until he finished. After a brief pause, his eyes flickered at Ruth before settling on Tippwick again.

'I told you, Sergeant,' he said, very slowly and brandishing the folder. 'The case is closed.' He turned to Ruth. 'I'm sorry, Doctor, but this is all coincidence and hearsay. I'm afraid police work involves evidence not coincidences – as well you know, Sergeant.' He had snapped his head at Tippwick and remained glowering him as he continued. 'I appreciate your concerns for Jim Clark, but I can't reopen a murder investigation just because of some highly strung eccentric.'

'But with respect,' Ruth said, 'the three of them coming from the same care home is –'

'A coincidence. The case is closed, isn't it, Sergeant?' Tiernay threw the folder at Tippwick. 'I expect that signed off and closed by this afternoon!' He turned on his heels and stormed out.

Tippwick shrugged at Ruth, who, after a moment's pause, followed the chief constable and shouted after him in the corridor. 'Perhaps I should explain all this to Inspector Anderson, then?'

Tiernay halted and turned about. He smiled, although his lips didn't widen much. 'I wish you good luck with that, I really do.'

Chapter Seventeen

'I'm sorry, Inspector, it's only eleven-thirty, I cannae serve you a drink.' Mrs Trout stood in the snug with one hand on her hip and a glass of orange juice in the other. 'This is all you can have. Ye know the law, surely?'

'Know it? Dammit woman, I am the bloody law.'

'Ye'll get no favours from me using language like that.' She sniffed, placed the drink on the table, turned tail and walked out.

Anderson scowled at the orange juice in front of him and took out his bottle of pills. He swallowed two dry and winced as they struggled to make their way down his throat. He looked across at Harrison, who was scratching a fork across his plate and had egg dripping from his wispy moustache.

Mrs Trout, re-emerged to replace their ashtray. 'Your elevenses all right?'

'Fine, thank you,' Harrison replied as the old woman flitted back out of the snug.

'Miserable old bitch,' Anderson muttered, before hearing her shrill voice filter back through the door.

'Oh, Doctor. If ye said you didn't want the room last night I could have let it oot.'

'I'm sorry, Mrs Trout, but have you seen the inspector, this morning?'

Anderson looked at Harrison. The sergeant's knife and fork clattered on his plate as Ruth walked in.

'What a load of bollocks,' Anderson said, causing Mrs Trout to drop an ashtray behind them. She'd been polishing the same one for the last five minutes as Ruth regaled them with her tale of Clark, Brennan and Michael.

Anderson smiled as she stormed out. *Nosey cow*, he thought. He turned back to Ruth. She looked like she'd been rollicking around the fields all morning. Covered in mud, with grass stains all up her backside. But she had tenacity, he'd give her that.

'Didn't you hear me, Inspector? Don't you think it's a coincidence they all went to this same home?'

Anderson shook his head, and sighed. At least they'd be leaving soon. He expected Phelps to call with the results from the choirmaster's autopsy at anytime, and once he'd called, Anderson could slink back to Inverness with a clear conscience, a bloated liver, and a fistful of receipts to put through expenses.

'Have you heard this, Harrison?' he said, hoping the atmosphere between the pair would be enough to send her packing.

'What's that, sir?' Harrison asked, pretending to take an interest in the ingredients that went into a packet of pork scratchings.

'She reckons that escaped nut killed the choirmaster.'

'And why would he do that?' Harrison said, not even looking up.

'Haven't you been listening? Father Walker had been abusing him. The others knew about it and said nothing, even when Michael was committed.' She stood with her hands on her hips, looming over them both and blocking the light.

Anderson was attempting to roll a smoke. 'And this fish fiddler, from where did you say? He told you all this, did he?'

'Lamb Holm, and not in so many words, but don't you think it strange they went to the same orphanage?'

'No, I think it's a coincidence, and you expect them on a small island.' He licked his roll up together and pointed it at her. 'Listen, even if your patient was buggered seven ways from Sunday, and was still all upset about it – he drowned!'

'Nobody's found a body yet, have they?' Ruth said.

Anderson placed his cigarette between his lips and reached for Harrison's lighter. 'No, but we know he didn't kill that choirmaster. There was a witness, apparently. And what about the heart attacks?' He lit his cigarette and blew a cloud of blue smoke across the table. 'How is he meant to give people coronaries – by scaring 'em to death?'

'I – don't know, but you must admit all these people having heart attacks can't just be coincidence, can it?'

'What else can it be?' He sighed; he had to admire her stubbornness. 'Look, you're telling all this to the wrong person. It's Tiernay and Tip-tip's investigation. Go and pester them with your theories.'

She fell silent, and Anderson grinned. 'Ah, I take it you have, and they sent you packing, ain't that right?'

She pursed her lips and looked about to protest when Mrs Trout re-emerged and interrupted. 'Excuse me Inspector.'

'What is it? You opened the bar, yet?'

'Ahem, no, another ten minutes. There's a telephone call for you.'

With the cigarette hanging from his lips, he gave Ruth a condescending smile. 'You're digging around for things that ain't there, love. Now, if you'll excuse me.'

He walked to the phone leaving Ruth and Harrison in an uncomfortable silence.

Tom sat rewording a press release from the Orkney Flower Arranging Association. Typing with one finger, the other held a cigarette that burned to his knuckles. He stubbed it out and relit another.

'Let's just be friends,' Ruth had said. He lost count of how many times he heard those words. He expected the elbow, though, but it still stung, even though the relationship was only a few days old. 'A sort of a holiday romance', was Ruth's description. Pah.

He made no mention of their conversation to Sophie, although he figured she had guessed. She'd taken the afternoon off school and was there when he returned from seeing Ruth. He rarely snapped at Sophie, but he lost his temper with her questioning. She was now downstairs, keeping herself scarce and tidying his room, but appeared every half an hour or so with a cup of coffee and a sympathetic smile.

He felt guilty, without Sophie he'd have nobody, although he knew that wouldn't last, either. She'd had several meetings with foster families over the last few months, and despite her best efforts to put them off, mentioning her record, and making up hobbies like the saxophone, one couple would come along, eventually. And then where would he be?

He looked at his copy on the typewriter, pulled the paper off the reels and screwed it up. No girl, no career, soon no Sophie. Alone and miserable – might as well go back on the powder. No, not that, never. Besides, he doubted scoring gear in Orkney would be an easy task. Just as well, as he knew when the black dog descended there was no telling what he might do, and the dog was barking like a bugger at the moment.

The sound of the hoover filtered up the stairs, and he decided to go down and apologise. After explaining about Ruth, he would cry on Sophie's shoulder and probably feel a hell of a lot better. *Yes,* he thought, stubbing out his smoke, *I'd be lost without Sophie.*

Chapter Eighteen

The cleaner moved the floor buffer around effortlessly, and in perfect time to *Derek and the Dominoes* pumping out from the ghetto blaster at his feet. He stopped when Anderson and Harrison marched across his newly polished floor.

Anderson scowled at the music volume. 'I'm getting sick of these *wog-boxes*, Harrison, bloody punk rock and heavy metal everywhere you go.'

'You're showing you're age,' Harrison said, as they rounded the corner and headed down a corridor. They stopped beneath a sign that read: 'Private Pathology.' A buzzing, like the sound of a dentist's drill, floated through door, and Anderson grimaced as he pushed it open.

An overpowering smell of ammonia and formaldehyde struck him as he entered, and Anderson took out his vial of pills, tipped a couple in his hands, before spotting Phelps at the end of the room. He was bending over a trolley and holding an electrical saw, which he wielded like a frustrated carpenter.

Anderson shuddered at the sound of sawed bone, which tickled his teeth. 'Hope you enjoyed your lunch, Harrison,' he said, gulping his pills down dry. 'You might be seeing it again,'

Phelps looked up, his toupee slightly askew. He switched off the saw and placed it on a nearby tray. 'Inspector, good afternoon.'

Gore covered his arms up to the elbows. He made pains not to drip any on the floor as he wiped his hands down his lab coat, which looked like a used butcher's apron, peeled off the sodden gloves, dropping them into a bin, before walking over and shaking Anderson's hand.

'So what's all the fuss about that you had to drag me into your meat shop?' Anderson asked, trying to keep his eyes from the trolley, but failing.

Naked and face up, with a cloth over his face, a dead man was lying with a Y-shaped scar running from below each shoulder to just above the navel.

Phelps pointed down at the cadaver. 'It's your fellow, Brennan, from the cathedral. I just don't understand it, Inspector.'

'Understand what?' Harrison asked, more interested in note taking than the corpse in front of him.

Anderson didn't like what he was hearing. He had just told that know-it-all shrink to stop jumping at shadows. Phelps had sounded so confident in the cathedral, and a change of opinion was unlike him. 'You said it was a heart attack?'

Phelps put his spectacles on. 'Oh, it is, but look at this.'

He walked to a small partitioned office at the rear of the laboratory and disappeared inside, re-emerging with a large glass jar. 'Look!'

He held the jar out to Anderson, who squinted at it, seeing nothing but a cloudy red liquid.

'What am I looking at?'

Phelps peered at the jar as if its identity was obvious. 'Pleural fluid, Inspector.' He nodded back over to Brennan. 'Took it out during his *thoracocentesis*, this morning.'

'His what?'

'Removal of fluid from the pleural space.' Phelps tapped his sternum. 'The chest cavity.'

'I'm still lost?' Anderson turned to Harrison for some sort of explanation, but the sergeant was chewing his tongue, presumably trying to spell pleural.

'Hold this.' Phelps plonked the jar into Anderson's hands and disappeared back into the office. He returned a moment later with another jar. 'I took this from that orderly from the psychiatric hospital.' Phelps raised the jar up to Anderson's face.

'Is this meant to mean something?' Anderson held the one jar at arm's length and grimaced at the sight of the other.

'Four pints in each,' Phelps said. 'There is not much that goes wrong with the human body that will produce that much ruddy fluid – about all the pleural cavity will hold.' For some reason he smiled.

'So?'

Phelps shoved the jar at Anderson, forcing him to balance both of them in his arms as the pathologist disappeared back into the office. He returned with yet another jar. Anderson staggered back at the sight of it. He knew little about pathology, but recognised a human heart when he saw one.

'Took this from that orderly. Meant to have put it back, but I've never seen one before, so I thought I'd preserve it.'

'What do you mean you thought you'd preserve it?' Anderson felt scandalised. 'You can't go around taking keepsakes from people's chests.' He craned his head round to the office, wondering what else Phelps was storing.

'You don't understand, Inspector.' Phelps unscrewed the cap, and plunged his hand into the jar, scooping out the organ.

Anderson, still clutching the two jars, jumped back as formaldehyde and gore dripped across the floor. 'Bloody hell, you dirty sod.'

Phelps smiled and prodded the organ with his finger. 'It won't hurt you, Inspector. Here.' He held the dripping monstrosity under Anderson's nose, 'These are the aortic sinus,' he said, pointing inside one of the main ventricles. 'They're like little channels. You can see here how flaccid they are?'

Anderson steered his nose away. 'And?'

'They're ruptured. That's what killed your orderly. Rupture of the aortic sinus.'

Harrison popped his eyes briefly over his notepad and spelled out a-o-r-t-i-c with his lips before returning to his scribbling.

Anderson shrugged. 'I've read your report. What of it?'

'Well, you'll remember I mentioned how rare it was. Well, when I saw that fluid, it made me think we might have two in the space of a couple of days. That's why I called you.' He placed the heart back into the jar, screwed the cap back on and took it back into the office. He returned and relieved Anderson of his two jars.

Anderson looked down at Brennan. 'So what? Two rare heart attacks. Coincidence?'

'You don't understand the odds, Inspector,' Phelps said, returning the other jars to the office.

Anderson felt relieved to see him re-emerge with nothing but two latex gloves, which Phelps proceeded to place over his hands.

'If I'm right,' Phelps said, snapping the gloves over his wrists. 'Then the odds are too high for it to be a coincidence. It's so rare, you see, Inspector. Only cases I've heard about were caused by prolonged syphilis. Ruled that out, of course.'

He walked over to Brennan, and slapped his hand on the

chest. 'Thought he had a case of arrhythmia, at first. Happens sometimes. Main cause of young-adult cardiopulmonary arrest, but then I noticed the pleural blood.'

Anderson shrugged at Harrison who had given up scribbling, but said: 'You already ruled out suspicious circumstances on the orderly, though, didn't you?'

Anderson nodded, but Phelps shook his head. 'Well, that's the rub. Isn't it?' He placed a hand in the Y-shaped incision on Brennan's chest. 'Nothing untoward could actually cause it, but if I'm right, and his sinus has ruptured too, then the odds of it being a coincidence are just too ruddy steep. Ten million-to-one. Perhaps higher.'

Anderson and Harrison looked at each other. 'And are you right?' Harrison asked.

'Well, there's only one way to find out,' Phelps said, as he pulled the skin on Brennan's chest apart, exposing the rib cage as if peeling a large banana.

Anderson could feel bile rise up his throat as he watched Phelps slide his hands inside the cadaver, up to the wrists, and with a squelch, like a Wellington boot emerging from thick mud, he lifted out the sternum and ribcage whole, dropping it on a side tray.

It was a perfect section of a human chest. Red-brown treacle dripped off the neatly sawed bone and on to the floor. Followed shortly by a splattering of bile, as Anderson threw up.

'How you feeling, sir?' Harrison asked, once they'd returned to the Rover. Anderson couldn't help but hear a sneer in the voice, and just grunted, blaming his ulcer. He rolled up a smoke as he thought. He still didn't understand why Phelps sounded so excited.

Determined not to show himself up any further, he stayed for the rest of the autopsy, enduring the grim sight of Phelps removing nearly all the choirmaster's organs.

He now understood why they called him the *Canoe Maker*. Because once Phelps had finished, having weighed and measured Brennan's organs, before lying them on the bench at the back of the laboratory, the empty chest cavity resembled a dug-out canoe.

Not being a medical man, it all reminded Anderson of offal, except the liver, which he recognised and wagered was in better shape than his own. But it was the heart that generated Phelps' excitement.

After weighing, and examining the organ under a lamp, he had shouted: 'Bingo!' and then shoved the grim artefact at Anderson.

Of course, Anderson couldn't tell what was wrong with it, but Phelps' words lingered uneasily with him, *It is the same, Inspector, and I'm not suggesting for one minute it's foul play – that's your job – and nothing one human being could do to another could cause a rupture like this. But I'm telling you, to have two, in the space of forty-eight hours, and within a few miles of each other. It's improbable to the point of impossible.*

Anderson hated impossibilities, as they tended to get in the way of putting a simple case to bed. He and Phelps went back a long time. And while a loose-legged shrink trying to make a name for herself, he could understand getting all excited about coincidences, Phelps had been in the game a long, long time. No, when someone like Phelps began flapping, Anderson knew he ought to listen, but he couldn't figure out what it all meant. If Phelps was right, and nothing, no blunt instrument, no poison, no electric shock or fiendish instrument could cause a heart to pop, then it must surely be a coincidence.

With Phelps' fervour, combined with Ruth's bleating about Brennan and the patient coming from the same orphanage, Anderson felt uneasy. His guts tingled – and he doubted his ulcer was to blame.

'So what do you want to do now?' Harrison asked, as the V8 roared into life outside the mortuary.

Anderson licked his roll-up together, placed it in his lips and pushed the car's lighter in with his thumb. 'I want to go and talk to that witness.'

'Who?'

'The boy that left his shirt at the cathedral. The one they reckoned might have seen something. I want to find out if he did see anything, and if he did, what exactly.'

'We'll have to get the details from Tippwick, then.' Harrison pulled out his notebook.

'You can speak to that girlfriend of yours, too.'

Harrison's face stiffened. 'Ruth?'

'Yes. I want to speak to that fish farmer she seemed so excited about, find out what he knows. And while you're at it, ask her to go over to Eynhallow and speak to that Sister Crowface woman.'

'McRowen?'

'Yes, if she's so confident the mad nun's hiding something, let her try to pry it out of her.'

'Okay. Anything else?'

'Yes, what time is it?' Anderson asked, as Harrison put away his notepad and pushed up the indicator stalk.

Harrison glanced down at his wrist. 'Just gone two, why?'

Anderson released a steady stream of smoke from his lips. 'Before we do all that, I need a swift drink.'

Chapter Nineteen

Anderson felt more irascible than normal. They'd located Ruth, sat in the pub looking forlorn. After Harrison asked her to visit Eynhallow for them, she gave Anderson that *told you so* look. Smug bitch. She did, however, supply the address for the fish millionaire, but suggested they tread carefully, saying he was in a delicate mental state. *Patronizing cow. Who did she think they were – Flying Squad?*

Their swift drink turned into several, though, and by the time they arrived at Tingwall station, the afternoon was half over. Rowland greeted them when they walked in and after Harrison explained they needed to see Tippwick, the young officer let them through the inner door and led them to the detective's office.

Tippwick, however, was not alone. Tiernay, wearing a golfing outfit and seemingly in a worse mood than Anderson, sat jabbing his finger at Tippwick, apparently giving the old detective a dressing down. 'Just four holes, that's all I had time for, thanks to you and this ridiculous business. Have you signed it?' he was saying as Rowland tapped on the door.

Both men turned to see Anderson and Harrison in the doorway. Tippwick twitched his moustache in agitation while Tiernay glared at the inspector. Rowland had the good sense to scamper off.

'If it isn't Special Branch's finest,' Tiernay said, with a sneer. 'Thought you'd be long gone by now.'

Anderson held a brown folder, which he passed to Tippwick. 'The pathologist's report from the cathedral body. Makes interesting reading.'

Tiernay snatched the folder from Tippwick's hands and flicked through the pages. He scanned them quickly before closing the folder and dropping it on the desk. 'As predicted. Natural causes.'

'But did you read his notes,' Harrison said. 'About it being unlikely that it was a coincidence.'

Tiernay shrugged. 'I go by facts, Sergeant, not surmising from eccentric doctors. It was made pretty clear to me yesterday that it was a natural death, wasn't it? How did you so eloquently put it, Inspector? Wipe your arse too hard and get crap on your hands – something along those lines, wasn't it?'

'That was yesterday,' Anderson admitted. 'I think you ought to listen to Phelps. He's been in the business a long time, cut up more bodies than I've –'

'–Are you telling me how to do my job!' roared Tiernay, getting to his feet. 'This is a CID matter. The escaped patient was your business, and he has drowned – you've already filed your report and closed the case, so I suggest you go back to whatever stone it was that you originally crawled out from under.'

Anderson clenched his fist and stepped forward, but Harrison held him back. Anderson wanted nothing more than to hit the chief constable, but knew his record wouldn't take another subordination hearing. So, gritting his teeth and brushing Harrison's hands off him, he turned about and walked out.

Ruth approached the island feeling satisfied that the police now took her seriously, and apprehensive at visiting Eynhallow again. Harrison didn't elaborate to the cause of he and Anderson's change of mind, but he not only asked her to visit McRowen, but also wanted Jim Clark's details. That concerned her. The clashing personalities of the ill-natured inspector and suicidal fish farmer could end badly. She warned Harrison about the shotgun, and he said they'd go prepared. She didn't know what he meant, but Clark was their problem. She faced something even more intimidating – McRowen.

Fog was closing in, and after she left the ferry, old Riley promised he'd wait but warned her not to dally – Eynhallow Sound being too treacherous during poor visibility, meaning she'd have to stay. Ruth promised not to be long. She had no intention of bunking up for the night in that hospital.

As she trudged off through the thick mud fronting the hospital, she twice slipped in the boggy surroundings, both times saving herself with wild, swinging arms. Thanks to her exploits at the quarry, she found herself forced back into her casuals. She doubted the sister would approve, but Ruth intended on seeing McRowen without mud and grass stains on her knees.

Sister Mary greeted her arrival, offering her usual welcome of refreshment. 'Dr Duncan, how pleasant to see you. Cup of tea?'

She still wore her dressing gown over her habit – Ruth remembered the chill around the place and understood why.

'Sister McRowen said you'd be calling,' Mary said, hastily filling a teacup. Ruth accepted the tea, hoping she'd find a pot plant on the way to McRowen's office.

She carried her teacup, balanced on its saucer, as Mary led her down the wards. Ruth caught sight of the languorous looks and gaunt expressions of some of the patients. Most ambled about unheeded, with a just a few sisters and bored-looking orderlies standing around the corridors keeping an eye on them. Ruth tutted at their neglect.

Mary led her to McRowen's office. She stopped, knocked, and after a screech told them to enter, Ruth took a deep breath and walked in.

After beating the top of the Rover with his fist, and shouting a word that made even Harrison blush, Anderson rolled a cigarette and slumped into the car. Harrison sidled in after. 'He was a bit out-of-order there, sir. Perhaps you should put in a complaint.'

Anderson, his lips pursed tight, still managed to let out a laugh. 'Don't worry about me, Harrison. I've a hide thicker than a rhino's foreskin.'

'At least we have the address for this fish farmer,' Harrison said, peering out into the afternoon. A mist was drawing in. 'Do you want to head over and see him, before it gets too foggy?'

'Aye, suppose so.' Anderson flicked his cigarette out the window, and proceeded to roll another, but paused when a figure bounded out of the police station and, after glancing behind him, ambled up to the car.

'Tipp-top?' Anderson said, as the whiskered detective leaned into the car.

'For what it's worth, sir, I cannae say I approve of yer methods, but there wisnae need for the chief constable to speak to ye like that.' He slipped a piece of paper through the window and Anderson took hold of it, reading an address in elegant handwriting.

'What's this?'

'The wee bairn who was with Brennan when he keeled over –

that's his school. If you hurry ye'll catch him.' Tippwick tapped his nose. 'But you disnae get it from me.'

Anderson smiled. ''Course not.' The pair exchanged a knowing glance and the whiskered detective jogged back to the station.

'Well, what about that?' Anderson said, waving the piece of paper at Harrison. 'Guess I got friends on this island, after all. I wonder if I could tap him for twenty quid?'

Harrison laughed and cranked the Rover into life.

Chapter Twenty

Tramping across the sports field, Anderson and Harrison followed the sounds of a whistle, several grunts, the thud of shoulders slamming together, and the eager shouts of fullbacks and number eights.

'Never understood rugby, Harrison,' Anderson said, as they neared the pitch and saw the players emerging through the mist. 'A game played by people who enjoy handling odd-shaped balls.' He shook his head at the scrimmage before them. The hands hooked through legs, shorts being grabbed around the groin, made him think of the last days of Rome.

'You not play, then?'

'Behave yourself. Only game worth mentioning is played at Ibrox.' He looked up and down at Harrison's lanky frame. 'Don't tell me you do?'

'First fifteen for the force. Blind-side flanker.'

Anderson shook his head and mumbled: 'Think you miss-heard 'em.'

A whistle halted the action on the pitch and all eyes stared at the visitors. The coach, portly, bald and red in the face, jogged over in a pair of rugby shorts two sizes too small. He stood panting on the touchline, gasping for breath. 'Huh ... huh... Can ... Cannae I help ... Huh huh ... help you?'

'You all right, pal?' Harrison asked, his face a picture of concern. The man's flushed cheeks had begun turning blue.

He waved a hand at them and slipped his hand into his shorts, retrieving an asthma inhaler. After sucking at it like a pregnant woman at gas and air, the vivid colour began receding from his cheeks. 'Sorry, gentlemen, but cannae I help you?'

'Are you Mr McGregor?' Harrison asked.

He nodded.

Harrison retrieved his warrant card and flashed it at the out-of-puff coach. 'The headmaster sent us down here. We need to speak to one of the boys. A Peter McCafrey.'

McGregor glanced over his shoulder. The boys stared back with arms crossed and surly expressions across their faces. 'Of course, yes.'

He jogged over to the boys. Anderson watched him mutter something to one of the players before blowing the whistle again, hustling the rest of the team farther down the pitch, leaving a single boy trudging towards the touchline.

According to Tippwick, McCafrey was not yet sixteen, but Anderson wouldn't have fancied his chances in an arm-wrestle. The kid had the upper arms of a power-lifter. His pectoral muscles, bursting through his green jersey, resembled dinner plates, and reminded Anderson of the pea-coloured body-builder in that ridiculous American TV show. His face was young, though. Blonde hair and skin not yet ravaged by the island's winds. Diffident too, keeping his eyes at his feet, even when Harrison spoke to him.

'Are you Peter McCafrey?'

He mumbled an acknowledgement.

'I'm DS Harrison and this is my colleague, Detective Inspector Anderson. We'd like to ask you a few questions regarding the death of your choirmaster.' Harrison reached for his notepad and flicked through a few pages. 'A Mr Ian Brennan?'

The boy fidgeted but kept his eyes to the floor.

'I understand you were there yesterday, when Mr Brennan died?'

The boy muttered something, but neither Anderson nor Harrison could hear him.

'What was that?' Anderson snapped. 'Speak up.'

The boy raised his head, eyes staring fearfully at them. 'I said yes, sir.'

'Could you tell me what happened?' Harrison asked.

The boy shrugged. 'I've already told Sergeant Tippwick everything. Mr Brennan just fell down – unwell, like.'

Attempting to roll a cigarette, Anderson gave up, releasing the cigarette paper to the wind. He pushed Harrison aside and glowered at the boy. 'Right. So how did he fall?'

'Sir?' The boy stepped back and fidgeted again.

'I want to know exactly what happened. Show me.'

'Sir?' The boy turned to Harrison with a quizzical look on his face. Harrison stared at Anderson with a similar expression across his.

'Show me,' Anderson repeated. 'Pretend you're Brennan. Do what he did.'

McCafrey looked at Harrison again, but the sergeant just shrugged. So after glancing over his shoulder at his team-mates, who were now behind the veil of mist, McCafrey began re-enacting Brennan's death.

Anderson slipped his hand inside Harrison's jacket and took out the sergeant's cigarettes. He lit one as he watched McCafrey with amusement. The boy walked toward them, staggered, slumped to his knees, clutched his chest, and pleaded to them with his hand out.

'And then what happened?' Anderson asked, after the boy finished his dramatics and began getting to his feet.

He shrugged. 'I don't know. I ran back to school.'

'Did you not get help?' Harrison asked, his pen hovering expectantly over his notepad.

The boy bowed his head. 'No, sir.'

'Why? Why didn't you can an ambulance?' Anderson snapped.

The boy just shrugged.

Anderson studied the tip of his cigarette, gently blowing on it, making the tip glow orange. 'So what were you doing before he had his funny turn?'

The boy's head snapped up suddenly, forcing Anderson's gaze away from the burning tobacco.

'Sir?'

'I said what were you doing. You and Mr Brennan. The rest of the choir had gone home, hadn't they?'

The boy's eye's dropped to his feet, and he shuffled uncomfortably. Anderson stepped toward him, the cigarette now in his mouth. 'Well?'

'Extra practice, sir.'

'You often have extra practice?' Harrison asked, his pen still hovering, still waiting for something important to write.

McCafrey just shrugged and fidgeted again.

'And where were you both?' Anderson asked. 'When he began having his turn?'

'Sir?'

'Were you standing near him?' Anderson added a little

suspicion to his tone, hoping a dose of fear might encourage the boy.

'N ... no, sir. Mr Brennan thought he heard a noise and had gone to check on it. He was standing in the crossing. I was on the other side of the transept, by the pillars.'

'A noise?' Harrison's eyes widened, and after a second, his pen realised its cue and began scribbling.

'What type of noise?' Anderson asked.

'Sounded like the door.'

'So you heard it too?' Harrison didn't look up from his notetaking.

'Yes, sir, but there was nobody there when he checked.'

Anderson leaned in, his smoke forming his words. 'But you never actually *saw* anybody?'

The boy coughed from the stale tobacco stench. 'No, sir.'

'Gloomy in there, though.' Anderson had returned to blowing the end of the cigarette. 'Somebody could lurk about and not be seen?'

'Yes it is, sir, but there was nobody near Mr Brennan when he collapsed. I ran right passed him, I would have seen.'

The whistle blew behind them and the coach, sucking on his inhaler, began checking his watch. Anderson tried to think of any other questions worth asking, but couldn't.

He nodded for McCafrey to go, and the boy ran off to join the game, disappearing into the mist after the ball. The detectives stood staring at each other. Harrison's expression suggested he knew no more than Anderson did.

Chapter Twenty-One

McRowen sat looking over her spectacles with her face emotionless as Ruth explained the reason for her visit. 'So you see, Sister. We think Michael might still be alive, after all.'

McRowen's features remained impassive even after Ruth finished speaking. She removed her spectacles, rubbed the impressions on the bridge of her nose, and shrugged. 'And what is it you want from me?'

Ruth narrowed her eyes. She expected something. Shock, surprise, a modicum of interest, even concern. On her last visit, McRowen demonstrated enough agitation over the subject of Michael Skye to lead Ruth into thinking she may have done away with him, but now, nothing.

'Want from you?' Ruth said, aware how their last conversation ended. 'I just thought you might wish to know he was still alive.'

'You said he *might* be alive?'

'We're fairly certain.'

'How? Has somebody seen him? I doubt that photograph I gave the police is a reliable source of verification – it is ten years old.'

Ruth sensed McRowen was attempting to convince herself, not her. 'We think he attacked somebody in Kirkwall.'

'Think?'

Ruth nodded. 'But we're not sure how.'

She expected at least some further questioning, but McRowen just leaned back. Her eyes seemed lost in thought above Ruth's head. The woman knew more than she was letting on. 'There's something you're not telling me, isn't there?'

McRowen blinked rapidly. 'And what makes you think that?'

'Why were you so frightened of Michael?'

She blinked again, but her eyes remained fixed above Ruth and she said nothing.

'We think he killed Barney,' Ruth said.

McRowen's gaze dropped to Ruth's face, but still she didn't speak.

'How's he doing it?' Ruth asked.

McRowen probed her features as if trying to judge her character. She placed her spectacles back on her nose and sighed. 'I don't know. But I know Michael is ... different.'

'Different, in what way?'

'If you'd met him, you'd understand. There was an evil about the boy. An ungodliness. The de'il's in him.'

'I think your choice of language is a little alarmist, Sister. I appreciate your faith but we're –'

'– Alarmist?' She leaned forward, her eyes, exaggerated behind the lenses, widened further, her large black pupils shining like buttons. 'Perhaps it is you that should be alarmed.'

The room fell silent and Ruth shivered, as if a chill had drafted in, only sweat trickled under her arms, and her top lip felt moist. Ruth broke the quiescence. 'You mentioned that Michael became agitated the day before Barney died?'

'Yes, and for no reason. He had been so good of late. Quiet.'

'And he was watching television?'

'Yes, he became uncontrollable. None of the other orderlies could do anything with him. So I had to call Barney.'

'Why Barney? What was so special about him?'

McRowen removed her glasses again, letting them drop on the chain around her neck. She breathed deep and clasped her hands together. 'Michael was frightened of Barney.'

'Frightened, why?'

McRowen shrugged. 'Perhaps his colour. I doubt he'd met any coloured men before his committal. But also –' She breathed deep again, as if searching for the right words, before dropping her head. 'I think Barney was being over-zealous.'

'You mean he used to beat him?'

McRowen nodded. 'I know I should have stopped it, but Michael was so difficult to cope with. Especially since the doctor died. Barney was the only one who could control him.'

'That was Doctor Franchard.'

'Yes.'

Ruth closed her eyes for a moment, not wanting to hear the answer to her next question. 'How did Dr Franchard die?'

McRowen paused for a moment, but the answer came and was as Ruth expected. 'Heart attack.'

Ruth's arms puckered in goose bumps. 'Was he with Michael?'

McRowen nodded, but only barely, and her taut features threatened to crack with tension. 'You could feel him.' Her voice was no more than a whisper. 'Whenever you went near him. Feel him inside you.' She slapped her breast, causing it to thud.

'And you think Michael was responsible for Dr Franchard's death?'

McRowen sighed, and placed her spectacles back on. 'According to the inquest, he died of natural causes. He was an old man. But –' She never finished her sentence and her last word lingered in the air.

'But you think it was Michael.'

'The De'il was in him. You may think of me as an alarmist, but how would you explain it, Doctor?'

Ruth couldn't. Not medically, but she was certain a rational reason lay behind it, regardless of what McRowen thought. Finding Michael was her priority, now. Everything else could wait until they located him. She wondered what could have set him off. Barney perhaps? After a moment's pause, she asked: 'What was Michael watching on TV?'

'I'm sorry?'

'When he became agitated. What was on the television?'

'The news.' McRowen's eyebrows narrowed. 'The patients only watch news or religious programming.'

'The news?'

McRowen nodded. 'Yes, the local news, why?'

Ruth bit her lip and realised she needed Tom.

'If somebody was in the cathedral, how did he do it?' Anderson said, peering through the windscreen. The road was getting hard to see. The mist had thickened into a soupy fog and the tail lights of the car in front kept dipping in and out of vision. The SD1 trundled slowly, with Harrison staring intently through the windscreen. 'You heard Phelps. Nobody could make a ticker go pop like that.'

Harrison shrugged, keeping his eyes fixed ahead as the car in front turned off. 'So what do you think we'll get from this Clark, then?'

'Not sure, but Miss Loose-breeches thinks he might know

something.'

'But you doubt it?'

Anderson sighed and pulled out his tobacco. He had no idea what was going on. Perhaps Phelps was having some sort of mid-life crisis and getting jumpy over nothing. *Ought to get himself a sports car and young floozy, like everyone else*, Anderson thought, but had to admit, coincidences seemed to follow contradictions on this case. Perhaps this cranky millionaire did know something, perhaps he didn't.

He placed his cigarette in his lips as a sign to Lamb Holm materialised through the fog ahead and Harrison slowed.

'This must be the barrier road,' Harrison said. 'I suppose we're over the sea now.'

Anderson peered through the window. Nothing but whiteness surrounded them, but it still made him feel bilious. He lit his smoke. 'You know where we're going?'

'Ruth says there's a turn off, somewhere up here on the left.'

A small cutting appeared and Anderson pointed at it. 'That it?'

Harrison drove down the trail, stopping at the padlocked gate stretching across the trail. 'Is this the right road?'

'How should I bloody know? It was your girlfriend who gave you the directions.'

'She said there'd be a bit of a walk.'

Anderson unwound the window to flick his ash outside. The fog meant he could see no more than a few feet from the car. 'So where's this trout farm, then?'

'It's a salmon farm – must be down there.' Harrison pointed through the gate and down the track, just as a sound echoed across the island. They both cocked their ears in the same direction.

'Shotgun,' Harrison suggested, as the report of another crack drifted across the isle. 'Apparently, he shoots a lot of seagulls.'

'Not in this fog, he doesn't.' Anderson threw his cigarette out the window, and looked grimly at Harrison. 'Well, what are you waiting for? Put your foot down.'

Chapter Twenty-Two

'It's not the first holiday romance you've had,' Sophie said, passing Tom his umpteenth cup of coffee.

'It wasn't a holiday romance!' he snapped.

'Yes, but she wasn't an islander. You knew she'd have had to go home soon.' Sophie stood with her arms akimbo and spoke sternly, like a mother nagging her child.

'I know, I know, don't go on. Hadn't you better develop those films from the fête?'

'Can't,' she said. 'Got to get back to the home. Some *loupers* coming.'

'Who?'

Sophie shrugged. 'Dunno, some couple from *Invie*, looking for a foster child.'

Tom felt his heart thud. *No, not Sophie too.*

His face must have given him away, because the youngster walked up and put her arm around his shoulder and gave him a comforting squeeze. 'Don't worry. By the time I explain about my record, and how I just love heavy metal and playing the drums – they won't be interested.'

'You don't play the drums?'

'Yes, but they don't know that.'

Tom tapped her hand. 'I'd be lost without you, Soph.'

'I know, but don't worry. I'm going nowhere.'

He was about to begin a sentence with a: 'What if,' when the phone rang.

'I'll get it.' Sophie said, reaching for the receiver.

'Thanks, the last thing I need is Mrs Trout or some other harridan moaning about the ferries.'

'Mainland Advertiser, Sophie speaking, how can I help?' She stared at Tom as she listened to the caller. 'Ruth! Well, I hope you're satisfied, Tom is in pieces –'

Tom threw himself across the desk and wrenched the phone from Sophie's grasp. 'Ruth, hi. Sorry, what is it?' Tom twisted the phone cable around his fingers as he listened. 'News schedule, what for? ... I see, yes ... Okay, I'll see what I can do. You still over there? ... I see. We'll meet you back at the Finn Man, then ... okay, see you in a bit.'

He hung up the phone and realised Sophie was glaring at him, hands on her hips again. 'What did *she* want, then?'

'Wanted to see if I could go over to Orkney TV and get the news schedule for the last week.'

'What for?'

Tom shrugged. 'Dunno, something to do with her escaped patient. I said we'd help.'

'You're too soft, Tom. She dumps you, and then has the nerve to ask for your help. And you agree!'

'She didn't dump me. We just agreed to be friends. So I'm helping, as a friend.'

'Yeah, yeah.' Sophie picked up her coat and slipped it over her shoulders. 'Well, c'mon then.'

'I thought you said you had to get back.'

'Well, it looks like I'll be late. Can't trust you not to do something stupid – like ask her to marry you or something.'

Tom smiled, shook his head, guzzled his coffee and followed Sophie down the stairs.

'Go around – across the grass!' Anderson shouted, as the third volley of shotgun fire reverberated across the island. The shot came from across the other side, and presumably from Clark's salmon farm.

Harrison span the wheel and pushed his foot down on the accelerator. The car screeched across the asphalt, bouncing over the kerb, and on to the muddy field to the side of the gate.

The wheels span to the noise of a throaty V8 roar and mud rooster-tailed behind them. Harrison struggled at the wheel to keep them straight as the rear axle fishtailed about. They soon lost sight of the gate and track as the car snaked across the field. 'Where's the trail?'

'Don't worry about it. Just straighten it up.' Anderson pointed ahead. 'That way!'

'You sure about this? We could end up driving into the sea!'

Anderson pulled his seatbelt over his shoulder, but didn't buckle it; the car bucketed around too much for that. 'Just keep driving. That way!'

The fog reduced viability to a dozen yards at most, far shorter than the braking distance on the wet grass, but Anderson felt confident they'd be okay. The trail they followed to the gate bordered the barrier road, and he'd seen a truck flash by in the mist. He knew if they kept going, they'd either rejoin the track, or arrive at the quarry.

He wound the window further down in the hope visibility would be better. It wasn't. The sun was hiding somewhere behind the fog, which thickened with every minute.

'Bloody hell!' yelled Harrison, pulling at the wheel and

causing the car to fishtail almost uncontrollably. A solid white lump of cloud had emerged out of the fog, followed by another, and then another. They darted about in front of them, running in all directions, attempting to avoid the speeding Rover.

'Sheep!' Harrison shouted, tugging at the wheel.

Dozens of the creatures began appearing out of the mist, scampering from the car as it careered toward them. Harrison swerved again.

'Keep going!' Anderson ordered, leaning out of the window to shout directions. 'Left, left – no right!

A loud thump sounded on the nearside wing.

'I think I've hit one!'

'Ignore it, just keep going.'

The sound of the bleating sheep almost drowned out the noise of the over-revving engine, but the animals soon thinned and the grassy field began to feel firmer. Rocks and stones started jolting the suspension and Anderson pulled his head back into the car. 'Stop, quick!'

Harrison slammed on the brakes. The car's wheels locked but failed to slow them.

'Pump the brakes!' Anderson shouted, seeing the grass field coming to an end and a wire fence bordering the edge of the quarry approaching alarmingly fast.

The car began bunny hopping as Harrison's right leg worked the pedal, but the car tyres refused to bite the ground and they slid towards the quarry, smashing into the wire fence. It saved them, sluing them to a halt with the bonnet hanging a couple of feet over the edge.

Both men exhaled.

Anderson stared through the windscreen at the quarry below, barely visible in the fog. Close. They'd not have survived that. He scanned the large pools of water and muddied floor, noting the lack of movement. He worked his eyes up the quarry face, stopping on the small cottage peeping out of the mist farther up the ledge.

He pointed at it. 'I reckon that's it.'

Harrison looked across. 'I've not heard any more gunshots.'

Anderson flipped open the glove box. A leather satchel fell forward. 'Best be safe than sorry.' He unzipped it and passed it Harrison, who slowly pulled out the revolver. 'You sure you know how to use that?'

'Yes, I passed the training.' Harrison clicked the gun open, span the cylinder and checked the barrel.

'All right, Roy Rogers. Put it away, you'll scare the sheep. And don't go getting it out unless I tell you to. I don't want a bloodbath on my hands.'

Harrison nodded, snapped the cylinder shut and shoved the gun inside his anorak.

'Right, you ready?' Anderson asked.

'Yes, sir.'

They opened the car doors in synchronisation and stepped out.

Chapter Twenty-Three

Mrs Trout busied herself with her ashtrays as Ruth sat quietly at the back of the bar waiting for Tom. Besides an old fisherman, who seemed as permanent a fixture as the old bar he sat at, the pub was empty.

Ruth drummed her fingers on the table as she waited, losing herself in a trance as she stared at the flashing fruit machine in the corner.

McRowen had thawed to the point of helpfulness, but she didn't understand what was going on any more than Ruth. Fear did funny things to people and Ruth understood why the sister attributed the events to her religion. Perhaps Michael was possessed. No, Ruth didn't spend her life studying psychiatry, a science, to resort to the supernatural because she didn't understand something. There had to be a rational explanation, but she couldn't think what.

Eventually, the door to the bar swung open, and two familiar faces walked in from the fog.

Ruth stood, and smiled weakly as Tom and Sophie walked over. Sophie scowled at her. Tom's smile was even weaker than Ruth's. She expected a frosty reception, and couldn't blame them. As always, she had been a bitch.

'Can I get you both a drink?'

'No thank you!' Sophie said, sitting down with her arms crossed.

Tom shook his head. 'No, we're fine.' He sat next to Sophie and Ruth took her seat.

'Look, I'm really sorry the way things happened. I shouldn't have led you on.'

'No, you shouldn't!' snapped Sophie.

Tom scowled at her. 'It's okay, honestly.' He pulled out his notepad and placed it on the table. 'Let's forget it. Friends?'

Ruth smiled. 'Friends.' She looked down at his notes. 'You've got it, then?'

Tom nodded and flicked through the pages. 'Not much news on the night in question,' he said. 'Lead was a fire burning down the carpet warehouse in Netherbrough.'

'We covered that too,' Sophie said.

'And the next?' Ruth asked.

'Appeal for a Rousay cancer patient.'

'Is she named?'

'Roweena something-or-other. Culley, I think.'

Ruth shrugged. The name meant nothing.

'The rest is just stuff on the Pope's visit,' Tom added

'Is that it, then?' Ruth hoped for more, but felt unsurprised. Michael suffered from schizophrenia; whatever upset him probably hadn't been rational. A look from the newsreader perhaps, or something trivial that sparked his paranoia. Any number of reasons could have triggered him to go after Brennan.

'Yes, unless you want a run-down of the Pope stories?'

Ruth saw no point. All the news channels ran the same stuff about the Papal visit. She'd seen it herself on TV in Inverness – the Mass in Glasgow's Bellahouston Park and his speeches at Murrayfield Stadium – but she nodded anyway. 'Might as well.'

Tom read from his notes. 'John Paul conducts Mass in Glasgow. Pope visits St Andrews for private prayer.'

Ruth shrugged but Tom continued reading: 'Pope approves former Orkney Father for ordination to bishop.'

Ruth's eyes widened. 'Say that again?'

'Pope approves former Orkney Father for ordination to bishop.'

'Was he named, this father?'

Tom looked down at his notes. 'Sorry only wrote down the headlines. Why, you don't think that's –'

'McKinnion!' Ruth said, her eyes as wide as snooker balls. 'Has to be.'

The Rover had halted lengthways across the muddied drive leading up to the cottage. The razor wire managed to wind around the front wheels, bursting one of the tyres that now hung over the quarry edge. Anderson shook his head as Harrison surveyed the damage.

'Leave it.' Anderson nodded up the trail to Clark's house. 'C'mon.'

The cottage cleared in the mist as they approached, revealing the hovel-like exterior. Anderson eyed it with contempt. It looked like a squat, with crumbling brickwork and bordered-up windows. 'Bloody hell, thought he was a millionaire. Doesn't like spending money, does he?'

'Seems quiet enough.'

Anderson raised his hand, halting Harrison. He stared at the blue front door, swaying lazily in its frame. He approached slowly, placing two fingers against the door, and pushed.

A figure dashed past him like a blur, and while Anderson felt certain he hadn't been barged into, he still found himself lying flat on his back.

He scrambled to his feet in time to see Harrison sliding over the bonnet of the car and giving chase down the trail, pursuing whoever had darted out of Clark's house. Anderson hesitated at the doorway, but decided to check inside. He stepped into the dimly lit hall.

He soon found Clark.

The parlour resembled an abattoir. The back wall was painted in blood, like red gloss thrown against the flock wallpaper, shimmering as it streaked and dripped into pools around the body lying slumped on the floor.

Clark's leg twitched in a rhythmic spasm and knocked against the skirting board. But he was dead. A double-barrelled shotgun rested under his chin, and while both hands still clutched at its breech, Clark lacked the back portion of his head, and bits of his brain and skull flecked the wall behind him.

The smell of cordite burned the back of Anderson's nose and he spotted empty cartridges scattered on the floor. He bent down and picked one up. Twelve bore. He sniffed it and coughed.

Turning around he noticed shot peppered the walls and chunks of plaster lay blasted to the floor. Anderson glanced back down at Clark and the hands clasping at the breech. *How did the intruder do that to him*, he wondered. *Clark couldn't have missed him, not in here, not with a shotgun. Unless he shot himself.* His head snapped back at the door.

'Harrison!' He slung the cartridge on the floor and dashed out.

Chapter Twenty-Four

Stumbling into the fog Anderson raced down the trail. He tried to slide across the car's bonnet, like Harrison, and very nearly ended up falling down the quarry, landing on his backside on the muddy trail.

He picked himself up and ran on as fast as he could, but his forty-a-day habit soon slowed his strides. Wheezing and gasping, his breath billowed out of him like a split radiator, but he ran on, straining his eyes through the fog, hoping for a glimpse of Harrison.

His eyes couldn't penetrate farther than ten paces. The fog was now as thick as bonfire smoke.

Anderson hadn't gone far before the burning in his lungs slowed him to a mere stagger. The trail wound its way down a ledge, so he ambled carefully, making sure to keep from the edge. Finally, his gasps and wheezes brought him to a halt. He bent double to make gulping at the air easier, until a shout snapped his head up.

'Stop!' shouted the familiar voice, echoing from farther up the track. With no short amount of wheezing, Anderson ploughed on, until another shout brought him to a stop.

'I said, halt!'

The sound of a gun followed Harrison's voice and a muzzle-flash momentarily cut through the fog, illuminating the trail ahead like a snapshot.

Harrison stood before him, thirty paces ahead, and standing astride a stile. His gun pointed in the air. Anderson caught a brief glimpse of a fleeing figure beyond, before the fog shrouded the scene from his eyes.

He heard Harrison call out again, telling the suspect to freeze, so Anderson ran on, reaching the stile. He rested on it for a moment, wheezing and huffing to satisfy his burning lungs, before clambering over.

While swinging his lead leg up, he slapped his testicles on the gate, causing him to howl. But he soon fell quiet and froze. With both legs astride the gate he whipped his head down the trail again as he heard Harrison shout: 'No, please!'

Another reverberating crack followed the plea, and again the muzzle-flash cut through the fog, burning a permanent Polaroid at the back of Anderson's eyes that he would later view in vivid and horrific detail.

Harrison stood the same thirty paces ahead, his right leg behind, showing him in profile. The figure stood farther away. No longer running but facing him. Not far off, but not close. Certainly not close enough for Anderson to ever fully understand what he saw.

In that split second, during the brief flash of gunpowder, he saw Harrison holding the gun in his hand. Only it wasn't pointing up and firing another warning shot, nor was it aimed ahead at the suspect. Harrison's arm was bent at the elbow, pointing the revolver back at his own face.

The muzzle-flash had emanated from under his chin, and in that split second of light, Anderson saw red confetti spray out the back of his head, before the scene disappeared behind the fog.

Anderson scrambled over the stile, glimpsing the assailant vanishing off into the mist. He ignored him, grabbing Harrison and turning him over.

Anderson's face contorted into a number of shapes as the mess presented itself. He expressed the grief and anger in a gag and whimper, before he turned away and threw up. After wiping his mouth with his sleeve, his lips stiffened, his teeth clamped-down tight and he looked down at the gun in Harrison's hand.

He reached for it, but retracted his fingers and balled them up in a fist. He got to his feet, screamed a cathartic: 'You bastard!' and sprinted down the trail.

The fog and darkness prevented him seeing anything other than his immediate footing, but he ran like a teenager for nearly a minute, ignoring his burning lungs and his pounding heart and his stiffening legs and the tears streaming down his cheeks. He ran faster than he'd run in twenty years and eventually caught a glimpse of whom he pursued.

Just visible in the mist, and only in silhouette, a figure was running ahead and faltering on the rough trail. Anderson shouted: 'Stop, you bastard!'

The figured faltered on his words, glancing around, but went on. Anderson careered after him, aware the rough ground began flattening under his feet. Asphalt.

He realised they must be running along the causeway, and could hear the wash of ocean over both shoulders and the sound of his loafers slapping the road as he ran.

The figure slipped in and out of the fog ahead as he fled.

'Stop!' Anderson shouted.

And he did.

With the mist swirling around him, the figure halted, and turned around.

Anderson scrabbled to a stop, his breath puffing out of him like a steam train. He rested one hand on his knee and gulped in air, staring at the barely visible figure before him.

The thick stew chilled Anderson's lungs as he gulped at the air, too breathless to shout. The figure seemed content to watch him, his outline appearing and disappearing into the mist like an apparition.

Anderson righted himself and squinted his eyes. 'You're coming with me, laddie!' The shadow slipped back into the veil of mist and Anderson stepped forward. 'Don't make me come and get you!'

The figure reappeared, the mist swirling behind him.

'I said, stop!' Anderson demanded, still feeling breathless. 'You're under arrest.'

There was no reply. Anderson could hear the sea bashing the rocks behind his right shoulder and knew he stood close to the wall at the edge of the road.

'You're under arrest!' he repeated, stepping confidently forward, his fist clenched behind him.

His breathlessness increased. His chest and throat began tightening, but he put it down to the sprint and stepped forward again. The pain increased. A shooting and stabbing, like a stitch, caused him to wince and falter. All the time the figure stood motionless in front of him.

Anderson clutched at his chest and staggered back. He found the pain ease as the silhouette fell behind the blanket of mist. But the figure stepped out and Anderson felt a crushing in his chest again.

He staggered back.

It eased.

The shadow stepped forward again, and Anderson's chest began to shoot with spasms. He tried to step back, but found his footing blocked. The dry stone wall edging the road pressed into the back of his legs. The ocean behind wafted up with a cold, moist wind.

The pain refused to subside, and all the while, the figure continued to approach, causing the squeezing in his ribcage to increase with every stride. Anderson screamed, clutching his left shoulder as his nerves began shooting alert messages up and down his arm.

He desperately tried backing farther against the wall, his heels kicking at the stone behind. He screamed, aware no sound came from his throat. He glanced around, as another spasm shot up and down his arm. The sharp stones of the wall now pressed into his gut; beyond lay the emptiness of the drop to the sea. Another cry from his nerves and he scrambled up, hauling his breathless body over the wall, using just the will of his mind.

As soon as he slumped on top, the pain eased, the shooting up and down his arms stopped and breath began to enter his lungs in joyous mouthfuls.

The respite didn't last.

The pain returned as intensely as before as the figure stepped forward out of the fog again. Anderson scrambled back along the wall, each inch relieving the screaming in his chest. Another cold draft blasted up from below and he glanced down at the nothingness, where the raging sea was hidden behind the mist swirling on the ocean.

He continued moving backwards and managed to scramble to

his feet, stepping away as the figure advanced. Each step the figure took felt like a puncture wound in Anderson's chest. But with every step Anderson took backwards, it eased. He edged back along the wall. The cold spray, wafting up from the abyss below, tickled his cheek, while all the time the figure advanced, matching him step for step.

And then Anderson ran out of wall.

The stonewall flanking the barrier road must have run in a dog-leg, because as Anderson stepped back, he found nothing under his sole and momentarily his foot hovered over emptiness. The crash of ocean shouted below, and the cold draft chilled his extremities. He pulled his foot in and regained his balance, just as the silhouette stepped out of the mist again and continued approaching.

He stood close enough that Anderson could have seen his face, if he cared to look, but the latest spasm of pain was so severe his eyes streamed with tears and he doubled over. He clutched his left arm as a jolt shot across his chest like a high voltage current.

His arms began to numb, and his feet began slipping on the edge of the precipice behind as he desperately tried to back away from the heart-squeezing pain. The sea sounded louder below, crashing and spraying, while water speckled his face.

He teetered on the brink, rising on tiptoes, trying to ease the pain, but it did nothing. His heart pounded so much that it reverberated through every bone in his body. The cold breeze from the sea only added to the numbing of his extremities.

The figure stepped forward once more.

The agonies in Anderson's chest increased to such a level he had little choice but to step over the void. Hovering his foot over the brink, until he could take the pounding in his ribs no longer, he stepped out, just as the crack of a shotgun caused all pain in his chest to stop.

His last memory was of the figure in the fog running off. He never saw the man who fired the gun, gravity had already decided Anderson's fate. With his arms swinging wildly, he wavered for several moments, before plunging off the wall toward the abyss below.

Chapter Twenty-Five

Anderson awoke to a dry coating in his mouth and a soreness to the throat that made swallowing difficult. Despite the blurred vision and his mind not having caught up with his memories, he could tell by the clinical smells and white sterility, he lay in a hospital room.

He coughed, the jolt causing his neck to spasm. The slightest movement of his head hurt the nape of his spine. Like whiplash. He began rubbing it, but paused, noticing a blurred figure before him.

For a brief moment, an overwhelming sense of fear gripped him, and his heart banged against his chest. Visions of the figure in the fog and the events at Lamb Holm began flashing through his mind like the stills in a flick book.

His palpitations eased when his eyes started focussing, and the figure leaned in, revealing herself.

'How are you feeling?' Ruth's voice sounded soft and compassionate.

Anderson felt confused as he tried to recollect the events from Lamb Holm, but all his mind would conjure up was the gruesome snapshot of Harrison, and a recollection of intense, intolerable pain, and then relief, followed by a throttling and choking.

He rubbed his neck again; it felt like someone had danced on it. 'I could do with a drink.' His voice sounded so cracked he didn't recognise it as his own.

Ruth understood him, though, and poured him a glass of water. He noticed she watched him sip it, her hands clasped anxiously on her lap. As he drank, he also became aware of a bleeping emanating beside the bed. Wires, connected to pads on his chest, fed back to a monitor, while a thin tube threaded its way from a drip across the bed and into a cannula in his arm. 'What happened? How long have I been out?'

'About eighteen hours. You suffered a minor heart attack last night.'

The nightmare feelings of his chest being squeezed resurfaced and caused the heart monitor to beep a little faster. He passed Ruth the water and flopped back on his pillows. His neck objected and stabbed at his spine. He winced and grabbed at the back of his head.

'The farmer did that,' Ruth said.

'Farmer?'

'Jerome, something-or-other. Pulled you off that causeway.'

Other than the lucid image of Harrison's death, permanently branded to his memory like an unwanted tattoo, his other recollections were hazy. He remembered the pain, and the phantom-like figure shrouded in fog, and he recalled the crashing sea and the flicker of cold spray across his face as he balanced on the wall. The wall!

He looked up, aggravating his neck again. 'I fell?'

Ruth explained Jerome, having heard the gunshots and the car tearing through the field, thought his sheep were under threat, so he grabbed his shotgun and crook, and charged out of the farmhouse.

Eventually, after hearing the commotion by the barriers, he came across Anderson on the causeway. Not being able to see what the two figures by the barriers were doing, he fired a warning shot. While the tormentor ran off, the shepherd, acting on decades of experience retrieving stricken ewes from the island's ledges, caught hold of Anderson with his crook just as he fell off the wall, hauling him back up to safety by his neck.

Anderson rubbed at the complaining muscles. 'No wonder it feels like Pierrepoint's had a go at it.'

She smiled at him, weakly. 'Tippwick and Tiernay are outside. They are waiting to speak to you. They want to know what happened to Harrison.'

He couldn't explain it. What could he tell them? That he shot himself! He couldn't do that to Harrison's widow. 'They found him, then?'

'Clark too. Dr Phelps says that both he and Harrison –'

'– Were murdered!' Anderson snapped, his neck complaining from the volume of his voice. 'What are they doing here? They should be out there looking for the bastard.'

'Tiernay ordered the barriers closed when you were found. They're still searching the south islands now.'

'Tiernay couldn't find a nipple in a bucket of tits.' Anderson pulled the pads from his chest, causing the heart monitor to begin wailing.

'Inspector, that's not wise, you need to rest.' Ruth began trying to push him back down.

'Get off me.' He swiped her hands aside and reached for his trousers at the side of the bed. The smell of grass, sea air and the sweat he expired on Lamb Holm still clung to them. He began putting them on, his neck and chest complaining about the exertion.

Ruth grabbed his shoulders and shook him gently as he

struggled to get his legs into the trousers. 'Stop. I know where he's going. I know who he's after.'

He looked up. 'Tell me.'

News of Harrison's death disturbed Ruth. She felt guilty, but didn't know why. Despite what happened, she liked Harrison and just wished it had ended better. How many times had she thought that?

Anderson looked weak and frail. His usual crude and acerbic defence mechanism did not mask the fear etched on his face. He remained quiet while she explained about McKinnion. Tom made some calls after their discovery and they learned the priest's ordination was taking place on Sunday. She explained all this to Anderson, who listened quietly.

'Where?' he asked, looking calmer. He still sat at the end of the bed but no longer tried to put his trousers on.

'Edinburgh. We think that's what triggered all this off. Michael hearing about it.'

She wasn't sure what reaction to expect, but Anderson seemed more agitated than when he thought Michael had escaped for good. He sat grinding his teeth, his one hand scratching at the cannula in his arm.

'At least we know where he's going,' she said.

His face remained grim, and he spoke with his teeth partly clenched. 'I'll not send any more coppers after him.'

She didn't know what happened on Lamb Holm, but from what she gathered from Tippwick and Tiernay, both Harrison and Clark suffered fatal gunshot wounds. Wounds from their own guns.

Whatever occurred, it had taken its toll on Anderson's features. His face looked haggard and pallid, and his eyes were red and vacant, like those of someone that spent a lifetime crying. He fixed them on her, a pleading expression across his brow, like one of her patients begging for medication to make the voices stop.

'How's he doing it, Ruth?'

She'd never heard him use her name before. Sounded strange. For a moment, he resembled her father. Sat in a hospital bed, looking helpless and pathetic. She shook her head. 'I don't know, Inspector.'

'But you definitely think he'll turn up, in Edinburgh? Seems a long way to go for a lunatic.'

'Michael may be mad, but that doesn't mean he's stupid. A lot of schizophrenics can be extremely clever, calculating and manipulative.'

'Then I'm going to have to speak to Kendrick.'

'Who's Kendrick?'

Anderson didn't answer, his eyes were lost in thought, but after a moment, he snapped to and continued getting into his trousers.

Chapter Twenty-Six

Wearing a surgical collar and new suit, which already looked like he slept in it, Anderson was among venerable splendour of paintings, thick red carpet and oak panelling. He sat uncomfortably in a leather-bound chair next to a low-slung table littered with magazines. He picked up a title, the stretching causing his chest to spasm. After reaching into his pocket, he retrieved the bottle of pills one of the doctors in Orkney thrust at him before letting him discharge himself, and placed one on his tongue.

His chest had twinged a couple of times on the journey down to Edinburgh, as the doctor said it would. But the nitroglycerine worked quickly, dissolving on his tongue and alleviating the pain almost instantly. It aggravated his ulcer, though, and he took out his other pills, tipping two in his hand. He sighed. His neck also hurt, but he was damned if he'd take more pills for that.

The receptionist said somebody would be down to attend to him shortly, and he fidgeted, leafing through a Woman's Weekly as priests and other diocesan officials bustled in and out of the arched door, his neck jarring every time they caught his eye.

A portrait on the wall opposite loomed over him, showing a pious-looking *God botherer*, with a sanctimonious face Anderson wished he could slap. The Church had not been helpful.

After he left hospital, Anderson spoke to Kendrick, the superintendent, but kept back a lot of the details concerning Lamb Holm. He still didn't know what to say. He did persuade the DSI, however, his report could wait until after the weekend –

they needed to speak to the church and get them to call off the weekend's ordination.

While the St Andrews Diocese welcomed the meeting, a muted response met any hint of postponement. The decision was Father McKinnion's, they said, and the soon-to-be bishop sounded not in the least bit interested, or alarmed, over the phone. Anderson would soon see about that.

According to Ruth, much of the blame for Michael Skye's vendetta lay at McKinnion's feet. And in Anderson's eyes, that meant he owned some responsibility for what happened to Harrison too.

He sat brooding with the magazine in front of him. By the time a young and effeminate-looking priest walked down the stairs and introduced himself, Anderson had learned how to knit a purl-stitched sweater.

'Inspector Anderson, I'm Father Wallace, Father McKinnion's secretary.' The young priest thrust out his hand. 'A real pleasure to meet you, Inspector.'

Wallace beamed a smile that few folk ever offered Anderson on meeting him, so he eyed the priest suspiciously, as he stood and shook his hand. 'Err, pleasure's mine.'

The father smiled again and pumped at his hand as if expecting to extrude water. Anderson began to think the man might have been deranged.

'I met several Special Branch officers during the Papal visit last week,' Wallace said. 'I must say, it seems such an exciting vocation it's almost made me wish I'd not taken the Holy Order. Almost.' He looked around furtively, before whispering: 'But don't tell Father McKinnion that.'

'Well, it has its moments,' Anderson said, surprised by Wallace's enthusiasm. *Definitely deranged,* he thought.

'You fella's are a bit like James Bond, aren't you?' Wallace said, still shaking Anderson's hand and causing the inspector's neck to ache.

Anderson pulled his hand free. 'Err, not quiet.'

'No? More like *The Sweeney*, then?'

Anderson straightened his shoulders and smiled. 'Almost, I suppose. Don't get as many birds as that fella Regan, mind.'

The young priest blushed and let out a little snigger, before nodding at the inspector's collar. 'Did you do that in the line of duty?' His face was full of admiration.

Anderson nodded and regretted it as his neck twinged.

'What was it, a *blagger*? The IRA?'

'No, a bloody shepherd tried to hang me.'

Wallace's eye's narrowed, but he tapped his nose. 'Ah, I understand. Say no more.'

Ruth would love this chap, Anderson thought, *definitely belongs in a funny farm.*

'Oh, my, what am I doing. You must be incredibly busy,' Wallace said. 'Here's me asking silly questions and you're here to see Father McKinnion. Please, follow me.'

Anderson, walking like a robot due to the neck brace hampering his gait, followed Wallace up a carpeted stairway as the priest jabbered on about how he admired the Branch and the important work they did.

Unaccustomed to such flattery, Anderson waited for the exuberant priest to take a breath, before changing the subject. 'Tell me, err, Father. Is the Bishop of Edinburgh with Father

McKinnion?'

Wallace stopped. They stood in a panelled corridor lined with oak doors. 'Cardinal White? Ah, sadly not. He's in Rome at the moment, but will be back in time for the ordination on Sunday.'

Anderson chewed his lip. He had hoped if his meeting with McKinnion didn't go to plan, he could have appealed to his senior to see sense. 'So what exactly happens during these ordinations?'

Wallace seemed bored by the question, presumably preferring to learn how many Irish dissidents Anderson had shot, but he answered. 'Quite a simple affair, really. The father.' He nodded to one of the oak doors lining the corridor. 'Is anointed by the laying on of hands by Cardinal White, and I believe the Bishops of Dumfries and Glasgow will take part.'

'Will many others be there?'

'Oh, lots. Very special occasions these ordinations, so senior priests all over Scotland will be in attendance, as will some important officials. Not the Secretary of State, though. I believe he has too much to deal with, what with the Falklands business.'

'And yourself?' Anderson asked.

'Oh, yes, as the father's secretary I have been made *thurifer*.' Seemingly bored with the questions, Wallace nodded at the door. 'The father's waiting in here.' He glanced around again, and added: 'Listen, if you need any help, I can be reached here at anytime. It would be my pleasure to assist Special Branch in any way.'

'I'll bear it in mind. I'm looking for a new partner.'

Wallace's smile almost split his head in two, before he realised Anderson was joking. The young priest walked to the door but before knocking, turned around and whispered: 'Be warned, the father can be a little –' He glanced around again. 'Prickly.'

'Wouldn't be the first prick I've met,' Anderson muttered as Wallace tapped on the door.

Anderson stepped in to a rather spacious and well-lit office. Three arched windows, bathing the room in natural light, overlooked the estate's gardens, while more pious-looking figures stared down from paintings adorning the panelled walls.

McKinnion stood in the centre of the room, wearing full ceremonial vesture, complete with scarlet mozzetta and red biretta. An attendant clucked at his feet, adjusting the hem and holding several pins in his lips. McKinnion turned his long face to Anderson. Two lazy, dark brown eyes looked him up and down, before he shooed away the assistant and nodded at Father Wallace to leave them alone. Both men left the office, with Wallace giving Anderson a wink as he went.

McKinnion offered Anderson a slender hand, eyeing the collar around his neck. 'Pleasure to meet you, Inspector. Been in the wars, I see?'

Anderson realised he still clutched the Woman's Weekly; he thrust it behind his back as he shook the Father's hand. 'Just a pain in the neck, nothing to worry about.'

His joke led to a moment's silence, broken when McKinnion offered him a seat. 'Please.'

A chaise longue and wide-backed chair sat in front of the windows. McKinnion carefully adjusted his rochet to ensure it remained uncreased and sat in the armchair. Anderson, hampered by the collar, lowered himself into the chaise long, slumping the last six inches and landing in an uncomfortable and recumbent position.

'I've already spoken to Superintendent Kendrick and told him there is no question of postponing the ceremony on Sunday – if that is what you are here for, Inspector.'

Because of the neck brace, and the way he'd slumped, all Anderson could see was the ceiling. He struggled to get himself in a more upright position, and finally managed it, his suit rolling up above his chest in the process. 'I know, but I'm here because I don't think you appreciate the gravity of the situation.'

McKinnion crossed his legs at the knee, still taking pains to ensure his vesture remained uncreased. He appeared younger than his seventy years, and spoke with a firm, authoritative voice, built up from a lifetime of sermons, no doubt. 'I'm sorry, Inspector, whoever it is you believe wishes to cause me harm, I can't delay my ordination, I am restrained by the orders of the Holy See.'

Anderson wasn't sure exactly what Kendrick had told McKinnion, but he felt certain neither the superintendent, nor Father McKinnion, took the threat seriously enough. Why would they? They'd not witnessed the events on Lamb Holm. 'I appreciate that, but –'

McKinnion raised his hand. 'The consecration of a Bishop must be conducted within a certain time frame. A delay would see me forfeit by position, Inspector. And I have worked too long and too hard to have it taken from me at the eleventh hour.' He smiled thinly. 'Besides, if Special Branch could keep the Holy Father safe during his visit last week, I'm sure you my protection shouldn't cause you too much trouble. Who is this deranged person, anyway? Your superintendent sounded very vague.'

'It's Michael Skye.'

The thin smile hardened.

Yes, now you look concerned, thought Anderson. 'I take it you remember the name?'

McKinnion stood up and walked over to the windows. He stared out over the gardens, his hands clasped behind his back. 'He was the boy that murdered Father Walker, in St Mary's, wasn't he?'

'The very same and he's already murdered two others from the same home, and one of my officers.'

'I thought he was locked up? Sectioned.'

'He got out.'

'And what makes you think he'd want to harm me. I hardly knew the boy.'

Anderson chose his words carefully. 'Certain allegations have been made, about Father Walker – and about your handling of the –'

McKinnion's head span around like an owl spotting a field mouse. '– How dare you! Whatever occurred all those years ago happened without my knowledge, I assure you. Oh, those allegations are not new, Inspector. They were made at the time, by the boy you mentioned. But they were unproven. Father Walker was a diligent and honest priest – who was murdered by that deranged child.'

'Well, he may still be deranged, but he's no longer a boy and is more than capable of carrying out his vendetta. I really think you should postpone this ceremony on Sunday.'

'Absolutely not!' McKinnion's taut face hardened further.

'You don't understand –'

'I understand all too well. As I said, there can be no question of postponement. You will just have to make sure there is ample security, won't you?'

Anderson gritted his teeth, but McKinnion turned his back to the window, and said: 'Now, unless there is anything else, Inspector, I am a rather busy man.'

Anderson then realised he was not getting off the chaise longue without help.

Anderson strolled through the tranquil gardens outside the diocese, rolling a cigarette, and only too conscious a pair of eyes looked through arched windows watching him leave.

Balls to McKinnion, he thought. *Would serve him right if Special Branch let Michael Skye get on with it. See how pious he'd be then, when his chest felt like an elephant sat on it.* Anderson's own chest twinged again, so he slipped another one of his pills on to his tongue as he opened the door to the Rover.

Kendrick sat in the driver's seat, the steering wheel cutting into his extended midriff, and the buttons on his suit strained to hold in the barrel chest and large gut. He looked like a bouncer from a cheap nightclub.

'So, how did it go?' he asked.

'What an arsehole,' Anderson said, slumping into the seat next to him and pushing in the cigarette lighter.

'You didn't upset him, did you?' Kendrick's flushed cheeks made him appear angry, and combined with his bull neck, shaved head and bristly beard, gave him a formidable countenance. But his voice sounded soft, almost effeminate, and in stark contrast to his appearance.

'I'm not the one wanting to kill him.' Anderson held the car's lighter to his cigarette.

'Do you have to do that, old boy?' Kendrick coughed and waved away the smoke. 'Look, I know what happened must be hard for you. Harrison was a good man, but I still don't understand all this. If this escaped patient is a big a threat as you say, we can just ramp up security, can't we? We've still got half of Scotland's firearms officers down here from the Pope's visit.'

Anderson jabbed his cigarette at him. 'No! I don't want any guns near the place.'

'Now c'mon, you're being unreasonable, old boy.'

'Am I?' Anderson had turned his gaze out the window as a trio of priests strolled past in the sunshine. His gaze remained fixed at the gardens, but he could feel Kendrick's eyes probe him and hear his thick breath preparing to speak.

'Isn't it time you told me what's going on, old boy?'

'I wish I knew.'

'Perhaps our man from Section Five may be able to help?'

Anderson snapped his head back to him. 'Do you think that's necessary?'

Kendrick shrugged his huge shoulders. 'I've not seen you like this before, so you obviously do.'

Anderson turned back to watch the three priests disappear into the offices. 'Okay. Set up a meeting.'

Kendrick nodded and turned on the ignition.

Chapter Twenty-Seven

It disappointed Anderson seeing the enclosure empty. He liked elephants. One of the few happy memories from his childhood came in the guise of a trip to Glasgow Zoo – a grand day out. He remembered the elephant enclosure being smaller than Edinburgh's, *but at least they had some bloody elephants.*

Strolling along the concrete wall, he realised how quiet the zoo seemed. Few families milled about, and no school parties stood jeering at the orangutans and apes. *Kids have too much to do these days,* he thought. The sun shone brightly and he wondered if the elephants might be inside enjoying the shade. Although he doubted a spring morning in Edinburgh compared to the Serengeti, or wherever they happened to come from.

The door swung noisily open and he walked into the elephant house, where a thick stench of manure, like the smell of the countryside magnified by a hundred, made his eyes water. He found it surprisingly stimulating, cutting through the fug of his mind.

His neck still hurt but he found the surgical collar too restrictive so had taken it off. His chest had not twinged for some time, and while physically he was on the mend, he'd be old bones before his dreams let him forget the events on Lamb Holm.

Two concrete pens divided the elephant house and Anderson walked along the observation gallery behind the visitor's rail that consisted of three steel tubes welded to the walls. No visitors were inside that morning, and while the first pen lay empty, in the next enclosure, Anderson saw his prize.

An African female lay in the enclosure with her giant bulk resting below the rail, where a woman in white coat and using a torch, examined the inside of the elephant's mouth.

'She's not ill, is she?' Anderson asked, leaning over the rail to pat the elephant's rear.

The woman turned round. 'Oh sorry, the elephant house is closed this morning.'

'Sorry, I didn't know. The door was unlocked.' Anderson patted the large beast again. The skin felt coarse and hairy, like a bristly doormat.

'That's okay,' the woman said, standing up and stretching her legs. 'Can't do any more. Wrong drill-bit.' She nodded to a *Black-and-Decker* electric drill plugged into an extension cord at her feet. 'Trying to sort out her molars.' She slapped the beast on the head.

'Ain't you worried she might wake up?'

'No, she's out for the count,' the vet replied, wiping her forehead with the back of her hand. She looked young, all freckles and no make-up.

'Must take one hell of a *Mickey Finn* to knock one of them out.' He stroked the thick hide again. 'How do you get a needle in there?'

She smiled, revealing a missing tooth on the bottom row. Anderson wondered how she had lost it. 'We dart them with *etorphine*, less stressful for the animal.'

They both turned their heads to the door as it swung open revealing a figure in the entrance.

The vet shouted over. 'Sorry, the elephant house is closed, today.'

The man didn't reply, but stood in the doorway smoking, the daylight behind blinding them to just his silhouette.

'It's okay,' Anderson said, giving the elephant one last pat. 'He's with me, and we're leaving.'

He walked toward the stranger, straightened his moustache with his fingers and nodded. The man smiled and raised a cigarette holder to his lips. 'You must be the famous Inspector Anderson,' he said, with an English accent. 'Let's go for a walk.'

Having followed him into the sunshine, Anderson noted the man cut an elegant figure. His suit had never been near a peg – the jacket alone must have cost a month's salary. The hair, white and neatly trimmed was side parted with a slight spread to cover the thinning, while his Italian brogues gleamed without a scuff or stain as he strolled with his cigarette holder held insouciantly between the fingers of one of his leather gloves.

Anderson shuffled next to him in ten-pound loafers, scuffed by last week's memories, a new but already stained jacket, and a roll-up shoved between his lips. He did have a clean shirt on that morning, although a coffee stain now ruined the effect.

They stopped opposite the black bear pit. The two bears lay in the sun, motionless, their thick coats patchy. Three children, leaning over the surrounding concrete wall and calling at the bears to do something, soon got bored and dispersed.

After sucking on his cigarette holder, the man turned to Anderson. 'So I hear you wanted to talk to me about a psychiatric patient?' He spoke in an accent without a region, like an announcer on the BBC, traceable to Oxbridge, but not before.

'You could say that,' Anderson said, leaning against the wall, and flicking his finished roll-up on the ground.

'Is he dangerous?' The Englishman's mouth moved very little when he spoke, yet his voice was strong and commanding.

'Killed my sergeant.'

The Englishman removed the cigarette from its holder, flicked the ash away from his suit and took out a silver cigarette case from his pocket. He offered Anderson one. 'They're Turkish.'

Anderson pulled out a leather pouch from his pocket and a packet of Swans. 'No thanks, I'll stick to Virginian.'

With a gold lighter that clicked open by touch, the Englishmen lit both their new smokes, and they slowly walked away from the bears. 'And you can't explain any of it?'

'Not in any way that'd make sense,' Anderson admitted.

The Englishman, holding his cigarette holder at a jaunty angle like a dandy, stopped at a cage full of monkeys and gibbons. 'Nearly all my life we've been at war,' he said, tiredly. 'Germans then the Russians.'

'And now the Argies,' Anderson said, joining him at the cage and staring at the bare backside of a baboon.

'I'd hardly call that a war,' the Englishman replied. 'Not compared with the arms race we're up against with the Soviets.' He turned around and breathed a stream of smoke from the corner of his mouth. 'And it's not all about conventional weapons, either.'

Anderson's eyes narrowed. 'What do you mean?'

'About a decade ago, the Americans got hold of some Soviet papers from the fifties. Seems Stalin was as obsessed as Hitler with pseudo-sciences.'

'Pseudo?'

'Yes, you know, all sorts of stuff. Religious artefacts, remote viewing, ESP – even levitation.'

'You're kidding?'

'No, all of it nonsense of course, well, most of it. There was this one piece of research that interested us. Some work they'd been doing in the Gulags, made quite horrific reading. But they seemed to have made a few advances. Got the Americans all excited, I can tell you.'

'Excited, about what?'

'Your psychiatric patient isn't the first to have displayed such –' He looked intently at the monkeys swinging around in the cage as he searched for the right word. '– such gifts.'

'So what do I do?'

The Englishman turned, his mouth smiled but his eyes remained cold. 'There's perhaps somebody who might be able to help.'

'Where do I find him?'

'Here, in Edinburgh.' The Englishman's thin lips widened and he reached into his pocket, pulling free a card. He handed it Anderson. 'Our top man in the field. Well, our only man if truth be told.'

Anderson stared at the card. It had the name of a psychiatrist at a city hospital written on it. The Englishman turned to walk away, leaving Anderson clutching the card and looking confused.

'Oh!' The Englishman stopped and turned around. 'You will remember to be careful, won't you? This boy could prove quite valuable.'

Anderson stared at him, his teeth clenched tight. 'I can't make any promises. He killed my sergeant.'

'May I remind you that you have your pension to worry about.' The Englishman smiled and walked down the hill to the exit.

Anderson watched him go and turned back to the baboon. The backside was still on display. He sighed, waited a couple of minutes, and shuffled off toward the turnstiles himself.

Emerging on to the street, the yellow rover sat rattling on the curbside. He opened the door and slumped into the seat.

'So, how did it go?' Kendrick asked, wedged behind the wheel.

'I'm going to need you to get hold of that shrink.' Anderson lit another cigarette and stared at the card.

'Shrink?'

'Yes, Ruth, the one who was on Orkney. I need her help.'

What an awful journey, Father McGuire thought. Not only did he have to stand most of the way from Inverness, but he now suffered the ignominy of being gawped at by some simpleton.

The compartment had had the only free seat on the carriage. And now McGuire knew why. A boy in tatty green shirt and pair of trousers that looked like they'd been stolen from a tramp stared with vague blue eyes and a mouth hanging open like a panting dog's. McGuire doubted he had a ticket. *Drug addict*, he thought, cursing Dr Beeching and British Rail.

The others in the compartment gazed deliberately elsewhere. McGuire sat sandwiched between a young woman, who chewed gum like a masticating camel and wore a skirt far too short, and a teenage girl wearing spectacles that remained focussed on a glossy magazine.

The occupants next to the strange boy seemed as

uncomfortable as McGuire did. A greying businessman having the fortune of a window to stare out of, but an elderly woman only had only her shoes to look at.

McGuire took his out his copy of the Catholic Herald, and sighed. Even he was tired of seeing pictures of the Pope's visit – a constant reminder of his having missed the occasion. He cursed his appendix. Why couldn't it have played up this week? Not only would he have seen the Holy Father, and accomplished a lifelong ambition, but wouldn't now be enduring such a horrible journey to Edinburgh – he found diocesan conferences a waste of time, anyway.

He pulled at the clerical collar around his neck. He felt a little unwell, but then the carriage was unusually hot. The boy's stares didn't help. Perhaps he should say something, McGuire thought – give him a piece of his mind. No, he'd search for a better seat after the next stop.

He didn't have long to wait. The dying afternoon greyness through the window soon illuminated to a bright yellow glow as they squealed into the platform, and the noise of the robust doors clunking open filled the train.

McGuire needed to stand to allow the short-skirted, gum-chewing woman out of the compartment. The businessman helped pull down her case, and reached out the window to open the compartment door – she rewarded him with a courteous smile – and when she disembarked, McGuire took his cue, reached for his hat and briefcase, and followed her off the train.

He knew how foolhardy looking for another seat among the throng of people on the train itself would be, so he walked down the platform until he found what he looked for. A first class carriage door revealed an empty compartment. He glanced about. He'd not spotted a guard all afternoon. Besides, he was unwell, and it'd be a brave British Rail employee that kicked a sick priest out of a first class carriage, no matter what price his ticket was.

He stepped up, slammed the door behind him and pulled down the window as far is it would go. He wanted to remove his clerical collar, but he didn't, nor had he ever in public, unlike so many of those modern priests. Besides, the cool air filtering through the window began cooling him enough.

He settled into the seat, pulling out his Catholic Herald as the slamming of doors and the shriek of a whistle preceded the slow jolt of the train pulling from North Queensferry station.

The sound of the compartment door slid open. He lowered the paper, hoping it wasn't the ticket collector.

It wasn't.

The boy in the shabby green shirt and dirty trousers stood in the doorway. McGuire opened his mouth to chastise him. This really was too much. But a breathlessness took hold, and his mouth hung open without any words exiting. The fever began raising his temperature again. A cold sweat started moistening his forehead as the boy's blank eyes just stared back at him.

Chapter Twenty-Eight

When Anderson asked her to meet him in Edinburgh, Ruth wanted to say no. She wanted to get away from Orkney and put all the memories and events behind her. But as she thought of Harrison, and remembered the look on Anderson's face in that hospital – especially his sorrowful, tired eyes that drooped like a dog's that had lost its master – she agreed.

Anyway, she was leaving for Inverness, and another day's diversion would do no harm. She had already said her goodbyes to Tom and Sophie. Not quite a warm parting, but she felt Tom understood, and knew their lives ran on different paths. She had her career to think of. No time for romance. Shame. Another life perhaps.

Anderson appeared brighter when she met him in Edinburgh, but unusually quiet, lacking any of his customary acerbic comments. They took a taxi from the station straight to their destination, and once there, he stamped out his cigarette on the floor and looked up at the hospital building.

'Is this it?' he asked.

She nodded, handing back the card he had given her. 'I've been here a few times, back in my study days.'

With each of its eight floors bizarrely striped either white or grey, the Royal Edinburgh Psychiatric Hospital always reminded Ruth of a council-built block of flats. Standing away from the other buildings, and separated by a car park and moat of grass, it seemed out-of-place, as if accidentally dropped in the middle of the field.

'I've about had enough of hospitals,' he said, nodding to the entrance. 'After you,'

The familiar curtness of an NHS receptionist greeted them once they walked in. 'Name-please-and-which-doctor?'

Anderson pulled his warrant card out and slapped it on the counter. 'We're not patients. We're here to see Doctor Kinnear.'

The woman frowned at the identification, and pulled out a box of index cards, flipping through them. 'Kinnear, you say? Geriatrics, that's seventh floor, next to ECT.'

'Thank you,' Ruth said, following Anderson who was already marching to the lift.

They travelled up to the seventh in silence, Ruth preening herself in the steel reflection and Anderson bouncing on his heels. Emerging into a typical hospital corridor, a row of elderly patients sat in wheelchairs before the lift, grinning at the visitors as they stepped out. Ruth's eyes remained fixed ahead, while Anderson's stared at the pensioners like a curious child.

'What's wrong with 'em?' he whispered.

'Dementia, Alzheimer's probably.'

He gave them a distasteful glance over his shoulder before Ruth found the door number the receptionist gave them. Anderson knocked.

The portly man who answered appeared flushed and sounded out of breath, as if he'd been up to no good. He grinned at them with Mr Toad-like lips and large bulging eyes. 'You must be Inspector Anderson?' His voice sounded thick, as if he was sucking a lozenge. 'Our mutual friend said you'd be calling.' He gave a rather obvious wink. 'I'm Dr Kinnear.'

Not much older than Anderson he had a few more grey hairs,

but a more affable smile. He thrust out his hand and Anderson shook it, and introduced Ruth. 'This is Dr Ruth Duncan, from Inverness,'

'Doctor?'

'A psychiatrist too,' she replied, shaking the man's hand.

'Ah good, might make all this easier to explain. Well, come in, come in, for heaven's sake.' He stepped back into his office, beckoning them to follow. 'Sorry it's so cramped'

Ruth and Anderson squeezed past a swollen bookcase and seated themselves at his desk. Books lay strewn before them, all lying higgledy-piggledy, and a model of brain rested precariously on the edge of the desk, next to which, and seemingly defying gravity and captivating Anderson's curiosity, a large cloudy jar containing what Ruth assumed was a pickled brain.

'I understand you're interested in my research? Something to do with a patient of yours?'

'Sort of,' explained Ruth. 'He escaped from a secure unit in Orkney.'

'Oh, what's his condition?'

'Acute paranoid schizophrenia, mixed with a whole heap of other personality disorders. Came from a care home –Catholic run. But I'm not quite sure I understand where you fit in, Doctor. I'm not sure geriatric research will help.'

The doctor laughed and plonked his leather elbow patches on the desk causing the jar to wobble. 'I only work here because there are no shortages of severe depressives in geriatrics. That's what my research needs, and it works out quite well. The only problem is that just when you are making progress, they go and die on you – it's most frustrating.'

'I see.'

Anderson was fiddling with the anatomical model on Kinnear's desk and dropped part of the forebrain to the floor. 'Sorry,' he said, reaching down and placing it back, upside down. 'You were talking about your work, Doctor. Exactly what is it you research?'

'Neuroprojection.'

'Neuro-what-now?' Anderson looked perplexed.

Kinnear leaned back on his chair, his thick lips curled into a contented smile and he clasped his hands behind his head. 'I suppose you've heard of telekinesis?'

'Isn't that mind reading?' Anderson asked.

'No,' Ruth said. 'That's telepathy. Telekinesis is the power to affect things externally with the power of the mind. Never been proved, though, a pseudo-science surely, Doctor?'

'So you say,' Kinnear snapped. 'We refer to it as neuroprojection. And I can tell you, it is certainly not a pseudo-science.'

Ruth raised her eyebrows at Anderson, whose face didn't hide his scepticism any better. 'I'm finding all this a little hard to swallow,' he said.

'Why?' Kinnear asked. 'Look at it this way. Nature is just a struggle for survival – an arms race if you like. One animal develops teeth and claws, and another, fast running legs. Neuroprojection is just another weapon in Mother Nature's arsenal.'

'If that's true, why can't we all do it? Why haven't I seen evidence of it before?' Ruth asked.

'Perhaps you have not looked hard enough,' insisted Kinnear.

'But it's a matter of need. I'm sure if a tiger were to run down this corridor now, you could probably run faster than the current world record holder. It's all about necessity. Would you say your patient has a history of trauma?'

'We think he was abused,' Ruth said, noticing Anderson now staring into space. 'His conditions in the secure unit were not good, either.'

Kinnear nodded. 'And he's injured how many people?'

'Left four dead.'

'Including a copper,' Anderson added.

Kinnear leaned forward, the pickled brain bounced in the air, but settled back on the edge of the desk. 'How?'

'Heart attacks, mainly. Aortic aneurysms,' Ruth said.

'Of course. I knew it!' He clapped his hands and slapped them on the desk. The jar bounced up again and finally toppled over.

'Come,' Kinnear said, righting the jar before standing. 'After I heard you were coming, I took the liberty in setting something up. I think it might just help.'

The pounding in McGuire's chest worked like an engine with a blown gasket – each thump in his ribcage raising his body's temperature. He pulled at his clerical collar. The white, starched band came loose in his hand. He clutched it while pleading to the boy to pull the emergency handle hanging above his head. But the boy remained motionless.

McGuire, his body feeling hot enough to boil the sweat off his skin's surface, tried to stand, but he fell to all fours, still clutching the dog collar in his hand. His fever continued to rise. He ripped at his shirt, the buttons flying across the floor and bouncing under the empty seats. Still the boy didn't move.

Driven by the need to cool his entire body and driven by the pounding in his chest, McGuire scrambled to the carriage door and its open window where the outside world whipped past. After ripping the shirt from his shoulders, and craning his head out of the window, he pulled with all his strength to get to his feet.

They were travelling over the Forth Bridge, the girders chopping the air as they hurtled over the black water. The wind bombarded his face, providing much-needed coolness. He gulped at the fast-moving air, hoping the speed of the train would force it into his lungs.

A hand, very gently touched his wrist. McGuire span around, still biting at the air for breath. The boy stood over him now, his hand prising the clerical collar from the father's grasp.

The boy then stepped back and picked up McGuire's shirt, clutching it while still staring at the priest. McGuire pointed at the emergency cord, but the boy remained still. McGuire, who now found even the blast of air through the window not enough to ease the burning of his body, turned back around and leaned out the window, as far as he could, his mind slowly closing as the lack of oxygen took its toll.

With each thump in his ribcage, his body seemed to heat exponentially. He felt his consciousness failing, and the intense fever making him feel as if he would spontaneously combust. McGuire leaned out farther. The more he stretched the cooler he became, but still not enough. In desperation, he reached for the door handle. He needed to get out. To be cool.

He plunged from the train, his mind just having time to

welcome the sudden cooling of his body before he hit the water.

Chapter Twenty-Nine

Kinnear led Anderson and Ruth to the top floor of the clinic. Anderson struggled to understand what Kinnear was suggesting and felt relieved Ruth had come with him. She and the doctor were prattling on about different disorders and conditions as they passed more geriatrics seated outside various rooms, all with disturbing grimaces across their faces.

Kinnear stopped outside a combination door at the end of the corridor. After entering the code, he led them to another set of double fire doors. Again he stopped, glancing up at a red light glowing above. He pressed a bell-button on the doorframe and stood patiently, until the red light went off and a young Chinese girl, in white lab coat and clutching a clipboard, opened it.

'Doctor, come in, we were just testing the equipment,' she said, in a strong Edinburgh brogue. 'We're all ready to go.'

'Is Mrs Dvorak here?' Kinnear asked.

'Yes, she's next door. I made her a cup of tea; she seems happy enough.' The young woman smiled at the guests.

'This is one of my finest graduates, Jenny Woo,' Kinnear said, with a smile almost the width of his head. 'Jenny, this is Dr Ruth Duncan and Inspector Anderson.'

'Nice to meet you,' she said, shaking Ruth's hand and offering it Anderson.

She was perhaps five years younger than Ruth, with jet black hair that shone brilliantly under the fluorescent tubes.

'Can we just get on with it,' Anderson said, ignoring her hand.

'You'll have to forgive the inspector,' Ruth said. 'Not very house trained.'

He gave her one of his sardonic smiles as the young lab assistant ushered them inside.

The laboratory looked like a TV studio with walls painted white and an array of lights mounted on the sidewalls. A small door sat at the back beside a tinted window that Anderson presumed was a gallery. Two bulky video cameras sat in the middle of the room, but rather than pointing at a TV set, they faced down to a small table. A single chair sat underneath, and other than a small transparent disc in the middle, the table lay bare.

Anderson walked over and picked up the clear plastic dish. 'What's this?'

Jenny appeared horrified. 'Careful!' she shouted, snatching the Petri dish from him. '*Clostridium Botulin.*'

Anderson looked blankly at Ruth, who explained. 'Botulism, perhaps one of the deadliest toxins known to man.'

Horrified, Anderson began rubbing his hands on the back of his trousers, while the two girls chuckled.

'Well, before your friend starts dismantling my experiment any further, I think we should take our positions,' Kinnear said, scowling at Anderson.

'I've put some chairs in the gallery,' Jenny said. 'I'll go get Mrs Dvorak and be with you shortly.'

She disappeared through the main door and Kinnear led Anderson and Ruth through the little door at the back of the studio.

A bank of four monitors provided the only illumination, and Anderson banged into one of the chairs in the darkness, letting out an expletive in the process. An array of dials, sliders and control panels sat before the screens, and after Kinnear prompted them, they sat down.

'Don't touch anything,' Ruth whispered.

Anderson decided to sit on his hands. Through the gallery window, he saw Jenny walk back into the studio, holding the door open. A woman shuffled in wearing a heavy overcoat and headscarf. He couldn't see her face, but by the way she walked, and dressed, she was clearly old.

'Mrs Anya Dvorak,' Kinnear said, as Anderson watched Jenny take the woman's coat and scarf, before helping her settle at the little table. 'She was born in Czechoslovakia, at the turn of the century.'

The woman sat with her back to them, rocking gently back and forth on her chair. Anderson turned to Ruth, but her eye's remained fixed on Kinnear.

'What's her condition?' she asked.

'Acute psychosis and post traumatic stress disorder,' Kinnear said. 'Brought about by her experiences in the war.'

'Why, what happened to her?' Ruth asked, as Jenny began whispering to the woman, holding her tenderly around the shoulders.

'Auschwitz Birkenau.'

A silence filled the room at the infamous name, until Ruth asked: 'Is she Jewish?'

Kinnear shook his head, 'No, her only crime was epilepsy, which was why the Nazi's placed her in Auschwitz – sometime in the spring of nineteen-forty. Soviets found her in forty-five.'

'She was there five years?' Ruth sounded surprised.

'Yes, that was what interested us, too. Few survived the camps for so long. I came across her in an asylum in Carlisle. Came to England sometime in the fifties. Been in and out of sanatoriums all her life.'

'What's she doing now?' Anderson asked, as Jenny began stroking the woman's head, causing the old lady to rock more fervently, as if becoming agitated.

'Hypnosis,' Kinnear said. 'It's quite all right, no physical harm will come to her, I can assure you.'

After Jenny made some minor adjustments to the cameras, she left the woman and made her way into the gallery. 'All set,' she said, taking a seat next to Kinnear.

'Ah good,' he replied, as Jenny fiddled with a couple of switches on the control panel. The two central monitors flickered on and two images wobbled on the screen.

'This one is a regular camera,' Jenny explained, pointing to the screen. 'It shows the entire desk – that's the Petri dish there.' She pointed with a ballpoint pen. 'You can't see the contents, of course, which is why we have got this camera.' She tapped the other monitor.

Anderson strained his eyes at it; the image was a lot less clear, a circular red blob surrounded by a blue hue.

'This is an infra-red camera,' Jenny said. 'The red you see is the botulism, it picks up the heat from the microbes.'

'I think we are ready to go, then,' Kinnear said.

Jenny nodded and leaned toward a small pencil-like microphone sticking out of the control panel. 'Mrs Dvorak, can you hear me?'

The old woman didn't turn around but acknowledged them

with a wave of her hand.

'Mrs Dvorak. I want you to listen to my voice very carefully,' Jenny said into the microphone. 'Okay, in your own time, I want you to cast your mind back forty years.'

Jenny turned off the microphone and they all watched Mrs Dvorak increase her rocking, her hands now clutching her head.

'Okay,' Kinnear whispered. 'Watch the infra-red monitor.'

Anderson followed everybody else's eyes to the screens in front of them, but couldn't see anything happening. He raised his head back up at the old woman. Her back was hunched over and she rocked slowly now, but jerking randomly.

The rocking stopped. She let out a wail and began sobbing. Ruth stared at the doctor, but he held his hand up. 'It is okay, she is recalling some of the events she witnessed in the camp. It's the only way for the effect to work.'

'Effect?' Anderson asked.

'There!' The doctor pointed at the screen.

Anderson looked back down but little had changed on the monitor. 'I don't see anything?'

'Look at the infra-red monitor,' Ruth whispered.

Anderson stared at the red blob on the screen, and sure enough, it began getting redder, before beginning to shrink, glowing brighter all the time.

'There, see?' The doctor shouted, pointing at the monitor again as the little red blob began moving towards the bottom of the screen. 'The bacterium, is moving away, see?'

Anderson watched as the red glow on the monitor finally settled at the bottom of the Petri dish. He turned to Ruth and stuck out his bottom lip. 'I'm sorry, but what does it mean?'

Ruth remained silent, staring at the screen, but Jenny answered. 'Those bugs are microscopic. For them to move as you have just seen, is the equivalent of you leaping from here to Fife.'

'What's the causal agent?' Ruth asked.

'We don't know,' admitted Jenny. 'What we do know is that there is nothing projecting directly from Mrs Dvorak.'

'No,' Kinnear added. 'It seems the energy is coming from the microbes themselves. It's not a case of Mrs Dvorak moving the microbes, more the microbes are moving away from her.' He jabbed a finger in the air with excitement. 'She somehow manages to manipulate the energy of the individual cells and gets them to release it – in an instant.'

'The reddening you see is the heat from this energy release, but it doesn't last long,' Jenny said.

Anderson squinted at the screen. The blob now looked a murky brown. 'Forgive me, it's very impressive, I'm sure, but I don't see how this helps us?'

Ruth scowled at him. 'That's how he's doing it. Don't you see? That's why there were no marks on the orderly or Brennan.'

'But what about Harrison?'

Ruth turned to Jenny. 'Does it only work with organic material?'

'Yes, we've tried with all sorts of things, iron filings, ball bearings, but she can only affect living tissue.'

'So it couldn't affect something someone was holding?'

Jenny shook her head. 'No, only organic tissue.'

'Ah,' Kinnear interjected. 'But it could be used to affect a hand holding something.'

Ruth shot a look at Anderson. 'What about the limitations,'

she said, turning back to the old woman through the glass. 'Does she have to be so close?'

Kinnear shook his head. 'There doesn't seem to be any limitation on distance, but line of sight is important. Mrs Dvorak has had cataracts, so needs to sit close to see the culture, but if better sighted, there's no reason to think the effect couldn't work from the other side of the room, perhaps farther.'

'We've even tried it through glass,' Jenny admitted. 'Doesn't seem to make any difference. As long as she can see it.'

'Let's run it again,' Kinnear said, leaning in to Jenny and whispering a few words.

'Are you sure?' she replied, looking through the tinted glass at Mrs Dvorak. The old woman had stopped rocking and sobbing, but remained hunched over.

'Ask her,' Kinnear suggested.

The young Chinese lab assistant got up and walked back into the studio. Anderson watched as she replaced the Petri dish and had a few words with Mrs Dvorak. The old woman nodded her head and Jenny turned, raising her thumb to the gallery.

'This time I have asked her to concentrate harder on some of the more terrible memories. It may be a little traumatic for her, and it pains me to have to ask her, but she has done this before so I ask you not to interrupt, no matter what happens.'

Anderson turned to Ruth whose eyebrows told him to remain quiet. He nodded, as Jenny returned and the experiment began again.

They settled down and stared down at the monitors and the faint red glow of the billions of tiny germs. Anderson's eyes kept flicking up to the old woman. She'd began her incantations again.

Trembling and sobbing as she rocked back and forth, only this time louder and more pronounced. Her cries made him feel uneasy and he moved his eyes over to Ruth, who seemed relaxed enough, presumably being used to such things.

The woman's sobs disturbed him. He hated hearing women cry, especially elderly women. Wasn't right. The sobbing didn't subside, instead she started wailing and her rocking increased, almost violently. She shouted in her native Slavic then started hitting herself around the head.

She seemed so distressed and agitated that Anderson thought she would implode with tension, and then Kinnear shouted and pointed at the screens again. 'There!'

Anderson's eyes followed his finger. The red glow of the bacterium began to move, as before. Only this time it didn't sink toward the bottom, but began forming a cross-shape in the middle of the Petri dish.

Ignoring the wails, screams and sobs from the woman next door, he stared at the screen until the blurred cross, slowly became clearer. Only it wasn't a cross, the ends of it had started to bleed at adjacent angles. After a few moments, Anderson's eyes widened and his mouth dropped open.

'Jesus Christ!' he said, as the familiar shape of a swastika took shape on the screen before him.

Chapter Thirty

Sophie lacked her usual bounce when she arrived for work that afternoon. Tom was busy typing up the edition's front page, involving the loss of two fishermen following an ill-fortuned expedition during a storm a couple of days earlier. The story was a big one for Orkney and had kept him busy. And kept his mind off Ruth.

Tom looked up from his typewriter, a cigarette drooping from his mouth, as the young photographer started going through her pictures. 'What's up, Soph?'

'Those bloody *Invies*,' she said, her camera swinging around her neck. 'They're coming back to have another look at me tonight. Like I'm a new pet dog or something.'

'I thought you said they wouldn't be interested?' Tom stubbed his cigarette out and sat back. He felt the room suddenly go dark, but knew the sun was still high in the afternoon sky.

'I tried everything?' she said, clutching the prints in her hand. 'Even nicked Roger's wallet.'

'Roger?'

'The bloke. Said it showed I had spirit. I'll give them spirit tonight. I'll show 'em. Might announce I'm pregnant.'

Tom smiled, but only with his mouth. It had to happen eventually. Ruth had gone, and now Sophie would follow.

She walked over to his desk. 'Don't worry about it, though. I'll make sure they choose someone else.'

'Why would I worry.' He found his voice sounded cold. 'I'm sure I'll get another photographer.'

For a moment he thought Sophie would cry – his words certainly made him feel like doing so, but she just stood with her bottom lip wavering. 'Is that all I am, then? Cheap labour.'

'Hey, don't get shirty,' he snapped. 'I'm still your boss.'

She eyed him carefully before throwing the prints on his desk. 'Well, *boss*, why don't you take your own photos, then?'

He shrugged. 'I don't know, perhaps I should. Your pictures have been lousy lately.'

She pursed her lips and scowled at him. 'You don't mean that.'

'Don't I? Listen, it's probably time you moved on, anyway. It's not healthy, a young girl hanging around with a bloke all day. People talk, you know.'

'Are you firing me?'

Tom lit another smoke. 'I think it's for the best.'

She lifted the camera from around her neck and placed it on his desk. 'If that's what you want.'

He stared down at his typewriter. 'It is.'

His eyes remained fixed at the copy. Even when he heard her footsteps run down the stairs and the door to the cottage slam shut. He wrenched the paper from the typewriter, screwed it into a ball and threw it across the room.

He then wiped the tears from his eyes.

Ruth sat in the hotel bar with Anderson and a very large man she'd been introduced to as DSI Kendrick. Few other guests were spending the bright Edinburgh Saturday afternoon drinking, but Anderson had consumed enough to keep the bar staff busy.

Kendrick, who sipped tea with is chubby little finger sticking out like a dainty old maid, placed his teacup down and turned to

Ruth. 'I'm not going to pretend I know what's going on,' he said, his soft voice an anachronism to his size. 'But are we sure your patient will be coming here? Edinburgh's a long way from Orkney, especially considering his condition.'

'Just because he's mentally ill, doesn't mean he lacks intelligence. A lot of schizophrenics are extremely clever and manipulative. Getting off Orkney wouldn't be too hard. He could have hitched a ride on the ferry, or even mugged somebody for the contents of their wallet, including their identification. You need to make sure the people arriving are who they say they are.'

Kendrick rolled his eyes, dismissing her as Anderson used to, until Harrison died. 'Well, they've all been told to bring their passports tomorrow – can't see what else we can do.'

Anderson downed his fifth glass of scotch. 'You got the list of everyone attending?'

Kendrick patted his jacket. 'Spoke to Cardinal White's secretary this afternoon. Should be a busy affair. I've enlisted nearly a dozen of the Branch, but without firearms, my biggest concern is how are we going to apprehend him – if he turns up.'

Anderson was rolling a cigarette. 'Been wondering that myself.'

'That psychiatrist you saw, no help?' Kendrick asked.

Anderson shook his head. 'Told us how he's doing it, not how to stop him.' He looked warily at Kendrick, as if an idea was brewing in his mind. 'You can shoot, though, can't you?'

Kendrick picked his teacup back up. 'Yes, you know I can, but I thought you didn't want any guns around?'

'I don't,' Anderson said, banging his scotch glass on the table. 'And I mean none within a mile of the place.'

Kendrick put his teacup down again. 'Then what are you on about?'

Anderson stood up, the sound of his chair sliding back awakened the bar staff, one of which grabbed another shot glass. But Anderson didn't turn to the bar, he placed his cigarette in his mouth and lit it. 'You leave it to me.' He turned about and began walking out of the hotel.

Kendrick stood also. 'Hey, where are you going?'

Anderson turned his head back over his shoulder. 'To the zoo.'

Kendrick looked down at Ruth, his eyebrows meeting in the middle from confusion. Ruth just shrugged.

Chapter Thirty-One

Ruth sat in the car with Kendrick. He smelled. Yet, she found the odour comforting. A mixture of sweat, stale coffee and cheap aftershave. The smell of machismo, which reminded her of hugging her father when he arrived home after a hard day's work. Before he became ill.

Despite his assurance he'd be at the cathedral that morning, Ruth hadn't seen Anderson since he left the hotel the afternoon before. She didn't know what he was up to, but strangely, found herself really wanting to see him. She couldn't for the life of her think why.

St Mary's RC looked unimposing for a cathedral. Set back from the main highway with a little access road, now blocked by the police cars and uniformed officers, it was sandwiched between a shopping centre and row of shops. The building could have passed for a library, except for the four spires, its only prominent features. She found it hard to imagine the Pope had visited there only last week, but then she knew little of the august nature of cathedrals.

Father McKinnion's ordination to bishop took place in less than an hour, and already a few of the venerable guests had begun arriving. The police cars across the access road prevented any vehicles from parking outside the front of the cathedral, except for the Rover she and Kendrick sat in. The officers at the cordon searched all the visitors thoroughly, regardless of whether they were priests, nuns, or friends and family of the soon-to-be Bishop. Sniffer dogs, tugging at their tight leads, inspected everybody's scent walking through the cordon, while the police padded everybody down.

A little gaggle of nuns, dismayed at having to go through such an undignified procedure, walked up the steps to the cathedral, shaking their heads at such disrespectful treatment, as did a group of priests after the police made them empty their pockets. Ruth understood the need for precautions, but had her own concerns about the security. What good would any of it be against Michael?

Kendrick was uneasy. He sat with the guest-list on his lap, and held a walkie-talkie, which crackled every time a new visitor arrived and the officers at the cordon announced the guest, allowing him to tick the name off his list. He and Ruth had sat there for the last three hours, the large man having earlier supervised the police as they scoured the cathedral for bombs and checked the guests who had already arrived, including the choir. Now, they both sat waiting for the rest of the guests to arrive, the bishops, Father McKinnion, not to mention Michael Skye.

'So where's the inspector?' she asked, watching the police frisk another group of priests at the cordon.

'He'll be here, don't worry.'

The radio began crackling again, and Ruth saw two black Bentleys sidle up to the police cordon, followed shortly by a black cab. Kendrick pulled open the door to the Rover and heaved his large frame out.

'Wait here,' he said, his arm supporting his bulk on the car's roof. 'I don't want you to get out of this car. Understand?'

Ruth nodded as he slammed shut the door and waddled over

to the police cordon, just as several officials and ceremonially dressed bishops stepped from the first car.

Ruth couldn't help but smile as the bishops, dressed in gold vestments, long smocks and tall mitres, went through the demeaning process of being frisked. Once satisfied, the police allowed them to walk up to the cathedral where they congregated on the steps of St Mary's.

She recognised Cardinal White, the Bishop of Edinburgh – his face was a regular feature on TV. And, stepping from the second car, dressed in similar regalia, Father McKinnion. It had to be. Wearing a red biretta and scarlet mozzetta, he walked through security with an air of arrogance, before ascending the steps to the cathedral with several diocese officials trailing behind, like pageboys at a wedding.

A lot of handshaking and discussions took place on the steps of St Mary's, while Kendrick discussed something at the police cordon with another of the clergy. He had got out the taxi alone and looked more conventional than the rest of the clerics, wearing only a plain white tunic. He carried a small leather case, which he handed to the superintendent, before following the other clergy up the steps.

Kendrick waddled back to the Rover. Ruth unwound the window as he leaned his weight on car's roof again, tilting the suspension.

'Is that McKinnion?' she asked, nodding to the elegant figure at the top of the steps.

'Yes, they're all here. The ceremony's about to start. I want you to stay put though, no matter what happens, stay in the car. Understand?'

Ruth nodded. 'Okay, but where's the inspector? He should be here by now.'

'He's inside,' Kendrick said, clutching the walkie-talkie in one hand, and the small leather case given him by the cleric. 'Now wait here.'

Ruth frowned. *When did Anderson arrive?* She'd been sat in the car for nearly three hours and should have seen him – the scruffy detective was, after all, difficult to miss.

Kendrick waddled back to the cordon, gesticulating orders to the police, as the bishops, priests and clerics filed into the cathedral. Ruth wished she had a cigarette.

'Oh, what now!' Jimmy snapped, yanking on the handbrake and causing the airbrakes to hiss like an angry snake. He looked down at the dashboard clock. He was already late. Another hour and the depot closed. Leaving him with an overnight stay and another night sleeping in the back of the cab.

Why the traffic? It's Sunday, he thought. While he knew it was blocked last week because of the Pope's visit, Leith Street should have been clear today.

He swore and took out a mint from the packet on the dashboard, and glanced back down at his clock. 'Oh, c'mon, c'mon.'

He drummed his fingers impatiently on the steering wheel. 'Bloody hell! What's going on?' he shouted to himself, after seeing police cars blocking the access road to the cathedral and leaving only one lane open to traffic.

The dashboard clock ticked relentlessly, and he bobbed his

head around in the cab to see if the southbound carriage was moving. He couldn't tell, but saw some dignitaries and bishops milling around the front of the cathedral.

'Bloody Catholics!' He snapped.

The car in front began moving and Jimmy lifted up the handbrake, causing another angry hiss from the brakes, only to have to slam his foot on them a moment later having moved only a couple of yards.

'Oh, bloody hell!' He could feel his pulse increase. Only fifteen minutes until the depot closed. He ate another mint and intensified his finger drumming. 'C'mon, c'mon.'

He began breathing rapidly. The stress would be doing him no good at all. His doctor already warned him about his blood pressure, saying a by-pass would be inevitable unless he sorted himself out. *Much chance of that*, he thought, watching the clock. His heart began pounding, his breathing increased to a pant and Jimmy started to feel unwell. He needed air and turned to wind down the window, only to see somebody staring at him. A priest. What was he looking at? Jimmy scowled at him, noticing the dishevelled clothing and wide glaring eyes, like those of an owl's.

The car in front moved forward. At last, progress. He crunched the gearbox into first, but suddenly his chest pounded. He understood why. Stress playing havoc with his blood pressure again, but what he didn't understand was why his leg began stiffening. It moved off the pedal and a gentle hiss indicated the brake's release. Then he found his foot over the accelerator, revving the engine. What was he doing? And why was he now lifting the other foot off the clutch? The truck lurched forward and Jimmy found himself depressing the accelerator and pulling at the steering wheel.

He mounted the pavement and the 22-ton articulated lorry picked-up speed and headed towards the police cars outside the cathedral.

Chapter Thirty-Two

Ruth watched as the last of the visitors climbed up the steps, entered the cathedral and a constable closed the doors behind them. He, and the policemen at the cordon, seemed relaxed. A couple of them took out cigarettes, but Kendrick, with his shirt hanging out exposing his big belly, paced up and down at the cordon, staring at every passer-by who dared to get too near.

Ruth looked at her watch. The ceremony was due to last two hours. Afterwards they could consider it all over. Except Michael would still be on the loose. Ruth half-hoped he wouldn't turn up. If Michael did show, she doubted he could be convinced to hand himself in. Not with his condition, and not after what he'd already done.

Her eyes fell on a call box on the pavement flanking the access road. Her thoughts turned to Tom and Sophie and she wondered how they were. She wanted to call, but wasn't sure why. Orkney seemed such a long time ago now and everything that took place since, felt surreal. She respected Kinnear, a psychiatrist with far more experience than she had, and was certain Anderson told the truth about Harrison's death, but it all seemed so unlikely. Perhaps McRowen was right, and the devil played a hand. She shook her head. Ridiculous.

Kendrick gave specific instructions to stay put, so she resigned herself for a long wait. She slid herself lower in the seat and yawned. Sleep had evaded her these last few nights and she struggled to hold up the weight of her eyelids.

A blink lingered a little too long.

She jolted awake almost as soon as she fell asleep. Several shouts drifted from the cordon and the sound of an engine, a big engine, began getting louder.

The sight of the HGV, mounting the pavement and speeding toward the police cars, played out like the slow motion on her Betamax video player. The lorry hit the first panda car and spun it like a Dinky toy. The car cascaded into two policemen, before the truck ploughed into the next one, causing several officers to flee. Kendrick, all twenty-odd stone, gambolled into the gutter. The tyre of the truck missed him by just inches.

Ruth sat horrified as a young constable, eyes fixed in the wrong direction got caught under the cab, the truck not even rising as the off-side tyres ran over his body.

The truck mounted the curb on the other side of the access road, ploughed into the call box, knocking it over like a domino, and then skidded abruptly to a halt, causing the driver to burst through the windscreen like a stuntman in a Hollywood action film. Except he didn't get up.

For several seconds Ruth surveyed the horror in front of her before reaching for the door handle and bolting from the car.

She stood motionless, the world mute, apart from a gentle hiss of steam from the lorry's radiator. After a few seconds, Kendrick and the policemen shook off their shock. The constable at the cathedral door bounded down the steps and several others began running around, shouting orders.

Ruth ran to the truck driver, and realised as soon as she crouched down to assist him that he lay dead. His eyes, wide open, stared lifelessly from a face peppered with glass and cuts. Nobody approached the policeman run over by the lorry. His death, evident to everybody who witnessed the crash, but two other officers lay squirming on the pavement, one trapped beneath a police car. Ruth ran over to help, along with Kendrick who barked orders into the radio, shouting: 'Code three, code three, St Mary's. Code three!'

After arriving at the smashed-up police car, Ruth saw one of the officer's leg was broken. The white of a bone protruded through his trousers. The other policeman, half-wedged under the car, appeared more severely injured. Although both men were conscious. Kendrick squatted beside her as she relayed her medical opinion while cradling the head of the officer under the car.

'Broken fibula,' she said, pointing to the one injured man. She could hear gurgling in the breath of the man on her lap. 'This one's lung's punctured.'

'The ambulance is coming,' Kendrick said.

Several commuters got out from their cars to assist, but Kendrick got up and ran over to corral them from the access road. 'Get back, get back! I said move! Put that bloody fag out – there's fuel about!'

The man in Ruth's arms began shaking and blood fountained from his mouth. 'Shhh,' she said, stroking his head. 'You're going to be okay. You're going to be okay, I promise.'

She glanced around, hoping to see the ambulance. She couldn't, but heard a siren in the distance. A second later, she broke her promise. The policeman died on her lap. Her eyes moved to the other injured man. While the broken leg had distracted him enough to miss his colleague's demise, her eyes told him the news.

The man began crying and she released the dead officer's head to console the other, just as a flash of black ran past her.

Ruth's head shot up and she saw a priest cantering up the steps to the cathedral. She watched as the large double doors slammed behind him. She looked over to Kendrick and waved her hands frantically for his attention, but the large man was busying himself with the other officers getting the road clear to make room for the ambulance.

After glancing from Kendrick to the injured policeman, she stood and hesitated. After glancing back a couple of times, she bounded up the steps after the priest.

When the outer door closed behind her, the sirens and pandemonium silenced. Kendrick had said Anderson was inside. She hoped he was right. Perhaps he'd already seen the priest run in, if not, she'd point him out. She pulled open the inner doors to the cathedral and dashed inside. The door banged behind. She stood motionless, panting.

The cathedral looked fairly modern inside and not as dour as St Magnus. Wooden chairs flanked both sides of the nave. Three quarters remained empty. The witnesses to the ordination all sat at the front, watching the ceremony in the apse taking place under an arched fresco. Or they were watching the ceremony. The rear rows all turned round after hearing Ruth burst in – the intrusion evidently not welcome.

She saw no sign of the priest that ran in before her. No wonder, at least fifty of them, identically dressed in black smocks, sat on the aisle seats, staring back at her. Michael could have been any one of them, if indeed it was Michael. She looked about hoping to spot one settling into a seat, but he'd had too much of a head start.

Ruth wanted to stop the service and warn everybody, but a diocese official, who stood flanking the door behind her, grabbed her, pulled her to the nearest aisle seat, and forced her to sit. She tried to protest, but he shushed her, and her feeble attempts at protest just generated more angry stares from the priests farther up the aisle.

Which one was Michael? She began scanning their faces, but they turned back round to continue their observance of the ceremony. Her thoughts then turned to Anderson.

Behind her, the diocese official had returned to his position by the door, and a few others lingered under the small pillars that flanked the aisles. The lighting far surpassed that of St Magnus, with electric bulbs providing enough illumination to reveal their faces. Anderson did not stand with them. Where was he then? She craned her neck to get a better view.

The ceremony at the altar proceeded despite her interruption. McKinnion sat on a throne-like seat beneath the giant vaulted arch. The angelic fresco befitting the soft voices of the choir, who sang lightly, and remained almost invisible behind the vaulted arch. Their voices provided nothing more than a background murmur as several ecclesiastical figures and two bishops, dressed in mitres and long gowns, stood next to Cardinal White who mumbled Latin sacraments before McKinnion.

The numerous candles flickering behind them surrounded the scene in an orange glow, and a couple of figures in plain white smocks moved around the bishops. One carried an incense burner, the smoke seeping out and thickening the air. The smell wafted as far back as Ruth's seat.

It all appeared a little amateurish, the man with the incense seemed to get in everybody's way, but she knew nothing of Catholic ceremonies and supposed the actions were in keeping with tradition.

The Latin speech reached a crescendo, as did the choir's soft voices. Cardinal White turned to face McKinnion and shouted another Latin utterance, before proceeding to place his hands on top of McKinnion's head. The other two bishops followed his motions and also placed their hands on his head.

The choir erupted into a Baroque falsetto, far louder than before, and Cardinal White began shouting, again in Latin, but sounding more like a rant.

Ruth saw very little from her position. She glanced behind. The diocese official no longer faced her direction, so she scurried a few rows farther forward, and glanced back. He'd spotted her move, and scowled, but seemed content to let her sit in her new position. The back row of priests were now only a few rows ahead, but she had no chance of spotting Michael, not that she knew what he looked like, they had their backs to her and eyes fixed at the ceremony, which she could now see more clearly.

The cardinal and two bishops still had their hands on McKinnion's head. Cardinal White continued canting in Latin as the acolyte with the incense walked around them. McKinnion's countenance looked solemn, his thin lips repeating the sacrament. Until Cardinal White, his hands shaking, removed them from McKinnion's head, and slowly, like a former drinker reaching for a glass, slipped them around his throat.

McKinnion's eyes then changed from solemnity to fear.

Chapter Thirty-Three

In the following seconds, the murmurs spreading amongst the pews, turned to chatter, to shouts, to panic and finally pandemonium. Priests stood and ran to the stage as Cardinal White throttled McKinnion. The two bishops either side began trying to prise his hands from around McKinnion's neck, as did several of the white smocked acolytes, except the one with the incense burner. He, like Ruth, stood and stared at the unfolding confusion.

With so many bodies running about, Ruth soon found her vision blocked. People bumped into each other with nobody knowing what to do. Clergy, clerics and diocese officials now surrounded Cardinal White, but judging by the screams and cries, they failed in their attempts to prise the hands from McKinnion's throat.

Ruth stood on her seat. She stared, not at the stage, but kept her eyes on the audience. All were in disarray, except one, who sat calmly, unmoved by the fiasco that played itself out in front of them. Ruth knew who it was.

She jumped from her seat and ran to the same aisle, and for a moment, just stared at him. He was a young man, no older than thirty with dishevelled hair and ill-fitting clothes. He looked filthy, his hair ruffled and greasy. His face, however, remained emotionless. Wide blue eyes stared ahead. Full lips wobbled as if uttering to himself. A face of contradictions. A face of tranquillity and confusion. A face of the psychotic.

She found herself unsure of what to do. She scanned around,

calling for assistance. Nobody paid her or the motionless priest any attention. All the priests, clergy and diocese officials piled in the apse, helping the bishops pull at the hands around McKinnion's throat. Shouting, screaming, waving their arms. Like stockbrokers clamouring for the last commodity on the floor. Until nothing could be seen except the backs of dozens of people.

Michael stood. Ruth knew he had to keep his eyes fixed on the melodrama ahead. His countenance remained placid, his eyes remained wide.

'Michael!' Ruth shouted, no more than a few yards from him, but she doubted her voice carried over the cacophony of screams, shouts and yells echoing around the vaulted building.

'Michael,' she shouted, again, louder.

He turned his head toward her.

A relief seemed to fill the voices around the bishops. She wondered if they had succeeded in freeing McKinnion, but she soon stopped thinking about anything other than the terrible pain emanating from her chest.

Michael stared at her with the same intensity as a blowtorch cutting through metal. His eyes pierced right through her, boring into her chest. She screamed a silent scream that did nothing but expel the last breath from her lungs.

She collapsed to her knees, appealing all round for help, but nobody paid her any attention. They were too busy subduing Cardinal White and administering aid to the stricken father. She saw McKinnion now, his face red, his once immaculate vestments ripped and torn. At least she had saved his life. But why? What did she owe McKinnion? What did anybody owe

McKinnion? A searing pain deep inside her chest interrupted her thoughts, as if her lungs had deflated to a size that would fit into a matchbox.

She gasped and tried to scream, but the light around her faded. One last hopeless appeal for help. A prayer. *Please God, don't let him kill me.*

And her prayer was answered.

Not everybody in the apse attended to McKinnion or subdued the Bishop of Edinburgh. As Ruth collapsed on to the pews, she spied the acolyte, who had so clumsily swung the incense burner around during the ceremony. He pushed his way through the thong of clergy and priests, shouting into his sleeve as he did so. Once clear, he ran toward the pews, just as the last of the oxygen burned itself in her body and she began passing out.

In her semi-conscious state, she had visions of the cleric jumping over the pews and leaping toward Michael. With his head back, he whipped it forward like a footballer receiving a header, smashing down on the unprepared psychiatric patient's face. He hit with such force, they both went tumbling over the pews into the centre of the nave.

And then Ruth fell unconscious.

Despite his annoying enthusiasm for everything Anderson said or did, Father Wallace proved incredibly useful. He said acting as *thurifer* for the ceremony was a simple job. All Anderson needed to do was swing the incense burner around, and keep from the getting under everyone's feet. Anderson found both tasks difficult enough wearing the cumbersome smock over his suit.

It worked, though. Being up front with Cardinal White and

the bishops gave him enough of a view to pick out Michael Skye. He almost missed him, though, having stumbled on his smock as the door to the cathedral first opened, allowing the disguised mental patient to slip in without Anderson seeing him. He caught sight of Ruth bursting in afterwards, and realised she pursued their quarry.

Plan A accomplished.

Plan B proved a little more difficult. In all the commotion, Anderson soon found his vision obscured by anxious priests and officials as Cardinal White began strangling McKinnion. Fortunately, Ruth spotted him, and Anderson realised she was one bloody brave bitch. She about saved McKinnion's life, although her presence in the cathedral alarmed him. Where was Kendrick?

Once Anderson spied Ruth in trouble, he knew he had seconds to react. He barked for the big man in the walkie-talkie, which he'd strapped under his sleeve, before launching himself at Michael. The Glasgow kiss crashed down on Michael's nose to a satisfying crunch, but after the pair cascaded over the pews, and Anderson got to his feet, plan B seemed to be going tits-up.

Ruth remained out cold, but he saw her breathing a few yards from his feet, but his biggest concern was Kendrick. Where was the fat bastard? Everything hinged on the big man. Anderson, righting himself and ignoring the bruises caused by the wooden chairs now lying scattered around the nave, began having doubts. Especially as a bloodied but pissed-off mental patient stood up before him.

For a moment, they stood facing each other. Anderson in his smock with Michael's blood smeared across his temple, Michael staring with those vacant blue eyes set back above a nose now smeared across face. He didn't even appear fazed or in pain, but simply glared. And then the pain in Anderson's chest began.

The rest of the congregation started to take notice of the disruption behind them, and Anderson noticed several priests stood watching the standoff. None moved. *Typical,* he thought, they soon ran over to save Father McKinnion, but when a hard-working copper needed a little help, they just gaped.

His chest contracted like a pair of bellows, collapsing him to his knees. The pain felt all too familiar. Thoughts of Lamb Holm began flashing through his mind as Michael's gaze took hold. Like before, the pain rippled through him like mains voltage electricity, sapping his strength, taking his breath. How long before his heart would pop? Not long. He knew his previous encounter with Michael did irreparable damage, even more than a lifetime's heavy drinking and smoking. *Another trophy for Phelps,* he thought, scrambling to reach the push-to-talk button on his walkie-talkie. He managed it, but had no breath to call for Kendrick.

He slumped face first on the cold mosaic floor, his eyes gazing at the door. As his vision began to fail and his chest began thumping faster and faster, he wondered if dying in a cathedral would give him any credit at the pearly gates. He doubted it. He lived life too hard. Still not a bad life really. Not too many regrets. Except perhaps Harrison. At least he'd get to apologise in person.

Here it came. Appearing at the end of the nave, the bright light he'd heard so much about. Would angels be taking him, or the others? Well, if Beelzebub wanted him, let him try, he'd give him hell. And then it came, appearing in the light and running toward him. An angel? Didn't look like one. Even the Italian's never painted them that chubby. A right fat-looking thing it was, causing the light to disappear behind its large frame. Then it stopped, shouted something Anderson couldn't comprehend before raising up its arm with the speed of a railway signal.

Anderson passed out. His last thoughts were that heaven must have got pretty rough if divine messengers now saw the need to be armed.

Chapter Thirty-Four

Heaven proved a disappointment. While the whiteness and bright lights were as his upbringing suggested, Anderson heard no soft harps or angelic voices, only an annoying bleeping and deep voices with English accents.

Typical, he thought. *Bloody sassanachs run the afterlife too.* Although, with his record, he felt lucky not to be burning in brimstone.

'I think he's coming round,' one of the voices said, as Anderson's vision started clearing and he prepared to take in the majesty of paradise.

Bloody hell. Damned nuns couldn't get anything right, he thought, seeing three ugly-looking angels looming over him. One was fat, another skinny, and the third who peered into his eyes, looked somewhere in between, only with a face like a sink plunger. Strangely familiar-looking too.

The figure leaned back and the fat one stepped forward and also peered into Anderson's eyes. 'Rest easy, old boy. It's all over now.' He had a soft voice and breath that could strip paint.

Kendrick.

'Are you dead too?' Anderson slurred.

'Nobody's dead, old boy. Although you gave a good go at it. They had to kick-start you twice in the ambulance. Thought you were a goner.'

Anderson's mind struggled to work out what Kendrick's words meant. He wasn't dead? Then where was he? The bright lights above him hurt his eyes so he rolled his head to the side and tried to focus on the other two men.

He now remembered who the man with the lips was. Kinnear. The mad old shrink. The other looked familiar too. Well-dressed and a smug face. Now he remembered. The Englishman from the zoo.

'You're going to have to stop waking up in hospitals, old boy,' Kendrick added. 'The cost of parking is bloody horrendous! Now keep still and rest.'

Anderson rolled his head around as his mind began catching up, but the rhythmic beeping beside him made thinking difficult.

'You better listen to the superintendent,' Kinnear said. 'You're full of *propofol*. You'll be out of action for a while.'

He had hazy recollections of being at a funeral, or was it a wedding? Something in a church. No a cathedral. A cathedral, and he was with a someone. A woman – his wife? No, of course not, the drugs weren't strong enough to make him believe he'd have gone near that bitch. But who? An image of a young woman on the floor suddenly appeared in his mind's eye.

'Ruth!' He rolled his head around anxiously and the beeping next to him increased. 'Ruth, how's Ruth?'

'She's fine,' Kendrick insisted. 'She's next door with the patient.'

'Patient?' Anderson struggled to keep his eyes open.

'Michael Skye,' said the Englishman. 'We got him intact – thanks to you.'

'Skye!' The beeping increased.

'It's okay, he's still out, and will stay that way,' Kendrick insisted. 'We were just discussing what to do with him.'

'Let me at the bash-tard,' Anderson slurred, feeling his eyes getting heavier.

Kendrick laughed. 'Well, at least he's feeling himself.' He leaned in. 'You've done your bit; let us worry about him. Now keep still and rest.'

'No ... let me shluppssss ... zzzzzz.'

Ruth watched the sleeping Michael Skye with some trepidation. Despite the button she clutched, which if he stirred, would give him another slug of *etorphine*, she still worried he might wake. She'd experienced first-hand the abilities he possessed, and didn't want to go through that again. Saving her life, nearly cost Anderson his. For that, she'd always be grateful.

She awoke on the flagstones of St Mary's in time to see Anderson writhing around in agony. Weakened she lay helpless, watching him, praying, and for the second time her prayers had been answered. Kendrick burst through the cathedral doors like a sheriff in a Wild West saloon. For a big man he couldn't half shift. He ran down the nave like a county prop forward before pulling out the gun. He shot Michael from at least thirty yards away, and while she was no expert on marksmanship, she knew it must have taken some skill.

For a moment, she thought the gun misfired, hearing no sound of seeing no muzzle-flash, but Michael's attention suddenly turned from Anderson to the tiny dart sticking from his neck. He slapped at it like a man stung by a bee, and for a moment he just swayed, his big, vague eyes, flitting from Anderson to Kendrick and finally to her. And then he collapsed.

Within moments, police swarmed through the cathedral doors, as did ambulance crews. Ruth recovered enough to see

Anderson having his chest pumped by several paramedics, while Michael was whisked away in an ambulance.

She'd sat by the inspector's bed all night, clutching his hand, until the doctors decided to wake him from the induced coma, at which time, Kendrick, Kinnear and the creepy Englishman, who forced her to sign the Official Secrets Act, asked her to sit with Michael. Special Branch had commandeered the ward. Policemen were positioned on both ends to the corridor and all but the most critical ICU patients had been moved. But somebody needed to keep an eye on Michael, they said. Not that they expected him to wake, but in a public hospital, Kendrick wanted to take no chances.

Ruth knew little about *etorphine*, except that vets used it, but she had knowledge enough to know Michael could be left permanently brain-damaged. If indeed, they managed to awake him at all. Perhaps, she thought, it *was* a blessing. She shook her head, thinking back to McRowen's words, and to how somebody like Michael managed to exist at all. She thought about what Kinnear had said. Trauma induced it as a defence mechanism. Michael deserved pity, not condemnation, and she cursed the abusive upbringing, which had brought it all about.

'How's our miracle?' said an English voice behind her. She turned to see Kinnear, Kendrick and the smartly dressed Englishman, who smoked from a cigarette holder, defying the no-smoking signage.

'How's the inspector?' she asked, looking at Kendrick.

The big man smiled. 'Wanting to take on the world. He'll be fine. Tough as my wife's steak that one. Don't you worry, lassie. Take more than two heart attacks in the space of a week to keep him on his back.' He turned to the other two men. 'Right, I best be off, got to go speak to the bishops – smooth things over.' He smiled warmly at Ruth and left the room.

The two other men stepped inside and peered at Michael. Kinnear lifted up the boy's eyelids and flashed a light into them. 'Still with the fairies, I see.' He took the auto-injector from her. 'Let's just hope we can wake him.' He looked up at the Englishman. 'Longer we leave it, the more chance there will be of cerebral damage.'

The man nodded and took a deep intake of smoke. 'I'm waiting to hear from Carstairs now, see if they have anywhere secure enough.'

'Carstairs!' Ruth stood up. 'You can't put him there; the place is almost full as it is. The patients wouldn't be safe.'

The man shrugged. 'Sadly, there is nowhere else I can suggest. A few military bases perhaps, mainly American ones, but Dr Kinnear here, is a little reluctant to place him under such security.'

'Would do him no good,' Kinnear said. 'I can't study him there. He'll need stimulus. Other people.'

The Englishman shrugged. 'Wouldn't be too happy giving our friends across the Atlantic unfettered access, either. But I don't know what else to suggest.'

'Well, we need to act quickly,' Kinnear said. 'Anything more than a few more hours and he may end up in a vegetative state.'

'Well, you're the expert, Doctor,' the Englishman said, flicking ash on the hospital floor. 'You know money's no object. Where do *you* suggest?'

Kinnear shook his head. 'Has to be somewhere remote and

secure, but also somewhere where he can stretch his legs.' He bit at his thick lip. 'Nowhere I can think off, even temporarily. No time to build anything.'

The Englishman shrugged.

'I have a suggestion,' Ruth said.

The Englishman raised his plucked eyebrows at Kinnear. 'Pray, please tell us, then, my dear.'

Chapter Thirty-Five

'You feeling better, old boy?' Kendrick asked, steering the Rover up the newly asphalted road leading from the jetty.

Anderson, his cheeks a shade of green, began rolling a smoke. 'Will be once I've had a tab.'

'For someone from a shipbuilding city, you don't half-hate boats. Thought the sea would be in your blood.'

'They built 'em, didn't bloody sail on 'em,' Anderson said, sticking the cigarette in his lips and staring through the windscreen. 'Bloody hell, you wouldn't recognise the place!'

The jagged stonework of Eynhallow was now covered in scaffold with workmen's vans parked all around it, and several ambulances and other vehicles sat on a new tarmacked car park. Kendrick halted the Rover next to one of the ambulances and yanked on the hand brake.

'Well, let's go see how everything is,' he said.

'If you ask me, we should have put him in The Maze with the other psychopaths,' Anderson said. 'Especially after what he did to Harrison.'

'We've been through this, old boy. The boy's sick, not a terrorist. He needs treatment. Don't worry, he's in good hands.'

Kendrick opened the door and stepped out, causing the Birmingham-made suspension to rock like a rowboat. Anderson felt sick again, but a quick puff on his smoke soon calmed his stomach and he followed the big man out of the car.

'Shame they can't do anything about the wind,' he said, pulling his jacket tight.

'Yes, it is rather bracing.' Kendrick nodded to the entrance, where a brand new glass door sat gleaming in the sunshine. 'Guess this must be the way in.' He waddled to the doors as Anderson took a look at the almost unrecognisable island.

The last time he stood there, he'd had one shoe on with Harrison berating him for his language. *Harrison*, he sniffed a melancholic laugh, and followed the superintendent inside.

In a fresh white-painted room, adorned with padded chairs and smelling of new carpet, Sister Mary stood behind the counter wearing a crisp, white gown with an over-sized name badge declaring her name. She smiled and greeted Kendrick with a cheery: 'Good morning, welcome t' Eynhallow Hospital, how may I help?' Her smile soon faded as Anderson shambled in behind. 'Oh, Inspector. I take it ye' gentlemen are here to see the administrator?'

'Yes, my dear,' Kendrick said, before turning to a tea and coffee machine in the corner and rummaging around in his pocket for some change. 'But would love a cuppa before we go in. Inspector?'

Anderson shook his head, noting Mary eyeing the machine with contempt. She leaned over the counter, furtively glancing around her before whispering like drug pusher: 'Psst ... I have some proper tea, if you'd prefer?'

Kendrick smiled, and the little woman, after glancing around again, magicked her teapot from behind the counter. 'Just brewed!'

Kendrick shoved his change back into his pocket. 'Ah, far better. Can't stand those machines.'

The sister grinned and poured the tea into a polystyrene cup.

'Sorry,' she whispered. 'We have to use these monstrosities – administrator's orders.'

'That's quite all right,' Kendrick replied, taking the steaming brew.

He blew it and took a sip, raising the cup in thanks as Mary stepped down from the box she was standing on and walked over to a recently installed security door at the back of the reception. She rolled up her sleeve, punched in a number that was scrawled on her wrist in to the keypad, and smiled with satisfaction once the electric bolt slid open. 'This way, gentlemen.'

They followed her through the hospital, which smelled of fresh gloss paint and where workmen hung off stepladders, rewiring, repainting and replastering the halls. Anderson didn't recognise the place. Even the patients, now wearing civilian clothes and playing ping-pong in the recreation room or watching the new colour television, seemed less *mental*.

Mary led them around the corridor to the office where Anderson had been scowled at by McRowen. She knocked on the door.

'Come in,' came the cheery reply, and Mary opened the door.

Ruth sat behind a desk in the freshly decorated room. Her face illuminated when she saw Anderson. She stood up and grabbed him around the neck.

'Hey, behave yourself, love,' he said, catching sight of Kendrick smirking.

She released her bear hug. 'Good to see you, Inspector. You too, Superintendent.'

Kendrick smiled and took a sip of his tea. 'Just a flying visit I'm afraid. Just checking on our guest.'

'I'll take you down,' she leaned around his large frame and nodded to Mary. 'You couldn't fetch the sister for me, could you?'

Mary nodded. 'Of course, dear. Would you like me to fetch you a cup of tea too?'

Ruth rolled her eyes. 'Okay, Sister.'

Mary scuttled off, and Ruth pointed to a dying pot plant in the corner. 'Poor bloody thing, has to put up with a gallon of the stuff most mornings.'

'Hey, what's that on your finger?' Kendrick asked, grabbing hold of her hand and peering at a tiny engagement ring.

'Me and Tom have set a date.'

Kendrick beamed. 'Well, don't forget our invitations will you?'

'Of course not. In fact –' She began blushing as she turned to Anderson. 'I was hoping you'd give me away.'

'Me?' Anderson bowed his head to the floor, aware that his face had probably gone crimson too. 'You know I ain't much good in churches.'

'I can't think of anyone else,' she replied.

'Well, if you put it like that.'

She grabbed hold of him again and kissed his cheek before they were interrupted by an austere cough from behind. Anderson turned to see Sister McRowen in the doorway, peering down her spectacles at him.

She looked younger than he last recalled, and even smiled when she saw the trio in Ruth's office.

'Ah, Sister,' Ruth said. 'You wouldn't mind doing the medication rounds, would you? I'm taking the officers to see Michael.'

'Of course not, Doctor.' Her voice sounded softer too. Relaxed.

'And you won't forget I've got to leave early today,' Ruth said. 'It's Sophie's parent's evening.'

'No, Doctor. I've made a note of it in my wee book.'

Ruth smiled. 'Thank you. Well, gentlemen. Follow me.'

She led them to where the old iron lift had sat, but had now been replaced by a modern steel elevator. The once bricked up archway now had a set of security doors on it too, which she opened, and led them down the stairs.

'So how you getting on with that mad old witch?' Anderson asked, noticing the stairs had a thicker shag than the carpets in his house.

'She can be a bit frosty, but she's a good nurse. I think she's happier in her new role, too. Certainly seems more relaxed.'

Ruth led them into the basement and Anderson couldn't believe the transformation. Gone were the cells and bare brickwork, replaced by an open plan room. It reminded him of a rumpus room and was better kitted out than the staff canteen at Inverness station, with pool table, colour TV and even a Betamax VCR. They walked farther down and then Anderson stopped. His heart gave a thump.

Michael Skye sat on a beanbag chatting to yet another familiar face, Kinnear. Michael spotted Ruth and the two men, and trailed off his conversation. Kinnear turned round, muttered something to Michael, walked to greet them.

'Ah, the men from Special Branch,' he said.

'Just checking on your guest,' Kendrick said, nodding to Michael.

Kinnear glanced back, before giving Kendrick his full-lipped smile. 'Absolutely, fine, in one regard. Far happier.'

Anderson noticed Michael staring at him.

His pains were less frequent now, and the doctors reckoned he'd be off the pills in a few weeks, but standing so close to Michael still unnerved him. His hand automatically squeezed at his chest.

Kinnear clucked his thick lips. 'Don't worry, Inspector. I doubt he could cause a state of hiccups now.'

Anderson narrowed his eyes. 'What do you mean?'

'Well, to the chagrin of our mutual English friend.' He raised his brows to Kendrick. 'Michael's abilities are weakening day-by-day. The happier he feels, the less effective they are.'

'Well, I can't say I'm sorry to hear that,' Anderson said.

'Neither am I,' Kendrick added, admiring the pleasant surroundings.

'Not a complete waste, though,' admitted Kinnear. 'I've already learned so much. Will take years to get it all down on paper,' He nodded back to Michael. 'Would you like to speak to him?'

'I'd rather not,' Anderson said, his lips taut.

Kendrick gave the inspector a frown. 'We are here to check, aren't we?'

'He can't hurt you,' Ruth said. 'I promise.' She squeezed him tenderly around the waist, and with Kinnear's assured hand on Anderson's back, they led the two men toward Michael.

Anderson could feel his heart beat rapidly as he neared. Its pace increased as the boy stood up.

'Michael,' Ruth said, stepping in front of Anderson. 'These two men are here to see how you are getting on.'

Michael fixed his eyes on Anderson, before bowing his head.

After a brief silence, he raised his head, again. 'I'm sorry,' he said, in the local accent.

Anderson glanced sideways at him. 'For what?'

'For everything. For what I did to your friend. For what I did to you. I wasn't –' He looked at Kinnear, and then to Ruth.

'Michael wasn't himself,' Kinnear said, placing a hand on the boy's shoulder.

'Is that a fact?' Anderson spoke with his teeth clenched.

'No, but I am still sorry, truly I am.' He looked at Anderson with wide eyes, eyes that seemed far less vague than the when they were glaring at him in the cathedral.

'So, am I, laddie,' Anderson said.

'You caused us all a lot of trouble,' Kendrick added. 'But I understand you are feeling better, now?'

The boy nodded, his eyes still fixed on Anderson. Moisture seemed to well in the corners and Ruth stepped forward and stroked his cheek. 'It's okay Michael. Nobody blames you.'

She turned to Anderson, her eyes wide and lips pursed. 'Do they?'

Anderson remained silent.

'No,' Kendrick said. 'We don't blame you, nobody does.' He gave Anderson a glare.

Anderson sighed, shrugged, shook his head.

Once back outside in the bracing breeze, Anderson took one last look at the hospital.

'Well, old boy,' Kendrick said, leaning across the car roof, much to the dismay of the Rover's suspension. 'All's well that ends well – to quote the Bard.'

'If you say so.'

Kendrick placed a hand on Anderson's shoulder. 'You can't blame the boy. Let it go.'

'Aye, I suppose so,' Anderson said, but couldn't help thinking of Harrison. He vowed to visit the sergeant's grave. Perhaps place some flowers and a can of real ale by the headstone.

'Back to Inverness, then?'

'I wanted to talk to you about that.' Anderson removed his tobacco from his pocket. 'I was wondering if I could take a little leave.'

'Leave? You?'

'Aye, I guess I'm due. Only a week or so. Going down south.'

'England? You? Whatever for?'

'Going to spend a few days with that daughter of mine, in Hampshire. See if I can mend a few bridges.'

Kendrick's brows rose upward. 'Of course, old boy, of course.' He smiled again. 'Aye, all's well that ends well. Clever chap that Shakespeare. Mind you when you get back, we're going to have to have a serious chat.'

'Oh, more trouble? What is it this time? The Irish? The Ruskies?'

'Worse than that,' Kendrick said, opening the car door. 'I've got to find you a new partner.'

The End

The Loch

An Inspector Anderson Mystery

Chapter One

Briers vaulted the gate and landed with a squelch. The slurry lapped over his wellingtons and speckled his face. He gagged. Then a clang echoed back in the darkness. He froze. Across the empty pens and between the hanging airlines, a figure, silhouetted against the blackness flitted across the back of the cowshed.

He had made a mistake in coming. Perhaps a fatal one, but he knew something was wrong when he arrived that morning. He could spot a reused ear tag when he saw one. That meant McGillivray Bovine Industries had been hiding cattle. Dead cattle. As a farming inspector that told Briers one thing. An outbreak. An outbreak of what, he didn't know, but the anonymous source that had tipped off the Ministry of Agriculture, Farms and Fisheries had said it was some sort of disease of the nervous system, something hitherto unknown, something new, something serious, something deadly.

Perhaps stealing in during the dead of night wasn't the brightest idea Briers had ever had, but if his source's suspicions were right, the outbreak could infect the food chain, the consequences of which could be catastrophic. It could migrate to humans.

On the face of it, the McGillivrays ran a reputable operation. They did everything onsite, from rearing and slaughtering, to butchering and packaging. That morning they had given Briers a well-orchestrated tour. They showed him everything, the cattle sheds, the abattoir, the loading bays. Everything except the lab where McGillivray's veterinarian kept his cultures and samples.

It was being renovated, they had said. Briers suspected they were lying.

The situation was too serious to rely on repeated letters, repeated inspections, repeated chances for the McGillivrays to hide their activities. MAFF was slow and it frustrated Briers. All too often outbreaks of this kind got swept under the carpet. The National Union of Farmers had a strong voice. Shame Maggie Thatcher didn't do for them what she did for the minors. As things stood, McGillivrays would more than likely get away with whatever they were doing. But not if Briers had his way.

He decided to act. Find the evidence he needed. And he knew where to find it. The lab. His scheme wasn't that well thought out, more a whim after he noticed the lapse security and absence of guard dogs, despite the signs, when he left that morning. The temptation proved too much.

The lock to the lab was easy to jimmy, and as soon as he opened the chillers, he knew on sight he had found what he was looking for. Normal brain tissue didn't look like that, not in healthy animals. He placed them in his coat and realised how lucky he had been. He had managed to sneak in unseen.

Then his luck ran out.

He didn't care about his job, although he'd certainly lose it if the McGillivrays called the police. But somehow, he knew they wouldn't. Couldn't. Not after what he'd found. So what would they do?

Another clang sounded behind him, only much closer. Panicked, Briers waded through the cattle waste towards the shutter, the only way out. The slurry acted like quicksand, slowing his strides. But he trudged headlong through it slurry, waving away the airlines hanging from the compressed air system.

He reached the shutter just as another clang and the sound of boots squelching in the slurry sounded behind him. He didn't have much time. Without looking back, Briers reached into the cattle waste and searched for the handle to the shutter, gagging and coughing as the effluent covered his arms. As he scrabbled around in the mess, he could hear the wading of boots behind. He didn't turn. His hand had found the handle. He yanked it.

Locked.

He turned around, his breath rising in silhouetted clouds in the darkness and slightly masking the figure stepping forward slowly, weaving his way between the suspended air hoses.

Briers scrambled to his feet and jumped to his right in an attempt at escape, but he stumbled, landing on all fours in the mire of muck. He got up, the sticky ooze dripping off his arms. He gagged, coughed, and then tried to dash to his left, but a side step blocked his way.

'Nowhere to go, Inspector,' his tormentor said, a gentle laugh under his voice.

'I'm just doing my job.' Briers' voice shook.

'You shouldn't have come back.'

'You've been hiding cattle.'

'Aye, that we have.' The man pulled a long cylinder from his belt, and even in the gloom, Briers identified it. He watched, terrified, as the man plugged it into one of the suspended air hoses and stepped forward.

Briers scrambled backwards, his back pressing against the shutter. 'What ... what are you going to do?'

The man laughed another deep, throaty laugh, and raised the cylinder. 'I'm going to make sure you keep quiet.'

Briers, his eyes fixed on the cylinder, held his sludge covered arms over his face. 'You ... you can't. I'm a government inspector!'

'Was,' the man said, pushing the cattle gun to Briers' temple. It hissed, like punctured tyre, and then Briers fell lifeless into the slurry.

When van Burgh's eyes grew accustomed to the darkness of the cowshed they widened as he saw what Joe McGillivray was hauling over the metal gate.

'Give me a hand, will you?' Joe ordered, his eyes far narrower than van Burgh's. Thick sludge covered his arms, as it did the body he'd pulled on top of the gate.

Van Burgh inhaled deeply. 'Joe ... what have you done?'

McGillivray rounded on him, pointing a finger that dripped with ooze. 'What had to be done! It's your damned fault, anyway.'

'Mine, how?' For a moment, van Burgh felt a sense of fear. The back of his neck tickled as if an electric current raced up and down his spine. He could see the bolt gun hanging from the air hose. He knew what Joe was capable of, the evidence lay slumped over the gate, but he also knew the McGillivray's needed him. For now.

Besides, he only had himself to blame. When he first met Joe McGillivray at a cattle rearing conference in Rotterdam, van Burgh had boasted how he could boost his profits three-fold. A combination of steroid overdosing and recycling rendered remains as cattle feed, could increase output and slash costs, he had said. It had worked in the Netherlands, made the Dutch cattle breeders the lead exporters of beef throughout the European Economic Community. Van Burgh promised the same rewards to the McGillivrays.

Joe hired him immediately, taking him on as a consultant and all was well for the first year. He did indeed increase the output of beef while at the same time reduced their costs. Until the epidemic.

The first cows started showing symptoms about eighteen months ago. It was something that van Burgh had never seen before. Not in cattle. In sheep, certainly. Scrapie was a familiar to all veterinarians, but he'd never seen the degenerative tissue in cows. The disease was eating away at their brains, mercilessly.

At first, they managed to contain it. Butchering and disposing of the odd cow without raising suspicion wasn't hard, but over the last eighteen months, things were getting out of hand. Nearly every day van Burgh would diagnose a new case. And hiding the problem became increasingly difficult.

They had to dismiss the local vet, who'd served the McGillivrays for years, as he was becoming suspicious, and it wouldn't have took him long to uncover what was going on. Van Burgh took on his responsibilities, and worked as hard as he could to identify the source of the epidemic.

At first, he had put it down to the steroids, but he had ruled that out as a possibility thanks to the samples he took from some of the dead carcasses. The samples Joe was now removing from the pocket of the dead man.

He waved them at van Burgh. 'If you hadn't left these in the lab, I'd not have had to do this,' Joe rasped. 'Why the hell did you keep them?'

'We need to understand what we're dealing with if you want me to solve the problem.' Van Burgh's Dutch inflection sounded even more alien as it echoed around the empty cow shed.

'Well, I need you to solve this problem first.' Joe nodded to the dead man slumped across the gate.

Van Burgh helped pull the corpse over the gate and it fell on to the concrete with a dull thud that reverberated around the empty cowshed for several seconds.

'So what you going to do with him?' van Burgh asked.

Joe straightened, his teeth catching the limited light as he grinned. 'You mean what you are going to do with him?'

Van Burgh cocked his head to the side, feigning miscomprehension. 'I don't ...'

'You can dispose of him in the same place you get rid of the infected carcasses,' Joe said. He pointed his filthy finger at him. 'And you can destroy those bloody samples too.'

Van Burgh nodded, took a deep breath, before bending over and removing the dead man's clothing. 'These will need to be incinerated,' he said, clutching the dead man's filthy clothes.

'You can do that when you get back.' Joe looked down at the dead man. 'Right, let's get him to the abattoir.'

Van Burgh grabbed the dead inspector's legs, Joe the arms, and they dragged the body across the cowshed, dumped it on a trolley and wheeled it across the yard.

They spoke in whispers as they entered the abattoir, where carcasses of dead cattle hung in ordered rows from the ceiling. However, two minutes after the fluorescent light flickered on, and the dead man had been heaved on to a bench, the bandsaw cutting bone, flesh and sinew, made further conversation impossible.

The road running along the north shore of Loch Morar stopped abruptly after about four miles. Van Burgh knew the road well. He turned the headlights off for the last mile, relying solely on the running lights. Not that he had to worry about somebody seeing him. In all his trips to dispose of carcasses, he'd never seen any other vehicles. And beside the odd farm and the campsite a couple of miles farther back, nobody lived along the north bank of the loch.

After reaching the end of the track, he steered the van around the trees and hedges, before edging the Transit down a narrow incline. He stopped well short of the edge, pulling on the handbrake.

The loch was deep here. And unlike farther up, where the waters descended gradually from the shoreline, natural erosion caused the loch to plunge straight down from the bank. One false step and van Burgh knew he would be way beyond his depth, especially since he couldn't swim.

He wasn't sure how deep it was, but he'd heard from some of the locals that Morar was the deepest body of water in all of Britain. A thousand feet in places. He didn't know what that was in metres, but knew it was deep enough. None of the remains he'd dumped had ever surfaced.

He got out of the van and carefully ambled to the rear, aware the wet grass meant he was only one slip away from oblivion. With a creak of rusted metal, he pulled open the doors. The stench of freshly butchered meat greeted his nostrils. While a familiar smell, he'd worked in the cattle industry all his life, he knew that not all the carcasses wrapped up in the muslin bags in the back were of bovine origin. He shuddered, aware of the gravity of the deed done that night. But there was no turning back.

He shook off his doubts with a deep inhale of breath before pulling out the first muslin bag. It was heavy. A quarter hind by the feel of it. With the wrapped up meat on his shoulder, he walked towards the water's edge. The running lights from the van provided just enough illumination. Still, he took care. He didn't want to disappear into the waters with the carcass.

After reaching the edge, he paused for breath. Then he placed one hand below the parcel of meat and shoved. A splash sounded as it hit the water and water sprayed on to his face. Then, after a few ripples and bubbles, he saw the bag of meat slowly disappear below the surface.

He sighed and stumbled back to the rear of the van. He heaved another muslin parcel on to his shoulder and edged back down the water's edge, aware this time, what he carried felt nothing like a quarter hind of beef.

Chapter Two

Mike felt relieved when the truck slowed. The noise of the sheep, combined with the smell and itchiness of the straw, made the journey in the back almost unbearable. He was glad of the lift, though. Hitchhiking meant he couldn't be too choosy. No buses went this far, and with limited funds, he found British trains too pricey.

The wagon stopped and Mike jumped off the tailboard, pulling his backpack with him. He walked round to the driver and thanked him for the lift.

'Aye, no problem,' the driver said, nodding towards the hills. 'Morar's o'er that way. No more than a mile or two.'

Mike looked across the barren glen before pulling the backpack across his shoulder. 'Do they have a campsite?'

The driver, a thick-haired and scruffy man, wearing a holey, knitted sweater, shrugged. 'Plenty o' campsites around these parts.'

'Well thanks again.'

'Nae problem. Take ken ye-self.' The driver crunched the truck into gear and moved off, the sheep baaing in the back as it disappeared into the distance and left Mike standing in what appeared to be the middle of nowhere.

'Ken of yourself?' he said to himself, shrugging. Despite his family's roots, he had found the Scotch tongue unfathomable since stepping off the plane in Edinburgh. Although he supposed his Milwaukee accent was probably just as hard for them to grasp, too.

He turned to face where the driver had nodded. The heather,

gorse and wild shrubs, seemed to stretch for miles, but he presumed the driver knew his business. So after clipping his backpack tight around his waist, he trudged across the scrub and up the nearest hill, presuming the walk wouldn't be far.

He was wrong.

He marched for nearly an hour, with each rise of a hill promising to reveal his destination at its brow. But it wasn't until three rests, the last of his potato chips and final can of Coke that he trudged up a hill and encountered the breathtaking view of Morar.

The Loch was nestled just off the coast. To his left right he could see the ocean, bordered by a vast silver beach that glistened under the sunlight. A tiny river cut its way through the sands, ran through a small village and fed into the loch. And what a loch. Dotted with islands and stretching as far to the east as the sea did to the west, the ice blue body of water sat between the hills and mountains like a long gash cut into the landscape. It was breathtaking, and he wondered if Sarah encountered the same view on her arrival. She'd have loved it.

He sighed. How long had it been? Seven, eight weeks? And still no word. He didn't care what the Embassy said. If she had some sort of accident, somebody, somewhere would know something. And that *somewhere* could be Morar. It was where the trail for Sarah went cold. Where she was last seen. If he had any hope of finding out what happened to her, Morar was the place.

From his vantage point, the vast waters of the loch and the surrounding hills dwarfed the little village sitting on the banks. But no matter how big it was, Mike presumed it would have a post office or pub where he could make enquiries—he'd not come across any part of Scotland without a pub. So he took a deep breath, loosened his backpack and began his descent.

Sergeant Betty Sandilands nodded intently at Mrs Trench. The woman had a strained look across her face but despite her evident trauma, she looked immaculate in long woollen coat, designer handbag hooked over her arm and hair lacquered in a stiff bouffant. 'You must begin an investigation at once, Sergeant, it's the law,' she insisted, wagging her finger at Sandilands.

Sandilands sighed. 'When did Mr Sheridan go missing?'

'Yesterday afternoon,' Mrs Trench said, removing a pressed handkerchief from her bag and dabbing it at her eyes.

'Well, I'm sure he'll turn up. He normally does.'

'But you must begin a search. He's been missing for over twenty-four hours. That's the procedure isn't it? You wait twenty four hours and then begin a manhunt.'

'Manhunt ...'

The police station door creaked nosily open and a young man in red skiing jacket and wearing a bulky backpack, squeezed inside. Sandilands gave him a smile, as if to say she'd be with him shortly, and gestured to the bench seat at the back. He removed his backpack and sat.

'Sorry, Mrs Trench, where were we?' Sandilands said, returning to the distraught middle-aged woman.

'Mr Sheridan, Sergeant. His search.'

'Oh yes. I'll ask about the village and get the constable to keep an eye out for him, but there's little else we can do.'

'Little else!' shouted the woman. 'That's hardly anything. You must do more. I don't know what I'll do without him.' She shook and let out gentle sob.

Sandilands sighed. 'Now, now, dry your eyes. He can't have gone far. Have you asked about the village?'

Mrs Trench dabbed her eyes again. 'Of course I have.'

'And nobody's seen him?'

'Of course not. That's why I'm here.' She softened her tone, and started pleading. 'You must find him, Betty, really you must. I don't know what I'll do without him.'

She began sobbing again.

'Look, pull yourself together. I'm sure he'll turn up. Perhaps you ought to tell me when and where you last saw him?' Sandilands reached for a pencil and took out her notepad.

Mrs Trench patted her hair and took a deep breath. 'Yesterday morning, just before breakfast. We were taking our usual walk around the loch. I thought he was next to me, but I turned around and he had gone.'

'He has gone off before, hasn't he, Mrs Trench?'

'Yes, but it's not like him to be gone for so long. I'm so worried, Sergeant.'

Sandilands sighed. 'With the chief inspector away for the week, there's only PC Featherstone and me here at the moment so there's very little we ...'

Mrs Trench wailed and Sandilands rolled her eyes and sighed. 'Okay, okay, perhaps I can take a description to pass about.' She licked her pencil and cocked her tiny eyebrows at the woman.

'Description? You know what Mr Sheridan looks like,' Mrs Trench snapped, her glossy lips pouting. 'Look, can't you just dredge the loch?'

'The loch's a thousand feet deep in parts,' Sandilands said, exasperated. 'I doubt we could do that for a human being, let alone a Highland Terrier.'

The young backpacker on the bench snickered, and Mrs Trench shot her head around and gave him a distasteful stare before turning back and pleading one more time.

'But what ... what if he's drowned? I mean, if he was chasing ducks again and went in the loch, he may not have been able to get out.' She started sobbing, and then blew her nose, unladylike, on the handkerchief.

'I'm afraid other than asking around the village, there's little I can do.'

Mrs Trench lowered the handkerchief, scowled, patted her perm and then sniffed. 'Well, if that's your attitude, perhaps I should speak to the chief inspector when he gets back. We'll see what he has to say. He plays golf with my husband, you know!'

She buttoned up her woollen coat, turned about and marched out of the station, flaring her nostrils at the young backpacker as she stormed past.

Sandilands shook her head, paused for a moment, until certain the woman had gone, and looked over at the young man. 'Yes, sir. How can I help?'

He stood up, leaving his backpack on the bench. He was tall, six foot or so, with a head of windswept mousy hair and swarthy skin.

'Hi, yes, I'm here about my sister.' His accent was an American, or Canadian, and he spoke with that distinctive drawl commonly heard in Morar during the summer season but less so at that time of year.

Sandilands frowned. 'Sister?'

'Yes, Sarah Cunningham. She went missing nearly two months ago.' He reached into his ski jacket and pulled out the dog-eared picture. 'This was taken just before she came to Scotland.'

Sandilands looked at the photo and frowned again. A young woman, blonde, early twenties. Pretty. 'Missing, you say?'

'Yes, ma'am,' He had large, brown eyes. Sad eyes. 'She spent the summer backpacking around here. We reported her missing at the end of August after she didn't call home.' The sad eyes lowered.

Sandilands put down her pencil and stared at the picture. 'Cunningham, you say?'

'Yes, ma'am.'

'Wait here, I won't be a minute.' She turned from the counter and marched into the back office, where she rifled through a filing cabinet until she found a folder, which she opened and read. She vaguely remembered the case. A tourist reported missing by the American Embassy. Enquiries were made, but they found no trace, not in Morar.

Sandilands returned to the desk with the folder. 'Sarah Cunningham. IC female, twenty-four, blonde, brown eyes, five foot one,' she said, reading the report. 'Reported missing by Michael Cunningham in August eighty-five.' She looked up. 'Is that you?'

'No, my father. I'm Michael Cunningham Junior.'

Sandilands smiled, the way American named their offspring after themselves amused her. 'Well, Michael Cunningham Junior, what can we do for you? There's been no more news, I'm afraid.'

'I know. That's what they told my father. But this was the last place she was seen, and I'm sure somebody must know something. That's why I came out here.'

'You've come all this way to find her?'

'Yes, ma'am. Nobody seems to know anything. She can't have just vanished.'

Sandilands felt a pang of sadness for him. He was obviously upset. Losing a sibling was difficult. She knew that better than anyone did. Her brother James died in a boating accident nearly ten years before. His death hit Sandilands and her parents hard. They moved away to Fort William, to get over it, but Sandilands eventually moved back when her father died from a heart attack a few years later. She and her mother seemed to drift apart after that. Became almost strangers.

She still thought about her brother and wondered what type of man he would have grown into. He would now be about the same age as the American standing before her. She shrugged off the memories and flicked through the folder.

'I'm afraid we made extensive enquiries at the time, but nobody had seen her since she checked out of the campsite.'

He placed his hands on the desk and leaned forward. 'Campsite, what campsite?'

'Lochside, over at Bracara. She checked in for two nights then went on her way. Mrs Fairbanks, the owner, didn't remember her, but the book was signed on August twelfth and she left on the fourteenth, owing a night's board, apparently.'

'Well, where was she going?' The American leaned over the counter and stuck his head in the folder. Sandilands pulled it back.

'It doesn't say. Mrs Fairbanks has plenty of visitors at that time of year, and many Americans. She doesn't remember the girl off-hand.'

He sighed. 'Perhaps I can speak to her, this Mrs Fairbanks.'

'That's up to you, but I don't think she'll be able to tell you any more than she told us.'

He shrugged. 'Well, I need to find a campsite for the night, anyway. Where is it?'

Before Sandilands could explain, the phone rang and she held her hand up to tell him to wait as she lifted the receiver. 'Lochaber Constabulary. WS Sandilands speaking.'

The gruff voice of the Chief Constable greeted her on the other end. 'Good morning. Chief Inspector Monroe, please.'

'I'm afraid he's on his holidays, sir,' Sandilands explained. 'There's just myself and Constable Featherstone here for the next week or so.'

'Drat,' snapped the chief constable. 'You'll have to do then, Sergeant. I need you to go to the station. There's a chap from Special Branch arriving.'

Her eyes widened. 'Special Branch, here!' She looked at the American as if the news should impress him too. He just tapped on the counter, impatiently.

'Yes, something to do with a missing inspector from the Ministry of Agriculture,' the chief constable said. 'A DI Anderson is arriving on the twelve o'clock from Fort William.'

'I see,' Sandilands said, glancing at the wall clock behind her. The train was due in fifteen minutes.

'Sorry about the late notice,' the chief constable added, but I didn't know myself until just now. You know what these Special Branch chaps are like, all cloak and dagger. But I want you to give him any assistance he needs. You're not too busy, are you?'

Sandilands looked at the American. 'No, nothing that can't wait.'

'Good, good. Let me know how things go.'

'Yes, sir.' She hung up the phone. 'Sorry about that. Where were we?'

He frowned. 'The campsite?'

'Oh, yes, Lochside. It's on the north side of the loch, about forty minutes walk. There's a path leading from the railway station. Look, I'll show you, I have to go and meet somebody on the twelve o'clock anyway.' She lifted up the hatch to the counter, steered the American out of the door, locked it, and led him down through the village.

Chapter Three

When Sandilands arrived at the railway station, the twelve o'clock was already in. Fuggy fumes billowed from the hot engine and the platform smelled of diesel. A few passengers were ambling towards her. Mr Calvey, on his way back from Glenfinnan from seeing his sister, Jenny Tavey, returning from college, and a local family that she recognised but whose names she couldn't remember. She smiled at them, but the father was too busy berating his two hyperactive children for running around near the train. However, there appeared to be no sign of the Special Branch detective she was meant to meet. And no sign of Mr Jordon, the stationmaster, either, which was unusual.

She walked farther down the platform and looked through the open carriage doors into the empty train. Empty. It wasn't until she arrived near the rear and the two first class carriages, did she see the bright yellow flag peeping through one of the doors.

'Mr Jordan?' she called.

The stationmaster turned round, flag in hand, a pained expression on his face. 'Thanks goodness it's you,' he said, shaking his head and glancing back into the train. 'We've got trouble.'

'Why what's the matter, Jim?'

'One of the passengers has been causing a disturbance. Tight as a drum, so he is.'

'A drunk?'

'Aye, sat in first class with only an economy ticket. When Mrs Kilkenny asked him at Glenfinnan to take an economy seat, he became abusive. Poor lass, she's had to have a sit down.'

'So why didn't you kick him off at Arisaig?'

'Well we tried, but—' Mr Jordon glanced back at the train. 'He says he's a policeman.'

'A policeman?'

'Aye, he's got a warrant card. Claims he's from Inverness. Special Branch if you please.'

Sandilands' mouth dropped open and she stood and blinked, repeatedly, unsure what to do. 'I err ... guess I'll have to have a word.'

She followed Mr Jordon on to the train where Mrs Kilkenny the guard sat shaking her head and clutching a ticket punch like a newborn baby. Sandilands gave the woman a tight-lipped smile. In return, Kilkenny, red faced and puffy eyes, shook her head and nodded to the door behind her marked first class.

'He's in there. Second compartment. He's singing now,' Kilkenny said, shaking her head at Mr Jordon. 'It's not on. Him being a policeman and all.'

Sandilands could hear a drunken chorus filtering through door.

There is a happy land, down in Duke Street Jail,

Where all the prisoners lie, tied tae a nail.

Breid an watter fur their tea, ham and eggs they never see,

There they live in miser-ee

God save the Queen.

Sandilands looked at them both. 'Okay, leave it to me. You two wait here. I'll have a word.'

The two British Rail employees nodded and Sandilands opened the door. The singing got louder.

There is a happy land by the `Red School'

Where Miss Macdonald stands, preaching like a fool.

Long legs and skinny jaws,

She can fairly use the tawse

On the wee bit bairnies' paws,

Three times a day.

She straightened her tunic, marched to the second compartment where the blind was pulled over the window, knocked and slid open the door.

Lying across the bench seat of the first class carriage, a middle-aged, greying, balding and sweat-laden man in a charcoal grey suit, the jacket of which lay strewn across the opposite bench. His tie rested over his shoulder, his teeth had a skinny roll-up clamped between them and his hand grasped a miniature bottle of Bells Whisky. More miniatures and fag ends littered the floor, as did his shoes, which accounted for the stench coming from his feet that almost overpowered the smell of alcohol and stale tobacco.

He stopped his Glaswegian chorus and looked up, pulling the skinny cigarette from his mouth and stroking his handlebar moustache.

'Good afternoon, da'lin,' he slurred, necking the remnants of the whisky before tossing the little bottle with the others. 'We in Morar, yet?'

'Yes,' Sandilands replied sternly. He looked more like a navvy than an inspector from Special Branch. And Mr Jordon was right. He was completely plastered. 'I take it you're Inspector Anderson?'

He sat up and belched. 'Aye.' He looked her up and down. 'Bugger me it's Juliet Bravo.'

She shook her head. 'Don't you think this sort of behaviour is unbecoming for an officer of the law?'

'An wash sort of behaviour—hiccup—is that?'

'You are drunk, sir.'

'How very dare you—hiccup—I'm not taking that sort of slander'ushness from a WPC.'

'Actually, I'm a WS. Sergeant Betty Sandilands.' She tapped her stripes. 'And I was told to meet you. I understand you're here to investigate a missing inspector from the Ministry of Agriculture.'

'Am I?'

'Yes, sir,' she snapped.

'Oh, right.' He got up, looked around the carriage and picked up his shoes. 'Be right with you.'

He fell back on the seat, his shoes falling from his hands.

'Here, let me help.' Sandilands knelt down and untied the laces, wincing from the foot odour, and slid the loafers on to his holey socks before fastening them as the inspector began singing again.

'There is a happy land, down in Duke Street Jai. 'Where all the prisoners lie, tied tae a nail.'

'You can cut that out,' she snapped, standing up and straightening her tunic. 'We need to get you off the train in an orderly manner. I don't want the whole village to know that a police officer is drunk.'

'I told you, I isnae drunk!'

She glowered at him and cocked her head to the side. 'Really?'

She stepped into the corridor and leant her head out of the window. The passengers had all cleared the platform, and only

Mr Jordan, flag clamped under his arm, and Mrs Kilkenny, ticket punch still in her arms, stood near the train. As British Rail workers, she trusted they'd keep quiet. She returned to the compartment, where Anderson now swayed in his seat and attempted to roll another cigarette, but was failing and dropping tobacco down his shirt.

'Right, do you think you can walk?' she asked.

'I'm not a bloody cripple,' he snapped, getting up and stumbling backwards on to the seat.

What was she going to do with him? He needed to sleep it off but she could hardly take him to the hotel, not in that condition. Mrs Trench would have kittens. She sighed. There was nothing for it other than to take him back to her flat. At least it wasn't far, and with any luck she could get him out of sight before any of the villagers saw him.

She picked up the inspector's battered old suitcase and steered him to the carriage door. She opened it. He fell out and landed flat on his face on the platform. She sighed again, helped him up, after which, he began walking in the wrong direction, so she spun him around. 'It's this way.'

'Okay, lead the way Sweaty Glands.'

'It's Sandilands,' she snapped, propping him up and escorting him out of the station.

Chapter Four

Sergeant Sandilands had been nice enough, Mike thought as he walked down the lane flanking the north bank of the loch. She didn't look that much older than him, perhaps closer to thirty maybe. Despite her austere appearance caused by the taut hair behind her cap, the sharp features and long Gaelic nose, she had a soft, welcoming voice with an accent he found far more appealing than the adenoid inflections of the girl's back home. He could have listened to her for hours and found himself captivated by the rolling r's and drawn out vowels.

She had pointed out the path to Lochside and said he could go to the station anytime if he wanted to discuss his sister's case. She also promised to speak to her chief inspector when he got back from his vacation. It did little to lift his spirits, though. Neither did the stroll down the narrow lane leading to the campsite.

It should have been idyllic. The clean, ice blue water surrounded by rolling hills was postcard pretty, despite the clouds of tiny gnats, which the Scots referred to as midges, that swarmed and peppered his face and made his hands ache with swatting them away from his eyes. But he felt forlorn. He wondered what on earth he was doing. If the police had no luck finding Sarah, how could he expect to?

Even when he saw the tents fluttering in the distance, it did little to lift his spirits. He hardly relished the thought of spending another night in a sleeping bag. Although Lochside looked better than many of the other campsites he had stayed at.

The tents, nearly all identical canvas types, sat in ordered rows before the loch, where the water glistened under the afternoon sun and a few kayaks and sailboats toed to a little jetty bobbed up and down. Further inshore, a concrete building housed what looked like a shower block, and judging by the signs outside, a cafeteria and bar. At least if this Mrs Fairbanks remembered nothing about Sarah, he'd get a good wash, a hot meal and pint of warm British beer, for which he had developed a taste.

Closer to the loch there was a small cottage with whitewashed walls just like in the village. Only as he approached, he realised because of the inflatable beds, net of footballs and various camping accessories hanging outside, it must have also been the shop and reception.

He walked through the campsite, smiling politely at the other campers and stopped outside the cottage. A family of tourists filled the little reception, pulling out maps and buying ice creams, so there was no room for Mike. He took off his backpack, dropped it to the ground and gazed out across the loch as he waited.

The crystal clear water by the shore darkened towards the centre of the loch. It must have been deep, he thought. Tiny waves cut across the surface and broke into surf along the little shingle beach beside the jetty. It was no wider than perhaps a mile to other bank where trees dotted the shoreline opposite and rolling hills rose up majestically, but the water stretched endlessly to the east. While to the west, a handful of small islands broke the stillness and uniformity of the water, and beyond those, Mike could just make out the village of Morar, which sat proudly before the landscape that equalled anything he had seen in Wisconsin.

He heard a gaggle of voices behind him and turned to see the family of tourists leaving the little shop, so he picked up his backpack and stepped inside.

Not having met Mrs Fairbanks, Mike didn't know what to expect, but the burly woman in tennis skirt, white vest and referees whistle around her neck, surprised him. She sat behind a counter surrounded by footballs, blow-up novelties, toy sailboats and a myriad of other souvenirs.

She was a pale woman, nearing fifty, with a thick neck and cropped hair. She stood and smiled as he walked in and he noticed she towered five inches above him. Yet she spoke in a soft, high voice that didn't match her daunting and butch physique. 'Good afternoon,' she said. 'Welcome to Lochside.'

Mike returned the smile and pulled the photo of Sarah from his jacket. 'Hi, my name's Mike Cunningham, are you Mrs Fairbanks?'

Her smile stiffened. 'Yes, laddie. How may I help you?'

'I'm here about my sister.' He handed her the photograph.

Mrs Fairbanks sighed as she studied the picture. 'The police told me about her.' She gave him a sympathetic frown. 'They've still not found her, then?'

Mike shook his head. 'No, that's why I'm here, I was hoping someone may know something.'

The woman shook her head, giving him that thin, sympathetic smile to which he had become so accustomed 'I'm sorry, dear, but I've no memory of her. We have so many people here during the summer, and lots of Americans. That's why we keep the book.'

She reached under the counter and lifted out a large red diary. After opening it, she began flicking through the pages.

'She was here in August, wasn't she?' she asked.

Mike nodded and leaned over as Mrs Fairbanks ran down the names with her finger.

'Ah, here she is,' she said. 'I'd marked it after the police came.' She turned the book around and Mike stared at the signature. 'She was only here for a couple of nights.'

On sight of his sister's name, Mike felt a sudden flood of sadness wash over him like the water from a breached dam.

Coming to Scotland had seemed like a big adventure. Hitchhiking up from Edinburgh and camping and hiking across the idyllic scenery, and meeting other backpackers and seeing the sights, all felt like a vacation. His trip had caused arguments with his father, who felt that should leave finding Sarah to the police. He didn't say as much, but Mike knew his dad was scared he might vanish too. For that, he felt guilty, but he couldn't sit around and do nothing.

Perhaps retracing his sister's steps was just a subconscious attempt to be close to her. Deep down, he knew he'd never find her, not alive. Now seeing her name written by her own hand caused this obvious reality to sink in. Sarah was dead. There was no other explanation. It hit him like a sucker punch. Unexpected, overwhelming, painful, and despite his best efforts to contain himself, he burst into tears.

'Oh, my,' Mrs Fairbanks said, sidling from around the counter and placing her muscular arm around his shoulders. 'I'm so sorry, love.' She gave him a gentle squeeze. 'If only there was something I could do. I'm really sorry, I just don't remember her.'

Mike managed to contain himself and she relaxed her manly embrace. 'I'm sorry,' he said, wiping his eyes with his sleeve. 'You must think I'm a right idiot.'

'Of course, not, and don't be silly, you've nothing to be sorry for. It must be awful, what you're going through.'

He pinched the corner of his eyes and took a deep breath. He felt embarrassed but he had come this far. He looked at Mrs Fairbanks, expectantly. 'Perhaps some of your workers may know something?'

'There's only the three of us here now the season is ending, but the police circulated your sister's picture and description to all the summer staff. I'm afraid nobody remembered her.'

Mike shook his head. Sarah, while small, was certainly not unnoticeable. She was an attractive girl, brazen and extroverted and always at the centre of things. Her outgoing personality was the reason she wanted to go backpacking in the first place. Mike remembered the rows. He couldn't believe it when his father finally agreed to it. *She'll go whether I permit it or not*, he had said. Now he sat back in Wisconsin a broken man, blaming himself for agreeing to the trip. And Mike's own departure would only be making things worse.

Mike looked back down at Sarah's signature. Knowing she had been there less than a couple of months earlier, standing where he now stood, made he feel a closeness he hadn't experienced since her absence. She had been here. There must be some trace of her.

'What about her things? Did you find any belongings you couldn't account for?' he asked.

Mrs Fairbanks sighed. Her breath smelled of mint. 'The police came with a description of some of her clothing, but we didn't find anything that resembled her stuff in lost property.'

Mike remembered giving them the description. When they waved her off at the airport, she had on her college jacket, but besides a few distinctive T-shirts, he and his father could give only sparse details. Knowing Sarah, she'd have also bought plenty of new clothes while travelling and probably lost or swapped many of her tops she took out with her. However, it was worth a try.

'Perhaps I could take a look, just in case I spot something,' he asked.

Mrs Fairbanks gave a sigh that was more out sympathy than resignation. 'Of course, laddie,' she said softly, twitching her head to the door.

She placed a back-in-ten-minutes sign in the window, Mike picked up his backpack and she led him through the campsite to a lean-to shed propped against the shower block. After fumbling with a set of keys, she unlocked a padlock and pulled the handle, causing a creak of protest from the old wooden doors.

'Sorry, there's no light in here,' she said, revealing the dark confines of the shed.

Kayaks, fishing gear and sporting equipment were stacked against the wall at the back, while several cardboard boxes sat on a set of shelves lining the sides. Mrs Fairbanks pulled two of the boxes down and dropped them on the floor. They were taped up, and on the top, written in large black letters, the words, lost property.

'That's all from this year,' Mrs Fairbanks said, retrieving a penknife from her pocket. She snicked through the tape and dragged the two boxes into the afternoon light.

Mike took a deep breath and pulled back the cardboard flap of the first box. None of the T-shirts, socks and other clothing items inside looked at all familiar. Still, he got it all out and checked it all thoroughly. Yet he recognised nothing. He returned the pile of unwanted garments to the box and looked inside the other. It contained another pile of unfamiliar clothes, which he removed and rifled through. Again nothing.

As he was about to return the clothing to the box, he noticed a sleeping bag rolled up in the bottom. He took it out and squinted at it. It was Brown with a bright orange interior. He felt his heart increase as he stroked the padded nylon as if were a family pet. Was it hers? It certainly looked like the one she'd bought for her trip. He couldn't be certain. He looked up at Mrs Fairbanks.

'This looks like hers! Where was it left?'

She raised a single eyebrow, but gave him another appeasing smile. 'I'm not sure. In one of the tents I think. It's a very popular design. You'll find plenty of people have one like it. We even sell them in the shop.'

Mike felt as deflated as one of the half-blown up airbeds outside her store. She was right. He couldn't be sure and there must be thousands like it. He dropped it back into the box. 'Nothing else?'

Mrs Fairbanks shook her head. 'Sorry, laddie.'

It was worth a try. He thanked her, but before walking away, he put his finger to his lip and said, 'You say there's three of you here, now?'

'Yes, me, my husband and Danny our son. He teaches water

sports.' She nodded to the kayaks in the shed.

Mike looked out over the loch. Sarah loved sailing and swimming and surfboards and boats and anything at all to do with water. If she was here, she'd have gone kayaking on the loch. She wouldn't have been able to resist. This Danny must have seen her. 'Perhaps your son might know something?'

Mrs Fairbanks shook her head. 'The police already spoke to him. I'm afraid he doesn't remember her either.'

'Maybe if I speak to him, he might recall something. Is he about?'

'Not at the moment,' Mrs Fairbanks said. 'But I'm sure he wouldn't mind speaking to you.' She looked down at his backpack. 'Will you be wanting to stay here?'

Mike nodded. 'Yes, if you have room.'

She nodded. 'We always have room this time of year. Only really busy in the summer. We do have a party of girl guides arriving tomorrow for an outward bound, which is why all those tents are up, but I'm sure we can squeeze you in. Come back to the reception and I'll book you in.'

Dejected and disappointed, Mike followed her back to the shop. Once inside, she pointed to a map of the campsite behind the counter and ran her finger across it. 'You can have pitch twelve-c. It's closest to the water so you'll have a nice view?'

'Thank you,' he said, pointing to a poster on the wall next to the map. It was of a sea creature, its head and several humps poking out of the water, reminiscent of similar images he'd seen around Loch Ness. 'Is that Nessie?'

'Och no, that's Morag, she's our very own beastie.' She smiled. 'You'll find all the lochs of Scotland have their own monster, not just Loch Ness, although I've been here twenty years and never seen it. Now, do you have everything you need?'

'Yes thank you.'

'I'll get Danny to come and find you when he gets back. Oh, and if you really want to see a monster, you can go speak to my husband, see if he remembers anything about your sister. He'll be in the bar. Although, if he's sober enough to remember his own name, it would very much surprise me.'

Chapter Five

Anderson awoke and felt as if the Black Watch were marching through his head. After sitting upright and taking a few hacking, chesty coughs, he looked around the unfamiliar surroundings and rolled a cigarette.

The room was neat. A large colour TV was wedged between a bookcase full of novels and a tall lamp, and he was sitting on a purple velour sofa, his back resting against plump, woollen cushions. On a small coffee table before him, somebody had left a glass of water and vial of aspirin. He lifted up the water, squeezed his stomach and looked about. His jacket lay on the back of the sofa. He slipped it on and removed a pill bottle from the inside pocket. After unscrewing it, he tossed a couple on his hand and knocked them back, before slumping back on the sofa, letting out a groan and a cough. He then fumbled for his lighter.

'I hope you don't think you are going to smoke that in here,' said a stern female voice.

Anderson turned his head, startled, which caused it to pay him back with a nauseating throb. A young woman in police uniform stood behind him, arms akimbo. She had a schoolmistress scowl across her lips, which sat beneath a long, hooked nose that spoiled her otherwise pretty features.

'Who the bloody hell are you?' he croaked, running a hand through his thinning hair.

'Sergeant Betty Sandilands, Lochaber Constabulary,' she said, walking around the sofa, hands still on her hips. 'And I hope you've sobered up, *Inspector*?'

'Where am I?'

'My home,' she said, snatching the cigarette from his lips. 'You were drunk. I had to carry you off the train from Fort William. Don't you remember?'

He screwed up his face and shrugged. 'Well, you can't blame me. Not much else to do on a bloody seven-hour train journey.'

She raised her eyebrows as he stood up, his hand supporting his forehead. 'It is not very professional, getting in that state. You're lucky nobody saw you.'

'Who said I was a professional?'

She scowled at him again. 'I take it you're the detective looking into the disappearance of the ministry inspector?'

He scratched his head. 'Oh yes, that's me all right. Somebody goes missing in the arsehole of nowhere and Anderson's your man.'

'The chief constable told me to offer any assistance you may need.'

He looked her up and down and sniffed. 'Well, right this minute all I need is a piss, so you can assist me with that, if you like?' He gave her grin, which she reciprocated with a tight-lipped scowl before nodding behind her.

'Toilet's through there.'

Anderson staggered into the bathroom, leaving the door open. 'So, they given me a WPC, have they?' He shouted over the noise of his stream, which sounded like a racehorse relieving itself.

' I'm a sergeant and I do have my own work to do.'

'You know Morar well?'

'As well as any round here.'

He walked back out, zipping himself up in front of her. 'Good, so do you know the McGillivray's cattle farm?'

'McGillivrays? Of course. Everyone knows the McGillivray's place. They're the biggest employer out here. It's just outside the village, past the dam. Why?'

'Because that's the last place our missing inspector visited.' He reached into his jacket pocket and took out his notepad. 'Made some inspection last week. Not been seen since.'

He took out his tobacco and proceeded to roll up another cigarette. 'How far is it?'

'Twenty minute's walk.'

Anderson frowned at her. 'And by car?'

'We'll have to go back to the station and call Featherstone. He's out in it at the moment.'

'You only have one car?'

'We're a small force, Inspector.'

'Well, we better get a move on,' he said, glancing at his watch. 'The pub'll be open in a couple of hours.' He lit his smoke and held his hand out to the door. 'After you Sweaty Glands.'

'It's Sandilands,' she snapped, before leading him out the door. 'And don't you think you have had enough to drink today?'

The bright red nylon tent Mike erected looked garish next to dozen or so canvas ones. Once he had finished, he collapsed on to his sleeping bag, exhausted. It was only mid afternoon, but the journey to Morar that morning, combined with the walk along the loch to the campsite, was farther than he'd walked in years. His feet burned, his legs ached and his eyelids felt like they were supporting lead weights. Yet he couldn't sleep.

His sister's signature in Mrs Fairbanks' guestbook had awoken feelings that up to now he'd locked away throughout his trip. Now, he was there, at the end of his trip, the last place Sarah had visited, yet he was no closer to finding out what happened to her.

He decided to pay Mr Fairbanks a visit after all. Not that he expected to learn anything. Mrs Fairbanks' glowing reference of her husband's character was hardly encouraging, but a cold beer, or more likely a warm Scottish one, may at least allow him to get a few hours shuteye that afternoon.

He strolled towards the concrete block in the middle of the campsite, and walked into the bar entrance, which was next to the shower block. The bar lacked the typical dowdiness of the English pub, with no oak tables and flock wallpaper, but plastic stools and plain white walls. It lacked decoration too, with just a stuffed fish above the counter and a faded fire notice poster, but the panoramic view of the loch through the long window provided ample scenery.

Mrs Fairbanks had been right about her husband. He was the complete antithesis to his athletic wife. Resting against the counter under the optics, reading a paper and sipping from a glass of scotch, a huge gut hung over his trousers, like that of a pot-bellied pig, and his face was ruddy.

He straightened at the sight of Mike, revealing a purple threaded nose. 'Good afternoon, what can I get ye?' he said, swaying uneasily.

'Just a beer, please.' Mike said, sitting on stool in front of the empty bar.

Fairbanks shakily pulled down a beer glass, placed it under the pump, and while rocking back and forth, poured Mike a lager. 'That's eighty pence please,' he said, placing the beer on the counter and spilling half the contents.

Mike paid him and Fairbanks, his tongue licking his lops as Mike sipped the beer, topped up his own glass from the optics. 'I think I'll join ye,' he said, swallowing the scotch in one mouthful before pouring himself another. He then staggered around the bar and slumped on the stool next to Mike. 'So you an American?'

'Erm, that's right,' Mike said, taking another sip of his lager.

Fairbanks, rocking from side to side, took three attempts to raise his own glass to his lips, but finally succeeded. 'We get lots of Americans, here. Good tippers,' he said, smiling. 'So you finding Scotland to your liking, laddie?'

'Yes, it's very beautiful.'

'That it is. How long you with us for?'

'Not sure, a couple of days, perhaps. I'm looking for my sister.'

'Oh?'

'She went missing seven weeks ago.' He took the photograph out from his jacket and passed it over. 'Perhaps you remember here?'

Fairbanks swayed in his seat as he studied the photograph. 'Nae, sorry, laddie. Pretty lass though. You're wife you say.' He handed back the picture.

'No, my sister.'

'I've got a wife,' Fairbanks said, frowning. 'Bitch.'

Mike remained quiet.

'She thinks just because she owns this place and has given me a job in it, gives her the right to tell me what to do. Pah! I had a business too, you know. A damned good one.' He drank the rest of his scotch and sidled back around the bar to pour another.

'What type of business were you in?' Mike asked, out of politeness.

'Fishing accessories and tackle,' Fairbanks said, slopping his whisky as he poured it. 'Biggest tackle shop in Lochaber. Do you fish?'

'Not much, no.'

'Och, there's nothing like it for a boy your age. Better than chasing skirt. Pah, they all turn into nagging shrews in the end. You met my wife?'

Mike coughed in embarrassment. 'Er .. yes. So what happened to your shop?' he asked, changing eh subject.

Fairbanks raised his glass at the window toward the loch, spilling half its contents across the counter. 'Nobody fishes round here no more. Nothing worth catching in the loch.' He slammed the whisky glass on the counter. 'Used t'be full o' trout and salmon. Used to pull 'em out the size of dogs. Now. Pah! Lucky if ye find a stickleback. All gone.'

'Maybe it's the monster, Morag.' Mike joked.

Fairbanks froze and one of his eyes bulged open while the other closed to a squint. He leaned close. 'I've seen her, so I have,' he slurred.

'Really?' Mike said, trying to mask his incredulity.

Fairbanks picked up his glass and pointed out the window again. 'A few weeks back when I was locking up this place. I saw her big black hump sticking out of the water. Right there, right in the middle of the loch.'

Mike looked out at the water and smiled. He imagined Fairbanks saw many things after locking up the bar, not just loch monsters, but probably pink elephants too. 'Perhaps the fish'll come back one day and you'll be able to reopen your shop.'

'Nae laddie, not while Morag's about.' He nodded at Mike's half empty pint glass. 'You want another drink?'

'Er, no thanks.' He lifted the glass, drained it and wiped his mouth with the back of his hand. 'Been a long day, think I'll go and have a lie down.' He thanked Mr Fairbanks, and walked to the door, but the old Scotsman called after him.

'Hey, Yankee!'

Mike stopped and saw Fairbanks staring at him with two steady eyes. 'Keep away from the water.'

Unlike the rest of their conversation, his words sounded sober.

Chapter Six

The Morar police car was a battered old Austin Allegro. Boxy with the rear and front of the car almost indistinguishable from each other, the shocks had gone, the handbrake didn't work and it was scratched and dented. Sandilands had been asking for a replacement for years but the constabulary kept ignoring her requests.

Anderson sneered at it, his lit cigarette pointing up in his lips like child with a thermometer in their mouth. 'Hope you don't get many armed robbers out here. Couldn't catch a paperboy in that thing.'

'It does us very well, thank you.' Sandilands suddenly felt very protective over the blue and white panda car. 'And you can put that cigarette out before you get in.

He moaned, but after flicking his cigarette to the ground, he slumped into the passenger seat. Sandilands sighed and sat beside him, adjusting the mirror before fastening her seatbelt.

'You're not on a bloody driving test,' he said, his tobacco pouch out. 'C'mon, sooner we get going, sooner we can get back. I wouldn't mind getting the last train out of this arsehole of Scotland.'

'Charming. Well, I'd let you drive, if you weren't over the limit.'

He flashed a sardonic grin and she fired up the engine, pulled from the curbside and headed out of the village past the hydroelectric dam, through the rolling pastures dotted with sheep and off the main road towards McGillivray's farm.

Judging by the colour of his face, Anderson obviously felt the worse for his earlier indulgence. He had large bags under his eyes and his skin glistened with clamminess. The cattle grids spaced along the track leading to the farm did little to ease his hangover.

'Bloody hell, ain't this thing got any suspension,' he said, holding his head as the car jolted up and down.

Sandilands smiled. Serve him right. She still felt scandalised at having seen him drunk, especially him being an inspector and all. 'Don't worry, it's not much farther,' she said grinning. 'So what do you think happened to this ministry inspector, then?'

Anderson shrugged. 'Probably had a nervous breakdown—sick of sticking his arm up cow's arses. He'll turn up. Either face down in a river somewhere or in a hotel with a rent boy. That's usually the way these things go, especially with civil servants. Most of 'em are queer.'

His face suddenly hardened and he scrunched up his nose and he took rapid sniffs of the air. 'Jesus Christ!' he yelled. 'What the hell is that?'

Sandilands laughed. 'McGillivray's place. It's just ahead.'

'Jesus, how you lot live in the country is beyond me.'

She smirked as he screwed up his face even tighter. 'You get used to it.'

She steered the car over a brow of a hill and the farm came into view. Below, row upon row of cowsheds laid out like a prisoner of war camp. Green roofed and corrugated walled, they covered several acres and lined up in perfect symmetry against the backdrop of the rolling hills.

A high wire fence surrounded the farm, dotted with bright yellow notices. Sandilands parked up at the security gate, which had further warnings of guard dog patrols. A guard, sat inside a little hut. He got out, frowned, opened the gate and waved them through.

'Here we are, then,' Sandilands said, driving over the cattle grid at the gate. She turned to see Anderson, thrust back in his seat, his jacket tight against his face, his hand waving her on.

The smell only increased as they approached, and by the time Sandilands parked the Allegro next to an articulated lorry in the main yard, Anderson, was squirming in his, his face pallid.

'Oh, Jesus, it reeks,' he gasped, lowering the jacket. 'How can you stand it, woman. With a hooter like yours it must be ten times worse.'

'You are about the most offensive and odious man I think I've ever met!' she said, opening the door.

'You obviously ain't been meeting the right men,' he spluttered, his face taut.

A few farm workers walked across the car park, eyeing the police car suspiciously. Anderson shook his head at them. 'How can they work here? They must have no sinuses. My God, you can taste it.' He stuck out his tongue and gagged.

'Well, you hardly smell fresh yourself, you know.'

He gave her another sardonic grin, spat a lump of phlegm to the ground and looked around the car park. A few cattle trucks and vans lay in the muddied yard, as did a muddied and dented Land Rover, but gleaming beside it was an olive-green Rolls Royce, the silver lady shimmering under the sun. He nodded to it.

'Whose is that?'

'Mr McGillivray's.'

'Well they do say there's money in muck. So where do we find him?'

A two-story office building, with McGillivray Bovine Industries written on a large sign was sandwiched between two of the cattle sheds in front of the Land Rover and Rolls Royce. Sandilands pointed to it. 'In his office,' she said, walking over. 'You coming?'

He nodded, pulled his jacket across his mouth and followed.

Sandilands had said that McGillivray's farm was one of the biggest and most successful in the Highlands, and as Anderson walked into the teak panelled office and stared across at the old man with his booze-addled face, he didn't doubt it.

The beef magnate was behind a large oak desk with nothing more than a crystal decanter and telephone before him. He wore a dark suit that hung loosely over his elderly and frail frame, had wispy grey hair slicked back with grease, tiny blue eyes glazed over with cataracts, and sovereign rings the size of knuckle-dusters adorning his fingers.

Next to him and sitting very close, a secretary, no older than twenty. She had a notepad in her hand, but by the way the old man patted her thigh, and judging by the size of her udders, which would have made any of the cattle on the farm jealous, Anderson realised she wasn't hired for her shorthand. *Yes*, he thought, *Mr McGillivray has done all right for himself.*

The old man looked up and smiled at Sandilands. 'Betty, how are you?'

With her cap under her arm and standing to attention like a drill sergeant, Sandilands smiled back. 'Very well, Mr McGillivray. This is Inspector Anderson, from Special Branch.'

'Oh, I see,' said the old man, his voice high-pitched and made up of only breath. He looked vacantly at Anderson before turning back to Sandilands. 'How's your mother?'

'She's fine, sir, but we're here on business. The inspector here wants to talk to you about a recent government visit.'

'That's nice dear.' McGillivray slurred, his vacant eyes now distracted by his secretary's cleavage.

He was showing obvious signs of dementia, but Anderson reckoned with access to McGillivray's cash, limitless booze and a blonde haired floozy like the old man's secretary, it wouldn't take long for him to become addled too. He knew one thing, though. While McGillivray owned the farm, he didn't run it, and probably hadn't for some time.

'I was hoping to speak to your farm manager,' he said, watching the old man pour himself a glass of brandy. The shaking hand meant the secretary had to lean over to help, resting one of her huge breasts on the delighted old man's shoulder.

'Farm manager? Oh, I don't have a manager. I like to keep a firm grip of the helm myself,' he said, livening up. 'Just me and my boy Joe. Family business is McGillivray's, and forever it will be so, as long as I'm breathing.'

Well that ain't going to be long, mate, thought Anderson, *not the rate you're going.*

'Where is Joe?' Sandilands asked. 'Can we talk to him?'

'Oh, I'm not sure.'

The old man looked to his secretary, who sighed. She leaned forward, lifted the phone and dialled a single number. 'Could you tell Mr McGillivray his father wishes to see him?' Her voice sounded bored. She waited for a reply and hung up. 'He'll be here in a minute.'

'Well, sit down won't you. Perhaps a drink?' the old man said.

'Not while on duty, thank you,' Sandilands said, remaining standing, her back rod straight. She took out her notebook.

Anderson shrugged and sat, leaning back in the comfortable wing back chair and took out his tobacco. 'That'll be very kind, sir. Thank you.'

Sandilands coughed and glowered at him, but Anderson ignored her. The old man, with the help of his buxom aid, poured him a drink, and after eyeing the tobacco pouch on the inspector's lap, reached into his drawer and pulled out a box of cigars. His secretary pulled one of the long, thick Cubans from the box, slid it out of the cellophane, bit the end, placed it in her mouth and lit it. After taking a deep puff, she placed it in the old man's mouth, who grinned like a teenager.

'Have one of these, Inspector.' McGillivray said, breathing out a deep lungful of smoke. Shakily he lifted the box and offered it over.

'Don't mind if I do, thank you.' Anderson took one of the cigars and offered it to Sandilands. 'Wouldn't mind doing me the same honours, would you?'

She curled up her lip in vicious scowl and glowered down her long nose at him. HE smiled and unwrapped the cigar, sniffed along its length and bit into the end. McGillivray's secretary leaned forward and lit it for him. Anderson grinned at the sight of the wobbling chest beneath his chin. He wondered if he qualified for a secretary. He'd ask the DSI when he got back.

'So, how long you been into cows?' he asked, after puffing a satisfying cloud of smoke to the ceiling.

The old man took a long intake of his cigar, his hand shaking as he held it to his lips as he thought. 'Over sixty years, man and boy.' His mind seemed to gain clarity as it delved into the past. 'Started with a bull and three heifers, and now I'm the second biggest beef producer in the Highlands.'

A tap on the door interrupted their conversation and everybody turned as in stormed a short man in Wellington boots, green body warmer and flat cap, stinking something awful.

He marched over to the desk and removed his cap, revealing red curls stuck to his forehead with sweat that suited the pale and freckly complexion. He eyed Anderson suspiciously before glaring at Sandilands. 'I understand you want to see me,' he said, not even acknowledging the old man.

'This is Inspector Anderson,' she replied, nodding to Anderson.

Anderson stood. 'And you are ...?' He winced at the stench emanating from the man.

'Joe McGillivray,' he snapped. 'Farm manager, and if you're here about farm business it's me you'll be wanting to speak to, not my father.' He scowled at the secretary. 'Dad's not well. He shouldn't be disturbed with such things.'

The busty girl just shrugged.

McGillivray junior then scowled at Anderson. 'If you want to know anything, you'll have to come to my office. I'm very busy, so it had better be quick.' With that he marched to the door. Anderson raised his cigar in thanks to the old man, gave the busty secretary a wink and followed the fiery red head out of the office.

Chapter Seven

While McGillivray Senior had an office panelled in teak and full of life's little comforts, McGillivray junior worked behind a mound of papers and three telephones, and the office stank of manure. He sat at his desk, his face frosty, as Sandilands and Anderson stood before him.

Sandilands didn't know Joe well, but she had a couple of run-ins with him in the past. On one occasion, she was called to the farm after a former worker had complained of an assault. She never got to the bottom of it. The worker, who had needed several stitches, dropped the charges. Paid off. But Sandilands knew Joe had a temper. Perhaps it was his stature, a Napoleon complex, or he was just highly stressed. His marriage was over, and if she believed the rumours about the frequency in which his wife walked into door, his wife had had a narrow escape. However, by the look of his red face and eyebrows arched into a vee, the divorce was doing little for his temper.

'As you've probably realised, my father is not well,' he said, looking sternly at Sandilands. 'You should have come to see me first.'

'Sorry, I wasn't aware your father was so ... ill.'

'He has been for some time. He hasn't had much to do with the running of the farm for about a while now. But he comes in everyday for a few hours, keeps him happy.'

'I bet it does,' Anderson mumbled, his face scrunched up from the smell. He sucked hard and deep on the cigar. 'Your father was just telling me how well you've been doing.'

'Well, it's not been easy. When dad first got ill, we got into some financial trouble, but we got through it. Now we are the largest beef producer North of Dundee.' He looked over at Sandilands again. 'So what's all this about?'

She nodded to Anderson. 'We just want to ask a few questions about a recent government inspection, that's all.'

'Inspections, pah!' Joe's eyes narrowed and his already flushed cheeks turned a darker shade. 'They're forever looking for fault. I tell you.' He jabbed a finger at Anderson. 'A man can't do well in this world without the government breathing down his neck. First it was the miners, now that bitch at number ten is having a go at us farmers.'

'Well, that's what we get for letting a woman run the country.' Anderson sniffed. 'I just want to know if you remember an inspector who came here last week.'

Joe leaned back in his chair. 'Yes, someone called Bryson, I think.'

'Briers,' Anderson corrected him. 'What do you remember about him?'

Joe shrugged. 'Not much, usual ministry jobsworth. Wanted to look round, so we showed him.'

'And what time did he leave?'

Joe reached for one of the telephones, picked it up and pressed a button. 'Gloria, bring me the visitor's book, will you.'

'Did he seem odd in anyway?' Anderson asked, as Joe hung up the phone.

Joe looked confused, one eyebrow cocked higher than the other. 'What do you mean?'

'Well, he's gone missing, see, and I'm just trying to trace his last movements.'

'Missing?'

'Aye, he'll probably turn up, but did his behaviour seem in any way erratic to you.'

Joe shrugged. 'Hardly spoke to him. Spent most of his time with my vet, Eric.'

'I thought Mr Kilkenny was your vet?' Sandilands asked.

'He was, but it made more sense to have our own full time vet on site,' Joe said, leaning forward and staring at Anderson as if measuring him up. 'We run a large-scale operation here, Inspector. We don't just breed cattle, but we slaughter them on site, butcher the carcasses, package them and despatch them straight to the supermarkets. Time is everything. When we get problems with one of our herds, I need it sorted straightaway. Can't stand around for six hours waiting for the local vet to get here. So I've employed my own.'

'Is there any chance I can have a word with this vet of yours then?' Anderson asked.

Behind, the door clicked open and a middle-aged woman with glasses propped on the end of her nose, strolled in with the visitor's book. She handed it Joe.

'Thanks Gloria,' he said, opening it up. 'Could you put a call out for Mr van Burgh, ask him to join us.'

'Yes Mr McGillivray.' The woman smiled officiously, turned about and walked out, closing the door behind her.

'Here we are,' Joe declared, turning the book around. 'Signed in at two o'clock, signed out at four.' He tapped the page with a dirty forefinger.

Anderson leaned over the desk and looked before letting out a sigh. 'Aye, well that's that then.'

'Probably got him on CCTV. Want me to dig that out for you, might take a while?'

'No, that won't be necessary,' Anderson said, turning the book back around. 'But I don't suppose you remember how he came and went, can you?'

Joe looked perplexed, his fuzzy eyebrows contorted again, and he shook his head. 'How do you mean?'

'We know he came up on the train, but it's a bit of a walk from the station.'

Joe shrugged. 'Must have got a taxi, I suppose. You'll have to ask Eric, my vet.'

'So I don't suppose you know which firm?'

'There's only one taxi firm in Morar,' Sandilands said. 'Shouldn't be hard to find who drove him up here and back.'

Joe smiled at her, but she noticed his eyes vibrating with anger.

Mike stood on the little shingle beach beside the jetty and stared out over the waters at the reflections of long trees shimmering on the water's surface. He still couldn't sleep and couldn't stop thinking of Sarah. Perhaps she had stood on this same spot, and then he shivered as the feeling of sorrow returned. What had happened to her? Murdered? Drowned? Perhaps she was still alive and in some hedonistic cult, or hooked up with a Hell's Angel. No. He knew whatever had happened to Sarah had prevented her from calling, from letting her family know she was safe. And only one thing would prevent her from doing that.

Footsteps on the shingle caused him to turn. A young man, taller than Mike but about the same age, with cropped ginger hair and wearing shorts, despite the sharpness to the wind, was walking towards him. He stopped, looked disapprovingly at the American, and said, 'My Ma says you wanted to see me.'

Mike held out his palm. 'Oh, you must be Danny. My name's Mike.'

'So what do you want?' Danny asked, ignoring Mike's palm.

'I'm looking for your sister?' Mike said, removing the photograph from his pocket. 'Her name is Sarah Cunningham, perhaps you remember her?'

Danny barely glanced at it. 'Sorry, don't remember her, so you're wasting your time.'

His was curt, short, abrupt, but Mike assumed it was just the choppiness of the accent. 'I know, but I was just hoping that you might remember something. Anything. Perhaps where she planned on going after Morar. Please take a look.' He thrust the picture at him.

'I told you,' Danny snapped. 'I don't remember her. Besides, the police have already been here asking questions. If I were you, I'd go back to America, and let them look for her. That's what they are paid for.'

'I just want to see if anybody remembers anything, that's all, Mike said, his voice slightly choked by the animosity.

'Well I don't.' With that, Danny unhooked a set of headphones from a cassette player on his belt, placed them over his ears, turned around and walked up the shingle beach to the cottage-cum-shop, where he disappeared through a side door to what Mike presumed was the Fairbanks' home.

Mike knew he was lying. He knew because of the way Danny spoke to him, by his defensive attitude, but most of all by the distinctive and familiar red Walkman hooked on Danny's belt.

After five minutes of waiting in uncomfortable silence, breached only by Sandilands attempts at pleasantries, a tap on the door to Joe's office was followed by the appearance of a tall and sinewy figure. Dark haired and with a crooked nose, the man wore a white gown with a selection of pens protruding from the top pocket.

He smiled at Sandilands and Anderson as Joe introduced him. 'Inspector, this is Eric van Burgh, our vet.'

'Pleased to meet you,' van Burgh said, in an obvious north European accent. He had long, thin fingers, which he extended.

Anderson shook the man's hand, and then wiped his palm down his trousers. 'I understand you spoke to Mr Briers last week.'

Van Burgh looked askance at Joe, before narrowing his eyes. 'Briers?'

'The ministry official, who came for that inspection.'

Van Burgh snapped his fingers. 'Ah, yes. Now I remember.' He glanced back at Joe again. 'What about him?'

'He seems to have vanished,' Anderson said. 'He was due back in Fort William the same day, only he never arrived. Seems that this was the last place he visited.'

Van Burgh shrugged. 'Well, what's that to do with us?'

'Probably nothing,' Anderson said. 'But did you notice anything unusual about him?'

'Unusual?'

'Aye, did he seem odd at all?'

'Odd?'

'Yes, distracted, perhaps.'

Van Burgh shook his head. 'Not that I can remember.'

'So what was the purpose of his visit?' Anderson pulled out his tobacco, having finished the cigar McGillivray senior had given him.

'Usual ministry business, you know. Wanted to check our tags.'

'Tags?'

'Ear tags,' explained van Burgh. 'It's how we identify the cows.'

'What for?' Anderson rolled up a smoke and placed it in his lips.

'Usual procedure. To check the origins of our livestock.'

'I see.' Anderson lit his smoke with a match, which he shook out and pointed at van Burgh. 'And did he say anything odd to you while he was here?'

'Not that I can recall.'

Anderson removed a piece of rogue tobacco from his tongue and shrugged. 'I guess that's it then. Thanks for your time.'

'Perhaps you'd like to have a look around while you are here, Inspector?' van Burgh said.

Anderson winced at the prospect. 'No, you're okay.' He nodded to Sandilands. 'Sorry to disturb you gents. It's all probably a wild goose chase anyway.'

'So what now?' Sandilands asked, as she and Anderson marched back to the car.

'Best go find this cabbie that picked him up,' Anderson replied, his jacket across his mouth again. 'Then perhaps I can put this thing to bed.'

'Shouldn't take long to find him. There's only a couple of full time cab drivers around here.'

'Good. Chances are Briers went for a long walk and didn't come back. They're like that these civil servants. Forever topping themselves.' He scrunched up his nose. 'And I'll top myself if you don't get me out of here. Jesus, what are they feeding these cows?' He started gagging again.

Joe stood in the yard, watching the battered old police car pull away. 'Why the hell did you offer to show him around?'

He spoke without turning, and even though he had his back to van Burgh, the Dutchman knew Joe was speaking through gritted teeth. Joe was an angry man, a paranoid man. His actions the week before testified to that. Since then, van Burgh had felt scared, really scared.

While he knew Joe needed him to sort out the epidemic, he also knew whose actions were to blame for the outbreak. And while that scared van Burgh well enough, what terrified him the most was being witness to murder. That made him complicit, and in Joe's eyes, dangerous.

'Thought we ought to be as open as possible. We don't want to cause suspicion,' van Burgh said, shuffling backwards. 'Do you think they suspect something?'

Joe turned round. His nostrils were wide, his eyes narrow, but he spoke calmly enough. 'They know squat.' He turned back around to the direction Anderson and Sandilands had driven off. 'You had better hope it stays that way. For your sake and theirs.'

Chapter Eight

Around the campsite, a few children ran about shouting and screaming and playing tag in the late afternoon sun, but Mike ignored them as he trudged to the relative quietness of his tent and ducked inside. He started rummaging around in his backpack and pulled free his Walkman.]

Other than being grey, it was identical to the one on Danny Fairbanks' belt. Mike had received his for Christmas that year. It was the very latest model with recording button and super bass loudness. They both got one, he and Sarah. Except she didn't like hers, said the grey looked too plain. Typical Sarah, always wanting to be different. So she took it back to the shop and exchanged it for a red one.

It had to be a coincidence, Mike thought, but it was so distinctive. Still, he couldn't very well go accusing him of having something to do with Sarah's death. Not because of a Walkman. But his imagination began taking giant leaps, and imagined Danny with his hands around his sister's throat. He tried to shrug off the thoughts, but just as he managed to convince himself it was all just a coincidence, Danny walked out of the little cottage, the Walkman still attached to his waist.

He watched as Danny walked to the shed, where earlier Mike had rummaged around in the lost property boxes. After disappearing inside, he reappeared hauling one of the fibreglass kayaks, which he dragged to the jetty and lay it face down on the wooden planks.

He then returned to the shed and dragged out another kayak, repeating the process until six of the bright yellow canoes lay on the little pier. As he watched, Mike imagined Danny dragging his sister like one of the canoes, dumping her in the loch. *Did he kill her?* Mike took a deep breath. He was letting his imagination get away from him. *But the Walkman?*

His eyes followed Danny after he returned to the shed, locked it up and walked back to the cottage. The little shop-cum-reception was now locked up, and Mrs Fairbanks was either inside, or somewhere else on the campsite. After a moment, he saw a shadow flicker past the curtain in an upstairs room. It must have been Danny in his room. Mike stared at the cottage, an idea hatching in his mind. A stupid idea. A crazy idea. But an idea he couldn't shake.

Before he left Lochside, he was going to take a look in Danny's bedroom.

After a brief radio call to the cab office, Anderson and Sandilands found the taxi driver who picked up Briers outside the railway station in his cab.

Sandilands pulled up behind the taxi and Anderson got out, rolled a cigarette, looked across at the station and swore. The last train out of Morar was departing. That meant spending the night in this damned backwater. He shook his head. At least his haemorrhoids would welcome the respite from another seven-hour journey.

Once Sandilands had slammed her door shut, the pair approached the taxi. The driver was asleep, feet up on his dashboard. Anderson banged on the window, causing the sleeping cabbie to awake with a look of sheer terror across his jowls.

'Ged heavens,' he screamed. 'What the ken are ye doing, man? You could have given me a heart attack.'

Anderson didn't doubt it. He was a big fellow, all gut and high blood pressure. The cabbie spotted Sandilands in her uniform and his eyebrows rose up his forehead. Anderson flopped open his warrant card. The cabbie glanced quickly from Anderson to Sandilands and back to Anderson again.

'What have I done?' he asked.

'Just need a word with you, pal,' Anderson said, striking a match and lighting his cigarette.

The taxi driver looked alarmed. He opened and closed his mouth without speaking causing his double chin to wobble like a turkey's wattle.

'It's Mr McKenzie, isn't it?' Sandilands asked.

'Yes, Sergeant,' he replied. 'And if this is about my tax disc, I'm just about to sort it, honest.'

Anderson chuckled out a breath of tobacco smoke. 'I don't care about your tax disc.' He leaned in. 'We want to talk to you about a fare you picked up last week. Name of Briers.'

The man shrugged.

'You picked him up from here and took him the McGillivray cattle farm,' Sandilands said, frowning at the tax disc on his windscreen and shaking her head. 'You then picked him back up a couple of hours later.'

'Aye, I remember. So what of it?'

'Anything odd about him?' Anderson asked.

The cabbie shook his head, causing his wattle chin to wobble again. 'Smartly dressed, that's all I can remember.'

Anderson breathed in another mouthful of smoke. 'And when

you picked him up later, where did you drop him?'

The man's eyebrows formed a vee as he thought. 'In the village.'

'Not here, at the station?' Sandilands asked. 'Why not?'

The man shrugged. 'I don't know. Perhaps he was going to get a bite to eat before the last train.'

Anderson stared at his cigarette for a moment then looked up as the sound of the five-fifteen departing filtered from the station. 'And what time was this?'

The cabbie shrugged again. 'Be about this time, I guess. Now you mention it, I thought he was cutting it a bit fine to get the last train.'

Anderson took another drag of his smoke, before flicking it to the ground and leaning into the car window. 'And did you see him again? About the village, perhaps?'

The cabbie screwed up his lips. 'I don't think so, but then I got a fare not long after.'

Anderson nodded, before straightening up. 'Guess that'll do.'

'Thanks for your time, Mr McKenzie,' Sandilands said, before tapping his windscreen. 'And make sure you get that tax disc sorted.'

He nodded meekly, and Anderson and Sandilands walked back to the car. 'What now?' she asked, leaning across the Allegro's roof.

Anderson looked back at the station. 'Sounds like a suicide to me. Probably had no intention of getting the train. Must have wanted a bit of scenery to end things. He'll probably float up from the loch.'

'You finished here then?'

'Aye, I suppose so, but as I've missed the bloody train-' He looked across the roof of the car and grinned '—how do you fancy taking me back to your place, then?'

She walked to the rear of the car, opened the boot, removed his suitcase and dropped it at his feet, and reciprocated his grin. 'Would love to, but I'm washing my hair. The hotel is just up the road.'

She pointed up the hill to what looked like a typical Scottish guesthouse. White washed stone and a sign outside offering bed and breakfast.

'But you best behave yourself. Mrs Trench doesn't take kindly to drunks,' She added, before getting into the car and driving off, leaving him to pick up his case and trudge towards up the hill, grumbling to himself.

Anderson cheered up a little when he arrived at the hotel and noticed it had a bar attached. At least he could spend the night drinking his expenses. His job did have some perks, after all.

Inside, the smell that greeted him was a familiar one. He'd stayed in plenty of bed and breakfasts in his time, and they all had the same aroma of overcooked vegetables mixed with *Shake and Vac*. The interior of the Morar Hotel was as typical as its exterior. Wallpaper from a decade ago, random pictures of thistles on the walls and guests in the dining room with an average age of seventy.

He dumped his battered suitcase at the empty reception counter, and rang the bell. Repeatedly.

'Heaven's above,' came a shrill cry from the back room, as Anderson increased his bell ringing tempo to a rhythm that would have befitted the drummer of a heavy metal band.

The woman that appeared had bouffant hair, make-up that looked like she applied it by a trowel and enough perfume on to warrant the need for a 'highly flammable' sign around her neck. She looked him up and down with her nose hoisted in the air and her lips grimacing with distaste.

'Can I help you,' she said, as a cloud of tobacco smoke wafted from the roll up clamped in his lips, causing her face to grimace even more.

'I want a room,' he said, not bothering to remove the cigarette, which bobbed up and down on his lips.

She gave an expression as if she had just smelled excrement on her top lip. 'I'm afraid we're full.'

Anderson removed his cigarette from his mouth and deliberately flicked ash on to the obvious well-vacuumed carpet. 'That's not what your sign says.'

'Still, we're full.'

He loudly sniffed down a ball of phlegm before reaching into his jacket. He pulled free his warrant card and flopped it open. 'I suggest you find room, otherwise you may find the drug squad down here ripping the place apart. Might cause a terrible scene.'

The woman glanced at the warrant card then at Anderson and back down at the warrant card again. 'I ... I suppose we can always make room for an officer of the law.'

He shoved the warrant card back in his jacket. 'Thought you might.'

Sandilands had been right, the woman was a stuck up bitch. He didn't quite know what to make of Sandilands, though. Generally, he didn't approve of women in the job. Wasn't right.

But out here, he doubted she'd have much in the way of armed robbers or drug pushers to deal with. Still, it made him wonder, *why would a bird would want to join up*? He usually thought of WPC's as either barren or not into men. He didn't have Sandilands down as a dyke and wasn't a bad looking bird, if you could get passed that big hooter. Shame he wasn't ten years younger.

Mrs Trench dropped a key, with an oversized wooden fob on to the counter. 'You're on the top floor. You want me to get my husband to help you with your suitcase?'

'Aye, tell him to dump it in my room. I'm off to the bar. Through here is it.' He jabbed his cigarette at the arched doorway leading to the dining room, at the end of which sat a smoked glass door.

'Yes, will you be wanting breakfast?'

'Do you do a full Scottish?'

'Not this time of year. Porridge or oatcakes.'

He sniffed in disgust. 'Then no.'

She rummaged around under the counter and produced the guest book, which she slid around to face him. 'You'll have to sign in. I'll just get my husband to attend to your ...' She looked down at his battered suitcase and gave that bad smell face again. '... luggage.'

She disappeared and Anderson picked up the pen chained to the counter and signed and printed his name. Ash fell from his smoke, and he leaned forward to blow it off the page, but stopped.

Halfway above his signature, a familiar name caught his eye. It took a second for it to register then he slowly pulled the cigarette from his lips and read the name aloud.

'Briers.'

Mike watched all night. He hoped Mrs Fairbanks and Danny would go to the bar or take a walk or do anything that provided the opportunity to steal a look inside the cottage. But neither emerged. Then after an hour of watching, a coach arrived at the campsite, its great big wheels crunching in the gravel. After a hiss, the doors opened and a hoard or young girls all wearing the same pleated skirts, blue shirts and yellow scarves swarmed out like ants from a nest and streamed into the campsite, giggling and laughing and shouting and squealing and signalling the end of any chance Mike had of seeing through his plan.

While Mrs Fairbanks appeared from the cottage and reopened the reception, Danny remained inside, his silhouette visible behind the net curtains at his bedroom window, watching the girl guides as they gathered around the cottage and shattered the quietness of the campsite.

A woman accompanied them. She was in her fifties but wore a similar uniform, including the pleated skirt that exposed her varicose veins. She and Mrs Fairbanks spent the best part of an hour chatting, while the girls milled about their tents making a hellish din.

Fortunately, after the umpteenth rendition of *Ging Gang Goolie*, night fell like a guillotine. The woman in charge of the girls clapped her hands and signalled it was bedtime. Mrs Fairbanks went back into the cottage, and an hour after the guides had been ordered into their tents, where they whispered and sniggered for hours keeping Mike awake, the guide leader crept to the bar and didn't return until close to midnight.

Mr Fairbanks came out after her, locked up and staggered home to the cottage. Mike watched as he zigzagged about, stumbling and staggering and falling all over the place.

But in all the time, Danny never once emerged from the cottage. The light from his bedroom window remained on for another hour, before it, and the rest of the cottage lights, went out, extinguishing the last remaining illumination in Lochside beside the partial moon. The darkness felt foreboding, eerie. As did the silence. The whispers in the surrounding tents had stopped and other than the wind rustling at the tents, all was quiet.

Not for the first time, Mike realised he was a long way from home. He zipped up his tent and slumped back on his sleeping bag. The Walkman lay beside him. He picked it up. The batteries had died days earlier, but he was in no mood for music anyway. He fingered it, opening and shutting the cassette tray.

Was he just being paranoid? Danny Fairbanks could have got his cassette player in all sorts of ways. Perhaps another tourist gave it him as a gift following a holiday romance. He looked the type girls normally went for. Athletic, broad shouldered, bad tempered. But it was still be a remarkable coincidence.

He cursed. He only needed a couple of minutes, and getting into the cottage would be simple enough. He noticed none of the family bothered locking the door when they went out, but the chance of Danny and his mother both going out one night looked slim, so Mike's plan was doomed to failure. It was a stupid idea anyway, he realised. He should leave it to the police. He'd speak to that Sergeant Sandilands in the morning. She'd know what to do.

Chapter Nine

An early morning chill signalled the onset of autumn. Mornings were always cold by the loch first thing in the morning, when the mist hovered over the water and the chill breeze wafted in from the sea. Sandilands always rose early. Even as a child, she'd find herself up long before her mum and dad. A day back then seemed to last so much longer. Growing up by the loch, meant a childhood full of adventure, boating, swimming, fishing, running around on the hills with her brother. She yearned for those days. For the excitement, the adventure. Perhaps that was the reason she joined the force, although a day's police work tended to disappear in a blur of paperwork and phone calls. Very little excitement and very little proper police work. Sometimes she wondered if it was all worth it.

She yawned as she strolled to the station, keys in her hand, ready for another day of Mrs Trench and her missing dog, altercations between farmers over insignificant stretches of land, and dishing out boating permits and fishing licences. Hardly action-packed.

She wasn't the first to arrive at the police station that morning. While walking up the hill, she saw the young American, Mike Cunningham in his bright red skiing jacket, propped up against the wall. Distracted by Anderson the previous day, she'd forgotten about Mike and his missing sister.

He stood up straight as she approached, so she gave him a smile and waved hello. 'Up early I see.'

He nodded. 'Couldn't sleep and wasn't too keen on facing Mrs Fairbanks' porridge. Was hoping to get a bagel at the bakery.'

'I doubt they'd know what a bagel is,' Sandilands said, unlocking the station door and pulling it open with a determined tug. 'I take it you're staying over at Lochside, then? Hear anything about your sister?'

Mike bit at his lip and glanced over his shoulders as he followed her into the station. 'That's what I want to talk to you about.'

'Oh!' She turned on the lights and lifted up the counter trapdoor.

'How well do you know of Danny Fairbanks?'

'Danny? Fairly well, I suppose.' Sandilands paused in the hatch. Danny has been in the same year as her brother at school. She and Danny had a few drunken dalliances over the years, but he had a roving eye, especially for the young girls that came to Lochside each summer. He was only a couple of years younger than she was, but had never grown up, not when it came to young girls, anyway. 'What about him?'

Mike bit at his bottom lip, hesitating. 'Well, it might be nothing. It's just that he has the same Walkman as my sister?'

'Walkman?'

He pulled out a silver cassette player from his jacket. 'Like this one, only red. I know you'll say it's just a coincidence, but it's a brand new model and I'm sure it's not out in the UK yet.'

She glanced at it. 'I don't understand. You're saying you think he has a Walkman similar to your sister's?'

'I know, it sounds paranoid, but he was very evasive when I spoke to him about her. Like he was hiding something.'

Sandilands should have been cross. Making wild accusations against somebody was serious, but she could sense the desperation in him. 'I'm afraid, that's just Danny. He's not the friendliest to strangers,' she said, almost adding, except to young women, but that would have heightened Mike's paranoia even further, and she knew it must be paranoia. Danny was many things, but a killer. Never.

'Isn't it at least worth asking him where he got it from?' Mike pleaded.

Sandilands sighed. 'Look, I'm really sorry about your sister, really I am, but you can't go around accusing people. I know the people around here, and nobody was as shocked as me when I heard about your sister's disappearance, but whatever happened to her, I'm sure it had nothing to do with Danny.'

'But can't you just ask him?'

'I'm sorry, not over a Walkman.'

Her radio crackled. She raised her hand and the lifted the walkie-talkie mounted on her lapel to her mouth. 'Go ahead Feathers.'

The radio crackled for a couple of seconds. 'Betty, are you at the station yet?'

'Yes, what's up?'

'I'm over at the dam.'

'The dam, why?'

'The night workers flagged me down on my way into town. They say they've found something in the water

'Found something, like what?'

'I think it's best if you just come over. Could be a body.'

While the words were almost lost in a crackle of static, Mike had heard them clearly. His eyes rounded, his mouth dropped open and his lip trembled.

'Now don't get ahead of yourself,' Sandilands snapped, staring into his eyes, her hand clutching the radio. 'Your sister is not the only person that's been reported missing around here.'

'Where's this dam?' Mike asked.

The radio crackled again and Feathers' voice sounded. 'You still there, Betty?'

She dropped her chin to the device. 'Okay, I'm on my way.' She looked back at Mike, his face a mixture of frustration and sadness. 'Look, go back to the campsite, as soon as I know anything I'll come and see you.'

'I'm coming with you,' he insisted.

'No you are not,' she snapped. 'I'll come and see you as soon as I've heard anything.' He looked like he wanted to protest but she raised her eyebrows. 'It's the best I can do.'

He nodded, reluctantly and she ushered him out of the station, just as a yellow-eyed and grey-faced gaunt figure, smoking a thin cigarette in between coughing up a lung, staggered towards them. It appeared Inspector Anderson and mornings were not good bedfellows.

'Good morning,' she said.

'What's so bloody good about it,' he muttered, giving Mike a wary stare.

She patted Mike on the back and gave him another sympathetic smile. 'I'll come see you later, okay?'

He looked at her, glanced at Anderson, looked back. 'Look, can't I come, I'll be no trouble.'

She glowered at him. He bowed his head, turned around and shuffled off back down the lane with hands thrust in his pockets. Sandilands shook her head in sorrow.

'What did that septic want?' Anderson asked.

'The what?'

'Septic tank—yank. He's an American ain't he?'

Sandilands sighed again. 'His sister went missing a few weeks back. Poor kid came all the way here looking for her. I'm glad you're here. I've just heard that they've pulled something out of the water over at the dam. It could be your man Briers.'

He lifted his head back and nodded. 'That might make sense, after what I've found out.'

She looked askance at him. 'What?'

'He checked into the hotel the day he went missing.'

'How do you know?'

'Spoke to that old harridan that runs it. Booked in, but never booked out. Didn't even sleep in his bed. Left owing her a night's board too. Reckon he must have gone for a long walk in the night and never came back.'

'I reckon it could be him at the dam then,' she said, relived. The last thing she wanted was for it to be the remains of Mike's sister.

Anderson snorted a lump of phlegm up from his throat and spat it on the pavement. 'Well, there's only one way to find out.'

Sandilands was too young to remember the controversy the building of the Morar dam caused after the war. She'd visited it when she was at school, though, and knew that by blocking the loch from the River Morar, which connected it to the Atlantic Ocean less than a quarter of a mile away, and forcing the waters through an intake, the small hydroelectric station provided enough power to serve Morar and the surrounding villages of

Lochaber.

All this she tried to tell Anderson as they walked the twenty minutes or so down the main road out of Morar. He was not the least bit interested, and instead spent the entire walk complaining about the distance while coughing and spluttering yet still smoking his thin cigarettes.

The police Allegro was parked alongside the concrete steps leading down to the power station and weir. Sandilands peered over the wall. She could see Featherstone. He was a gangly lad. Tall, thin, arms and legs like a daddy longlegs. His uniform always looked too small, but he had one of those frames where nothing fitted properly. Still, he was a good PC, sensible, diligent, not rash or prone to bravado. They got on well.

He was standing on the metal gantry running along the slipway. Beside him, a pair of power station workers. One was in a lifejacket, shaking his head at a something at Featherstone's feet. The other was wearing a wetsuit, complete with oxygen tank, and appeared to be pulling in a red inflatable dinghy from in front of the sluice as the waters cascaded over and dropped a yard or so into the river.

'Best see what they've got,' Sandilands said, coming away from the wall and leading Anderson down the metal steps, past the unimposing and small concrete power station and down to the gantry.

Spanning less than twenty yards, the still waters of the loch fell only a few feet over the spillway before turning into a foaming madness on the river, and the crashing, roaring and splashing rose to deafening levels as they descended.

Featherstone, his police helmet clamped low over his brow,

spotted Sandilands and Anderson as they made their way along the gantry, and he walked over to greet them.

'Sorry to drag you all this way on foot,' he shouted, his voice barely audible over the din of cascading waters.

Spray from the spillway speckled at Sandilands face so she wiped it off with her hand. 'That's okay, it's not that far,' she yelled, turning to Anderson only to see him clutching the handrail, his knuckles and face white as he peered over the railing at the surging waters below. 'Oh, this is that Special Brach inspector I was telling you about.'

'You both had better take a look at this,' Featherstone shouted, leading them over to the two dam workers. They were looking at a black bin liner lying in the middle of the gantry.

'Found them blocking the filter to the intake about an hour ago,' the dam worker in the lifejacket shouted. He was a middle aged, bearded chap with a stomach that pushed up the life vest so it barely covered his chest.

His colleague in the wetsuit was younger, shorter, thinner, he pointed to the bag at his colleagues' feet.

'Them?' Sandilands crouched down and opened the bin liner, revealing the contents. She looked at Anderson, whose lips parted as he saw what was inside. He then looked at Featherstone, who looked at the two men, and then everybody looked down at the collection of bones at Sandilands' feet.

Chapter Ten

Mike returned to Lochside and slumped into his tent, his mind racing with thoughts and fears and anxiety. Was this it? Had he found out what had happened to Sarah? He didn't want to believe it, wanted to think she was still out there somewhere. Perhaps Sandilands had been right and it wasn't her. Perhaps she was still alive. No, he knew he was just fooling himself.

Around him, Lochisde bubbled with the noise. The sounds of singing, squealing and girlish giggles surrounded him as the girl guides ran around in a fever. Some cooked breakfast, filling the damp morning air with the smell of bacon and eggs. Others walked past and waved and flirted their eyes at Mike, but he just sat and stared ahead.

If his sister had been found dead in the loch, then somebody was responsible for it. Somebody was hiding something. Sarah could swim like a fish, she would never have drowned. Not accidentally. And as far as Mike was concerned, there was only one person in Morar that was hiding something.

If creeping into the Fairbanks' house at night wasn't possible, that meant he'd have to try sometime in the day. As he pondered the deed, his mind flip-flopped. He didn't even know what he could possibly expect to find. He tried to think of anything distinctive he could remember Sarah owned. Other than the Walkman, he could think of nothing. Besides, he reasoned, if Danny had been involved in her death, he was hardly likely to hang on to her belongings. But what if he did? What if he decided to retain a keepsake or a trophy, Mike had heard of killers doing such things.

By eleven o'clock, the sun, hanging above the loch, turned the air humid and oppressive. Mike was used to such temperatures, Milwaukee had plenty of balmy days, even in September, but Scotland's Indian summer brought with it a humidity that made every inch of him sweat.

This perspiration chilled when he saw all three members of the Fairbanks family emerge from their home, leaving the cottage empty.

Mr Fairbanks came first, bleary eyed and unsteady on his feet as he trampled up to the bar. Next, Mrs Fairbanks dressed in a tennis skirt and vest, displaying tree trunk legs and the upper torso of a wrestler. Then Danny sauntered out of the cottage in tiny shorts that exposed his hairy thighs while his T-shirt showed off his defined but pale biceps. He strutted around like a cock in a hen house, flashing sly smiles to the more attractive and mature girl guides, as his mother busied herself handing out life vests and sorting through the oars and kayaks on the jetty.

The chaos of girls, dashing around the camp, quietened when the rather pale guide leader emerged, black bags under her eyes like two used teabags, and Mrs Fairbanks blew her whistle causing the gaggle of guides to line up like marines on parade.

'Right, then, listen up girls,' Mrs Fairbanks shouted, giving her whistle another peep. She walked up and down on the jetty like a sergeant major inspecting the troops. 'We want no silliness this morning. We want you to have fun, but the loch can be dangerous, so listen carefully to what I am about to tell you.'

She paused and scanned the girls with her eyes under unplucked brows to ensure all were listening. 'I promised the arkala here, I'd look after you all.' She nodded to the guide leader who stood clutching her head and looked very much as if she were about to puke. 'I can only do that if you all pay attention and behave yourselves. Now I want you all to watch how to put on the life jackets. Danny.'

Mrs Fairbanks slipped one of the life vests over her muscular chest and turned around for her son to tie it behind her.

'Watch how he does it,' she said, as Danny thrust a knee in her back and tightened the jacket like a maid fastening a corset. 'That's right, ensure it is tight.'

'Are you joining us Danny?' One of the young girls asked, fluttering her eyes.

'Danny will be on the shore as spotter,' his mother said, her life vest now squeezing her muscular torso. 'I won't be able to keep an eye on you all, so Danny will be the eyes in the back of my head.'

A couple of the girls tutted but Danny mollified them with a wink, which caused giggles and flushed cheeks.

Once everybody had secured their life vests, Mrs Fairbanks corralled them into a linc again by blowing hcr whistlc, and one by one, she and Danny helped the girls into the canoes that Danny had taken out the shed the day before.

While he, his mother and the guide leader oversaw the girl guides on the loch, and with Mr Fairbanks probably already drunk in the bar and the rest of the campsite all but deserted, Mike realised this was his chance.

He sat in his tent waiting, watching. Eventually, the girls were all in the water, so was Mrs Fairbanks, paddling about and blowing her whistle, while Danny looked on from the bank. Everybody was engaged, focussed, eyes away from the cottage and its front door. Everybody except Mike.

The melodious hum of the generator was loud, but quieter than the random crashing of waters on the weir, which is why Sandilands and the others took the grisly finds into the power station control room. The giant green dynamo turning the power of the water into energy for half the homes in Lochaber was visible through the panoramic window above a control panel that consisted of dials, switches and lights that flashed in rhythmic patterns, like a massive fruit machine. Resting against it, a dented and bent grille, similar to those that cover air vents, only much larger and dripping wet.

The dam worker in diving suit said he had removed it from the dam's intake when pressure dropped, only to find the bones that Sandilands now tipped on the control room floor.

'So what do you think?' the diver asked, staring down at the macabre collection, his wet suit tied around his waist. 'Human?'

Sandilands bit her lip, pulled out her truncheon and prodded at the bones. 'I'm not sure.' She turned over one particularly long bone. It looked like a limb to her, tibia or fibula perhaps but not human, although she couldn't be sure.

'They look like animal bones to me.' She said, looking across at Anderson for confirmation.

He was rolling a cigarette. 'Do I look like a bloody pathologist,' he snapped, shoving the stick-like smoke into his mouth.

'Could be sheep,' Featherstone said. 'They sometimes fall off the hillside into the loch.'

'Aye, we've pulled them out of the intake before,' the chubby dam worker said, still wearing his lifejacket. 'But normally whole carcasses.' He nodded to the bones, his face showing a mixture of revulsion and suspicion. 'Not like this. Look how clean they are.'

Sandilands nodded as she prodded at the bones, realising he was right. They were ivory white and polished, almost porcelain, with not a morsel of flesh or sinew stuck to them. 'Well, whatever they came from, they look like they've been in the water quite a while.' She looked up at Anderson. 'That rules out your ministry man.'

'Why don't you take them to Mr Kilkenny,' the portly and older dam worker said. 'He'll tell you whether they are man or beast.'

Sandilands stood, stretching out her back. 'Good idea.' She looked across at Feathers. 'What time does he get to his surgery?'

Featherstone glanced at his watch. 'About this time, I'd say.'

'Who is he?' Anderson asked, letting out a puff of blue smoke. 'The doctor?'

'No, local vet.' Sandilands replied. 'But he'll be able to us what these belonged to.'

Anderson removed his smoke like with thumb and forefinger, spitting a flake of tobacco from his tongue. 'Then you best get that lot bagged up, hadn't you.'

She sighed, crouched down and began prodding the bones back into the black bag with her truncheon.

Chapter Eleven

The veterinary surgery sat between a between a row of holiday cottages and tourist shops that sold everything from bucket and spades to postcards and potatoes. After dropping off constable Featherstone back at the station, Sandilands parked the old Allegro outside. After retrieving the black bag full of bones from the back seat, she slung it over her shoulder. Then, like a postal worker carrying a rather grim sack, she ushered Anderson into the surgery.

The door tinkled open and a dour looking receptionist, spectacles perched on the end of her nose, looked Anderson up and down, screwing up her face, before casting her eyes on Sandilands.

'Oh, Betty, how are you dear?' she said, rising from her padded seat behind the desk.

'I'm Fine, Mrs Travers. How's the old man?'

'Still the same, I'm afraid,' the woman tutted. 'Left him this morning as stiff as a board.'

Anderson's one eyebrow shot up his forehead.

'He's got a bad back,' Sandilands said.

'Bad!' Mrs Travers said. 'The poor wee soul is crippled by it.' Her eyes fell on the sack on Sandilands shoulder. 'I take it you're here to see the vet?'

'Yes. This is Detective Inspector Anderson from Inverness.'

Mrs Travers looked incredulously at Anderson's suit, before nodding to an adjacent door marked, surgery. 'He's with the McFinnigan's poodle. You can go in, if you like.'

Sandilands smiled her thanks and Anderson followed her

through the surgery door, in which they found a portly, tweed-wearing, fifty-something with a sour face and a pair of jowls hanging below his chin. The vet was stood over a table and grappling with a dyed-pink poodle that appeared to dislike being prodded because as Anderson and Sandilands walked in, it snapped and bit the vet across the palm.

'Damn ye, ye heathen!' yelled the vet, jumping back from the poodle. The dog then snarled at Anderson and Sandilands, causing the vet to turn round and notice he had visitors. 'Oh Betty, how nice to see you. Now, don't get too close!' he warned her, rubbing his wounded hand. 'Hercules here is in a terrible mood.'

Anderson smiled at the sight of the bouffant hound. 'Hercules?'

'Mr Kilkenny, this is Detective Inspector Anderson, from Inverness.'

'Oh, how do you do?' the vet said, just as Hercules snapped at him again. 'Damn it, I only want to clip you toenails, ye devil hound.' He left the dog on the examination table, which took the opportunity to lie down and lick itself.

'So what can I do for the police?' Kilkenny asked, walking over to the sink where he rinsed his hand under the tap and examined the dog bite.

Sandilands lifted up the black bag. 'Got something we're hoping you can identify. The dam workers found them stuck in the intake to the weir.' She placed the bag on another metal trolley on the other side of the surgery to the dog. 'We're hoping they are not human.'

She carefully tipped out the contents, which caused the dog to stand up and wag what was left of its docked tail as it eyed the bones.

Kilkenny, his eyebrows hunkered low, approached the trolley carefully. 'What do you have here, then?'

'We were thinking perhaps a sheep had fallen into the loch,' Sandilands said, as Anderson attempted to pat the poodle. A snarl made him retract his hand.

Kilkenny lifted one of the bones and scrutinised it 'Oh, definitely not a sheep.'

Anderson turned his attention from the dog. 'You think they could be human?'

Kilkenny smiled a broad grin and shook his head, causing his jowls to judder. 'Oh, heaven's no. Bovine by the looks of them.' He picked up another bone. 'Yes, definitely cattle.'

Sandilands let out a disappointed sigh. 'Well, excitement over. I guess a cow must have fallen into the water.' She shrugged at Anderson who tutted at the waste of time and took out his tobacco pouch.

'Doubt it.' Kilkenny said, shaking his head and causing his jowls to wobble like a bulldog. 'This animal was dead long before it was in the water.'

Anderson's fingers paused on his cigarette paper. 'And how can you tell that?'

'It's been cut, see.' Kilkenny brandished the bone at him, which caused an excited pant from the dog. 'By a bandsaw, I'd say.'

Anderson shrugged. 'I guess somebody must have dumped their Sunday lunch then.'

'I don't think so, Inspector,' Kilkenny said, still brandishing the bone. 'These come from several animals.' He placed the bone back down and picked up another. 'These are both right foreleg femur. That one's a rib, and there, they are both the same shoulder joint.'

Anderson licked his roll up closed. 'So what are you saying?'

'Well, unless somebody round here eats more than one cow for lunch, I'd say they are from dumped carcasses. And I bet I know who dumped them.'

Sandilands raised her head. 'Only one cattle farm around here—McGillivray's.'

Anderson frowned, the cigarette drooping from his lips, and remembered where he had heard Kilkenny's name mentioned before. 'Ere', didn't you use to work for the them?'

'That's right, until they gave me my marching orders just after Christmas. They'd got their own man in and said they didn't need me anymore, but I reckon that was just an excuse.' He nodded down to the bones on the table. 'And this could be the reason why ...'

'How do you mean?' Sandilands asked.

The vet shook his jowls, as if having second thoughts. 'It's probably nothing.'

'No, go on.'

'Well, the McGillivrays have got really industrial with their practices of late.'

'How do you mean?'

'Well, they brought in this Dutch consultant, a vet, although I use the word in its loosest possible sense. He got them to start pumping the cattle full of steroids and feeding them bone meal, practices I abhor, mind you.'

'And you reported them, is that it?' Anderson said.

'No, not for that, it's not illegal. Doesn't make it right, though.'

Anderson waved his unlit cigarette at him. 'So what's your point?'

'Well, at the end of last year, I noticed something odd in a few of their cows.'

Anderson struck a match and lit his smoke. 'Odd, like what, extra udders?'

'It looked like an outbreak of sorts.'

'Outbreak, of what?' Anderson shook out his match.

Kilkenny shrugged as he examined his wounded hand. 'Damned dog ... I'm not sure, Inspector. Had all the signs of spongiform encephalopathy.'

Anderson looked blankly at him. 'Spongy-what-now?'

'Scrapie,' Kilkenny said.

'Scrapie! I thought that only infected sheep?' Sandilands said, talking out her notebook.

'It does, but some of McGillivray's cows were showing similar symptoms.'

'Excuse my city-boy ignorance,' Anderson said, blowing out a lungful of smoke. 'But what's scrapie?'

'A degenerative brain disease found in sheep,' Kilkenny said. 'But I saw several cows demonstrating the same symptoms. I couldn't really explain it, still can't, but I'm convinced they were trying to cover it up. I mentioned it to Joe McGillivray, but the next time I went round to the farm, the infected cows were gone. Oh, several cattle were wearing the same ear tags, but I'm sure they weren't the same animals.'

Sandilands paused from her note taking. 'Did you confront

him about it?'

Kilkenny took out a pair of nail clippers from his pocket, eying the dog, warily. 'Of course, but he said I was mistaken, and then couple of days later he calls me up to give me my marching orders.' He pointed the nail clippers at the table of bones. 'They could very well be from those cows.'

'Shouldn't you have reported all this?' Anderson asked.

'I did. Called the Ministry of Agriculture, Farms and Fisheries a few months back, but I had no proof, and you know how slow these civil servants are.'

Anderson tapped his lips, the cigarette still burning between them. 'So you think McGillivray could have dumped these infected cows into the loch?'

'If there was an outbreak and he wanted to hide it, swapping the ear tags and getting rid of the carcasses would be the way to do it. He doesn't have an incinerator over there. So my guess is, yes, he slaughtered them and dumped them in the loch.'

Sandilands scratched her head with the end of the pen. 'But you can't prove any of this.'

'No, but it makes sense. And I'm a Dutchman if those cows I saw at the farm were the same ones that had been sick.' He approached Hercules again. The dog snarled as he neared.

Sandilands tapped the pen on her notepad. 'Didn't that vet at McGillivray's place say Briers was interested in the cow's ear tags?'

Anderson took the cigarette from his mouth and stared at the lit end. 'Aye, he did that. And he *was* a Dutchman. So what could that have caused the outbreak, the steroids?

Kilkenny approached the dog, nail clippers outstretched,

tentatively. He paused and faced Anderson. 'No, if it's a bovine form of scrapie it is degenerative, but it's still not on, filling cattle with hormones like that. Might have been spread by the bone meal, I suppose, and even if it wasn't, feeding cows ground up cattle bones is immoral in my opinion.'

Kilkenny shook his head and rested his uninjured hand on Hercules' behind. The dog didn't like it and went for him again.

'Blast!' Kilkenny shouted, shaking his hand, which now had an identical wound to the other one. He dashed to the sink and rinsed it under the tap. 'I don't mean to be rude, but unless there's anything else, I really do have to get on.' He gave the dog a contemptuous scowl.

Anderson nodded slowly, before pointing his cigarette at the bones. 'Don't forget those,' he said to Sandilands, who sighed and bundled the bones back into the black bag.

'Thank you Mr Kilkenny,' she said, slinging the bin liner back over her shoulder. 'You've been most helpful.'

'My pleasure,' he replied, staring at the ill-tempered poodle.

They filed out of the surgery and closed the door behind them, just as the sound of barks and snarls and blasphemes filtered back through it.

Chapter Twelve

The girls on the water squealed with delight, splashing each other, paddling in circles, some doing Eskimo rolls. It all looked like exhilarating, but Mike's heart thumped with its own excitement.

He sidled up to the cottage and glanced back at the water. Mrs Fairbanks was paddling around, preventing the girls venturing too far from the shore, while her son marched along the banks, shouting instructions to keep their hands central on the oars.

Mike looked up at Danny's bedroom window, before resting his hand on the open front door. After one quick look back to the loch, he took a couple of deep breaths and dashed inside.

Once in the hall, he rested the door back on its frame, but didn't shut it completely. He'd rehearsed this in this mind all morning, but still couldn't believe he was actually doing it. Turning around, he faced a staircase lined with trophies and medals. He panted breathlessly in his excitement and cantered up the stairs two at a time. He turned on the landing and dashed through the door opposite. Danny's room.

Pictures of half-naked women covered the walls, interspersed with a few football posters. Danny apparently supported Partick Thistle. A double bed took most of the space, but the room also had a wardrobe and chest of drawers. Mike quickly rummaged in the wardrobe, but saw nothing but clothing, before he fell on his knees at the chest of drawers.

One by one, he rifled through the drawers, but found nothing he could attribute to his sister, and nothing he could claim was sinister, apart from a pile of pornographic magazines and a small tin containing cigarette papers and a lump of hashish.

He felt frustrated. He was certain Danny had something to do with Sarah's disappearance, and he expected to find something, anything. Resigned there was nothing to find, he sighed, stood up, cursed his own paranoia, and then turned to the door, where Danny Fairbanks now stood, his face red, his lips curled back in anger.

'So what do you think?' Sandilands asked, as she threw the bag of bones into the boot of the Allegro.

Anderson flicked his cigarette to the ground and immediately began rolling another. 'About what?'

'What Kilkenny said about the possibility of the McGillivray's dumping cattle.'

He stuck a match and cupped his hands to light his smoke. 'Unless they're shoving heroin up the cow's arses, it's a job for the ministry.' He shook the match out. 'And we've only got the word of James Herriot in there.'

'Yes, but if it's true, it would give McGillivray a motive for Briers' disappearance.'

'Seems a bit of a stretch, to kill someone over a load of old syphilitic cows, or whatever it was they had?'

Sandilands nodded. It did sound unlikely. Joe was many things but she couldn't imagine him resorting to murder, even to protect the farm. Although he did love the place. As the largest employers in Morar and the surrounding villages, people treated him as some sort of laird. If all that was threatened ...

'But we do know Briers left the hotel that night,' she reminded him. 'Perhaps he went back up to investigate.'

Anderson's mouth let out a cloud of smoke. 'In the middle of the night? He was an inspector for farms and fisheries, not James bloody Bond. Besides, I told you, these ministry types are all manic-depressives. I'll bet my right bollock he is huddled under a bush somewhere with his pants down his ankles, his tadger in his hand and his wrists slashed open.'

'Nice image.' She wafted away the tobacco streaming her way. 'There's a chance though. Don't you think we ought to speak to him again? Ask him about the cattle bones.'

He stared down at the end of his smoke and rubbed his head, as if trying to remove an imaginary ink stain. 'Aye, I suppose so, but if I'm going back up to that crap factory, I want a drink first.' He glanced at his watch before nodding o the hotel at the bottom of the hill. 'C'mon, it's opening time.'

She pulled at her tunic, reminding him she was in uniform. 'Anyway, you are out of luck. Mrs Trench doesn't bother opening up in the day. Not this time of year.'

His jaw fell open. He looked like a child waking up to an empty Christmas stocking. He looked down the hill at the hotel with disbelief smearing his face. 'She has to. She has a bloody moral obligation.'

Sandilands' laughed, just as the radio on her lapel crackled into life. 'Go ahead Feathers.'

'How did it go with Kilkenny?' the constable said, after a fizz of static.

'Sorry to disappoint you but they were only cattle bones.'

'Tsk, ne'er mind. Anyway, where are you? We've had a call. There's been a burglary up at Lochside.'

'Burglary!'

'Aye, had a call from Mrs Fairbanks. Somebody broke into their cottage by the sound of it.'

Sandilands swore. That damned American. It had to be. 'I'm on my way.' She released the talk button and swore again.

'Bad news?' Anderson asked.

'Bloody fool.'

'Hey!'

'Not you. That American kid. Och, never mind, but if you want a drink that badly, you can come with me. I've got a visit to make at Lochside. Their bar'll be open.'

Anderson flicked his cigarette to the ground, grinned and jumped into the passenger seat. 'Well come on then, what you waiting for.'

Sandilands drove down the loch road that served the few small hamlets and farms on the north shore. It only ran a few kilometres and tractors comprised the only regular traffic. As a result, rutted grooves and potholes aggravated the worn shock absorbers on the Allegro's suspension, causing a tirade of oaths from Anderson as he bounced up and down on the passenger seat. At least the jostling prevented him from rolling his ghastly cigarettes.

As the trees cleared, revealing the waters of the loch and a few dinghies sailing around the islands, Anderson sniffed and pointed out the window.

'How come there ain't any anglers? It only needs to rain and leave a puddle in Glasgow before half a dozen bampots are dangling their rods in it.'

'Fishing has dried up of late,' Sandilands said. 'They reckon pollution or algae have wiped out the trout and salmon. Local papers are always on about it.'

She pulled off the lane towards the campsite, slowing as she negotiated the gravel drive. Instead of stopping in the car park next to the coach and smattering of cars, she decided to approach in the car, driving carefully down the grassy incline past the tents, and beeping the horn to move the crowd, consisting mainly of semi-nude young girls standing outside the cottage.

After yanking on the handbrake, Sandilands got out and placed her cap on and walked over to where Mrs Fairbanks was waving at her.

'Hey!' Anderson shouted. 'Where this bar.'

Sandilands sighed and pointed to the building in the middle of the campsite.

'Oh Betty, thanks for coming,' Mrs Fairbanks said, running up to her. 'Danny's caught someone breaking into our house.'

'Danny, where is he?'

'Standing guard. He's locked him in his bedroom.'

'Okay, you can leave it to me. Could you get everybody away?'

Mrs Fairbanks smiled and nodded, turned around and blew her whistle. 'Okay girls, the police are here now. I want you all back in the water. Chop, chop.'

Sandilands waited for everybody to disperse, before stepping into the front door. She found Danny Fairbanks sat on the top of the stairs, rubbing his knuckles.

'How you doing, Betsie?' he asked, flashing her a familiar smile.

He had always called her Betsie when they were young. She hated it. 'It's WPS Sandilands when I'm on duty, if you don't mind. What's going on?'

'It's that American that booked in yesterday. Knew he would be trouble. Bloody thief.'

'Where is he?'

'In my room. You remember where that is, don't you?' He winked at her.

She ignored it and pointed to the front door. 'Go wait outside.'

He handed her a key, stood up and marched out of the cottage. After he shut the front door, Sandilands went upstairs, unlocked Danny's door, pulled it open and gasped.

The face that looked up at her, bore little resemblance to the Mike Cunningham she had seen that morning. He sat slumped on the floor by the bed using his now bloodied T-shirt to dab at his wounds. A split lip, swollen eye, bleeding nose, reddened cheek. *Damn you Danny Fairbanks.*

She bent down. 'Are you okay?'

'Guess you think I deserve this.'

She removed her handkerchief from her pocket and wiped some of the blood from around his face. 'What the hell were you thinking?'

'I just thought I might find something, especially after hearing what you'd found.' He winced as she wiped the cut on his lip.

'Sorry,' she said, handing him the handkerchief. 'All we found were some old cattle bones. I told you not to jump to conclusions.'

His head dropped. 'I was just convinced Danny knew something.'

'Because of a Walkman?'

He bowed his head. 'Stupid, I know.'

Sandilands helped him up and lowered him on to the bed. 'Listen, I knew how you feel.' His brown eyes looked unconvinced. 'I lost my brother a few years back.' Sandilands felt moisture filling the corner of her eye. She inhaled deeply. 'I know how easy it is to blame other people, but you can't go breaking into people's houses over something as trivial as a Walkman.'

'I know. But look at me. The guy's an animal.'

'Maybe, but how would you react if you found a stranger in your bedroom?'

He sighed. 'I guess you're right. So what happens now? Am I going to jail?'

'Considering the pasting Danny's given you, I might be able to convince the Fairbanks to drop the charges and let me just give you a caution. By rights, I should be charging you both. Him with assault and you with burglary.'

By propping her arm under his, she helped him up and he hobbled to the stairs. 'Come on. You can wait in the car while I sort things out with them. Then we'll get you back to the station and clean you up a bit.'

His broken lips formed a smile. 'Thank you.'

'Don't mention it. But if you intend hanging around any longer in Morar, you'll have to find somewhere else to stay. I can't see that you'll be welcome here any longer. There's a hotel in the village.'

'That's okay. I don't suppose there is much point in staying. I guess I might as well go home.'

Sandilands felt both relief and disappointment, but wasn't sure why.

Chapter Thirteen

Mike sat in the back of the police car, dabbing at his wounds with Sandilands' handkerchief. His face stung. Danny's assault had been ferocious. When Mike turned to see him standing in the doorway, he'd tried to explain, apologise. Danny was in no mood to listen and punched him square in the face. The blow sent Mike barrelling over the bed, where Danny leapt on top of him and punched him about the head, repeatedly. Each blow fell harder than the last and Mike could do nothing but squirm and kick helplessly.

Now, as he leant over the front seat and examined himself in the rear view mirror, he could see the damage Danny's handiwork had done. His lip was split, both cheeks were bruised, and dried, crusted blood caked his nostrils.

Outside he could see Danny standing with Sergeant Sandilands. She kept pointing back to the car and wagging her finger in an authoritative, censuring, reprimanding way. Danny's face responded with aloof and uninterested expressions, casting occasional surly looks in Mike's direction. At least the girl guides were not about to witness Mike's humiliation. They were back on the water with Mrs Fairbanks, who appeared to be demonstrating Eskimo rolls, dipping her head under the water and spinning the canoe upright. It looked cold.

After further heated gestures from Sandilands, Danny skulked past the car, snarling his lips at Mike as he stomped back to the loch, where he propped himself against a tree, staring out at the water and the kayaking guides while occasionally sending dirty looks in Mike's direction.

Sandilands then walked to the car and tapped on the window. 'Just going to have a word with Mrs Fairbanks.'

Mike nodded and watched as she called the woman in from the water. Mrs Fairbanks blew her whistle and ordered the girls out of the loch, before paddling up to the jetty and pulling herself free. Sandilands helped her to her feet, and as the girl guides made their way to the shore, she and Mrs Fairbanks walked slowly away. A muted conversation followed, with Mrs Fairbanks making solemn nods and occasional glances at Mike.

He felt ashamed. The woman had been kind to him. A kindness he'd repaid by breaking into her home. He couldn't hold her gaze, so kept his eyes fixed on the girl guides clambering out of the water. He could see Danny with the guide leader, offering a few of the older girls a hand on to land. Laughing, joking, grinning.

One canoe remained on the water. Whether the girl had not heard the whistle or she was having too much fun, Mike didn't know, but she continued barrel rolling in the water, her splashing lost amid the gaggle of squeals and songs erupting on the bank. Through the windscreen, he watched her for a few moments as she splashed about, laughing to herself every time she managed to plunge in the water and right herself. A small girl, no older than twelve, she went over and over in the water, again and again.

Danny had seen her too and called her to shore. She couldn't hear, too engrossed in her Eskimo rolls. Danny waded a little in the water and called again, but his orders were lost among the squealing and giggling of the girls around him.

Another roll in the water was one too many. The girl never

managed to right herself, and slipped from the canoe. After a moment submerged, she appeared, bobbing in the water, laughing to herself, trying to swim back to her upturned kayak. However, it was drifting away towards the centre of the loch. Hampered by her paddle and lifejacket, she couldn't swim properly and the kayak got farther and farther away. She released the paddle and kicked hard.

Then the water erupted around her and something broke the surface. Something big.

The next moment lasted a second, no longer, but it replayed in front of Mike's eyes, and later through his mind, as if in slow motion. It was a large black shape, almost formless. Bigger than the girl, much bigger. It broke the water, lazily, not like a dolphin or whale, but like a piece of flotsam, bobbing up to the surface. Then it was gone.

And so was the girl.

The paddle and upturned canoe continued drifting across the loch, but of the girl, nothing.

Mike couldn't comprehend what he saw. One moment she was there, the next ... what? What was it he had seen? He looked across at Danny. He too was staring out at the loch to where the girl had been. None of the girl guides seemed to have seen anything, but eventually one turned round and pointed to the drifting canoe. She shouted.

'Emma? Emma!'

A few more girls turned round as did the guide leader.

The singing stopped.

The squealing stopped.

Screaming started.

Anderson walked into the little bar overlooking the loch, cigarette in his mouth, pound notes and loose change in his hand. He slumped on to a bar stool, and said, 'Scotch, large one,' before slapping a handful of cash on the counter.

'Yes, sir.' The ruddy-faced bar tender already looked half cut. He poured a drink from the optics and said, 'Think I'll join ye,' before handing Anderson the large whisky and pouring himself one. 'You not from round here, are ye?'

'No, thank God.' Anderson downed the Scotch and waved his glass for another. 'Glasgow born and bred.'

The barman downed his Scotch, shuddered, and poured them both another. 'Ye on business then?' He handed Anderson one of the glasses.

'Aye, you could say that.' Anderson necked the scotch in one mouthful, waving the glass for another.

Fairbanks breathed deep, and gulped down his before pouring another couple of drinks. 'So, what type of business ye in.'

Anderson pulled out his warrant card. 'Inverness Special Branch. DI Anderson.'

He swayed slightly before handing Anderson the scotch. 'Polis Inspector. Well, ye can have the next ones on the house then. Always like to look after polis *orificers*. The names Fairbanks.'

'Thank-ee.' Anderson took the glass, but only downed half of it, before pointing his glass above the bar and the large stuffed trout mounted on the wall. 'You catch that?'

Fairbanks took a swig of his scotch, turned around and grinned. 'Aye, a twenty-five pounder. Pulled it out of the loch a couple of years back.' He shook his head and poured the rest of the whisky down his throat. 'Won't find a fish that size in those waters now, though.' He lifted his glass, as if to offer Anderson another.

Anderson drank what was left of his existing whisky and handed Fairbanks the glass. 'So I hear. Problems with pollution, so I gather.'

'Pah,' Fairbanks said, pouring two more drinks. 'Them waters are as clean as a priest's tadger.' He handed Anderson the drink. 'Isnae pollution that's been killing all the fish,' he slurred.

'No, what then?' Anderson asked, taking a big mouthful of whisky.

Fairbanks placed his glass down and leaned his great bulk on the bar. 'Morag.' His eyes bulged almost out of their sockets as he said it.

Anderson frowned 'Who's Morag?'

Fairbanks straightened, closed one eye and stared out the window. 'I've seen her, so I have.' He curled up his fingers and waved his fist. 'A great big black beastie, eyes as big as this hand.'

Anderson lifted glass to his lips and swayed unsteadily in his seat. 'And how many of these had you had?'

Fairbanks shook his head, causing the rotund belly hanging over his trousers to wobble. 'Pah, ye can mock, Inspector, but I'm telling ye. I've seen it with my own eyes. T'was big enough to swallow a man whole.'

Anderson laughed. 'Yer pullin' my dobber.'

Fairbanks leaned forward, one eye open, the other closed, his breath caustic with whisky. 'I'll tell ye this much.' He turned his head to the window. 'Ye won't catch me on those waters. Not for all the whisky in Glenturret.'

A squeal and a scream caused both men to turn their heads to the window. Anderson realised some sort of excitement had broken out among the girl guides along the shore. 'What's up with them?'

Chapter Fourteen

Security locks prevented Mike from getting out the backdoors of the Allegro, so he sat stricken as he watched the pandemonium. The girls gathered on the shore to the loch, screaming, shouting. He'd seen Sandilands dash among them along with Mrs Fairbanks and the guide leader. After a few minutes of commotion, Sandilands helped the women into two canoes, after which they paddled out toward the upturned kayak drifting towards the centre of the loch.

The cacophony on the shore died down as everybody watched the two women circling on the water, eyes fixed beneath the surface. They searched for several minutes, but eventually Mrs Fairbanks lifted up her head and shook it at Sandilands on the shore.

Some of the girl guides started crying, and after a few more minutes of looking, Mrs Fairbanks and the guide leader returned to shore with the upturned canoe. Sandilands waded out to meet them. She helped the women clamber out and they dragged all three canoes out of the water. Then all the girls started crying, hugging each other and wailing.

As Mike watched it all unfold, he noticed Danny Fairbanks had skulked off back to the cottage. He'd seen what happened just as well as Mike had, so why wasn't he saying anything?

Mike tried the doors again, and even unwound the window, but it only went down so far, not enough for him to reach out and open the door, so he clambered over the front seats and pulled at the driver's door handle. It opened. He fell out of the car and ran toward Sandilands.

She had her notebook out, speaking to Mrs Fairbanks and the guide leader. Both had their heads bowed, hands rubbing at their foreheads. Mike approached warily. He knew Mrs Fairbanks would not be best pleased to see him.

'I saw what happened,' he said. 'I saw it.'

He had been right. Mrs Fairbanks scowled at him and the guide leader scowled and Sandilands scowled.

'It's your fault,' Mrs Fairbanks snapped, pointing her finger at him as if holding an imaginary dart. 'If you hadn't broken into our house, I wouldn't have been distracted.'

'You should have put the girls' safety first,' the guide leader said, rounding on Mrs Fairbanks.

'And where were you when one of your girls was drowning?' she retorted. 'Nursing your hangover. Aye, my husband told me how long you stayed in the bar last night.'

'Ladies, please,' Sandilands said, raising her hands to prevent the two women from coming to blows. She turned back to Mike. 'Go and wait in the car.'

'But I saw it,' he said.

'I'll take a statement from you in a minute.' Her eyebrows met as she frowned at him.

'You don't understand. I saw what it was that took her.'

Sandilands' eyebrows now formed a vee and she pointed at the car. 'I said wait in the car.'

'Please, wait ... you don't understand, it was a creature, an animal.'

'Now listen here!' Sandilands stepped forward, and for a moment, Mike thought she was going to hit him, but a voice caused everybody to turn round.

'Ye best listen to the laddie.'

Mr Fairbanks stood behind them swaying next to the scruffy, middle-aged man Mike had seen with Sandilands at the police station. He didn't know who he was, but he and Mr Fairbanks both looked drunk. Everybody stared in silence, broken only by the scruffy man, who hiccupped.

Morar police station only had one interview room, and with nearly a dozen people to speak to, Sandilands was forced to commandeer the dining room of the hotel, much to Mrs Trench's dismay. She clucked about offering tea, but was none too pleased about having a room full of teenage girls, especially ones who were crying and blowing their noses on her best napkins.

Sandilands and Featherstone conducted the interviews as best they could, despite the bereft sobs of the girl guides. Mrs Fairbanks, Danny and the guide leader all gave statements, as did the girls, although nobody had seen anything. The victim, Emma McFee, a fourteen-year-old from Fife, fell out of her canoe unseen. She'd not resurfaced.

Sandilands assumed she must have got caught in some reeds in the loch bed. The volunteer rescue service had sprung into action. It consisted of a couple of local farmers, the butcher and even Mr Kilkenny, who arrived at the loch sporting bandages on both hands. They turned up within fifteen minutes and were still searching the waters in their dinghies now. But so far, nothing.

It all sounded like a terrible accident.

Once they'd taken all the statements, Sandilands agreed with the guide leader and Mrs Fairbanks it best if the girls remained at the hotel. After the events of the day, it had been agreed that the girl's camping trip should be cancelled, but it was too late to go home now. Until the rescue service had finished their sweep, they would stay with Mrs Trench – If they did find the body, nobody wanted the girl's to witness it being dragged ashore. It was now getting dark. Sandilands suspected they wouldn't find her today.

She left Featherstone to keep an eye on everybody, while she walked back to the station. She needed to speak to the only person left to give a statement. Mike Cunningham.

Under the circumstances, she felt it best if he waited in the station. The boy had made some wild claims, but then, she knew because of his circumstances, he was a little unbalanced. Inspector Anderson was meant to be keeping an eye on him. Only when she walked in, she found the inspector sleeping with his feet up and Mike nowhere to be seen.

'Where the hell is he?' She demanded to know, kicking the inspector's legs off her desk and waking him up.

He sniffed, grunted and coughed. 'Ugh, what, who?'

'The American. The one you were meant to be watching.'

Anderson scrunched his eyebrows up and rubbed his face with his yellowing fingers. 'In the cells, where do you think?'

'What? I didn't say lock him up. For crying out loud.'

She walked out the back to the custody suite, where Morar's only two cells sat in a damp, dim corridor. They didn't get much use. Just the occasional drunk locked up for the night. They were relics from when the station was built sometime in the last century, and it was normal for those gaoled to toilet in a bucket.

She unlocked the cell and saw Mike sat on the bed, head down, arms hooked over his knees. He looked up at her through one good eye. The other was no more than a slit. His lip had swelled too.

'C'mon,' she said. 'Best get some ice on that face of yours.'

She led him into the office, where Anderson, rolling a cigarette, had his feet back on the desk. 'I thought I asked you to clean up his wounds?' she snapped.

He sniffed. 'Who the hell do you think I am, Florence bloody Nightingale?'

'Have you spoken to Danny?' Mike asked, as Sandilands sat him down.

'Yes, why?' She retrieved the first aid kit from the wall cupboard and opened it.

'Because he saw it too.'

Sandilands sighed. 'We'll talk about what you saw in a minute. Let me get you cleaned up first.' She dabbed at his wounds with an alcohol wipe, causing him to wince and stiffen. 'Well, I don't think you're going to need stitches.'

'No but you're going to look a bloody mess tomorrow,' Anderson said, unhelpfully, while blowing smoke rings at the ceiling.

'Can't you make yourself useful and get some ice.' She snapped, nodding to the fridge in the corner of the office, where she and Featherstone kept their sandwiches.

Anderson tutted but trudged over and removed the ice cube tray from the freezer department. 'He'll need to put steak on that, not ice,' he said, handing it Sandilands.

She snatched the tray from him and emptied a couple on to her hands. Mike still had her handkerchief, so she took it, flapped it out and wrapped the ice cubes in it. 'There, keep that on your eye, it should reduce the swelling.'

Pressing the bundle of ice cubes on his one eye, Mike appealed at her with the other. 'You think I'm mad, don't you?'

'No, but I think you are upset about your sister, that's all.'

'I swear to you, I something take that girl, something big. Ask Danny.'

Sandilands sighed. 'I've already spoken to Danny.'

Mike removed the ice pack from his face. 'What did he say?'

'The same as the others. He didn't see anything.'

'No, he's lying. He saw it. He must have done.'

'Now calm down,' she said, pushing the ice pack back on his face. 'I know you think you saw something, but it was an accident, that's all. A terrible accident.'

'Has the bairn turned up?' Anderson asked, his face looking almost genuinely concerned.

Sandilands shook her head. 'No. Rescue service is still down there, but so far, nothing.'

'Poor lass.' He took another suck of his roll up. 'Guess you'll have to call the divers in.'

She exhaled and nodded. It required divers to find her brother's body. They spent two days scouring the loch, eventually making the grim discovery in the reeds near one of the islands.

'If you want, I can call Frazer the Frog for you,' Anderson said, breathing out a mouthful of smoke.

She frowned. 'Who?'

He placed his cigarette in his teeth and smiled.

Chapter Fifteen

Gordon 'The Frog' Frazer learnt to dive during the war, in the navy, when he spent his national service planting limpet mines on German warships. He loved it. After he demobbed, Frazer knew whatever line he fell into, it would involve a diving regulator on his back.

During the fifties, Frazer spent a financially unfruitful career teaching tourists to dive in the ice-cold waters off Aberdeen. But that all changed when the police approached him to help in the search for a child, missing for nearly a year. Frazer agreed, and after two days scouring the depths of Inchgarth Reservoir, he found the boy's body. Despite the grim nature of his discovery, Frazer felt an unusual sense of satisfaction. It not only gave a family with a body to grieve over, but also provided enough evidence to convict the child's killer. It also turned Frazer into the Highland's first professional police diver.

Eventually he formed the Highland Underwater Search Team, Scotland's first fulltime diving unit, and he spent the next thirty-five years diving in Scotland's great lochs, rivers, canals and seas. He'd found everything from guns and knives, to drugs and bodies. Mainly bodies.

Six of them now comprised the Search Team, but with leave and sickness, only three sat with him in the van as it approached Morar that morning.

Young PC Jimmy Selkirk was in the back, helping Frazer check and recheck the equipment. Navy habits died hard. Jimmy had a pale face, shaved head and rugby playing shoulders that Frazer reckoned would only hinder his performance in the water.

Mostly they dived amongst piles of detritus, shopping trolleys, traffic cones, old tyres, all dumped in the waterways. Time would tell, he supposed, but as a probationary diver with only twenty hours dive time, for this trip, Jimmy would remain on shore.

Sergeant Foster drove the van. He always drove the van. He'd been with Frazer a long time. A stoically quiet man, with long, thin limbs, he swam better than anyone Frazer had ever known. They had dived together for years. More than once Foster had saved his life. But as he was recovering from a bad case of gastroenteritis, probably earned on their last outing in a cold, rat infested canal, he too would not be going in the water this trip.

That left PC Ramsey. Also a new recruit, and while he had less experience than Foster, Ramsey, like Frazer, had served as a Navy clearance diver, and like Frazer, had seen his fair share of action, mostly in the Falklands, blowing up Argentinean mines and defusing unexploded torpedoes lodged in British ships. A misjudgement onboard HMS Atlantic left him badly burned on his left side. While his injuries had ended his military career, Frazer was only too happy to have him.

Frazer and Ramsey would take it in turns to dive alone. Rules, devised by Frazer, stipulated that for every man in the water, three had to be either in the rubber support boat or onshore. It was a rule Frazer occasionally broke, but he'd promised his wife he'd take no more chances. He only had a year left before his pension kicked in. After that, it would be a life of travelling, diving in the barrier reef and warm waters of the Caribbean.

He'd not dived in Morar for a few years, and was looking forward to it. Besides being the deepest loch in Scotland, it had crystal clear waters, unlike the peat and silt blackness of Loch

Ness. Normally he worked in near zero visibility, in filthy quagmires, relying on fingertip searches. Through sludge, through silt, through debris, finding anything at all tended to be more art than science. Morar would make a nice change.

The village was basking in sunshine as the van pulled up outside the tiny police station. Ramsey gave a yell that they'd arrived, pulled on the handbrake and Frazer and the team piled out the back.

'Okay lads,' Frazer said, arching his back. 'Stretch your legs and I'll find out where we're going, but don't wander off.'

He marched into the police station where a young policewoman greeted him with a smile from behind the counter. Behind her, a familiar face, feet up on a desk, a customary fag stuck between his teeth.

'How you doing you old flatfoot,' Frazer said, as Anderson stood up and thrust his hand over the counter. 'Not seen you since that business up in Lomond.'

'Don't remind me,' Anderson said, shaking his head at the memory. 'Still makes me queasy thinking about it.'

'Not managed to get your sea legs sorted yet, then?'

'Pah, if God wanted me to swim, I'd have a fin where my arsehole is.'

The young policewoman, her hair tightly bunched behind her cap, shook her head. Anderson nodded to her.

'This is Sergeant Sweaty Glands,' he said, slapping her on the back.

'It's Sandilands,' she snorted, scowling at him and extending her had to Frazer.

'He's an old charmer, isn't he? Please to meet you.' Frazer

gave her a gallant smile, the one he kept for barmaids, attractive ones, before turning back to Anderson. 'So what we looking for?'

'Don't ask me. I'm just an observer.' He nodded to Sandilands. 'It's her shout.'

Her taut features tightened further. 'A drowned girl. Fourteen-years-old. Fell in the loch on the north shore. Didn't resurface.'

Frazer shook his head. 'Damn shame.'

'Her name was Emma–'

Frazer halted her with his hand. 'I don't need to know.' He tried never to think of the bodies he searched for as people. Would make the job too difficult. Especially with children. A name only made things harder. 'Just show me where.'

'Okay, you can follow me up.' She looked round at Anderson. 'You coming?'

'Okay, but I want to go back to that farm at some point today. See what McGillivray has to say. With any luck, I might be able to make the afternoon train and get back to somewhere where the pubs open when they are meant to.'

Frazer laughed. 'You don't change, do you?'

Mike had risen early. While the bed at the Morar Hotel provided better comfort than he'd experienced in days, he had hardly slept. His face stung. The swollen lip, black eye and bruised cheek, made lying on his side difficult, but that wasn't what kept him awake.

He sat in the dining room in the hotel nursing the same cup of tea and bowl of muesli for near two hours. Eventually, Mrs Trench politely told him to go. She needed to clean. He heard her mumble about the mess left behind from the girl guides, who were also all staying at the hotel. Thankfully, they were not there when Mike descended the stairs. Their leader had apparently taken them for a long walk in the hills, to take their minds of the tragedy. Mike doubted it would work

Realising he'd outstayed his welcome, he left the dining room and stepped out of the hotel. While bright and cloudless, he found the morning chilly, even under his skiing jacket, so he decided to warm himself with a walk. Morar was a pretty place and he'd seen very little of it since his arrival. Besides, a walk might help him make sense of what he had seen, or thought he had seen the previous day.

He headed along the path to the south shore of the loch. His legs carried him automatically as his mind wondered back to the events of yesterday, but no matter how far he went, and he walked a good distance, little was making sense.

Had he imagined it? Yet as he strolled along the south bank of the loch, his eyes staring at the rippling water, he knew something was down there. He had only glimpsed it for a fraction of a second, but he'd replayed the scene over and over again in his mind. Each time, a splash, followed by the dark hump bulging out of the water, and then the girl was gone.

Certain at what he saw, Mike knew Danny had seen it too. He had to have done. So why hadn't he said anything?

Before the incident, Mike had decided to leave, to go home back to Milwaukee. Now he knew he had to stay. He had a feeling whatever was lurking in the loch had something to do with Sarah's disappearance, and whatever it was, Danny knew more than he was letting on.

By the time he stopped for a rest, it was well into the afternoon. The south shore wasn't as pretty as the north. It had no proper road traversing the water's edge, fewer trees, not as many farms or pretty hamlets, and nothing but midges and sheep to look at. It was only when he looked over to the other shore, and saw the little jetty and the tents fluttering in the breeze, did he realise he was opposite Lochside.

The distance between the two shores wasn't far, so he sat on the bank leading down to the water and watched. The campsite bustled with activity. Sandilands was there, not that he could see her, but he recognised her police car parked close to the water's edge. Beside it sat a van, and several figures gathered about it. He knew what they were.

That morning, he'd overheard Mr Trench explaining to one of her customers that the rescue service hadn't managed to find a body. Police divers had been called in. Mike assumed that must be them. Perhaps, he thought, they might find more than one body in the loch.

The campsite was quiet. The girl guides had come for their belongings and left that morning. And the few other guests either were out, or had been ordered by Sandilands to keep their distance.

She stood on the jetty and watched the divers make their preparations. Frazer looked comical as he emerged from the van in his scuba gear. He waddled past her like a proud duck, in flippers, a black wetsuit — his middle-aged spread bulging in the rubber — a hood that covered his head and a diving mask on top of it.

Two of the other team members, both in the same black wetsuits, had inflated a yellow dingy, complete with outboard motor. It now bobbed on the water by the jetty. After a brief discussion with Frazer, the two men clambered aboard, started the motor and headed out into the loch, towing a thin line behind them.

The other member of the team, clutching a handheld radio and dressed in civvies, jeans, T-shirt and big heavy boots, tied off the guide rope to a weighted stand on the jetty. He then tied another line around Frazer's waist, before securing that to the guideline with one of those metal clamps climbers used. Two scuba tanks sat on the jetty, and the young officer helped Frazer place one on his back. After a few checks, a yell to the support boat and several thumbs up all round, Frazer stepped off the jetty with his front leg outstretched and plunged into the water with a splash.

Sandilands watched him submerge, the bubbles foaming on the surface above him. Memories of years before flashed through her mind. She'd not watched the divers trawling the loch for her brother, but she'd imagined it plenty of times.

She watched as his breathing apparatus bobbed on the surface as he scanned below the water line. The search was methodical. Frazer made his way along the guide rope towards the dinghy. After ten minutes, he broke the surface by the boat, pulling his mask up and gesturing with his hand.

The dinghy then moved off a few yards farther up the loch, and the young man onshore, moved the weighted stand along the bank, keeping it parallel to the dinghy. Then Frazer submerged again.

Splashes and bubbles showed his path back to the shore, where he emerged minutes later before making further gestures. Again and again he went under. Each time the dinghy and guide rope moved farther and farther down the loch. Eventually, after spending over an hour on the water, the dinghy headed back inshore and Frazer waddled out of the loch on to the sandy beach and pulled up his mask.

'Nothing in the shallows,' he said, wiping water off his face as he walked up to Sandilands. 'We're going to take a breather then try further out. The water gets deep there though, so I'm not sure how far we can go.'

Sandilands nodded. Morar's depth was something about which the people of the village boasted. But not today. The deepest loch in Scotland and deepest body of water in Britain was now a deep grave.

The rest of diving team scrambled off the dinghy. Despite the grim nature of the task, everyone remained in good spirits. A few lit cigarettes. Frazer waddled to the van, retrieved some sandwiches and distributed them among his men and they all ate them on the tailboard, Frazer still with his flippers on.

Even Anderson and Mr Fairbanks came to assist, carrying a tray of beers and crisps. 'For the lads,' Anderson said, but Frazer shook his head.

'Sorry, Inspector. Not until the dive's done for the day.'

Anderson and Fairbanks exchanged shrugs and took two pints each. 'Not found her yet, then?' Anderson asked, sipping the head from one of the beers.

Water still clung to Frazer's wetsuit hood and it sprayed off him as he shook his head. 'As I was just telling the sergeant here.

It gets deep pretty quick away from the shore, but there are still plenty of reeds to look through near the shallows, and if she's anywhere, it'll be there.'

'You watch yon back,' Fairbanks said, raising one of the pint glasses in his shaky hand. 'There's something unearthly in those waters.'

The eyes of all divers fixed on Fairbanks. All had the same expression on their faces. Anderson cocked his head at the drunken old man. 'Apparently Nessie's cousin is down there.'

Laughter erupted from the divers and Frazer hopped off the back of the van, a big smile on his face. 'I've seen plenty of strange things under the water, pal, but yet to come across a loch monster.'

'Yeah, well you ain't seen my ex missus taking a bath.' Anderson said, causing everybody to erupt into more laughter. Everybody except Fairbanks.

Chapter Sixteen

'How do you want to do this, skip?' Ramsey asked, as he, Frazer and Foster chugged out in the dinghy. 'Drop arc line?'

Frazer scratched at his wetsuit hood and nodded. Yes, a drop arc line would be the best way to examine the deeper waters. It involved a weighted line dropped overboard and the diver, which in this case would be Frazer, connected to the line by a climber's metal-sprung carabiner and a safety line around his waist. He would descend the drop line and search in an arc around it, keeping the safety line taught. Gradually he would let out more line, spiralling out, examining a wider circumference. It took time, but it was the only way they could search deep water like this thoroughly enough.

'I'll do the first sweep,' he said. 'You can do the next. We'll take it in turns until we can't go any deeper. It drops off pretty steeply but I doubt she's far from shore.'

While Frazer doubted the mild current of the loch could have carricd thc young girl's body too far from the shore, if she was anywhere below a hundred and thirty feet, she would be down there for good. Frazer had set that as a limit and never dived lower. Ever. It represented to much risk. Oxygen toxicity, nitrogen narcosis and decompression sickness were all killers.

Foster lifted the radio to his mouth to let Selkirk know what was going on, while Ramsey checked Frazer's tank and tied a line around his waist. They all knew the drill.

While all three men had wetsuits on, only one would be in the water at any one time. The other two in the dinghy would ensure the line remained straight, while Selkirk would watch from the shore, keeping an eye out for boats, changes in weather, anything that threatened.

Frazer devised the diving system years before. It worked. In all the searches he had conducted, in the great lochs, in the swirling rivers, in the stormy seas, and in the murky, rubbish littered canals, he'd never once lost a man. Not yet. And he planned to keep it that way.

Selkirk's voice crackled back on the radio and Foster gave a thumbs up. Ramsey dropped the weight into the water and connected Frazer's safety line to it using the caribiner. Following a good luck pat from both men, Frazer grabbed his underwater light, placed the regulator in his mouth and fell backwards into the depths.

He lingered on the surface for a while, allowing his body to acclimatise to the cold. His skin shrivelled at the shock and his limbs shook and trembled. He was getting old. The layer of water in his wetsuit took far longer to warm him than it used to, but eventually, the shaking subsided, and after gesturing an okay sign to those in the dinghy, he submerged, head first.

During the first search, in the shallows, visibility had been excellent and Frazer could see the loch bed clearly. The reeds, stones, little fishes darting beneath him. Here, the sunlight struggled to penetrate the greater depth.

He turned on the underwater light and pointed it down as he descended the guideline. A steady stream of bubbles floated across his mask from his regulator. He kept his legs still, flippers barely moving, allowing his body to sink slowly.

At sixty feet, measured precisely by his depth gauge on his wrist, the bottom of Loch Morar finally appeared below. The bed sloped away steeply. While directly beneath, Frazer could see the sparse forest of reeds blowing around in the gentle current and the pebbles and rocks and stones littering the floor, a little farther out, it all disappeared out of sight as the loch floor dropped downwards.

At eighty feet, he floated just above the reeds. He released the line and allowed himself to drift until the safety rope around his waist tightened. Gently he kicked, swimming in a circle around the guideline. His head down, underwater light extended in his arms, eyes transfixed on the bed below.

Occasionally he had to drop among the larger reeds, pulling them clear to ensure nothing hid among them. But in the main, visibility remained good. Once he completed one arc, he released another five yards of line from his waist and began another.

This time, as the arc swept him farther away from shore, he had to drop lower to keep the loch bed in view. Ninety feet by his gauge. And the deeper the bed fell, the denser the reeds became. He swam among them, carefully scanning the silt and sand. Still nothing.

He knew he could maybe manage one more arc, perhaps going as far as fifteen yards from the guideline, which would also be another ten or fifteen feet down. Already, he could feel the pressure squeezing his chest and the bubbles from his regulator became too numerous for his liking. But he pulled free another five yards of line and searched as before. The dark waters now hid the vertical guideline descending from the boat, but he kept the line around his waist taut, ensuring he was just one tug from safety. Still, this was as far out as he'd dare dive.

With a longer circumference, the search took more time. Near the shallows, he skimmed over areas he'd already searched, but following the downward slope of the loch bed, he took his time, carefully checking among the reeds and swimming carefully between them, like a flatfish looking for a meal.

As he reached the farthest point away from shore, his depth gauge told him he'd gone beyond a hundred feet. Farther out, the loch bed plunged even steeper and deeper, the bed dropping away dramatically. He knew in places it exceeded a thousand feet where no diver could reach such depths, but he doubted the little girl's body would have found its way that far from shore. Still, even at just a hundred feet, the light from his underwater torch failed to penetrate more than a few fathoms and he had to squint and strain his eyes.

Then he saw something, something among the reeds and pebbles. Strange objects his eyes couldn't make sense of. Rocks perhaps, although their blanched colour looked far paler compared to the other pebbles and stones. Curiosity overpowered his squeezing chest and the rapid expulsion of bubbles from his regulator. After loosening a few more yards of safety line from his waist, he kicked his flippers and dived lower to where his depth gauge needle flickered into the red, pointing past a hundred and ten feet, far deeper than he'd dived in years.

What were they?

He darted down among the reeds until the blanched stones were within arm's length. Only they weren't stones, he could tell that now.

Bones. Hundreds of them.

They dotted the loch bed in all shapes and sizes. Leg bones, ribs, vertebrae, even skulls. But they weren't human. Judging by their size, they must have been either cattle or horse. They littered the loch bed like some mass grave, as if an ancient battle took place under the water and hundreds of slain animals lay where they fell.

Bubbles cascaded from his regulator as his surveyed the macabre field of remains. He'd not found the missing girl, but clearly he'd found something. He'd not bought a net with him to take any of the bones back up, but he would make sure Ramsey did when it was his turn. He was younger, fitter, could dive deeper.

Aware his heart thumped like an ungoverned piston, he took one last look and tugged on his safety cord and made his way back to the vertical guideline. Once he'd caught hold of it, he stretched his head back, faced his mask up and gently kicked, floating slowly up.

He rose slowly, keeping his speed on a par with the rise of bubbles from his regulator. He'd seen in the war what decompression sickness, or the bends as they called it, could do to a man. The nearest decompression chamber was a hundred miles away and he didn't intend to spend the rest of his life a paraplegic.

Then a dark flash from below caught his peripheral vision and he halted his ascent. He peered into the gloom. *What the hell was that?*

It looked big, but then he knew the depths had the habit of playing tricks on divers. Even a modest sized trout or salmon could cast a shark-like shadow. Must have been a pike or salmon, or even an eel. He knew they grew pretty big in the lochs. He dismissed it, looked back up the guideline and kicked gently again.

Chapter Seventeen

Mike watched the divers from the opposite shore for over an hour. As far as he could tell, they'd not found anything. He knew they wouldn't. Whatever it was in the loch had ensured of that. He shivered at the thought.

His stomach finally made him stand up, dust himself off and begin the long trek back to the village. His appetite had returned with an angry growl.

He walked back with both his legs and mind wandering uncontrollably. Perhaps Sandilands was right, perhaps he was losing his mind, perhaps he did only see what he wanted to. Yet somehow, he knew in his wildest imaginings, he couldn't conjure up something so bizarre, so weird, so monstrous.

If only she would listen to him. Let him explain properly. The only person he could think of who seemed to have any belief in what he had seen was Mr Fairbanks. Perhaps he should have listened to the old drunk more carefully. He thought about paying him a visit, but Sandilands had warned him not to venture near Lochside, and Mike doubted Fairbanks ever ventured far from his precious bar. Besides, the people of Morar were hardly likely to listen to the town drunk any more than a mixed up American. No, Mike decided as he climbed the hotel steps and walked into the dining room, it was down to him to make people listen.

Mrs Trench was now serving afternoon tea to the smattering of guests at the hotel. An elderly couple Mike had seen at breakfast, a couple of late season tourists enjoying tea and cakes and a chubby man with square glasses and an unshaven face, sitting at the back.

Mike sat down and waved over Mrs Trench, who took his order or baked beans on toast, a cup of tea and a chocolate éclair. His American accent seemed to cut through the sound of clattering china and muted Scottish chatter and he felt several pairs of eyes on him. In particular, the chubby bespectacled man gave an intense, curious stare.

After Mrs Trench returned a few minutes later with his meal, the man sidled over. 'Are you an American?' he asked, a cup and saucer wobbling in his hand.

'Er ... yes, sir,' Mike replied, his mouth full of beans.

'Mind if I join you?' The man gestured to the empty seat with his cup and saucer.

Mike shrugged. 'Sure.'

The man thrust out his hand. 'The name's Greg Hanson, how do you do.'

Mike shook it. 'Mike Cunningham. You from round here?'

The man sat and placed his cup and saucer on the table. 'No, Fort William. I'm here on business. How you enjoying your holiday?' He touched his cheek. 'Been in the wars, I see.'

Mike rubbed his wounded face. 'Something like that. Not been much of a holiday.'

Hanson nodded, solemnly and picked up his tea. 'I suppose not. I heard about the drowning on the loch yesterday. These sorts of things would put a downer on anybody's holiday. Terrible business.'

Mike dropped his head.

'You didn't know her, did you?' Hanson asked.

Mike shook his head and sighed. 'No, but I was there.'

Hanson's teacup clattered back on to its saucer. 'You saw what happened?'

Mike nodded. 'I guess so.'

'That must have been awful. It's the family I feel sorry for, especially as she was so young. Such a terrible accident.'

Mike couldn't help but sniff. He alone knew there was more to it than just an accident.

Hanson's eyes opened wide. 'What? Do you know something?'

Mike shook his head. 'Oh, nothing. I doubt you'd believe me if I told you. Nobody else does.'

'Try me,' Hanson said, clasping his hands together and leaning forward like a comforting padre.

Mike sighed. What did he have to lose? Everyone else though he was crazy, so what would it matter if one more person did. 'Before the girl disappeared, I saw something in the water?'

'Something, like what?'

Mike shrugged. 'I don't know. All I remember is that she was splashing about and the next thing this big, black shape appears out of the loch. After it disappeared, the girl was gone.'

'Can you describe it?' Hanson asked, his hand slipping gingerly into his jacket pocket.

'No, I only saw it for a second ...' Mike realised that Hanson had pulled out a notebook and pen. He looked down at it. 'Sorry, you never told me what business you were in.'

'Didn't I? My apologies. I'm chief reporter for the Lochaber News,' Hanson said, grinning.

'Bones, what do you mean bones?' Anderson asked, as he had Sandilands' listened from the police car. They were about to go back to McGillivray's farm, Anderson still had his investigation to finish and all these distraction meant his chances of leaving town that afternoon were getting slimmer and slimmer.

Sandilands turned off the ignition, causing an audible sigh from Anderson. 'What type of bones?'

Frazer stood at the car window with one of his divers. Both men still had their wetsuits on, although their flippers now hung at their hips. Frazer nodded back to the other diver who removed his hood and revealed a scarred face that looked to Anderson as if somebody had taken a blowtorch to it. He had a bag at his feet. He lifted it up and tipped upside down, spilling out a selection of bones on to the grass.

'They're either cattle or horse,' Frazer said, looking down at the grim finds.

'And there's lots more where that came from,' added the scarred man. 'That's all my bag would hold.'

Sandilands hung her head out the window to examine them, before looking back at Anderson, her eyes wide. He leant across her lap and peered through the window.

The bones looked like the ones found by the dam workers, all polished, porcelain white. 'There's more of them, you say?' he asked, staring at the discovery.

'Hundreds of them,' Frazer said. 'I tell you, I've never seen anything like it. If you want them taken out, it will take weeks.'

Anderson looked up at Sandilands, who appeared uncomfortable with his skinny frame strewn across her lap. 'No, that' okay. Just keep looking for the girl.' He pointed down to the bones. 'But pack that lot up and put it in the boot.' He slid back into the passenger's seat. 'It appears your pal McVet was right.'

'So he does have more questions to answer. This gives him even more motive for Briers' disappearance, wouldn't you say?' Sandilands said.

Anderson hated to admit it, but she was right. While the few bones found at the dam and the vet's admission was one thing, this was another. If Frazer was right, the McGillivrays must have been dumping cattle for months, perhaps longer. The ministry clamped down hard on such things. If Briers had suspected something, McGillivray was not only looking at losing his farm, but gaol too. Anderson knew men would do almost anything to avoid that. Damn it. Was he ever going to get out of this place?

'Right,' he said, his teeth clenched tight. 'Let's get over there.'

'So, can you describe this thing?' Hanson asked, his notebook in hand.

Mike stared down at his beans. They had started to go cold, developing a wrinkled film across the top. He pushed the plate away from him. 'If I knew you were from the papers, I wouldn't havc said anything. I don't want you to print this. People think I'm mad as it is.'

He stood up to leave.

'Too late, Mr Cunningham,' Hanson said. 'Tell me, is that one 'N or two?'

Mike stopped and turned round. 'I don't want my name in the papers. I'm in enough trouble with the police as it is.'

Hanson's grin widened. 'Well, we can do this one of two ways, Mr Cunningham. I can either quote what you've said, or you can tell me the whole story, and I'll leave your name out of it.'

Mike sat back down. He felt he had little choice.

Chapter Eighteen

The animal squirmed when van Burgh loaded it into the metal yoke, as if it knew what was coming. A hiss sounded from the bolt gun and the cow slumped into the metal collar, dead.

Van Burgh pressed the release button and the cow dropped down the chute and on to a trolley.

'Keep it away from the other carcasses,' he said, as one of the abattoir workers pushed the trolley away. 'And make sure you clean the saws after you've butchered it. With solution, not water.'

The worker nodded. 'Yes, Mr van Burgh.' Then he scuttled off, giving Joe McGillivray an awry glance as he stood watching the slaughter, arms folded, eyes narrow, cheeks flushed red.

'How many more is there?' he asked, as van Burgh corralled another cow into the yoke using an electrical cattle prod. 'Those four and six more possible,' he said, pointing the prod at four more cows lined up in the holding pen. Behind those were the regular pens, where over a hundred cattle waited to be turned into fine cuts of beef. But normal operations had been suspended that morning, after van Burgh had found more animals demonstrating symptoms of disease.

'Six, you sure there's no more?' Joe asked, his lip curled up.

Van Burgh shook his head. 'I don't think so, no.'

'You don't *think*?' Joe walked over and jabbed his finger in van Burgh's chest. 'You didn't *think* feeding my cows ground up cattle bones would do them any harm either, did you?' He began mimicking van Burgh's accent. 'It will save you money Mr McGillivray. Increase your yield Mr McGillivray.' He pushed van

Burgh backwards towards the holding pen. 'I should have known better than to listen to some tulip eating foreigner.'

Van Burgh looked at his feet. Having worked with animals all his life, he knew eye contact was the easiest way to antagonise them, and Joe was more animal than man. '...I told you, Mr McGillivray ... it's something new, I couldn't have ...'

'Ahem.'

The cough caused both men to turn round. Standing behind them and looking uncomfortable in the bloody surroundings of the slaughterhouse, stood one of the security guards. 'Mr McGillivray, sir.'

Joe frowned at him. 'Yes, what is it?'

The man took off his cap. 'Sorry to disturb you, but that police inspector has just pulled into the gates with Sergeant Sandilands.'

Joe's eyes widened, as did his nostrils, and his face turned red as if his head it had been boiled. The security guard scuttled away, sensing the tension.

'Thcy ... thcy know, don't thcy?' van Burgh said. He didn't know what he feared the most: the police, prison, or Joe McGillivray.

Joe snatched the cattle prod from van Burgh's hands and thrust it under the man's chin. 'All this is your fault.'

Van Burgh found himself on tip toes, shuffling backwards until his back was pressed against one of the doomed cows in the holding pen. The animal mooed.

Joe removed the cattle prod and held it an inch from van Burgh's eyes. 'We're going to have to deal with them the same way we did that farm inspector.'

'But, Mr McGillivray, sir, they're the police,' van Burgh protested.

Joe turned the cattle prod on. It caused van Burgh to jump as it buzzed and a sparked in front of his face. 'I know exactly what they are,' he said. 'Now go and bring them here.'

Anderson had again pulled his jacket across his face as they arrived at McGillivray's yard. The day had been hot and sticky, making the smell even stronger. Sandilands didn't mind it herself, and found it rather bracing, but Anderson was positively green.

'Jesus,' he said. 'I forget just how bad this place stank.'

'Thought you'd have got used to it by now,' Sandilands said, as she pulled out the black bag full of bones from the boot of the Allegro. 'So what's the plan? We going to arrest Joe?'

Anderson lowered his jacket and looked down at the bin liner. 'I think we'll need more than that. Besides, we don't know if Briers even came back here. The *ee'jit* didn't tell anybody what he was up to. Bloody civil servants. I blame their public schooling. Puts silly notions into their head. That and a penchant for buggery.'

'Then what are we doing here, with this?' She waved the bag of bones at him.

Anderson bobbed his eyebrows up and down. 'Let's see if we can't smoke 'em out.' Suddenly his smile dropped and his nose scrunched up as a gust blew across the yard, intensifying the smell.

'Ugh,' Anderson said, gagging. 'Next time I'm bringing a bloody gas mask.'

Sandilands laughed again and the pair walked across the yard towards McGillivray's office but had to jump out of the way after a horn sounded and the green Rolls Royce squelched past them in the mud and ground to a halt beside the Land Rover already parked in front of the office.

The Roller's passenger door opened and the young busty secretary they had met on their previous visit got out. A moment later, wearing an immaculate suit over his frail frame and sporting a pair of driving gloves, the doddering McGillivray senior clambered out of the driver's side.

'You there,' he said, scowling at Anderson. 'Shouldn't you be in the milking shed by now? And where's your overalls?'

Anderson and Sandilands gave each other a frown. 'This is Inspector Anderson,' Sandilands said, putting the bag of bones on the ground. 'You met the other day.'

The old man's face indicated he had no memory, but he feigned recollection. 'Ah, yes, of course. How are you?'

'Not as bad as some,' Anderson said, his eyes glancing down at the exposed cleavage of McGillivray's secretary, who was stood with a sullen, bored look across her face, eyes rolling to the top of her head. 'Your boy Joe about?'

'Should be,' the old man said, pulling off his driving gloves. 'More than likely with that damned kraut vet in the slaughter room.'

'You mean Mr van Burgh?' Sandilands asked.

McGillivray shook his head and screwed up his wrinkled face. 'Oh, you know the bugger do you, Betty?'

'Not personally, but we met the other day.'

'Damned foreign swine,' McGillivray snapped. 'Whatever was

wrong with Mr Kilkenny is beyond me. At least he didn't steal our cows.'

Anderson and Sandilands exchanged another bemused glance. 'Steal your cows?' Anderson said, still wincing from the smell of the yard.

'Yes, bloody thief,' snapped McGillivray. 'He thinks nobody knows what he's up to, but I'm on to him.'

'Why, what is he up to?' Sandilands asked.

'He's damned well nicking our heifers, so he is. Thieving Hun swine.'

Anderson's eyebrows rose in scepticism at the old man's ramblings. But Sandilands pressed him further. 'What makes you think he's been stealing your cattle?'

'I've seen him. He thinks because he does it late at night when nobody is around it has gone unnoticed, but I know what he's up to.'

'What is he up to?' Anderson asked.

'Loading our prime beef into one of our vans and disappearing. Ruddy German thief. I blame the Common Market. We didn't fight two world wars to have these bloody Hun come over here and steal our cattle, did we? I'll catch him at it one day, and by God he'll be for it then!'

Sandilands and Anderson exchanged glances again, just as the subject of their conversation strolled across the yard towards them.

'Talk of the devil,' Anderson said, as the thin, wiry, foreign accented vet, wearing a lab coat and clutching a clipboard, appeared out of one of the cattle sheds and waved at them, before walking over.

This caused a tut and scowl from old man McGillivray. 'Damned kraut,' he hissed, clutching his secretary around the waist and doddering off towards the office, glancing caustically behind him as he went.

Anderson's eyes followed the secretary's rump as it disappeared into the office. 'Fascinating.'

'You mean about van Burgh driving around late at night with a van full of cattle?' Sandilands said, quietly, as van Burgh approached.

'Oh, yes, that too,' Anderson said, turning to greet the vet.

'Hello again,' van Burgh said, cheerily.

'Is Joe about?' Sandilands asked as she picked up the bag of bones and slung it over her shoulder.

Van Burgh's eyes lingered on the bag and one eyebrow slowly rose up his forehead. 'Perhaps there is something I can help you with?'

'I'm sure there is,' Anderson said. 'But I need to speak to the organ grinder first.'

'I beg your pardon?'

'Joe, where is he?' Sandilands asked.

Van Burgh waved his clipboard in the direction of one of the cattle sheds. 'He's in the slaughterhouse. If you follow me, I'll take you to him.'

Chapter Nineteen

They had searched as far out from the shore as possible. Besides all the cattle bones lying on the loch bed, they found no sign of the little girl. Frazer was losing any optimism of finding her. He decided to move the team farther away from the campsite, more westerly. The slope descended even steeper here, which meant a deeper dive, perhaps a hundred and twenty feet, but the gentle current in the loch could have possibly carried the drowned girl's body at least this far. If she wasn't there, he doubted she would ever turn up. Morar seemed intent on keeping her.

It was his turn to dive again. Knowing he would be going so deep, Frazer opted to dive with nitrox in his scuba tank, as it would allow him to stay down longer. The added nitrogen was better under pressure than a regular air mix. It would be deeper than he'd dived in years, but he wanted to be thorough. He owed it to the little girl's parents. Having a body meant a lot to people. It gave them something to bury, to mourn.

He checked his gear carefully and ordered the others to keep a close eye on the guide rope after he dropped the weight in the water. He knew they didn't need telling, but diving so deep unnerved him, even after all these years. Ramsey was better suited to such a deep dive, but since he had taken the last dive, the rules, which Frazer had devised himself, said he needed a break.

So after finishing his preparations, Frazer again plunged backwards into the water and for body to acclimatise, before swapping okay signs with the others in the dinghy then Frazer placed the regulator between his teeth and dived headfirst into the depths.

With the underwater light in one hand and the guide rope in the other, Frazer pulled himself down, slowly. It took several minutes before he neared the bottom of the loch bed. According to his depth gauge, he was close to a hundred and twenty feet and as deep as he'd ever gone on a search.

Visibility was poor. Even with the underwater light pointing at the downward slope of the loch bed, it was dim, dark, gloomy. While plenty of reeds blew in the current, strangely, he could see none of the animal bones that seemed so plentiful farther inshore. That was weird. It was as if the current only caused them to congregate in that area. Or something had deposited them there.

He plunged between the reeds of the sloping loch bed. They were longer, stretching as high as they could to reach the feeble sunlight that barely penetrated this far down and towered over Frazer like the canopy of a great forest, swaying in the current just like branches of trees in a storm.

The farther out towards the centre of the loch he dived, the more it darkened, and if it wasn't for the underwater light, he would have seen nothing, and even with it, his eyes struggled to penetrate through the dense underwater foliage. Often, the torch would snag in the reeds, as would his safety line, and Frazer would have to tug at them. It made the going difficult, slow.

He'd been underwater for nearly twenty minutes before he managed to complete his first arc. He checked his levels and reckoned he would have enough time for another. Although, another five yards out from the guide rope would mean at least ten feet deeper to dive. A hundred and thirty feet. The limit. But the nitrox was working well. His chest didn't feel as tightly squeezed as before and the bubbles from his regulator not as numerous.

He loosened more safety line, and dived farther down the incline and in between the reeds, using his hands to pat and scratch the loch bed. Because the reeds were denser, Frazer believed he was in the right place. Bodies tended to float, the fact the girl hadn't emerged indicated the current had taken her to the bottom and she'd become snagged on the underwater foliage. If she were anywhere, she would be here.

He searched meticulously, using fingers more than eyes. Whenever he felt something beneath his hands, a rock or a dense mass of reeds, he'd use the light to examine it. But after halfway through his second arc, nothing.

Being so deep, he checked his levels and depth gauge regularly. He didn't want to get caught out without enough time to surface safely. Going up too quickly and decompression could set in. Frazer feared that more than drowning.

It was while glancing at his wrist that the shadow flashed in front of him. His peripheral vision only caught a glance, but it was big. Looming.

Startled, Frazer glanced about, but the shadow had disappeared into the gloom. He peered into the depths, his body floating upright just above the loch bed, the reeds swaying around him.

What the hell was it?

Then it flashed by again. This time to his side. His head spun around, but the bubbles pouring rapidly from his regulator obscured his facemask and he could see nothing. When they cleared, the shadow had disappeared again.

What the hell is it?

He turned his head left and right, almost frantically. Whatever it was, it was big. Far bigger than an eel or a salmon. Far bigger than he was.

Then it came from behind.

One moment Frazer was floating upright, the next, a powerful force slammed into his back, dislodging the regulator from his mouth and sending him spiralling through the water.

The safety line snagged taut, bringing him to an abrupt halt upside down in the water. He hung there helpless for a moment, not sure of his orientation. His regulator dangled in front of him, filling the water with bubbles or air. After a frantic moment of squirming, Frazer reached for it, shoving it back in his mouth, and kicking gently with his flippers, he righted himself.

Then it hit him again.

This time, Frazer saw it clearly. Yet he had no idea what it was. It approached head on, charging through the gloom like a torpedo, its mouth gaping. A hideous mouth. A mouth with thick, bulbous lips. A mouth sprouting long, tentacle-like tendrils. A hideous, ugly, monstrous mouth.

An instant later, darkness enshrouded him and Frazer felt an almighty squeeze around his chest. His arms were pinned to his body, and horrifyingly, he realised his upper body was inside this creature's mouth, whatever it was.

Helpless, he kicked and squirmed and struggled, but the crushing on his chest increased and the creature shook him, like a dog with a ragdoll.

Then the safety line pulled tight against his waist, squeezing and cutting into his midriff as the creature tried to carry him away.

Then it let go.

The scuba tank on his bank must have meant he was too much of a meal for the creature to swallow, because the pressure around Frazer's chest subsided, and a moment later he was free. Spat out like an unwanted piece of chewing gum.

He'd lost his underwater light and regulator and Frazer screamed silently in the darkness, water filling his mouth, filling his lungs. Panic consumed his body. He kicked and clawed at the water, but the safety line held him tightly in place. He unhooked it. And in frenzied panic, he ascended rapidly.

Too rapidly.

He broke the surface. Coughing, spluttering, ejecting water from his lungs, screaming for help. He heard shouts and yells, splashes as divers hit the water to retrieve him. Hands pulled at him, people called his name. He felt his body slumping on to the floor of the dinghy. Then the shakes started, and the aches and the convulsions and spasms and tremors, and just before he blacked out, he heard somebody shout out.

'Jesus, he's got the bends!'

Chapter Twenty

If the smell outside was bad, the putrid stench generated by the hundreds of live cattle mooing inside the shed made even Sandilands gag.

The shed was enormous. Hundreds, if not a thousands of cattle stood in dozens of different pens, each with barely enough room to move. Workers dressed in white coats and clutching cattle prods stood between the pens. And after a buzzer sounded, the metal gates clanged open and after some coaxing and a chorus of moos, all the animals were shifted from pen to pen down the shed.

'What are they doing?' Sandilands asked, as they followed van Burgh. She had the bag of bones over her shoulder while Anderson, his jacket across his face, had gone a pallid shade of grey.

It looked inhumane. The electric cattle prods seemed to cause significant pain to the animals, but the vet seemed nonplussed. 'They are all being slaughtered today,' he said, pointing to the far end of the cow shed. 'That's where we herd them to the final holding pen, see?'

Sandilands could see the last pen funnelled into a long gangway and ended at metal shutter. The cows lined up in single file and when the buzzer sounded again, the shutter opened and a worker coaxed the cattle down the gangway where they disappeared when the shutter closed, and then the gangway slowly filled again with more cows coaxed down by the workers.

'You slaughter them behind there?' Sandilands asked, pointing to the shutter, a deeply unpleasant taste forming in her mouth.

'Yes, and it is where we'll find Mr McGillivray,' van Burgh said. 'Overseeing the slaughter. The partition is to prevent the animals from seeing what fate has in store for them. Without it, they'd be difficult to control. We could end up with a stampede.'

Anderson, his jacket still clamped around his mouth, suddenly swore, looked down, and began hopping as he realised he'd stepped in something. 'Don't stop 'em shitting themselves though, does it?'

Van Burgh laughed. 'Should have brought your boots, Inspector.'

When they arrived at the shutter, van Burgh opened a small doorway cut into the metal at the side and Sandilands saw something that would replay in her nightmares for years to come and put her off eating beef for life.

Behind the shutter, the gangway full of cattle carried on until it reached a gate. Beyond that was a row of metal yokes where a bank of white coated workers, all clutching cattle prods stood with Joe McGillivray who also brandished a cattle prod. He used his like a conductor wielded a baton, orchestrating the workers, as one by one, they walked to the gate, opened it, coaxed out a cow and led it to a yoke. After clamping the metal around the animal's neck, they nonchalantly placed a cylindrical bolt guns to the cow's heads. A loud hiss sounded and the animals fell lifeless into the yokes. The white coats then released the catch and the cows slid down a conveyor to where other workers waited who tied chains around the dead animals' legs, hoisted them to the ceiling, and a conveyor carried them down the shed.

Dozens of animals hung suspended from the ceiling, moving

slowly down the conveyor, where further down the shed numerous workers greeted them with electric saws, knives and various other instruments. Slicing, dicing, cutting, disembowelling, until nothing but prime shanks of beef hung in ordered rows and were loaded straight on to trucks that had with their tailgates open at the shuttered gates at the rear.

It was so clinical, so matter-of-fact. Workers chatted, joked, butchered animals by the dozen.

Sandilands was appalled and dropped the bag as the slaughter unfolded before her. She placed her hands over her jaw, holding in a mouthful of vomit. She couldn't believe the systematic nature of it all. 'My God, it's so—'

'Efficient?' beamed van Burgh.

'Barbaric was more along the lines I was thinking,' Sandilands snapped.

Van Burgh stopped and frowned.'I can assure you this is the most humane method of despatching cattle.'

Sandilands felt faint. Seeing the cows herded down the shed and despatched so clinically seemed like something from a horror film. This was not how farming should be. She knew animals needed killing, but here, it was so industrial.

'I hope the sight doesn't put you off your Sunday dinner,' Joe McGillivray said, stepping down from the yoke and marching over to greet them with the electric cattle prod resting on his shoulder. He smiled, broadly.

Anderson removed the jacket from his mouth, winced at the smell, gave a phlegmy sniff, spat.

'Seen worse,' he said, his nostrils bellowing like the blowholes on two whales.

Joe smiled. 'And what can I do for you, Inspector?'

Anderson nodded to Sandilands, picked up the bag from the floor and tipped it upside. The cattle bones scattered on to the sawdust.

Joe looked at them, van Burgh looked at them, but while the latter's face turned pale, pupils dilating, eyes widening, Joe just shrugged. 'Been to the butcher's shop, I see.'

'They pulled these out of the intake vent at the dam,' Sandilands said.

Joe's lips shrugged.

'And we have divers at the loch that have found more – A lot more,' added Anderson.

'So why you telling me,' Joe said, turning round to gesticulate with the cattle prod at the white-coated workers. During the conversation, the slaughter seemed to have stopped, much to Sandilands' relief. However, following Joe's prompt, the white coats carried on their work, prodding cattle to the yokes and despatching the animals.

'We believe somebody dumped these remains into the loch on purpose,' Sandilands said, trying to make her voice heard over the din of moos and clanging metal and that disturbing hiss from the bolt guns. She kept her eyes down, avoiding the slaughter.

'And you think it was us?' van Burgh asked, his eyes fixed on Joe.

'Who else has a cattle farm around here?' Anderson asked, removing his tobacco pouch from his pocket. 'And if it was you who dumped these carcasses you did so for a reason, didn't you?'

'And what reason would that be, Inspector?' Joe asked, turning away to watch a worker leading a cow from the gangway.

He walked over and rested his arm over the gate, gently tapping his cattle prod over his shoulder.

Sandilands noticed van Burgh fidget, and he dropped his gaze to the floor.

'I think you were trying to cover up an outbreak,' Anderson said, shoving a cigarette in his lips and walking up behind Joe.

'An outbreak of what?' Joe asked, his back to Anderson. Another white coat coaxed a cow from the gangway. Joe assisted him by poking the animal on the backside with his cattle prod. The cow jumped, mooed, but was corralled into the yoke. A hiss. Sandilands jumped, so did the cow before it slumped lifeless.

'Don't ask me. I'm no expert,' Anderson said, lighting his cigarette and looking unaffected by the slaughter.

'And you have evidence of all these allegations? ' Joe asked, turning around and glowering at Anderson.

Anderson scrunched up his nose and shrugged. 'No, but I reckon if I tell the ministry about it they'll send have a team of inspectors up here before you can say bullocks.' He beamed a grin. 'Thcy'll go through this placc likc a dose of the trots. Bound to find something.'

'We have nothing to hide,' Joe said, defiantly. A broad grin then stretched across his lips. 'We've not had an outbreak of anything, have we, Eric?'

Van Burgh glanced at everybody like a frightened rabbit. 'No, Mr McGillivray. All our animals are healthy.'

Anderson poked his cigarette to the bones and nodded at Sandilands to pack them up. 'I wonder what else those divers will find in the loch,' he said, as Sandilands bent down to shove the bones back into the bag.

In the corner of her eye, she saw Joe's face lose its smile. Gritted teeth replaced his broad smile.

Anderson removed the cigarette from his lips and jabbed in Joe's direction. 'We'll be seeing you soon, Mr McGillivray. Real soon.'

Sandilands slung the bag on her shoulder and nodded goodbye. Van Burgh's face had gone taut, his eyes bulging.

'We'll see ourselves out,' she said, following Anderson towards the shutter. She felt relieved to be going. She doubted she had ever been anywhere so unpleasant.

'Watch how you go, Inspector,' Joe yelled at them. 'This is a dangerous place.'

A clang of metal sounded behind them, followed by a rumble, like the noise at the start of the Grand National. Sandilands turned to see the gate to the pen wide open and four cows, about two tons of prime beef stampeding towards them.

'Down!' she yelled, grabbing Anderson and diving to the floor. Within seconds, the cows crashed into the shutter. Hooves thundered around their heads, kicking up sawdust. Sandilands screamed, the sound of her voice lost amid the panicked mooing. One of the cows kicked at her arm but she felt a hand grab at her, dragging her through the door of the shutter, and she and Anderson rolled into the main shed.

They lay there for a moment, Anderson clutching his stomach, Sandilands her arm.

Then the buzzer sounded and the shutter started opening behind them.

'Quick,' she grabbed Anderson, hauled him to his feet and pulled him away. Within moments, the cattle burst through like a bovine tsunami. One fell, one bucked like a bronco, others charged, all mooed.

Screams, shouts, yells erupted from the various workers and they ran around trying to contain the animals, while Anderson and Sandilands huddled together at the side as the cattle stampeded past them.

A moment later, as Sandilands lay gasping on the sawdust and the workers had managed to contain most of the loose cows. Joe appeared under the shutter, the cattle prod in his hands.

'I told you it was dangerous,' he said, his lip curled up in a sneer.

Chapter Twenty-One

'We should have arrested him,' Sandilands said, as they arrived at the Allegro and she dumped the bag of bones in the boot. She rubbed her arm. It was bruised, sore, but not broken.

'For what?' Anderson was holding his guts, his face contorting with obvious pain.

'What about attempted murder,' she snapped. 'He let those cows go on purpose.'

'And do you think that would stick? We'd be lucky to pin a breach in health and safety on him, let alone attempted murder.' He winced and clutched his stomach tighter.

'Here, let me look.' She lifted up his jacket and untucked his shirt. He took an intake of breath, So did Sandilands, she couldn't help it. The blue welt on his stomach looked terrible. 'We need to get you to the doctor.'

He snatched his shirt from her. 'No quacks. I just need a drink.'

'I think you've broken your ribs.'

'That's nothing to what I'm going to do to Joe McGillivray.' He pulled out his tobacco pouch, and despite his obvious pain, proceeded to roll up a cigarette.

'So are you going to call the ministry, klike you threatened?'

'Pah, these ministry officials need paperwork signed in triplicate before they take a piss.' He gazed at her. His eyes lacked the normal cynicism. They were narrowed, serious, angry. 'Besides, what do I care for sick cows? I want McGillivray for murder.'

'So you're convinced he did it then?'

'I am now.'

'Then how we going to nail him?'

Anderson looked round to the meat shed where they had just narrowly escaped being trampled to death. 'I hope you don't have plans tonight.'

She shook her head, just as a crackle sounded from her lapel. Sandilands lifted the walkie-talkie to her mouth. 'Go ahead Feathers, what's up.'

'You best get up Lochside,' he said, his voice barely audible behind a fizz of static.

'Lochside, whatever for?'

'There's been an accident,' came the reply. 'One of the divers ...' The last part of his sentence died in background noise.

'Say again Feathers.'

'One of the divers ... seriously injured.'

By the time Anderson and Sandilands had driven back through Morar and along the loch road, in her pitifully slow driving style and even slower car, nearly half an hour had passed since they'd received the radio message. On their approach, a helicopter had thundered overhead, and Anderson knew what that meant. Whoever was injured required an emergency airlift.

They saw the helicopter when Sandilands pulled into the campsite entrance. It had landed a good distance away from the tents and several figures were carrying a stretcher towards it.

Anderson saw two of the divers running alongside the stretcher with the paramedics, and as Sandilands switched off the engine, he was out of the car and hobbling to meet them, despite the considerable pain coming from his stomach and ribs.

'What happened?' he shouted, as he closed on the group at the chopper as they loaded the stretcher into the back of the helicopter.

One of the divers turned round and shook his head. It was the one with the scarred face. It looked grim. 'He came up too quickly. He's got decompression sickness.'

Anderson peered over and saw Frazer on the stretcher, still in his wetsuit, wrapped in a blanket. The other, tall, thin diver was clutching his hand as the air ambulance team secured him inside the chopper, while the third member of his team, stood shaking his head, disbelief etched on his features.

'Something spooked him,' the scarred man said, as Frazer's face flopped weakly towards Anderson. It didn't look good. One side drooped, as if he'd had a stroke, and his eyes looked too big for their sockets, and his mouth dribbled and the veins of his face protruding through translucent skin.

'What do you mean, something spooked him?'

The diver shook his head, solemnly. 'I wish I knew.' He looked over at the loch, where the rubber dinghy and equipment lay strewn on the jetty. 'Something down there caused him to panic.'

'Panic? Frazer the Frog, what the hell are you talking about, man?' Anderson couldn't believe it. In his line of work, he knew some brave men, but few compared to Frazer. Not only was he a war hero, but also he'd been diving for decades and had come face-to-face with some the grizzliest sights a man in his profession could encounter. Nothing had ever spooked him before, not bodies, not mutilated remains, not even dead children.

The air ambulance crew gesticulated for the divers and

Anderson to step back. As they did so, the engine whirred and the rotors started spinning, creating a gust that made them step back farther.

'What happened?' Sandilands asked, jogging over and clutching her cap with one hand to prevent the draught from the helicopter carrying it off.

The divers shrugged, as did Anderson. 'I wish I knew,' he said, staring at the loch.

'I'm afraid we'll have to call the search off, ma'am,' the tall diver said. 'We've not enough men to continue.'

Sandilands nodded. The helicopter lifted off, its downdraught now physically beating at Anderson's face, but he didn't move. He just stood and stared as the chopper disappeared over the valley.

He felt Sandilands touch his shoulder. 'C'mon, let me buy you that drink.'

Chapter Twenty-Two

Sandilands and Anderson sat at the side of the road in the Allegro. They'd been there for hours, since before sunset. It was now nearly midnight. Mostly they sat in silence. Anderson was still in obvious pain. His hand kept grasping at his wounded ribs, but no matter how much Sandilands nagged, he'd refused to see the doctor. Besides, she knew his silence was mainly caused by pain of another sort.

She had called the hospital to find out Frazer's condition. The news wasn't good. Critical, they had said. And even if he did recover, they doubted he would ever walk again, let alone dive.

She knew he and Frazer went way back, but Anderson hid his emotions well. She'd asked him what he thought had happened. He just shrugged and said, 'Just one of those things. Took his eye off the ball. It happens.'

She knew it had affected him badly though. He had become withdrawn, quiet. Gone were his sarcastic comments, cynical quips, one-liners. Instead, after leaving the bar at Lochside, he ordered her to park up here, where he sat silently and smoked cigarette after cigarette until a thick fug filled the car sending Sandilands dizzy.

She coughed and waved the odious smoke from her eyes. 'Tell me again, what exactly are we doing here?'

Anderson threw his cigarette out the open window and adjusted the side mirror to get a better look behind them. 'I told you. We're going to see what our visit earlier today flushes them out.' He winced, grabbing his ribs. 'It's called bluffing. I take it you've never played poker?'

'What happens if Joe doesn't fall for it?'

Anderson took his tobacco pouch out again and rolled another smoke. 'He will. He won't want to take the risk. Too much at stake.'

'I still don't understand what you expect to happen.'

In the gloom of the car, a flicker of light flashed across Anderson's face.

'Look.' He pointed his cigarette at the rear view mirror. 'Turn the ignition on.'

Sandilands did as she was told and glanced behind her. A set of headlights was snaking up the road from the farm, heading their way. The lights grew larger and eventually, a van passed them by. In the darkness, she couldn't see its occupants, but Anderson cast his cigarette out the window and pointed at it as it disappeared down the road.

'Go on then. Follow that van.'

She put the car in gear and drove off, causing a tiny screech from rear wheels. In all her years in the force, she had neither taken part in a stakeout nor pursued another vehicle. Tonight she was doing both. It excited her.

They followed the van through Morar, until it turned down the track that followed the north shore of the loch, past Lochside, where they'd watched Frazer being airlifted out only hours before, and on to Bracorina, a quiet area consisting of a few sheep farms, but nothing else. She wondered where the van was going.

'Keep your distance,' Anderson snapped. 'I don't want him to see us.'

She slowed down, allowing the taillights of the van to

disappear into the darkness ahead. She knew there was no chance of losing it. The lane only ran halfway along the north shore and other than a few tracks leading to the various farms, it went nowhere, just came to a dead end.

They drove on in the darkness, and after a mile or so passed Lochside, the two distant red dots of its rear lights reappeared in the windscreen. The van had stopped.

'Kill the lights,' Anderson ordered.

Sandilands turned the headlights off and slowed to a virtual crawl.

'Pull over,' he said. 'Let's see what he's up to.'

She cut the engine and Anderson opened the door.

'Jesus,' he complained, hauling himself free of the car, cursing and clutching his wounded ribs. 'I think my arse has gone to sleep.'

Sandilands got out, pulled free her truncheon and leant back in to take her torch out from the glove box. She turned it on and they both crept down the lane towards the taillights. It was dark. Black. Eerie. Silent.

Ahead, a splash sounded as they closed. Startled, Sandilands let out a quiet yelp.

'Shhh,' Anderson hissed, as another splash sounded. He crept up to a line of bushes offering cover beside the loch and peered over. 'I knew it,' he whispered. 'It's that Dutchman. He's chucking stuff into the water.'

Sandilands, her heart beating rapidly, crept up to the bush and peered over too. Sure enough, the van was ahead with its rear doors open. Van Burgh, his gangly silhouette easily recognisable, had something on his shoulder. He gingerly walked the water's edge, stopped and threw it in, causing another loud splash.

'Cattle carcasses, I bet,' Anderson whispered, looking down at Sandilands' hands. He snatched the torch from her and smirked at the truncheon. 'Well come on then, let's go and see what he has to say for himself.'

He pointed to the left of the bush. 'Go that way, but stay out of sight. I'll go around to the right'.

She nodded and crept around the foliage and waited. A second or two later, she heard Anderson's voice so peered over the bush.

'All right, sunshine. Hold it right there.' Anderson had the torch pointing in van Burgh's direction and stood by the front of the van.

The Dutchman had just pulled another large muslin parcel from the rear and had it on his shoulder. He froze, like a married man caught with his trousers down. His eyes rounded in the torch light and he raised his hand to shield them.

'What do you think you're up to, then?' Anderson asked, taking a few steps forward.

Van Burgh glanced about, as if looking for somewhere to run. 'Don't you dare,' Anderson said. 'You and me need to have a little chat'

Van Burgh ignored him and dropped the parcel from his shoulder, but Sandilands now appeared and stood blocking his way, truncheon in one hand, her other palm out, halting him.

He stopped, hesitated, and then ran backwards, attempting to get around the rear of the van, but the incline was steep and he lost his footing, tripped, skidded, wavered, and then plunged into the loch with a splash.

'Help!' he screamed, as he thrashed about in the water. 'I can't swim.'

The water looked deep, because he kept going under and waved frantically. Sandilands edged down the incline and extended her truncheon. 'Here, grab this.'

Van Burgh splashed about, and while spitting out water, reached for her outstretched hand, but Anderson dashed up, grabbed Sandilands' arm and pulled it back.

'What are you doing?'

He pointed the torch at the struggling vet, illuminating him in the water like a spotlight. 'I think if Mr van Burgh wants our help, he ought to answer a few questions first.'

Van Burgh, his arms flailing about, squealed and spluttered. Then his head went under. He soon re-emerged, spitting, coughing, thrashing about, desperate to keep his head above the water. 'Help ... please ... ugh ... pull me out.'

'Tell me about Briers,' Anderson said, clutching Sandilands' arm so that the truncheon wavered tantalisingly close to van Burgh's outstretched hands.

He tried to reach it but fell short, his head momentarily plunging beneath the water again. 'Please ... I'll tell you,' he said, emerging and spitting out a mouthful of the loch. '... ugh ... just pull me up.'

'He's drowning,' Sandilands protested, but Anderson pulled her arm back and shined the torch into van Burgh's eyes.

'Tell me what happened to Briers?'

Van Burgh thrashed and struggled and kicked and spat. 'It was Mr McGillivray ... Ugh ... He did it.'

'Joe McGillivray?'

'Ugh ... yes ... please ... pull me out.'

'What did he do?'

Van Burgh's head disappeared below the water again, but he came up, spitting and squealing. 'Please ... help me.'

'What did Joe do?' Anderson asked.

'Ugh ... he ... ugh ... killed him.'

'And you'll put that in a statement?'

'Yes ... anything ...ugh ... just help me.'

Anderson released Sandilands' arm. 'Okay, pull him out.'

She reached forward and van Burgh grabbed hold of the truncheon, but just as she began hauling him in, something exploded from the water causing a torrent of spray that forced her and Anderson backwards on to the slope.

Anderson's still had the torch pointed at the water, and see van Burgh and whatever it was that had emerged from the depths, but what exactly it was, she couldn't tell. It was big, formless and as black as the water surrounding it, and an instant after bursting from the depths it came down on top of the struggling vet, creating another splash that soaked Anderson and Sandilands on the shore.

Momentarily blinded, Sandilands wiped the water from her face the thing had disappeared. So had van Burgh. All was still, except for bubbling foam on the water's surface.

Then Anderson scrambled back from the edge and pointed his torch at the water. 'What the bloody hell was that?'

Chapter Twenty-Three

After the events of the previous night, Sandilands first instinct had been to warn the village, put up signs, keep people out of the water. While neither she nor Anderson knew what they had seen, the danger it posed was evident. It had taken van Burgh right before their eyes, and more than likely was responsible for what had happened to Frazer and the poor girl guide.

However, Anderson told her not to be hasty. Not only would they risk sounding like a couple of 'bampots' as he put it, but also, with van Burgh dead, they now had nothing on Joe McGillivray. But Joe wasn't to know that the vet was dead, and after the Dutchman failed to return from his nightly sojourn, he would be left sweating, wondering what had happened. Perhaps, Anderson had reasoned, if he thinks they had collared van Burgh, it may force Joe's hand.

She only hoped Anderson knew what he was doing. What Joe would do was anybody's guess, but after hearing from van Burgh that he had indeed killed Briers, whatever it was, it was bound to be rash. Yet Joe was Anderson's concern, she was more interested in keeping people away from the water. And how she would do that without letting on what she had seen she still wasn't sure even when as she walked to work the next morning.

After the events of the previous night, Sandilands arrived late in Morar, but the place was unusually busy for that time of year. Cars beeped and honked, many were double-parked, and despite it being early, the village was full of people standing about on corners, chatting and rummaging around in the shops.

She saw Featherstone outside the station, gesticulating at a small gaggle of people surrounding him. 'What the hell is going on?' she asked.

'Thank God you're here,' he replied, his voice raised over the demand for directions and other enquiries. 'I take it you haven't seen the papers this morning.'

He pointed over at the newsagent, where an A-board brazenly announced the morning's news: 'Unidentified Creature Blamed for Girl's Death at Loch Morar.'

She gaped at the headline and then realised who all these people were. Press. Reporters. Dozens of them, notebooks in hands, accosting everybody and anybody that happened to pass by. Even the BBC was there, their outside broadcast van was parked outside the hotel where a broadcaster was doing a piece to camera.

And mixed in with the reporters were morbidly curious tourists. It seemed every crackpot between Morar and Fort William had turned up. Teenagers wearing Iron Maiden T-shirts gathered in the shops grabbing Morag merchandise by the armful, while anglers armed with heavy duty fishing gear were haggling with the locals on the jetty where all the rented boats were moored.

'But where the hell did they get their information?' she asked, before her mind answered her own question. Her head shot to the hotel. Only one person she knew had made such wild claims. The American, Mike. Although she now knew they weren't wild claims at all.

One of the reporters thrust a tape recorder under her nose and asked for comment as she tried to sidle past into the station. 'Is it true a diver was killed in the loch yesterday?'

'No, it's not.'

'Have you seen the beast yourself?' asked another.

'What? Look, go away, will you.'

Featherstone shook his head at her. 'You're going to have to do something. Give a press conference, at least.'

And say what? She could hardly admit there *was* some beast swimming in the loch. Instead, she told Featherstone to keep an eye on everyone while she disappeared into the station and slammed the door shut.

As Anderson hobbled out of the hotel late that morning, he saw Sandilands outside the police station with a piece of paper in her hand and a rabble of what he presumed were reporters gathered around her. At first, he thought she had said something about the previous night, but he then realised their arrival was too soon for that. They must have been their because of girl guide. Nothing like a dead little girl to get the nation's press excited.

He hung back, smoked a roll up and watched. The last thing he wanted was to get involved in a media scrum. Despite the best part of a bottle of scotch, he'd not slept well. Not only were the events of the previous night still playing on his mind, along with what had happened to Frazer, but also his stomach felt as if it had been kicked by a bull. Which, in all intents and purposes, it had.

Sandilands called the crowd to order. 'Thank you all for being so patient,' she said, her long nose buried behind the paper. 'Two days ago, a young girl drowned in the loch whilst canoeing with a group of girl guides. Despite what you may have heard or read, the incident is being treated as a tragic accident.'

Grumbles and chatter erupted from the crowd of reporters. One shouted out, 'What about the sightings of a loch monster.'

Sandilands shook her head. 'I repeat. The incident is being treated as a tragic accident.'

'So nobody reported seeing something in the water shortly before the girl drowned?' Another reporter shouted.

'Yeah, and what about the police diver. Is it true, one was attacked by something.'

Sandilands pulled tight her tunic. 'Due to circumstances beyond our control, the dive to recover the girl's body had to be called off, but it will begin again in due time. I have no further comment.'

More questions, shouts and clamouring erupted, but Sandilands ignored them and turned about and walked back into the station. Anderson was impressed. He cast his cigarette to the ground, and made his way through the congregated crowd of media, ignoring the stabbing pain in his stomach as he shoved them aside.

'Out the way,' he ordered, pulling a reporter away from the door.

The journalist turned round, startled. He looked Anderson up and down, before asking, 'Are you a police officer?'

'Inspector,' Anderson said, pulling open the station door. 'Department of mythical beasts.'

He left the man gaping as he walked in.

Sandilands had her head in her hands, coffee steaming in front of her next to a bottle of aspirin.

'We have to do something,' she said, on sight of Anderson. 'I can't hold them off forever. Besides, there's folk going out on to the loch to the look for the bloody thing.'

Anderson sat down and, while wincing from his battered ribs, put his feet on Featherstone's desk and rolled a smoke. 'What do you reckon it is then? Some kind of shark?'

She shook her head. 'Not in freshwater.'

'Then what?'

She pinched her eyes. 'I don't know. It was too dark. I didn't get a proper look. Perhaps an eel of some kind.'

'Big bloody eel.' Anderson lit his cigarette. 'But whatever it was, it swallowed the only chance we had of nailing Joe McGillivray. But if we can make him think we have the Dutchman under lock and key ...'

'But how long will that take? And in the meantime, how do I keep people out of the water?'

Anderson shrugged.

'Besides,' she continued. 'What makes you think he'll fall for it?'

'He's desperate enough. Bumping off a ministry inspector's proof of that.' He raised his chin. 'Where's the van?'

'Where we left it, I suppose. Why?'

'Send that constable of yours to go and get it. Ask him to park it out front where McGillivray can see it.'

'Okay, but you are going to have to fend for yourself after that. I need to find out what the hell is in the loch and how to get rid of it before it grabs somebody else.'

'And how are we going to do that?'

She bit her lip, shook her head, and then stood up, chair scraping the floor.

'Where you going?'

'To find that American. We're not the only ones to have seen it and he saw it during the day. I want to know what it is we're dealing with.'

'You know who else you should speak to.'

'Who?'

'That old drunk back at the campsite. He seems to know a thing or two about it.'

'Fairbanks? Christ, it comes to something when you need help from the town drunk.'

'Don't knock it. We old sops can be quite helpful when we want to be.'

Chapter Twenty-Four

Mike had hoped his conversation with the reporter would come to nothing, but when he went down for breakfast that morning, he knew just what a big deal it had become. The press had gathered in the hotel lobby, and the entire village was abuzz with people all talking about the same thing: the monster in the loch.

He knew he had to get out of the village. Sergeant Sandilands may only have been a rural British cop, but it wouldn't take her long to realise who had tipped off the media. And he doubted she would be best pleased. He felt stupid. Blabbing about what he saw would only make matters worse. Besides, he didn't even know what it was he had seen. It could have been anything; flotsam, maybe or a log. No, as much as he wanted to dismiss it, he knew what he saw.

He decided to take the same walk as he'd taken the day before. No matter how much trouble he'd caused Sandilands, he doubted she'd look for him along the south shore of the loch. Her banged up old clunker would have trouble negotiating the muddied trail. He doubted any vehicles ventured up there.

But he was wrong, because after a mile or so, he saw a van parked along the water's edge. It was a small, rounded VW. The type the hippies of San Francisco drove to Grateful Dead concerts. Only this had no tie-dyed paintwork on it, but did have a large antenna protruding from the roof and a rack loaded with stuff and covered in tarpaulin.

A strange looking man sat outside cooking what smelled like bacon. And on sight of Mike, he stood up and waved hello. He had a long, straggly beard and shoulder length dreadlocks, which gave him somewhat of an aged appearance.

But as Mike closed, drawn more by the smell of bacon than the unusual looking fellow – he'd not eaten that morning and the smell was intoxicating – he realised the man was probably no older than he was. He was scruffy though, wearing ripped jeans, a thick sweater that looked self-knitted, a woollen hat and trainers of no discernable make.

'Good morning to you,' the man said. His accent was English, not Scottish, and he had a slight lisp. His eyebrows also rose slightly as Mike neared. While the swollen eye, cheek and thick lip had gone down, Mike realised he was probably still a bit of a sight.

'Hi, how you doing?' Mike said, glancing down at the source of the delicious aroma.

'Oh, you're an American.' The man clapped his hands together. 'I don't suppose you come from the North West, do you? Always been fascinated about the sasquatch legends.'

Mike narrowed his eyes. 'Er, no, sorry. Wisconsin.' He glanced back down at the pan again. He'd begun to drool. 'The name's Mike Cunningham.'

The man smiled and thrust out a fingerless-gloved hand. 'Robert Freely, but most folk call me Freaky Freely, on account of my work. Not that I mind, really.'

'Work?' Mike shook his hand. He seemed jovial, happy and friendly enough.

Freely smiled. 'I'm a journalist.'

'Oh.' Mike rolled his eyes. Damned reporters.

'I write for Crypto Zoology Monthly,' Freely continued. 'Just got here from Loch Ness. I came as soon as I heard the news on the radio this morning about that girl.' He rubbed his back. 'Hell of a drive, took nearly four hours.' He sat back down and took a fork from his pocket and turned over the bacon.

'Sorry, crypto-what?' Mike couldn't help but glance at the bacon, which was now looking crispy, the way he liked it.

'Crypto zoology,' Freely said, rummaging beneath a deckchair and producing a loaf of bread. He took a couple of slices out and using the fork, dropped a piece of bacon between them and bit into it. 'I study cryptids,' he said, his mouth full. 'Animals that are not formally recognised by science. Nessie is my speciality.'

'Is that so,' Mike said, not really listening. His eyes were transfixed on the sandwich.

Freely smiled. 'I'm sorry, my manners are atrocious. Would you like a bacon butty?'

'Only if you have one spare,' Mike said, nodding like a hungry dog.

Freely took another couple of slices of bread out of the bag and deftly flipped a rasher of the bacon between them, before tipping out the oil from the frying pan and turning off the gas stove. He handed Mike the sandwich and he instantly tore into it.

'So, you on holiday here, then?' Freely asked.

Mike held his hand to his mouth while he chewed. 'Ugh ... something like that.' He swallowed. 'I originally came out here to find out what happened to my sister.'

'Sister?'

'She went missing six weeks ago. She was backpacking around these parts. Nobody's seen her since.'

Freely shook his head. 'Sorry to hear that.'

Mike dropped his head and a silence took hold, until Freely, his mouth full of bacon sandwich, said, 'I don't suppose you've seen it, have you?'

'Seen what?'

'The loch monster. Apparently, a witness saw it take that girl guide the other day. Most often, these things turn out to be just some crackpot telling wild stories. But there might be something in it. Morar has a history of sightings.'

Mike paused with the sandwich to his mouth. 'Actually, I think I might be the crackpot.'

Freely looked at him, his head cocked to the side like a curious puppy. 'Oh?'

'Seem to put my foot in it with a reporter, yesterday.'

Freely's face dropped with disappointment. 'You mean there was no sighting?'

'Well ...' Mike realised he probably couldn't get into any more trouble, no matter what he said. He looked at the calm, still waters of the loch. 'I *was* there when the girl disappeared, and I suppose I did see something, but I don't know what.'

Freely stood up as if he'd sat on a tack. 'Wait there.' He dashed into his camper van. The van rocked and creaked and oaths and curses filtered out. And then a moment later, he re-merged, clutching a pile of papers. 'Tell me, what you saw, was it anything like these?' He laid the papers on the ground.

They were photographs and sketches. Some looked familiar, such as a fuzzy and grainy black and white snapshot of a long necked beast, which Mike had seen in various magazines and books. Others looked more bizarre. Squid-like creatures with giant tentacles wrapped around fishing boats, drawings of dinosaurs, and even some pictures of sharks.

Mike, having finished his sandwich, scratched his head. 'I only saw it for a split-second, but it looked nothing like any of those.'

'Describe it.' Freely's tone suddenly got excitable.

Mike shrugged. 'I'm not sure I can. I only caught a glimpse. It was just a dark shape.'

'How big?'

Mike shrugged again. 'Could have been twenty feet.'

Freely looked down at his collection of images, his hand rubbing his chin. 'Can you remember anything specific, anything that might help me identify it?'

Mike looked out across the water and the events of the day before last played vividly in front of his eyes, as if a projector were beaming a film on to the loch. He saw the girl, splashing and laughing. Then the creature. Big, dark, shapeless. No form, no hump, no long neck, no tentacles.

Wait.

Something.

He looked at Freely, whose eyes were expectant and wide. 'It had spikes coming out of its mouth,' Mike said.

'Spikes?' Freely's face became animated, the eyes buzzing around in their sockets.

'Yes, sort of like antennas, or whiskers perhaps.'

A smile formed on Freely's face, which got wider and wider, and then wider still.

The entire nation's press seemed to have congregated in the reception of the Morar Hotel, clamouring to use the only phone to file their copy, much to the chagrin of Mrs Trench.

'Oh, Betty, thank heavens,' she said after Sandilands made her way through throng of reporters. 'You must do something.' Tension had wrinkled her face like a prune.

Sandilands shrugged. What could she do? The Scottish media had decided to descend on Morar and unless another story broke somewhere else, they would be here for a day or two, at least. Longer, if they got wind of what Sandilands had seen the night before, but she was not going to be blurting that out anytime soon.

She smiled thinly. 'Sorry, there's nothing I can do.' She then shouted over the noise of the newsmen. 'Which room is the young American in?'

Mrs Trench frowned, told the gaggle of reporters surrounding her to quieten down, and then checked the register. 'Fourteen, but he's already gone out for the day.'

'Out, where did he go?'

'Away from this madness, and who could blame him?'

Frustrated, Sandilands trudged out of the hotel and stood on the steps, unsure what to do. She had left Anderson back at the station, still nursing his ribs and waiting for Joe McGillivray to come sniffing about. If he ever did. Van Burgh's transit was now parked outside the station and Anderson was hoping it would stir some reaction. What that reaction would be, Sandilands had no idea, but knowing Joe McGillivray, it was bound to be hotheaded. But he was Anderson's problem. She had something just as dangerous to deal with. Yet she wasn't sure how.

With no sign of Mike, there was only one other person in Morar that could possibly help her comprehend what she was dealing with. And as it was now only lunchtime, there was a slight chance would be relatively sober. So she took out her car keys and walked to the Allegro.

The Land Rover idled on the side of the road opposite Morar police station. Joe's knuckles were white on the steering wheel. He'd been there a couple of hours and had seen the young constable park the van outside. But had seen no sign of van Burgh.

When the Dutch vet didn't come back the night before, Joe knew something was up.

Was he in there now, spilling his guts, telling that damned Glaswegian inspector everything? Of course he was. Eric had no balls, a spineless, clog-wearing, tulip eater. He should have done for him a long time ago. All of this was his fault — the disease, Briers, everything, all down to him and his so-called farming methods. And now he was in there giving the police all they needed to put them both away for life.

Not if Joe had anything to do with it. He'd invested his whole life in the farm, building up his empire, and he was damned if he was going to let an inept Dutch vet and scruffy copper take it from him.

Without van Burgh's testimony, they'd have nothing. And Joe was not going to let him take the stand and bring him down. Not while he still had breath in his body. How he would stop van Burgh from giving evidence against him, he wasn't sure, the man was currently tucked up safe and secure in Morar station's cells. Changing that would require a plan.

And that plan started forming the moment he saw Sergeant Sandilands trounce out from the Morar hotel and get into the battered old police car.

Joe pulled from the side of the road and followed.

Chapter Twenty-Five

The VW was a mess. Empty wrappers and packets littered the floor, the dashboard was split and cracked and held together by black tape, an old mattress lay on the floor in the back, and camping equipment, old clothes and papers and cameras and other equipment, some of it looking pretty expensive, were strewn all over the place. There was also a familiar sweet, pungent aroma filling the van that reminded Mike of college, as did the abundant supply of long cigarette papers sitting on the dashboard.

Freely appeared immensely proud of the old van though, and he whispered encouraging words and stroked the dashboard every time they negotiated a rough bit of track or when the VW had to climb a hill, which it struggled to do in anything but first gear.

'You sure this chap might has seen it?' Freely asked, as the Lochside campsite came into view.

With Freely desperate for more information, Mike could only think of one other person that believed the loch contained something unexplainable. Although Mike doubted the ramblings of a drunk would be of much use. Yet Freely was insistent and demanded he take him.

The campsite was quiet. The coach that had brought the girl guides was no longer there, and most of the tents had been taken down, leaving just a bare field.

'Positive,' Mike said. 'Didn't stop talking about it last time I saw him. But as I told you, he might not be the most reliable of witnesses.'

'So where do I find him?' Freely asked, as he steered the VW into gravel car park.

Mike pointed to the building in the centre of the field. 'In the bar.'

'And he'll definitely be there?'

'Certain of it.'

Freely looked wary. 'You sure you don't want to come in?'

'Positive. As I told you, I'm not too welcome here.' He had already mentioned he was *persona non grata* at Lochside. He didn't go into details and Freely didn't press him.

'So, what's he like, this Fairbanks?'

Mike smiled. 'I think you'll like him.'

Freely smiled and pulled on the handbrake. 'Okay, see you in five,' he said, getting out and leaving Mike alone as he trotted off to speak to Fairbanks.

Mike contented himself by fiddling with the CB on the dashboard, listening to the truckers chatting in their almost unfathomable Scottish. But as he listened to the rhotic, rolling Rs, he happened to look up and saw somebody that made his spine stiffen. Danny Fairbanks.

He was walking out of the campsite, hands in his pockets, a smug, arrogant smile on his face. Mike knew he should just sit in the van. Say nothing. Behave himself. But he caught sight of his own face in the rear view mirror. While the swelling had subsided, his lip was still split and his cheek bruised and tender.

He felt anger bubbling up from his guts like a dose of acid reflux. Not because of the beating but because of the statement Danny had given after the girl's death. He had made Mike sound foolish. Hysterical. A crackpot. Yet Mike knew Danny had seen that thing in the water too. So why did he lie? Mike needed to find out.

He bolted out of the van and marched over to confront him. Danny stopped and removed his hands from his pockets.

'What the hell are you doing here?' he snapped, fists clenched at his side.

Mike raised his hands. 'I don't want any trouble.'

Danny sneered at Mike's face, content at his handiwork. 'I bet you don't.'

'I just want to know why you lied to the police.'

'About what, you being a thief?'

'About the girl on the loch.'

Danny gave another sneer. 'What about her, she drowned?'

'You saw it, I know you did.'

Danny turned to walk away. 'I don't know what you are talking about.'

Mike grabbed him. 'You've known about it all along, haven't you? Did it have something to with my sister's disappearance too, is that why you don't want to talk to me?'

Danny pushed him off, and thrust his finger under Mike's chin. 'If I were you, I'd go back to America. You won't find any answers here.'

'What are you trying to hide?' Mike said, refusing to back down.

'Get out of my way.'

'Not until you tell me what happened to my sister.'

Danny slammed both hands into Mike's chest, shoving him back. Mike stepped forward and Danny grabbed him, so Mike pushed his hands off. Then Danny hit him. Mike staggered back.

Danny hit him again, and again. Then Mike launched himself at Danny.

The next moment, both were on the floor, grappling, punching, rolling around.

'Oi, stop that, now!' shouted a voice. A moment later Mike felt a hand on the back of his jacket, hauling him up. Danny was still thrashing and swiping at him, but a familiar dark blue figure stepped in between the two of them.

'What the hell are you two doing?' Sandilands asked, her arms outstretched, keeping Danny and Mike apart, teeth flashing, eyes vibrating with anger.

Despite her presence, Danny tried to take another swipe at Mike, but Sandilands pushed him back. 'Do you want me to nick you, Danny?'

He didn't look at her. His eyes continued glaring at Mike. 'He started it,' he insisted.

'And you just had to finish it,' she rasped. 'Now unless you walk away, you can spend the next twenty-four hours in the cells.'

Danny stood firm for a moment, eyes still glaring at Mike, lips curled back in a snarl. Then he spat on the floor, scowled and walked past them both, deliberately shoulder barging Mike as he went.

They watched him walk out of the campsite and up the lane towards Morar, before Sandilands turned her indignation on Mike. 'What the hell are you doing back here?' She shook him as she asked, as if he were a naughty child. 'I told you to keep away.'

'I know,' he said, head bowed. 'It wasn't my idea.' He looked back at the VW. 'I was just showing somebody the way.'

Sandilands frowned. 'Who?'

'Err ... just somebody I met in Morar.'

'A reporter?'

Mike didn't say anything.

'You're the one who tipped off the papers, aren't you?' she snapped.

'I didn't mean to, it just ... I was tricked into —'

'Well never mind that now. I need to speak to you about what you saw.'

'Saw?'

She pointed across the field, over the tents. 'In the water, when the girl died. I need you to give a statement.'

Mike raised his head, confused. Why the sudden interest? She had already dismissed him as being unhinged. He studied her face. Her eyes had lost the initial anger of seeing him and Danny fighting, but they looked just as serious.

'I already told you everything already,' he insisted. 'You didn't believe me, remember?'

Her features softened somewhat and she breathed in deeply. It was her turn to bow her head. 'I may have been a bit hasty.'

Mike looked at her for a moment. 'You've seen it, haven't you?'

She breathed in deep again. 'I'm not sure what I've seen, that's why I need you to explain precisely what it was you saw.'

'I told you, I don't know.' He looked back at the VW. 'But I think I know somebody who might.'

Chapter Twenty-Six

Fairbanks was in his usual position behind the bar and speaking to a longhaired, scruffy looking character who Sandilands presumed was the person Mike had escorted to Lochside.

They both turned around as she and Mike walked in. 'Sergeant, nice to see you again,' Fairbanks said, beaming a sincere if slightly wary smile. While he didn't look drunk, the glass of scotch in his hand indicated he was hardly sober. 'If you're after our Danny, he's gone to Morar. I hope he's not been causing you bother again?'

Sandilands took off her cap and placed it on the bar. 'I've just seen Danny, and no, it's not him I need to speak to, it's you.'

Fairbanks eyebrows rose an inch up his forehead. 'Me? Whatever have I done, lassie?'

'Nothing. But I'm hoping you can help me with something.' She looked across at the scruffy man, who had a pint glass in his hand. 'Are you Freely?'

He looked back at Mike, his eyes asking for clarification. Mike nodded.

'Yes,' Freely said, rather sheepishly.

'She's seen it too,' Mike said, his head turning to the window and the calm, benign-looking waters of the loch. 'Whatever it is.'

Sandilands propped herself on a bar stool next to Freely. 'I need to find out what it is,' she said, looking at Fairbanks and Freely in turn. 'And more importantly, how to get rid of it.'

'Morag is nae of this earth,' Fairbanks said, turning round to the optics and pouring a drink. 'She's the de'il, so she is.'

Sandilands sighed. She knew this was a waste of time.

Fairbanks stopped talking sense when he fell into the bottle six months ago. He'd always been eccentric, but after his fishing shop closed, he'd become the village clown. Nobody took him seriously.

'Actually, I think I might have an idea as to what we're dealing with,' Freely said, taking a sip of his beer. He put the glass down and wiped the froth from his mouth. 'Having spoken to Mr Fairbanks here.' He looked across at Mike, who was still staring out of the window. 'And after your description this morning, I think I may be able to identify it.'

'What description? I told you, I only caught a glimpse of it,' Mike said, turning back from the window.

'But you remembered seeing its barbells,' Freely said.

Mike frowned. 'Barbells?'

Freely smiled. 'The whiskers, antennas protruding from the mouth, remember?'

Mike screwed up his eyes and nodded.

'Well, when I heard you mention those, it made me think of a theory about loch cryptids that I've been thinking about for a while now, and after speaking to Mr Fairbanks,' he smiled at the old sop. 'It's all starting to make sense.'

He paused as everybody stared at him.

'And?' Sandilands said.

'*Siluriforme*,' Freely declared, jabbing his finger in the air.

Sandilands frowned, as did Mike, while Fairbanks downed his scotch and poured another.

'And what is this Siluri-whatever-you called-it when it's at home?' Mike asked.

'You have catfish in America, don't you?' Freely said.

'Catfish, yes, of course, why?'

'Well, in Britain we don't have any native species. But during the last century, a couple of species, the wels and the bullhead, were introduced by anglers.'

'What I saw wasn't a catfish, it was huge,' Mike insisted.

Freely rose his hand. 'And because of its size, we can rule out the bullhead, but the wels is a different matter. Back in the rivers neat the Baltic where they originate, Russian fishermen regularly pull up wels catfish in excess of ten feet. Some weighing three hundred pounds.'

'So you think it's some over-sized fish?' Sandilands said.

Freely nodded. 'It makes more sense than you might think. The wels was introduced into Britain at the end of the nineteenth century, about fifty years before the first sightings in Loch Ness. Now, the wels is an interesting fish for three reasons. Firstly, they grow throughout their entire life depending on the amount of food available. There doesn't seem to be a limit to how big they can get, either. If they have enough food, and enough time, they can grow massive. Secondly, they can live to be well over a hundred years old. And thirdly,' he looked at everyone in turn, like a teacher ensuring his pupils were listening. 'They eat almost anything.'

He paused to take a sip of his beer.

'Now, just suppose they found their way into Scotland's lochs at the end of the nineteenth century,' he continued. 'There would be no natural predators to attack them, and with enough food, they could grow to huge proportions over the next thirty, forty or fifty years. And that would coincide to when we get the first sightings of loch monsters. Most famously at Loch Ness, but here too.'

'But what would it eat?' Sandilands asked. 'The fish in Morar is sparse to say the least.'

Her eyes fell on Fairbanks who started nodding. 'Nae enough in that water for a fish supper let alone to support yon beastie.'

Freely screwed up his lips. 'Around the valleys surrounding most of Scotland's lochs there are plenty of sheep. They must occasionally fall into the loch, and would sustain a large wels.'

'Then why is this thing all of sudden attacking people?' Sandilands asked.

Freely shrugged. 'Who knows? Maybe it wasn't always big enough. It will only target food that it can fit in its mouth. Perhaps it was too small but suddenly got access to a glut of food, then it could have had a growth spurt, making it large enough to pose a threat to people.'

Sandilands sat back, a realisation forming in her mind. McGillivray. If, as she and Anderson suspected, the McGillivrays had been dumping cattle parts into the loch for last year or so, it would explain how this thing has suddenly grown so big. She then had another thought. Kilkenny. He had said Joe McGillivray had been filling his cattle up with steroids. She knew little about the effects of anabolic medicines, but did know they encouraged an increase in muscle mass.

'It still sounds a bit far-fetched to me,' Mike said. 'A shark I could believe, but a giant pond fish?'

'So what do you suggest it was that you saw, then?' Freely snapped, sharply. 'Some creature from the Jurassic period that has somehow managed to survive the mass extinction of the dinosaurs? Pah!' He took a large sip of his beer, leaving foam all round his beard. 'Look, it is just a theory but it fits.'

Sandilands scratched her chin, unsure if this Freely was really the expert he made out, or just another crank. 'I'm going to need more than a theory,' she said, knowing what the chief constable would say if she started making claims a giant fish was loose in the loch.

Freely stood up, his face excited, the eyebrows raised high up his head. 'I have some equipment in the van that may help — an underwater camera, a sonar buoy and ...'

'Now hold on,' Sandilands said, standing up and looking sternly at Freely. 'I don't want anybody going out on that loch. Not until we know for sure what we're dealing with.' She had already seen anglers from out of town on sail dinghies looking for this blasted thing. 'You leave it to me. The last thing I need is another accident'

She screwed her cap back on her head. 'But I may need to speak to you all again, so I'd appreciate it if you stay in town.' She glared at Mike. 'But stay out of trouble.'

While the young constable, Featherstone, rattled around the office, answering calls, keeping busy, saying very little, Anderson chain-smoked.

He was getting bored of waiting. It was well into the afternoon and there had been no sign of Joe McGillivray.

He rubbed his ribs. He felt certain his ruse would work because he knew McGillivray's type. Ruthless, desperate. He'd had met Irish dissidents of the same vein, schoolteachers by day, all caring and altruistic, who became merciless thugs by night who'd think nothing of smashing in somebody's kneecaps just because of their religious or political beliefs. The same was true of Joe McGillivray. He may have come across as a hardworking businessman and farmer, but beneath beat the heart of a true psychopath.

Then why hadn't he shown himself, done something, anything? He couldn't know van Burgh was dead. He'd have to assume he was in custody. That should have rattled him. Yet time was running out. They'd have to report van Burgh's disappearance soon. Although he had no idea what he was going to write in his report.

He wondered if Sandilands was any closer at finding out what the thing was. He'd seen many a strange thing in his line of work, but loch monsters had their place in the pages of fairy tales. Yet they had both seen it. He thought about calling Kendrick, his Superintendent, to get his opinion, but he doubted he'd know what to do anymore than Anderson did. Strangely enough, nobody had ever got round to writing up a contingency plan for loch monsters. Besides, he'd think Anderson had gone mad.

Whatever it was, it was Sandilands' problem, for now. His priority was nailing Joe McGillivray, which meant he was going to wait as long as possible for him to make his move. If he ever did.

Chapter Twenty-Seven

Sandilands drove out of Lochside even more confused than when she drove in. She hadn't a clue what to do. If what Mike's friend Freely said was true, and they were just dealing with just some oversized fish, how would they to get rid of it? They could hardly pluck it from the loch on a rod and line. And what if there was more than one? She hadn't thought about that. She gazed over at the waters, shimmering in the afternoon sun. There could be a whole family of the things down there. She shuddered.

She'd not gone far, when she slowed the car. A Land Rover was blocking the narrow trail. It appeared to have broken down. The bonnet was up and she could see the backside of somebody bent over trying to fix the engine. Great. That's all she needed. She'd have to lend a hand. There was no way round.

She stopped, yanked on the handbrake, got out and screwed her cap on.

'Trouble?' she asked, walking over.

No reply. Whoever had broken down was obviously too absorbed with fixing the engine.

'Do you need a hand?' she asked, approaching the raised bonnet and remembering she had some jump leads in the car somewhere.

'Yes, that would be nice,' came the reply.

The bonnet of the Land Rover suddenly slammed shut and the face of Joe McGillivray grinned at her. He had something in his hands. A cattle prod. But before she could say anything, do anything, he raised it up to her neck and an intense spasm of pain flooded her body.

'Do you really think it is just a big fish?' Mike asked, as he and Freely sat in the bar, with Mr Fairbanks pouring them regular drinks and not asking for any cash. Already, Mike could feel his head spinning.

'As I said, it's just a theory, but it makes more sense to me than any other ideas milling around about loch cryptids. He spun around on his seat and looked Mike straight in the eye. 'The thing about catfish, particularly the wels, is they are not really predatory in the same sense that a shark is. They have no teeth and tend to swallow their meals whole. But they'll eat anything, whether alive or dead, fish or mammal, it makes no difference to them so long as they can swallow it.'

'Been no fish in the loch worth a bite for over a year,' Fairbanks said, shaking his head and sipping at his scotch.

Freely looked out at the water. 'That makes sense. If there is a big wels in the water, they have voracious appetites. They will even eat each other, and in a loch this size, that means I doubt we are dealing with more than one specimen. Competition would be too high, as soon as one got large enough, it would devour all the rest and every other fish of any reasonable size.'

'How do you think the police are going to deal with it then?' Mike asked.

Freely took a gulp of his fresh pint. 'I doubt they will. The problem with being a crypto zoologist is that until you can show people evidence, they just dismiss you as a crank.'

'But Sergeant Sandilands seemed pretty interested.'

'I'm sure she is, but what can one policewoman do? She'll have to convince others that what we're saying is true.' He shook his head mournfully. 'And in my experience, nobody will listen.'

'Then we have to get proof,' Mike declared, looking at both Fairbanks and Freely in turn.

'You heard her,' Freely said. 'We're not to go out on the loch.'

'This equipment of yours. Is it difficult to set up?'

Freely shook his head, his long dreadlocks swinging. 'No, not at all. Just have to drop the sonar and camera buoys in the water. They are all automatic.'

'Then what are we waiting for. Let's drop them in the loch and see what they pick up.'

'Steady on.' Freely held up his hands. 'It's not quite as easy as that. We need to find the right place, besides, where do we get a boat?'

Fairbanks placed his glass down and leaned over. His whiskey breath causing Mike's eyes to water. 'If it's a boat you are after.' He pointed out the window of the bar, to where the dinghies bobbed and jostled next to each other along the jetty.

Mike turned to Freely. 'Can you sail?'

Freely shook his head. 'No, can you?'

Mike shook his head too, and then both of them looked at Fairbanks, who began to cackle. 'I'll take you, laddies. I've a score to settle with yon beastie.'

Sandilands awoke to intense pain in her arms, a burning, stretching pain. At first, as her mind cleared and her eyes opened, she thought she was paralysed. Breathing was difficult, she couldn't move her legs, couldn't speak. Full consciousness then brought with it a terrifying realisation.

She was suspended, tied by chains to the ceiling, mouth

gagged by tape. It was dim but she could still make out other forms hanging beside her. Reddish in colour, dripping blood, skinned. Cattle carcasses. And she was hanging helpless like just another piece of meat.

She struggled. The resulting pain in her wrists and arms caused her to scream, but the duct tape over her mouth muffled any sound.

'So you are awake, then?' said a familiar voice in the gloom below.

A clunk of machinery sounded followed by the whirr of a motor. Sandilands felt the sensation of movement. She was being lowered. Following another mechanical clunk, she came to an abrupt halt, causing another spasm of pain in her arms and wrist. Her feet still dangled above the ground, but she could now see her tormentor, grinning, just below her chin.

'Sergeant Betty Sandilands, how nice of you to hang around.' Joe laughed at his joke, but his face soon straightened and he stepped forward. She could see the cattle prod in his hands. He held it up, stroking the blouse beneath her tunic. 'I think you and I are going to have to have a little chat.'

He jabbed her with the prod and a jolt of intense pain rippled up her body and she struggled and squirmed and tried to scream as her body spasmed and trembled.

Joe chuckled and thrust the cattle prod beneath her chin. Then, with one swift motion, he pulled the tape from her mouth. It stung, like a slap in the face during a cold day and she screamed.

'Joe ... what the hell are you doing?'

'Shaadup,' he rasped, shoving the cattle prod under her arm.

He zapped her again.

She screamed, this time her cries echoed around the abattoir.

'That's okay,' Joe said, chuckling at her torment. 'I'm afraid there is no one around to hear you. My workers have all gone home. It's Saturday. The slaughtermen won't be back until Monday. And none of the farm hands would dare come in here, no matter what they heard'

He prodded her under the arm again. Sandilands screamed once more, kicking, squirming, shaking in pain.

'Now,' Joe said, stepping close, so his face was inches from hers. He held the cattle prod up to her face and let the spark arc in front of her eyes. 'Let's talk about Eric and what he's told you.'

Chapter Twenty-Eight

Freely had been right, it wasn't as simple as Mike had thought. It had taken the crypto zoologist hours to ready his equipment and test it all, especially the sonar buoy. It had been in a large case at the back of the van. It was fairly large, about the size of a bass drum, painted bright yellow with a box of tricks and flashing light on the top. With it, Freely had a small computer monitor hooked up to a radio transmitter and a set of headphones.

'Does it work?' Mike asked, sitting cross-legged on the jetty, getting impatient as Freely continually fiddled with the device. The sun was now dropping below the valley, which meant it would be dark soon, and Mike didn't want to be on the loch when night fell.

'Of course it works,' Freely snapped. 'Here,' he handed Mike the headphones and waved his hand at the monitor.

Mike placed the headphones over his ears. He could hear very little but crackle and fizz, but when Freely tilted the buoy to its side and waved his hand under it, a loud succession of pings accompanied a fuzzy green shape on the monitor.

Mike took off the headphones and handed them back. 'Where did you get it from?'

Freely smiled. 'It's old navy equipment. I have a source.' He tapped his nose.

'Shouldn't we wait until morning,' Mike said, as Freely loaded his equipment into the boat. 'It'll be dark soon.'

'We've got time,' Freely said, checking one of the camera buoys had film in it. 'Catfish are more active at night so long as we get these installed before nightfall we have a good chance of getting something. We can sit in the van and monitor the sonar and come back in the morning and see what the cameras have picked up.' He pointed to a couple of smaller green buoys beside Mike. 'Just need to load the film into the cameras and I'm done. You best go get Fairbanks, tell him we're about ready.'

'Have you heard anything from Betty?' Featherstone asked, as Anderson was dozing, feet up on the desk, a cigarette burning in his lips, in the station.

He pulled the cigarette free. 'Sweaty Glands, no why?'

'She's not answering her radio,' Featherstone said.

The young constable had a perplexed expression on his boyish face. Anderson could never get used to how young coppers were these days. 'Maybe she's busy.'

'Aye, maybe, but she normally calls in if she's expecting to be out past her shift.' He checked his watch. 'Especially when she is using the car.'

'When was the last time you to spoke her?' Anderson asked.

'Earlier this afternoon. She said she was going up to Lochside to speak to Mr Fairbanks, but that was hours ago.'

Anderson suspected Featherstone was holding a candle for WS Sandilands. He could see why. There wasn't exactly an overabundance of petticoats in these parts. Although he doubted Featherstone would know what to do with a bird like Sandilands if she ever gave him the chance. Which he doubted she would.

'So, what do you want me to do about it?' he snapped, wishing he was a decade or so younger. In his prime, he'd have shown her a good time.

'Nothing,' Featherstone replied. 'Just wondering if you'd seen her, that's all.'

'Don't worry about Sweaty Glands. She's big enough to look after herself.'

Anderson had more pressing things to worry about, namely Joe McGillivray. He knew he couldn't keep up the bluff about van Burgh for too long. He'd have to inform the procurator fiscal sooner rather than later. Although he still didn't know what to put in the report. He could hardly go around blaming Morag the loch monster. They'd section him.

Van Burgh's disappearance would have to be accounted for, though. Somebody would start asking questions sooner or later. Everybody had somebody. A girlfriend, wife, doting mother, anxious employer. Anderson had hoped in van Burgh's case that that somebody would be the latter, but there had been no sign of Joe McGillivray all day, not a phone call, not a visit, nothing.

He was coming to the conclusion his ruse wasn't working. The frosted window on the station door had now darkened. Day was slipping away on Morar, and with it, his hopes of flushing out Joe McGillivray. He decided to give it another hour, then go to the pub. He really needed a drink. As he sat, smoking, waiting, eyes staring at Featherstone, who kept checking his watch, no doubt wondering when Sandilands would get back, the phone rang.

Featherstone stared at it for a ring or two before snatching the receiver from the cradle. He held it to his ear, his eyes lighting up as he heard the voice on the other end.

'Betty, where the hell have you been? Yes ... yes, he's still here.' Featherstone's eyes fixed on Anderson, and he held out the receiver. 'She wants to speak to you.'

Anderson sighed and snatched the phone from him. 'Yes,' he

sighed.

'It's Sandilands,' the voice on the other end said.

'Where are you?'

The phone went quiet for several seconds. 'I'm at McGillivray's place,' she finally said.

'What you doing there?'

'I have something to show you,' she replied. Her voice sounded distant and it echoed, as if she were speaking in a cathedral.

'What the hell for?'

Silence for another few seconds.

'Just come,' she said. 'And I need you to bring van Burgh. It concerns him too.'

'What the hell are you talking about?'

'Just bring him,' she insisted, before the phone went dead.

Anderson, the phone still held to his ear, looked at Featherstone. 'We're going to need help,' he said. 'You best call whoever it is you call when you need backup.'

Featherstone frowned, eyebrow hunkering over his eyes. 'Backup?'

Anderson pulled the receiver from his ear and stared at it as he gently placed it back in the cradle. 'Yes, backup, and preferably armed.'

When Fairbanks arrived, only then did Mike realise how small the fibreglass dinghy was. It was barely large enough for Freely and Mike, let alone the equipment. But Fairbanks was a big man, and he doubted the boat could even hold his weight.

'I think we need a bigger boat?' he said, as scenes from the film *Jaws* flashed through his mind.

'She'll do just fine,' Fairbanks said. He threw a pair of lifejackets at the two boys, but didn't bother with one for himself. Mike doubted they did them in his size.

Fairbanks then hiccupped. He was blind drunk and Mike realised this was a bad idea. 'Perhaps we should wait until morning.'

'You can stay here if you're afraid,' Freely said, still checking his camera.

'No, I'm fine.'

Freely nodded to the boat. 'Then get aboard. It's time to go.'

Mike tentatively stepped into the craft. It bobbed violently as he took his seat at the front. Freely clambered aboard next and sat next to him, the three buoys at their feet. Then Fairbanks stepped in. The little dinghy bobbed so ferociously Mike thought it would capsize. He felt a wave of nausea bubble up from his stomach, but the large man soon settled on the bench behind the sail and the bobbing eased but the water level was perilously high.

'You lads ready?' Fairbanks asked, before belching.

'I'm starting to think this is perhaps not a good idea,' Mike said, battling to keep the four pints he'd drunk in his stomach.

'Too late for that, laddie,' Fairbanks said, unmooring the boat from the jetty. He then gave a wave in the direction of the cottage, where unbeknown to Mike, Mrs Fairbanks had been standing outside the shop-cum-reception, arms on hips, head shaking with incredulity.

Before Mike could say anything else, Fairbanks pulled on the boom and the sail unfurled and the light evening breeze caught it, gently pulling them from the jetty.

Chapter Twenty-Nine

Featherstone and Anderson were in Kilkenny's Volvo. The young constable had borrowed it from the vet when it became apparent Sandilands was in trouble. And she was in trouble. Big trouble. Anderson knew his ruse to flush out Joe McGillivray had worked, but had perhaps worked too well.

Both Sandilands and Anderson knew that van Burgh was dead, drowned, loch creature fodder, but Joe didn't, and her insistence that van Burgh be brought to the farm was proof she was in danger, and that, clever girl that she was, she hadn't let slip that to Joe that van Burgh was dead. Yet. And the moment she did would probably mean the end of her. Anderson had been right about Joe. The man was clearly psychopathic.

Anderson made Featherstone turn off the lights as they reached the brow of the hill overlooking the farm. While the sun had only just set, outside of the village there were no lampposts, so the road was dark, and only a few lights twinkled in the distance from the farm below.

'Wait a moment,' Anderson insisted, staring through the windscreen. There must have been a dozen cattle sheds on the farm, and with just the two of them, it could hours to find Sandilands down there. 'When did you say help is arriving?'

'Could be hours,' Featherstone said. 'I had to call the superintendent over at Mallaig at his home. He's getting people together now, but we don't have much experience of this sort of thing out here.'

Anderson took out his tobacco and quickly fumbled together a cigarette. 'Well, she could be dead by then.' He thrust the smoke in his mouth and lit it, using the Volvo's cigarette lighter. 'I guess it's just you and me then, kid.'

'You ... you really think Joe would ... hurt her?' Fear crackled his voice.

'He's killed before. And he's desperate enough to do anything.' Anderson nodded down the hill. 'Take it slow. Let's not announce our arrival.'

There was little sign of activity, even the security gate didn't have anybody on duty and other than the sound of mooing cattle drifting on the breeze, all was quiet.

The gate was pulled across and a chain hooked around it, but when Featherstone got out of the Volvo, he unravelled the chain and opened the gate.

'Unlocked,' Featherstone said, as he got back into the car.

'Seems like somebody wanted us to find our way in,' Anderson said, wincing at the smell.

Slowly Featherstone drove in, headlights still off, and both men looked eagerly about, checking for any activity. Nothing. No workers, no security, the place seemed to be deserted, other than the cattle, which mooed incessantly from the surrounding sheds.

Driving at a crawl, they arrived at the yard where McGillivray's had their office. That was quiet too, but a Land Rover sat where McGillivray senior normally parked his green Rolls Royce.

'There's at least one person here,' Anderson said, nodding to it. He stubbed his cigarette in the erstwhile clean ashtray and got out of the car.

Featherstone followed, placing his domed helmet on his head. The young constable then removed his truncheon and looked warily about the yard.

Anderson slapped him on the back. 'Relax, just keep your wits about you.'

As far as Anderson could tell, the office was locked up and deserted, as were most of the cattle sheds. In fact, the only sign of activity were the lights coming from the abattoir he and Sandilands had the misfortune to visit the day before. Anderson rubbed his ribs. They still ached terribly.

'Right,' he said, looking at the truncheon held in Featherstone's hand. 'Come on *Charlie Barlow*, this way,' he said, walking towards the abattoir.

'Charlie who?' Featherstone whispered, scuttling after him.

'Didn't you watch Z Cars?'

'Bit before my time, sir. I've started watching The Bill, you seen it?'

'Don't get chance to see much telly, these days,' Anderson replied, as they reached the main door to the abattoir. He pulled at the door handle. It too was unlocked.

The large metal door opened without discretion, clanging and creaking and echoing around the large expanse of the abattoir.

The smell was just as bad as Anderson remembered but there were now no cows in any of the pens. A few weak emergency lights cast everything in gloom and long shadows. All was quiet. Too quiet.

Despite the lack of lighting, Anderson could see the shutter where he and Sandilands were almost trampled to death the day before. It was half-open. He twitched his head towards it, and he and Featherstone made their way along the pens in silence.

On reaching the shutter, the pair ducked underneath, which

caused Anderson ribs to throb in pain. He clutched at them as he righted himself in the slaughter room. And then another spasm of pain shot through his body, only this wasn't caused by his broken ribs but several thousand volts of electricity coursing through his body.

Mike and the others had been on the water for about an hour, during which time the sun had sunk below the valley plunging the loch in near darkness.

Freely had a torch strapped to his head and was peering over the side. 'This could be a good place,' he said, much to Mike's relief.

They had sailed up and down the loch looking for a likely spot for what seemed ages, but Freely always found fault with every location, either it was too close to the shore, too shallow, or too many reeds that would cause interference with his precious sonar. Now they were near to the loch's islands and closer to the village, its lights twinkling in the distance.

Freely placed the buoy in the water, slipped the headphones over his ears and fiddled with the monitor. 'Yes,' he said, after a few moments. 'This may just do.' He looked over at Fairbanks, who was sitting content, sipping from a hip flask. 'How deep are the waters here?'

'Deep,' Fairbanks replied, taking a slug of whisky from the flask. His face then screwed up and he tipped the flask upside down. 'Bah, it's time to get back.'

'Okay, just give me a minute.' Freely gesticulated to Mike. 'Give me a hand with the camera buoys, will you.'

'Sure,' Mike said, passing one of the green buoys. 'But will these see anything?'

'They have underwater flashes. If anything gets close they'll go off and we should get something.' He pressed a button on the underside of the buoy and suddenly in synchronisation to a muffled clack, a blinding white light flashed, followed by a muted whirr.

The light had been intense, causing shadows to dance in front of Mike's eyes. He rubbed them. 'You'll probably blind the damned thing,' he moaned, as Freely dropped both the buoys in the water and tethered them to the sonar.

'I've angled them away from each other. Should give us the widest field of view,' he said, nodding to Fairbanks. 'Okay, let's get back.'

Fairbanks leaned from his seat and unfurled the sail, causing the boat to bob dangerously. Mike grabbed hold of the gunwale with his free hand and slowly the boat started to turn. And then a clack sounded and a white light flashed under the water from one of the buoys.

All three heads on the boat turned back to the buoys.

Another flash, this time from the other buoy.

'Blast,' snorted freely. 'They must be malfunctioning.' He shrugged at Fairbanks who pulled on the tiller and turned the boat back towards the buoys.

Another flash, and then another.

'Damn, there'll be no film left at this rate,' Freely said, as the boat gently drifted towards the buoys. He leaned over and plucked one from the loch, dripping cold water in the boat and all over Mike

Frustrated and feeling cold, Mike cast his head down, and

noticed something on the small portable monitor. It was a green shape, appearing and disappearing on the centre of the screen. He leaned close and could hear something coming from the headphones, a relentless, continuous stream of clicks.

'Does that mean anything?' he asked, pointing to the monitor.

Freely, the buoy still in his hands was checking the camera and looked across. 'Does what mean anything?'

'That,' Mike said pointing at the monitor, but before Freely could investigate, a flash from the buoy cast the boat in brilliant white, burning ghosts on to Mike's retina and temporarily blinding him.

Mike rubbed his eyes, and then the buoy flashed again, but this time he was ready for it, keeping his eyes cast over the side, where for a few milliseconds the loch illuminated in an intense, dazzling light, and he saw a great black shape just beneath the surface.

'Jesus,' Mike yelped, rubbing his eyes and moving as far from the side of the boat as possible. 'Did you see that?'

'See what?' Freely asked.

Mike pointed over the side. 'It's there, in the water.'

Freely peered over the side, the torch strapped to his head no match for the darkness. Fairbanks had bought a more powerful flashlight with him, so he switched it on, its beam settling as a spotlight on the water. 'I can't see anything,' Freely admitted.

'It was definitely there, in the water. It was huge,' Mike said, his voice panting.

'Are you sure?' Freely asked, as Fairbank's spotlight scoured the water.

But before Mike could answer, a thud underneath the boat

caused all three of them to sit upright. And then the boat rose perilously in the air, threatening to tip over.

'What in God's name!' Fairbanks shouted, falling backwards on to the mast and causing the boat to rock ferociously. It soon settled, the mast slowing like a metronome running out of energy. But nobody spoke. All eyes were on the water. Fairbanks had dropped his torch, but picked it up again and pointed it at the blackness around the boat.

With one hand gripping the gunwale, he leaned over. 'I cannae see it,' he admitted.

Then it broke the surface, emerging right in the middle of the spotlight. A huge, black, hideous head with tendrils poking from bulbous, thick lips that looked like a truck's inner tube. It dived again.

Silence. Everybody looked at one another, then at the water. Then a loud thud sounded from below, water exploded around them and the boat capsized.

Chapter Thirty

When Anderson came to, he found he couldn't move. His head thumped angrily, but no worse than the average hangover. His ribs hurt too, made worse by the position of his body. He was bent over, hands chained, much like being held in a set of stocks. Lying on the floor near the shutter, he could see a shape. Featherstone, domed helmet tipped off his head. Whether he was still breathing, Anderson couldn't tell, the light was too dim. But despite the gloom, he could see Sandilands hanging between the shanks of meat ahead of him. Or he presumed it was her. Cattle didn't wear police uniforms.

And she was alive, because he could see her kicking and squirming, her eyes bulging in his direction, and then he realised the true horror of his predicament.

The chute gave it away. Only the day before had he seen a slaughtered cow slide down it, before being hoisted to the ceiling to the conveyor from which Sandilands now hung. This meant he was shackled to the yoke where he'd seen the cows despatched. He then realised why Sandilands was squirming and staring in his direction. Somebody was behind him, breathing heavily.

'So glad you could join us.' It was Joe's voice, and he spoke close to Anderson's ear. 'But there appears to be somebody missing from our party. Where's Eric van Burgh?'

'Taking it easy in one of the cells,' Anderson snapped, defiantly. 'Exactly where you are going to be before long.'

'Is that a fact,' rasped Joe, tapping something metallic on the side of Anderson's face. 'So who's watching over him? The sergeant is tied up, the young constable's taking a nap and that old fool Inspector Monroe is still on his holidays.'

'They've sent some boys down from Mallaig,' he said, struggling in the chains. 'They're on their way here too. So you best do yourself a favour and untie me because otherwise when I get free—' He raised his voice to a shout. 'I'm gonna stick my hand up your arse and pull your balls through your jacksey!'

A loud crackle sounded near his cheek, and a moment later an intense jolt of pain shot down his spine and played on his broken ribs like they were a xylophone.

He screamed, clenching his teeth together.

Joe then zapped him again, the pain much worse, but Anderson refused to give him any satisfaction.

'Arrgh ... lower, lower, you've missed a bit.'

Joe started chuckling. 'Quite the comic, aren't you. But perhaps I can wipe that smile off your face.'

He stepped from behind and walked to where Sandilands hung struggling. Gently he stroked her with the cattle prod and Anderson could see her squirm in the chains.

'Perhaps, if you won't speak, she will.'

He then jabbed the cattle prod into her body. She stiffened then went limp then kicked and squirmed. But she didn't scream, until Joe ripped the duct tape across her mouth. She then groaned and panted.

'So, Betty, are you going to tell me about Eric?' Joe asked.

'Screw you Joe,' she snapped, spitting straight in his eye.

Good for you girl, thought Anderson, as he watched Joe wipe the spittle from his face. Joe jabbed her with the cattle prod, and she screamed an ear-splitting, blood-curdling scream that bounced off the walls and echoed around the cattle shed.

Anderson pulled and tugged at his chains, shouting, swearing, blaspheming, but Joe ignored him and continued his torment of Sandilands.

'I think you better start talking, Betty,' Joe said as she kicked and squirmed in her bonds.

'Screw you,' she shouted.

Joe laughed, but rather than poke her with the cattle prod again, he tossed it to the floor and walked back to the yoke where he slapped Anderson around the face. 'Quite the tough girl, isn't she, Inspector?'

Anderson tried to bite his hand, but Joe removed it and cackled. He then stepped to the side and reached for one of the compressed air hoses dangling from the ceiling. After a little fumbling, he connected a metal cylinder to the end of it. Joe held it before Anderson's eyes, waving it menacingly. He fired it, a hiss sounded, and a bolt, about eight inches long, suddenly shot out the end.

'I'll ask you again, Betty, where is van Burgh.' Joe pushed the bolt back into the gun and pressed the cold steel end of it against Anderson's temple. 'I'll give you to the count of three.'

'Joe, don't,' she pleaded.

'One.'

'Joe, please,' she screamed. 'We can talk about this. Stop before it's too late.'

'Two.'

'I'll tell you, but please, put that down.'

'Don't,' shouted Anderson. 'He's bluffing. He's not got the balls.'

Joe pressed the gun hard against Anderson's temple. 'Three.'

'He's dead,' spluttered Sandilands. 'Van Burgh's dead.'

'No!' shouted Anderson. 'Don't listen to her.'

The cold steel tip of the cattle gun retreated from Anderson's temple. 'Dead, dead! What do you mean dead?'

'He fell in the loch last night, Joe ... he's gone,' Sandilands admitted, her voice barely a whisper.

Instead of sounding relieved that they no longer had a witness to his activities, Joe roared at them, his voice booming around the slaughterhouse. 'You mean all this ...' He waved the cattle gun at Anderson. '... Was a waste of time?'

He started snorting and breathing heavily through his nose. Anderson realised that now that Sandilands had played their only hand, Joe could hardly let them go. Kidnap and torture of police officers was as serious as murder, perhaps more so. Joe would realise that, which meant he would have only one option.

Anderson squirmed and pulled at his chains, but the jangling did nothing but catch Joe's attention. He grabbed Anderson's hair and yanked his head back, the metal cylinder waving close to his eye.

'You think you're so clever, don't you,' he hissed. 'Ruin me, will you.' He pushed the end of the bolt gun hard against Anderson's temple.

'Joe, don't,' Sandilands pleaded. 'We can talk about this.'

'The time for talking is over,' Joe snapped, as Anderson closed his eyes and prepared for the inevitable.

'Joe, no!' Sandilands yelled.

'Say goodbye, Inspector.'

The water was cold, body-numbingly cold. Mike splashed and

kicked and gasped for several moments, and after getting over the initial shock of immersion, he became aware of somebody else struggling in the water beside him. He reached out and grabbed a handful of sodden dreadlocks.

'Mike ... ugh ... is that you?' Freely shouted, his mouth full of water.

'Yes, are you all right?'

'I can't ... swim.'

'It's okay, you're life jacket will keep you afloat. Just kick. Those islands are close, we can make it.'

'Where's Fairbanks?' Freely shouted, as Mike helped pull him towards the wooded islands.

Mike scanned the dark waters around him, but other than the upturned boat, could see nothing, no Fairbanks, no giant fish.

'Maybe he's already ashore,' Mike said, his teeth chattering, as he kicked towards the nearest island.

They swam for a minute or two and after slipping beneath some overhanging trees, Mike felt the bottom of the loch floor. While dragging Freely with him, he waded on to the island, falling into a mesh of bushes and bracken and thistles.

They lay shivering for a moment, shaking, teeth shattering, lips quivering, until Mike got his breath back. He stood up and called out. 'Mr Fairbanks, sir, are you okay?'

His voice echoed out into the night, but no reply came back.

'Sir, Mr Fairbanks?'

'Can ... can you see him?' Freely asked, shivering.

Mike shook his head. Before them, the water was still, quiet, calm. They could see the dark bulge of the upturned dinghy, but of Fairbanks, nothing.

They continued calling, their voices carrying across the water, but not receiving any replies. Before long, tiredness and coldness made them give up, and they slumped back into the thistles and bracken, shivering.

'We need to get warm,' Mike said, trying to unbuckle his lifejacket. But his fingers were numb, making it difficult, but with some perseverance, he soon managed it and helped Freely out of his.

'I still have my lighter,' Freely said, struggling to reach into his pocket. Mike helped him, and pulled out a small tobacco tin. He opened it, revealing Freely's stash, sodden and useless, but the thin plastic lighter still sparked.

With their hands so numb, making a fire and setting it alight took what seemed like hours, but they managed it. And as the heat thawed the veins in their fingers, they huddled together, shivering on the little island, keeping their eyes transfixed on the loch, hopeful that Fairbanks would emerge from the water, alive, safe, unharmed.

Chapter Thirty-One

Instead of the hiss, followed by internal blackness, Anderson heard a grunt, the sound of metal clattering on the floor and felt Joe's grip loosen on his hair.

He opened one eye, and then the other.

Joe was no longer beside him. Instead, he was at the bottom of the steps, clutching his arm, making a groaning noise. Standing before him, the thin, wiry frame of PC Featherstone, helmetless and truncheon over his shoulder.

Oh, good lad, thought Anderson. *Just in the nick of time*. Joe scrabbled for something on the floor and within seconds was standing up, the cattle prod back in his hand.

Featherstone stepped back as the arc of electricity buzzed from the end. Featherstone lunged with his truncheon but Joe sidestepped, bringing his cattle prod down and pushing it against the young constable's chest. Featherstone went down below Sandilands, who was still squirming and kicking. Joe went in for the kill, jumping on top of the constable.

But his face was too close to Sandilands, who hooked her legs around his neck.

'Quick,' she shouted. 'Untie the inspector.'

Featherstone scrambled to his feet as Joe struggled to get free from Sandilands' thighs. He ran over and started unhooking the chains from around Anderson's hands, freeing him from the Yoke. Then Sandilands screamed.

Joe had used the cattle prod and managed to free himself. But with Anderson now free, and Featherstone with the truncheon back in his hand, he was outnumbered.

So he ran for it.

'Get her down,' Anderson yelled, pointing at Sandilands before darting after Joe.

Joe was quick and Anderson's forty a day habit didn't help catch him. He gave chase through the slaughterhouse, past the empty pens and out into the yard, where he caught sight of Joe's shadow sprinting towards the Land Rover.

'Oi,' Anderson yelled, in between gasps and pants.

Joe didn't slow or turn around. Instead, he jumped straight into the driver's seat and turned the engine over. Anderson sprinted towards him, but only got half way when the Land Rover's tyres span on the loose gravel and its headlights bore down on him.

Anderson had nowhere to go. He was too far from the entrance to the cattle shed and the corrugated sides of the buildings offered no protection. He stepped to the left, then to the right, but the headlights followed his movements, and before he knew it, his ribs exploded in pain and he was catapulted into the air, landing flat on to the bonnet with every ounce of air expelled from his lungs.

He lay helpless, his leg caught in the bull bar while the Land Rover careered through the farm. He flailed about as Joe picked up speed and headed towards the gate leading out of the farm.

The cattle grid at the entrance vibrated under Anderson, almost throwing him clear but he clutched one of the windscreen wipers.

They headed up the hill into the night. Anderson screamed and shouted. The Land Rover was now doing more than fifty and the scenery whipped past in alarmingly fast. Anderson, spread-eagled on the bonnet, clung on, one hand on the wiper the other clutching the wheel arch.

The Land Rover rounded a left hand bend causing Anderson to slip across the bonnet, his head dropped over the side, inches from the front wheel. But his foot was still wedged in the aluminium frame of the bull bar, preventing him from falling, but he flailed and banged against the wing like a cowboy on a runaway horse that had his foot caught in a stirrup.

Upside down, Anderson could see another sharp bend ahead that led to Morar. As Joe wasn't slowing, it didn't look as if he was going that way, which meant he was taking Anderson on a hell ride down the main trunk road leading to Mallaig. If he came off the bonnet now, there'd be little left of him to scrape off the road.

But just before they reached the turn off, a sight and sound filled Anderson with hope. In the distance and heading toward them, a set of blue lights accompanied by the wail of police sirens. Featherstone's backup coming from Mallaig.

Joe must have seen them too, because he slammed on the brakes, causing Anderson to rise off the bonnet. But his wedged foot kept him attached to the Land Rover as Joe veered sharply to the right towards the village, throwing Anderson across the bonnet and flat on to the windscreen.

As he bounced towards Morar, Anderson could feel his trapped foot loosen and he started slipping off the bonnet. He slapped his hands across the windscreen, desperate to get purchase as the dam flashed by on the right, the powerful spotlights around it lighting up the night to near daylight visibility, but it flashed past in a blur as the Land River hurtled onwards.

Anderson, still pawing at the windscreen, glanced over his shoulder, and squealed in terror as he realised they were hurtling towards the hump back bridge running over the river feeding from the loch.

Whether Joe had seen it or not, Anderson wasn't sure, but if he had, he didn't lift off, brake, or attempt to slow the Land Rover in anyway. And the inevitable happened.

With Anderson still slapping at the windscreen, obscuring the road from Joe's vision, the Land Rover hit the bridge fast enough to lift the two-ton vehicle off the asphalt. And while it was hardly a scene from Hollywood, the wheels barely airborne, it was enough for Joe to lose all control. The Land Rover landed with a thump sending Anderson flying into the air, spinning and cartwheeling. And although he braced himself for the terminal impact of hitting the road, his landing was much wetter and colder than he expected.

Joe must have veered completely out of control and burst through the wall lining the river leading from the loch, because not only did Anderson plunge into the cold, cold waters, but also a split second later, a massive eruption nearby that sent water cascading down on his head, signalled the arrival of the Land Rover.

Anderson had never learned to swim. Never saw the need. But as he thrashed and kicked and swallowed mouthful after mouthful of water, he wished he had. He was out of his depth, but the Land Rover, which had plunged nose first into the water, had its back wheels spinning above the water line.

Despite the throbbing pain of his ribs, despite the cold, cold water, Anderson splashed and lunged at the upturned vehicle in an ineffective doggy paddle, desperate to save himself from drowning. His head went under the water repeatedly and his lungs filled with water, but his hand caught hold of something hard and metallic and he managed to raise his head.

Using the back door of the Land Rover to keep himself afloat, he gasped and panted, spitting out mouthfuls of water. His ears were full of it too, because he could see flashing blue lights of the Mallaig officers' cars lining the road by the illuminated dam, but he couldn't hear the sirens.

No matter, he was alive, safe.

Or so he thought.

The water bubbled around him and suddenly something exploded from the depths. Anderson remembered what he and Sandilands had seen in the loch, and he first thought it was the shapeless creature that had swallowed van Burgh, but when a hand grabbed him around the face and forced his head under the water, Anderson realised he wasn't the only one to have survived the crash.

Despite his tiny stature, Joe was a farmer and used to hard graft. He had hands like shovels. Besides, being out of his depth and nursing several broken ribs meant Anderson was pretty much helpless. He flailed and kicked and tugged, but Joe was not letting up and Anderson lungs filled with water again. In desperation, Anderson bit into Joe's palm and he felt the grip weaken. Anderson broke the surface, gasping and gulping and biting at the air, but Joe pushed him down again.

Under the water, Anderson could see nothing. The water was ink-black and cold, so very cold. Numbness and lack of air slowed his flailing limbs and the black water got even blacker, but as he was about to black out, he suddenly found himself flying through the air.

It happened quickly. One moment he was gulping in water with Joe on top of him, the next, something exploded beneath him and launched him out of the water.

His back hit the partly protruding Land Rover and the impact expelled what breath was left in his lungs, and he plunged back in the water, helpless, limp, used up.

While he could barely see, barely hear, he could just make out something silhouetted in the dark water, big, black and shapeless. And it had something squirming in its mouth.

Anderson mustered a yell. He then became aware of the cries and shouts coming from the bank. He could see several uniforms under the lights of the power station, standing on siding of the dam and slipway where ring buoys lined the gantry. A copper threw one into the water, which landed far too far away for Anderson to reach it. Yet he found himself was moving towards it, moving towards the bright lights of the power station, to safety, to help, to salvation. Or so he thought.

He then realised he was being carried by the current of the water that cascaded over the weir. And it was not only dragging Anderson towards it, but as he glanced back, he realised it was dragging the big black shape following him too.

Another copper threw a life ring, which Anderson managed to grab. He clutched it desperately as he drifted further towards the cascading water under the spotlights on the power station. The water around him brightened, and he stole another glance back, and then in vivid detail saw the horror that followed him.

It was long, over twelve feet, its body like a giant slug, shapeless, distended, slowly scything through the him. Yet the front of the creature was the most terrifying, not just the pouting lips, the whiskers protruding from each side, but also the pair of wellington boots hanging out of mouth, still kicking.

Fortunately, its undigested meal meant it could fit nothing else into its mouth, but that didn't stop it from trying. It charged, its great tail thrashing frantically. It slammed into Anderson, forcing him under the water as the ring flew from his grasp.

The current beneath the water was so much stronger, and the lights from the power station that managed to cut through the water revealed exactly why. The inlet fan that drove the power station's turbine was just below him. The exposed inlet fan. It was a spinning wheel of death, churning up the water and somersaulting Anderson and the creature in a vortex of swirling water.

They span and twisted, Anderson swallowing mouthfuls of water, unable to see, hear or tell up from down.

And then he blacked out.

Anderson came to on the gantry, cold, frozen, drenched, covered in several police tunics and aware of several faces looking down at him, but only one he recognised.

'How are you feeling?' Sandilands asked.

She looked in a state. Her blouse was ripped and torn, a bruise covered her left cheek and her hair was free of its normally taut bun.

'What ... what happened?' he asked, before coughing up a mouthful of water.

'You nearly drowned, that's what.'

He tried to stand, but slumped back on to the hard metal of the gantry, letting out an 'oomph' as his battered ribs panged in protest.

'Stay still,' Sandilands ordered. 'An ambulance is on its way.'

'How did you get here?'

She crouched down and pulled one of the police tunics higher up his chest. 'The boys from Mallaig picked us up. What happened to Joe?'

Anderson craned his head back. The Land Rover was still in the middle of the water. 'Fish food,' he said, slowly sitting upright, ignoring her protests and attempts to push him back down.

'It's Dead,' she said. 'Got smashed up in the intake fan. Blocked it up. Saved your life in a way, although there is not much left of it.' She nodded to the other figures looking down at him. They were all in police uniform, minus their tunics. 'They fished you out.'

Some of the officers stepped aside as a stretcher and two ambulance drivers arrived.

Anderson wanted to protest and explain how much he hated hospitals, but he didn't have the strength. He had more broken ribs than intact ones, cold had numbed his entire body, and his lungs felt pleuritic. So he let them carry him to the ambulance, where he passed out again.

Chapter Thirty-Two

They found Fairbanks' body washed up on one of the islands the next morning. While his great bulk had been too much of a mouthful for the fish, he'd drowned. Sandilands, still battered and bruised from the night's exertions had to break the news to his family. Danny didn't take it well. He ran out of Lochside, tears streaming down his face.

Mike and his friend, Freely, were picked up in the early hours after an angler spotted them waving on one of the islands. They were taken to hospital with mild hypothermia, but both were expected to make a full recovery.

Morar was awash with police and scenes of crime officers. Nobody knew what to make of the night's events, or the creature found minced in the inlet fan, so they came to a consensus and put Joe's death down to a drowning and made no mention of a giant catfish in their reports. She didn't blame them, with nothing but fish pulp, they had little evidence it existed at all, and nobody wanted to put their head abovc thc parapct and admit to what they had seen.

Inspector Monroe had telephoned that morning, having been called by the Superintendent from Maillag. He'd agreed to cut short his holiday to give Sandilands and Featherstone some much-needed relief. Featherstone was sporting a bandaged head and suffering from mild concussion, but would be all right. He had proved to be a right hero. Sandilands started to see him in a different light.

Of the inspector, he'd called from the hospital earlier that afternoon, having just discharged himself, so she sat in Morar station awaiting his arrival.

However, when the door finally creaked open, it wasn't Anderson who stepped in, but Danny Fairbanks, face red, eyes squinting.

'Danny? What are you doing here?' Sandilands asked from behind the counter. 'You ought to be with your ma, she'll need you more than ever now.'

He stood in the doorway, eyes glistening under the fluorescent lights, and nodded. 'I know, but I needed to speak to you about that American.'

Sandilands sighed. 'Danny your father has just died, can't you let your grudge go?'

'It's not about that, it's about his sister.'

Sandilands frowned. 'His sister, what do you mean?'

Danny bowed his head and sat on the bench, eyes cast down at the floor. Sandilands lifted the counter flap and sat beside him, placing a gentle hand on his knee. 'What is it, Danny.'

'I lied,' he said, eyes still burrowing into the floor.

'What do you mean?'

'About his sister, I know what happened to her.'

Sandilands released his leg. 'I think you better tell me everything.' She tried not to sound too scolding, but her tone was assertive.

He looked at her with eyes streaming with tears. 'I liked her.'

'Mike's sister?'

Danny nodded. 'She was only here a couple of days, and ...' he shrugged. 'I just wanted a bit of fun.'

Sandilands felt uneasy. It was the way he said it. *I* just wanted a bit of fun, not *we*. 'What happened, Danny.' Her tone was now more accusing, sharp, demanding.

'I thought she was just playing hard to get.' He burst into tears.

Sandilands gave him a moment, before prompting him to continue. 'Go on, Danny, you need to tell me.'

He sniffled back the tears. 'I managed to convince her to go kayaking during the night, just the two of us.'

'And what happened?'

'I thought if I got her alone, she'd be more ...'

Sandilands didn't need him to finish the sentence, she knew where this story was going, and didn't like it one bit. 'What did you do Danny?'

'I didn't do anything, I promise.' He bowed his head. 'I just took her to one of the islands, where it was quiet.'

Sandilands looked at him, but said nothing.

'Okay, I tried it on with her, but nothing happened.' He bowed his head again.

Sandilands felt anger rise from her stomach, but she contained herself. 'Go on?'

'We ended up having a fight. I told her I would leave her there unless she ...' He looked pleadingly at Sandilands. 'I just wanted a bit of fun. She pushed me off, and ran into the water, saying she would swim back.'

He breathed in deep, and stared intently at the floor again, as if the memory was playing before his eyes. 'I saw her swim off,' he admitted. 'She was good, a strong swimmer, but then ...'

'Then what, Danny?'

He looked up, his eyes streaming with tears. 'That thing, the thing that took the girl guide, I saw it. It grabbed hold of her. One minute she was swimming to shore, the next she was gone. Just disappeared.'

'Why the hell didn't you tell anyone, Danny?' Sandilands almost shouted the question, and even though he didn't answer, but just shrugged, she knew why. He tried to force himself on the girl and didn't want to admit to it. To himself or anybody else. As a result, people had died, including Danny's father. Danny must have realised his responsibility for that, which was why he was there, confessing all.

She said nothing else and after sitting on the bench seat crying for a few minutes, he got up and walked out.

Shortly after Danny's departure, Anderson arrived. Considering his ordeal the night before, he didn't look in bad shape. His arm was in a sling and he limped and coughed something awful, but that didn't stop him smoking one of his God-awful roll ups.

'Just came to say goodbye,' he said, holding up his battered suitcase.

'Shouldn't you be resting? Why don't you stay for another day or two,' she said, stepping around the counter.

'Don't take offence, but I've had enough of this place to last me a lifetime.'

She smiled. 'Well things are certainly going to be a lot quieter when you are gone.'

'Any one would think you were going to miss me.'

She sniffed a laugh then opened up her arms. 'Come here.' She gave him a gentle hug.

'Ouch,' he yelled.

Then the door opened so both turned round.

Mike was stood there, slightly pale but looking okay.

'I've just seen Danny Fairbanks,' he said, his eyes narrow. 'Told me you have something to tell me.'

Sandilands nodded. 'I do. You had better sit down.'

Anderson picked up his suitcase. 'I'll leave you to it.' He then winked. 'Been a pleasure, Sergeant. Be seeing you.'

He then walked out of the station.

The End

Paradise Woods

An Inspector Anderson Mystery

Chapter One

'Shhh!' Jason's eyes rounded in the torchlight.

'Sorry,' Helen whispered, as she clambered through the open window.

Philip and Sarah helped her down, but the noise they made as they lowered her to the tiled floor annoyed Jason further. He shone his torch in their eyes and glared balefully.

'Let's keep it down, people,' he whispered. 'If security hears us, it's all over. They have dogs, remember!'

The three of them nodded like apologetic schoolchildren following a scolding. Jason could be intimidating when he was angry, almost frighteningly so. But he was passionate, Helen understood that, and he'd been planning tonight for weeks. If they were discovered now, all that reconnaissance and plotting and nights spent in the woods watching and taking notes would be for nothing. They would also end up in trouble. Serious trouble. Breaking and entering would mean jail, especially with Helen's record. Worst of all, failure meant the animals they'd come to save would have to endure even more suffering. That would hurt Jason more than any custodial sentence. And Helen would do anything to prevent that.

She loved him.

He must have known. She'd made it obvious enough. Around camp, she'd bring him something to eat every time she cooked, washed his clothes and would share her cigarettes and dope with him whenever she had any. And at every demonstration, she made sure to stand next to him. That made life tricky. He was well known to the police. They always targeted Jason first. And whenever they'd drag him into a police van in cuffs, they'd drag Helen with him too. She'd spent more nights in a police cell than she'd care to remember. But the cause was worth it. Jason was worth it. If only he would notice her.

She'd hoped volunteering for tonight would make him pay her more attention, but her clumsiness hardly had the mission off to a good start.

And a mission it certainly was.

Paradise Woods Research Centre sat nestled in its eponymously named forest smack in the middle of the Cairngorms. It stood just off the main B-road, but few people would ever have noticed the place. It could easily have been just another farm, albeit a rather strange and perfunctory-looking one compared to the tumbledown farmhouses that normally dotted the Cairngorms. Perhaps a few people may have thought the razor wire fencing around the perimeter a little bit odd.

But nobody would have conceived the sheer horror hidden inside the innocuous looking complex.

Jason knew about it. So did the rest of PAAR—the People's Army for Animal Rights. And despite spending the last year and a half telling the world about it, nobody did anything.

Paradise Woods could not have been more improbably named. For animals, the research centre was pure hell. And despite PAAR's protests and the petitions and the leafleting in nearby villages, and despite the support from the local people, most of whom were aghast at such atrocities on their doorstep, it still went on.

But not any longer.

Direct action, Jason had called it. He couldn't sit by while animals were tortured and mutilated. None of them could. Animals could not defend themselves, so somebody had to protect them, which was why Helen, Jason and the others were there: to steal in during the middle of the night and let them out. All of them.

It was risky, and Helen had never done anything like this before. Yet, so far, it had been relatively easy. The security had been surprisingly lax. Two security guards spent most of their time in the little hut fronting the complex. They regularly walked the perimeter with two Alsatians, like guards patrolling the fences of a POW camp, but their regularity was their weakness.

Helen and the others had watched the complex for weeks now. Not only had they located all the CCTV cameras and found a blind spot at the rear, but also they knew the schedule of the guards. They were as regular as clockwork. On the hour, every hour, one took a dog and circled the perimeter. At the same time, the other would enter the building with the second dog, presumably to patrol the corridors. After fifteen minutes, both would return to their hut for a cup of tea and a smoke, leaving the dogs outside. The Alsatians preferred to laze by the front gate rather than venture off on their own, so Jason and the others had plenty of time to get in, get the job done and get out again.

All this meant Jason and the others had forty-five minutes. Cutting through the fence at the rear of the building had taken fifteen. It took another ten for Jason to jimmy the window—they couldn't smash the glass, it would have been heard—which meant they had a little over twenty minutes to free the animals and escape.

Unless Helen's stumbling alerted the guards or their dogs before that.

She flashed Jason an apologetic smile, then all four looked at each other, eyes wide glinting in the torch light. All nervous and bristling with tension.

Even Sarah looked nervous and she'd been a protestor for all sorts of causes over the years: Greenpeace, free Mandela, CND; that was where she and Helen first met, at the women's peace camp. They had talked and realised they had a lot in common and promised to meet up again. But it wasn't until Helen met Jason at university and joined PAAR that she contacted her again. The short, stout and shaved-head professional protestor took little convincing when she heard about Paradise Woods and turned up at camp on the first day.

Out of the four of them, Helen didn't know Philip that well. While he had been at the University of Aberdeen too, they swam in different circles. The only thing they had in common was Jason, and Helen half suspected the tall, blond rugby player had as much of a crush on him than Helen did.

They'd only planned the protests at Paradise Woods to last the summer then they'd return to Aberdeen, but they couldn't stop, not now, so Helen had put her law degree on hold. All of them had. But that was okay, the cause was worth it.

Jason was worth it.

Even now, in the darkened room, his face stiff and grim, eyes determined, lips tight, she felt like bursting into tears and wrapping her arms around him. Although, she had to admit, the feeling could just be nerves and adrenalin.

Now they were all inside, they turned on their torches. The window they had crawled through led into what appeared to be some sort of storeroom. Two long benches ran down either side, both littered with vials, flasks, boxes, microscopes and other equipment. The thought of what it would all be used for caused Helen to shudder.

Jason twitched his head to the door at the far end, raised his hand to order the others to stay back, placed the torch in his teeth and approached with the crowbar.

The door opened with a crack as the wood around the lock splintered. Everybody froze, listening.

Nothing.

He gestured with his torch and the four of them stepped into the darkened corridor, circles of torchlight before them.

It wasn't what Helen expected. She thought an animal testing laboratory would be bland, sterile, hospital-like, but the carpeted floors, pictures on the walls, pot plants and the soft, leather couch in what Helen presumed was some sort of reception area, reminded her of a regular office. It looked innocuous, harmless.

Perhaps Jason had it wrong, perhaps Paradise Woods was not an animal testing centre. Then what was it? No, she had complete faith in him.

They stopped at a set of double doors at the end of the corridor. 'I think this is one of the laboratories,' Jason whispered as he peered through the frosted glass. 'I can see movement.'

Helen felt her heart quicken, the thumping in her chest audible in her ears. She glanced about, her torch scanning the corridor behind as Jason squatted at the door, crowbar in hand.

A clang, loud and echoing, caused them all to freeze as he broke open the lock. A long moment passed as they listened for any sound of discovery. On hearing nothing, Jason pushed open the doors.

And they all sucked in their breath.

It was true.

The room was full of metal cages. Dozens of them. All full of small white, furry animals.

'Rabbits,' Helen said, rather too loudly, which caused another scowl from Jason.

'Poor things,' Sarah whispered.

'What do you think they have been doing to them?' Philip asked, as they ventured into the laboratory, their torches causing a flurry of activity among the rabbits.

'Probably injecting them with everything and anything,' Jason said, undoing the fastening on one of the cages and opening it. He pulled free the frightened bunny inside, which kicked and struggled as he lifted it out. 'We're going to have to work fast.' He handed Sarah the rabbit, which was still kicking and struggling. 'You girls run back to the way we came in and drop them out the window. Philip and I will get the rest out of the cages.'

Chapter Two

It took nearly fifteen minutes to remove every rabbit from the laboratory, with Helen and Sarah scuttling up and down the corridor, dropping the bunnies out the window. But finally, they had freed them all.

Jason checked his watch. 'We still have some time,' he said, poking his head out of the laboratory. 'And we haven't checked down that corridor.' He shone his torch down a side passage. At the end, another set of double doors.

They approached and stopped as Jason's torch shone on a sign on the door.

Danger!
Contamination Control Area
No Unauthorized Personnel!

'I'm not sure we should go in there,' Helen said, her eyes fixed on the sign.

'Pay no attention to that,' Jason said, as he crouched down, removed the crowbar from his jacket and heaved at the lock. 'They just stick those up to keep people out. I bet most the people that work here don't even know what is truly going on.'

As the lock splintered and the door sprung open, a pungent smell, musky and sweet, wafted out.

'Oh, my God,' Philip said, as his torchlight fell on the contents of the darkened room.

A cage sat in the centre, much larger than the ones containing the rabbits. Its occupant was much larger too. It glared at them, its eyes wide under Philip's torch, its teeth bared in a frightened grimace. It then let out a shriek and backed away.

'A chimpanzee!' Helen said, pushing past the others and stepping into the room.

'Don't get too close,' Sarah said. 'They can be dangerous.'

The chimp's eyes fixed on her as she neared. It tilted its head and blinked before raising one of its hands, as if trying to reach out to her. It looked sad, forlorn, lonely.

She touched its fingers and it bowed its head. 'Look at him.' She turned to the others, a tear tricking down her cheek. 'How could they?'

Jason walked over and placed his hand on her shoulder. 'I know, it's barbaric. You'd have thought it was the Middle Ages, not nineteen-eighty-five.'

He lifted the padlock fastening the cage, before wedging the crowbar behind it. 'Don't worry. We'll soon have him out of here.'

'Hurry,' Philip hissed. 'The security will be doing their patrol in a minute.'

Jason prised open the lock, causing a loud clang. Sarah and Philip glanced down the corridor and gestured for him to hurry. Jason then opened the cage.

The chimp shrieked a loud, shrill scream.

And then launched itself at Jason.

Jason went flying, knocking into Helen who hit the floor, the wind expelling from her lungs. The noise was deafening, terrifying. She lay helpless as the chimp's shrieks blocked out the screams from Jason who tumbled across the laboratory, the animal stuck to his face.

Sarah and Philip stood motionless, their torches fixed on Jason as he knocked over flasks and stands while blood splattered on the pasteurised walls. Glass smashed, papers flew everywhere and Jason screamed and kicked while the chimp clawed and bit and scratched and tore at his face and arms, its shrill cries as unrelenting as its attack.

'Do something,' Sarah shouted, running up to Helen, her torch fixed on Jason, now on the floor, twitching, writhing, blood pooling around his body.

Philip ran up to him and tried to kick the animal free, but it lunged at him too, sending him barrelling backwards. It then fixed its eyes on the girls.

Sarah screamed as the chimp jumped at them, but Philip managed to kick the animal in mid-air before getting to his feet. He pushed the two girls out of the laboratory, his arms and hands bloody from where he had fended off the assault.

'Run,' he shouted, as a screech sounded behind. 'Run for it!'

Helen didn't look back. She charged down the corridor with Sarah, Philip's footsteps close behind, and the screams from the chimp following.

They dashed straight into the storeroom. Philip threw the door closed and slammed his shoulder against it. His body jolted as the berserk primate thumped against the other side. 'Get out! Quick! Quick!'

The two girls glanced at each other, their torchlights flitting around the room like drunken fireflies. 'What about you?' Helen said, as Philip jolted against the door again.

'I'll hold it back. Just get out.'

Sarah ushered Helen to the open window. Helen clambered through and dropped outside. She could hear the sounds of dogs barking and men shouting.

'Quickly,' she said, helping Sarah out. She noticed a nasty wound on Sarah's forearm as she hauled herself free from the confines of the window. It looked like a bite. 'You're hurt!'

'I'm okay,' Sarah said, turning round and pointing the torch back inside the storeroom. 'Phil, hurry.'

A second later, he was at the window, both hands on the frame, hauling himself out.

Then, as if sucked by a vacuum, he was dragged back in, arms flailing. A horrendous, inhuman shriek sounded in the darkness, followed shortly by a more human but equally chilling scream for help.

'Phil!' Sarah and Helen ran to the window, torches aimed into the blackness. Neither could see him, just blood covering the walls and benches. Sarah leaned in. 'Phil!'

Then a face appeared at the window. A non-human face, teeth bared, blood and gore dripping from its mouth.

'Run!' screamed Helen, pulling Sarah with her. 'Run!'

Chapter Three

Two police cars blocked the small track road. Two officers, helmets low over their eyes and wearing thick day-glow jackets to keep out the stiff breeze and drizzle, raised their hands. Jennings slowed and rubbed his strained eyes. The winding roads running through the forest were dark, ominously so, and after a long drive, it was all he could do to keep the Volvo on the road.

One of the officers leaned over the car and tapped the glass, gesturing for Jennings to unwind the window. 'Road's closed, sir,' he said, poking his head right in, as if trying to take a respite from the weather.

Jennings took out his warrant card and handed it to the officer. 'Special Branch. DS Jennings. This is DI Anderson.' He twitched his head to the form beside him. Anderson was asleep, an extinguished cigarette hanging from his bottom lip, which rose up and down as he snored.

The officer studied the ID. Moisture dripped from his nose on to the laminate. He then handed the warrant card back and gestured for his colleague to move one of the cars to open up the road.

'Who's here?' Jennings asked.

'There's a superintendent come up from Aberdeen,' the officer said. 'Goes by the name Garrick. You'll probably find him inside. The pathologist has just arrived too. Can't miss the place.' He raised his sleeve and pointed it down the road, where the vague flashing of blue lights cut through the early morning gloom.

'You say the pathologist is here?' Jennings' frowned his eyes. 'I thought this was just a break-in?'

This was only his second assignment for Special Branch. The Highlands of Scotland were hardly a hotbed of political intrigue or terrorist plotting. His first assignment with Anderson was a suspicious package delivered to a councillor in Inverness. Turned out to be a turd. Somebody obviously wasn't happy about something the council had done. It hardly warranted a full-scale Special Branch investigation and the case was dropped.

For the last three weeks, Jennings had been twiddling his thumbs, regretting the move from CID, until they got a call several hours earlier. Details had been sketchy. All he knew was that some sort of government-funded research facility had been broken into. Their job was to assess if it posed a national security threat. And bodies certainly leaned in favour of that, and dead people meant overtime, and with his wedding coming up, that was something he desperately needed.

The officer didn't seem to share Jennings' eagerness. 'Don't ask me. I'm just freezing my dangly bits out here.' He had that brogue Aberdeenshire accent that made him sound depressed, which, given his duties that wet and torrid night, he probably was.

The other constable had moved the car, and after glancing behind, the officer slapped the top of Jennings' car. 'I guess you best get down there.'

Jennings nodded, put the car in gear and pulled down the road to where more police cars, ambulances and what looked like forensic vans were parked outside a bland but modern-looking building. It was a strange-looking place, one floor, but large and oddly shaped, a bit like a fifty pence piece. A sort of miniature Pentagon.

He pulled up at the barrier at the front, flashed his warrant card, and after the constable raised the barrier, parked among the emergency vehicles.

Beside the car park, a moat of grass ran around the building, hemmed in by barbed wire fencing. On it, a dozen or so uniforms walking slowly in a line, heads down, eyes focussed on the grass. A couple more stood by the front entrance, taking notes and more than likely using the overhang on the building to shield from the weather.

Jennings looked at the sleeping inspector next to him, coughed gently then tentatively jabbed him in the ribs. 'We're here, guv,' he said softly.

Nothing. Anderson continued to snore, the fag end bobbing up and down gently.

'Sir, we're here!' Jennings repeated, louder, shaking Anderson by the shoulder.

The snoring got louder, but he still didn't wake.

'For love of ... wake up!' Jennings shouted.

'What the f...' Anderson bolted upright as if somebody had given him a suppository made of cold metal. He coughed a loud hacking, phlegmy cough, groaned, shook his head like a dog drying itself after a bath, and then checked his watch. 'About bloody time. You drive like an old woman.'

'How would you know?' Jennings said, rubbing the back of his neck. 'You've been asleep since Inverness.

'I was just resting my eyes.' Anderson peeled the dead cigarette butt from his lip, threw it in the foot well then rolled a fresh one and popped it in his mouth. 'Who's in charge?'

'There's a superintendent from Aberdeen overseeing everything. Goes by the name of Garrick.'

'A super? Wonder what's dragged one of them down?'

'I think it's juicier than we first thought,' Jennings said, turning off the engine. 'Copper out front said the pathologist is here. Must be a body.'

'Is that right, Sherlock? Nothing gets passed you, does it? No wonder they promoted you.'

Anderson got out the car and lifted his jacket collar as he looked around. *What is it this time? And why is it always in the middle of nowhere*? He arched his back. He was getting too old for all this running around the country. At least he had someone to help with the legwork now. God knows why it took so long for them to sort him out a partner. Anyone would have thought he was hard to work with.

He wasn't sure about Jennings, though. Too clever for his own good. He had a degree of all things. The first copper Anderson knew with letters after his name. He was young too, and he didn't smoke and hardly drank, which made him dubious in his eyes. He half-suspected he was queer, but apparently, he was engaged. Proof, if there ever was any, that you didn't need brains to get a degree.

He was also too eager, forever running around and getting excited. Even now, after a four-hour drive, the fresh-faced sergeant was chatting to a couple of constables, assessing what was what.

Anderson shook his head. He'd soon knock that eagerness out of him. Then something caught his eye. The grass, where the line of police patrolled up and down, was covered in what looked like bits of wool. It was everywhere, and patches of dark moisture glistened under the temporary lights erected by uniforms doing the search. Blood. It looked as if a sheep had stepped on a landmine.

He jabbed his cigarette at the mess as Jennings returned with one of the constables. 'What the bloody hell has happened here?'

'Rabbits,' said the uniform, his face streaming with moisture.

Anderson squinted at him. 'Are you having a laugh?'

The uniform, a youngish, tallish fellow, shook his head. 'Er ... no, sir.'

'This is PC Ferguson, guv,' Jennings said, offering the constable an apologetic half-smile. 'He was just telling me that they think it was animal rights protestors. Looks like they broke in and released a load of rabbits.'

Ferguson nodded to the grass. 'The guard dogs got to 'em before security could do anything about it.'

Anderson laughed at the irony. So much for saving the animals. He then scowled and rubbed his backside, which was stiff and numb from the journey. 'So why have they called us out?'

Ferguson shook his head. 'I can't say, sir. I've not long got here.'

'There has been a fatality, don't forget,' Jennings reminded him.

Anderson sighed. 'The way things are going today, it'll probably turn out to be Elmer bloody Fudd.'

Chapter Four

Superintendent Garrick was a tall man, imposing too, with broad shoulders, a steely stare and hands that looked as if they could dig trenches. Despite the early hour, his uniform looked clean and fully pressed, top button done up, cap screwed tightly on his head.

He seemed to have organised things pretty well. Besides the search outside, forensics milled about inside the research centre, scraping and swabbing, while several uniforms took statements from the various employees.

When Anderson walked in, a skinny roll-up clamped between his yellow teeth, ash cascading down his shirt and his jacket looking as if he'd slept in it, the superintendent was standing with a couple of security guards, both clutching savage-looking Alsatians by their choker chains.

'Pleased to meet you,' Garrick said, after Ferguson introduced both Anderson and Jennings. 'Sorry for calling you out at this ungodly hour, Inspector.' Garrick's Aberdeen accent was rich and rhotic; the sort of voice you'd hear on BBC Scotland.

Anderson grumbled and didn't approach too closely. The two dogs seemed to be staring and baring their teeth at him.

'So, what exactly has happened?' Jennings asked, removing a notebook.

'We're just trying to piece it all together,' Garrick said. 'It appears as if some animal rights activists broke in during the night, although we're going to struggle to identify them.' He pointed down the corridor. 'It's a terrible mess back there.'

'It was them, all right.' The voice was female.

Anderson turned to see two women sitting on a smart leather sofa in the corner of the room. One of the women was young, fresh-faced, if not a little bookish, with a blonde ponytail down her back and a white lab-coat covering her skinny frame. The other was older and less pleasant to look at. She had a stern face and piercing eyes, and short hair. Anderson was yet to meet a woman with a man's haircut that wasn't trouble.

The stern-looking woman passed a pile of folders to the younger woman. 'I'll join you shortly, Dr Long,' she said. The younger woman got up and disappeared into an adjoining room while the older woman approached, her eyes going from Jennings to Anderson where they stopped and blinked disparagingly as he puffed on his roll-up.

'Inspector, this is Dr Cunningham,' Garrick said. 'She is one of the scientists that work here.'

'I'm the research coordinator,' she said, rather sternly. 'And you are from Special Branch, I understand?'

Anderson could hear a hint of English in her accent so instantly took a dislike to her, but he didn't say anything, as one of the dogs was struggling against its chain, snarling at him.

'Will you take those two bloody things outside?' he said to the security guards. 'Before one of them takes a chunk out of me.'

'You needn't worry, I think they've already eaten,' said Ferguson, a smirk on his face, which caused a frown of disapproval from Garrick, Cunningham and both the security guards.

'Aye,' said Anderson. 'I've seen the X-rated version of Watership Down out there. But I'd rather not end up missing one of my vitals.'

Ferguson nodded to the security guards and one of the men handed his dog choke to the other, who dragged both animals outside, causing Anderson to relax.

'Right, so who are you again?' he asked, looking Dr Cunningham up and down.

She looked your typical career type. Forty-something, hawk-like nose, granny spectacles, and a face that could have done with a lot more makeup and a touch of waxing on the top lip. She also wore an unflattering trouser suit that exaggerated the size of her backside. She tapped the laminated name page on her lapel. 'I'm Dr Harriet Cunningham. I'm in charge here.'

'Not anymore,' Anderson said, stamping out his cigarette on the carpeted floor. 'So, would you mind telling me exactly what has happened, other than the mass butcher of bunnies I saw on my way in?'

Dr Cunningham scowled at him, but after a pause, pulled off her glasses and pointed them down the corridor. 'Last night, a group of animal rights activists broke into the laboratories and released some of our research subjects.'

'It resulted in them losing their lives,' Garrick said, gravely. 'The pathologist is with the bodies now.'

'What killed them?' Jennings asked, removing his pen and notebook.

'Mauled to death by the looks of it,' Garrick said.

'By the guard dogs?' Jennings asked, waving his pen and notebook around.

'No, no, by one of the research specimens they let out,' Cunningham said.

Anderson, patting at his pockets for his tobacco, paused. 'What? They were killed by a rabbit?'

'No, Inspector.' Cunningham rubbed the bridge of her nose. 'The rabbits were not the only thing the activists released last night. They also let out a chimpanzee.'

'Chimpanzee as in a monkey?' Anderson said. This was getting queerer and queerer.

'A chimpanzee is an ape, not a monkey, Inspector,' Cunningham replied. 'And yes, they let it out after they released the rabbits.'

'And you are telling me this chimp attacked and killed them?'

'They can be very powerful animals,' Cunningham said. 'Aggressive too, if provoked.'

Anderson let out a gentle laugh. 'Bloody hell, somebody ought to tell the folks at PG Tips.'

'So, where is it now?' Jennings asked, as Anderson found his tobacco and began rolling up another smoke.

'We don't know,' Garrick said. 'We think it escaped through the same window the intruders used to break in. It is one of the reasons we called you out. I think we need to authorize a hunt for it. It could pose a significant risk to the public.'

'So why did these protestors break in? What is it that you do here?' Anderson asked, lighting his smoke.

'This is a non-smoking building,' Cunningham replied, her nose flaring as his smoke wafted towards her. 'And I'm afraid I cannot go into details about our work. It is classified.'

Anderson stabbed his cigarette towards her. 'You *will* go into bloody details. If there is a mini-version of King Kong roaming about the countryside who is pissed off because you've been dripping shampoo into his eyes, I want to know about it.'

Cunningham glared at him. 'We are a government-funded medical facility. We do not drip shampoo into the eyes of animals. And I will tell you everything you need to know to assist you in your enquiries, but I am not permitted to go into details about our research.'

'You'll do as I bloody say, otherwise I'll have you banged up, you uppity cow!'

'Making friends, I see,' hollered a voice from down the corridor.

Anderson turned and saw a friendly and familiar face.

Chapter Five

'If it ain't the butcher of Blythe,' Anderson said, as Phelps, the chubby, tweed-wearing pathologist walked up to him ahead of four ambulance men carrying stretchers laden with the two bodies covered by plastic sheeting.

'I take it you know each other?' Garrick said as Phelps placed down his medical bag and ordered the stretcher-bearers to stop.

'The inspector and I go way back,' Phelps said, pumping Anderson's hand before his eyes rested on Jennings. 'They haven't given you another partner, have they?'

Jennings straightened slightly and thrust out his own hand. 'Philip Jennings, formerly Edinburgh CID.'

'Maurice Phelps, formerly good looking and virile.' He winked and smiled genially as he shook Jennings' hand. 'I hope you've got good life cover, laddie.'

'That'll do,' Anderson said, as Jennings gave a half-smile, half-frown. Anderson then looked down at the two bodies on the stretcher. 'These the victims?'

'What's left of them,' Phelps said, arching his back and gesturing for his ambulance men to put down the stretchers. 'Want to take a look?'

'Not this side of breakfast,' Anderson said, grimacing.

But Jennings was curious and stepped forward towards the nearest. The orderly looked at Phelps, who nodded, so the man whipped back the sheet covering the body.

'Jesus Christ,' Jennings shouted, jumping back.

Anderson had turned away, his hand protecting his vision from the sight, but Jennings' reaction caused him to peep. He wished he hadn't.

He'd never seen anything so horrific. Whoever was lying face up on the stretcher, no longer had a face. All that was left was some tufts of hair, one eye, which hung out of its socket, and tissue and sinew where the skin had once been.

'Cover it up, for Christ's sake,' he shouted.

'Bloody hell. A chimp did that?' Ferguson said, stepping forward for a look.

Phelps gestured to the orderly to cover the man back up. 'The other one is not in any better shape. There are ruddy bits of him all over the storeroom back there. I've ordered a clean-up team to come in once forensics have finished, but I can't imagine the place will be sorted today.'

'Any identification on them?' Garrick asked, his face creased and grim, his eyes fixed on the now sheeted figure.

Phelps shook his head. 'No wallets, and unless their fingerprints are on file, you're going to have a problem getting a formal identification.'

'We know who they are,' Cunningham said, her voice lacking any emotion. 'They're from that damned animal rights camp.' She glared at Garrick, hands on her hips. 'We've asked you dozens of times to do something about them, Superintendent. I told you something like this would happen, eventually.'

'Hang on,' Anderson said. 'What's this about a camp?'

'There's a group of animal rights activists camped on the field by the woods,' Ferguson informed him. 'Been campaigning about this place for a few months now.'

'And none of you have done anything about it,' Cunningham snapped.

Garrick raised his hands. 'Protesting is not illegal, Doctor. And up until now, they have not broken the law.'

Her nostrils flared.

'And now two people are dead and we have a specimen on the loose.'

'And a ruddy dangerous one at that,' Phelps said, shaking his head, the obvious hairpiece on his head shifting from the movement. 'I've not seen wounds like that before. This was some sort of ape, did you say, Dr Cunningham?'

She nodded. 'A chimpanzee, yes.'

He glanced back down the corridor. 'Well, considering the frenzied nature of the attack, there might be a good chance some of the others are injured too.'

'Others?' Garrick's eyes narrowed at Phelps.

'Why, yes. I'm no expert on forensics, Superintendent, but there were more than two sets of footprints in all that blood back there. I'd say there were at least four of them.'

Garrick looked at the security guard, who until now had remained quiet, head bowed. 'Did you not see anything last night, anything at all?'

'No, nothing. Just heard it.' The security guard's voice wavered, no doubt worried about his job. 'By the time we got here, the two kids were dead, almost made me sick, so it did, but there was no sign of the others, or the chimp.'

'Haven't you got cameras?' Jennings asked, waving his notebook at the man.

'Aye, but they must have staked the place out because they didn't show up on any of the videos. They came in through the back, where the cameras can't see.'

Phelps gestured for his stretcher-bearers to pick up the bodies. 'If you don't mind, Inspector, I need to get these two to the mortuary and inform the fiscal. So, unless there is anything else?'

Anderson shook his head. 'No, you be away.'

The pair shook hands again, and after Phelps disappeared with his two orderlies, Anderson pinched his forehead with his fingers as a cigarette burned between them. 'Let me get this straight. We've got two dead animal rights protestors, killed by a mad monkey, which could now be anywhere from here to Aberdeen and could potentially attack anybody it comes across.'

'About the long and short of it,' Garrick said.

'I think apes are territorial animals,' Jennings said, as he made a note.

'How do you bloody know?' Anderson asked.

'I read a little zoology at Edinburgh.'

'Did you now? Well, I watched David Attenborough's latest series, but it doesn't make me Charles bloody Darwin. So let's stick to what we know for certain, not what we've read in the Ladybird A-Z of animals.'

'Your sergeant is right, Inspector. That woman I've just been speaking to is our animal behavioural expert. She suggests it probably won't go far. Certainly not in the short term,' Cunningham said. 'So the sooner you endeavour to recapture it and bring it back here, the less likely it will pose a risk to the general public.'

Anderson glared at her. 'Recapture it! Bring it back here! Are you mad, woman? It's just ripped off the faces of two people. If we find it, it'll be destroyed.'

'You will do no such thing,' Cunningham protested. 'That is a very valuable specimen. I want you to bring it back here.'

He thrust his cigarette in her direction. 'Listen here, *Dr Cunny Lingus*, or whatever your name is. We've two dead people because of your bloody chimp, so, when I say we're going to destroy it, we're going to bloody well destroy it. Is that all right with you?'

Her face stiffened. 'How dare you speak to me like that? Who do you think you are?'

'The law, and you're damned lucky I don't charge you with manslaughter. If you had proper security, this wouldn't have happened.'

The security guard shifted uncomfortably and looked as if he were about to say something, but Anderson's scowl told him to keep his mouth shut.

Garrick coughed. 'Perhaps I ought to call in an armed unit from Aberdeen. It may take a day or two to organise, but we haven't the manpower here for a full search. There is too much terrain.'

Anderson shook his head. 'A couple of days is too long. The bloody thing could be anywhere by then. We need to get out there now before it pisses off. That means we need somebody that could track this bloody thing.'

'What do you suggest?' Garrick asked. 'I can contact the zoo in Aberdeen, see if they have anyone.'

'No, we need somebody local, who knows the lay of the land.' He stared at the tip of his cigarette as he thought. Then he looked up. 'I take it they do deer stalking in these parts?'

Ferguson nodded. 'Yes, July through to September.'

'Then we need to find ourselves a half-decent gillie. Somebody that knows the place and is good with a rifle.'

'You'll be wanting old Brophy,' Ferguson said. 'He's head gamekeeper up at the estate. You'll not find anybody that knows the woods and mountains better than he does.'

'Where do I find him?' Anderson asked.

Ferguson shrugged. 'You best go speak to the laird up at the house.'

'You go with them, Ferguson,' Garrick said. 'I think I'll send some cars up to that protest camp and bring a few in for questioning, see if they know anything.'

Anderson shook his head. 'That can wait. I want to speak to those animal rights nutters too, but if I were in your shoes, I'd get as many flatfoots as I can out and about to warn the locals to stay indoors.'

Garrick sucked air through his teeth. 'That's not going to be easy. The only real conurbation is Monymusk. Mostly, it is farms and hamlets around here. There's also a lot of campsites and holiday cottages.'

'Just do the best you can.' Anderson then looked at Cunningham. 'I hope for your sake this bloody orang-utan, or whatever it is, doesn't go for anyone else.'

She glared at him, and he felt her eyes still boring in his back long after he stepped outside.

Chapter Six

The police were still swarming all over the centre when Shannon Long sneaked off to the laboratories. They were asking questions, awkward questions. Shannon didn't have the answers, and had questions of her own. So once the forensic team had finished and the bodies had been taken away, she slipped into the laboratory wing to avoid further interrogation and to see for herself what had happened.

The entire wing of the complex looked like something from a video nasty. Blood plastered the corridor, puddles of it dotted the floor and gloopy red streaks dripped down the walls.

She approached the laboratory, where she normally spent her days, and saw distinct handprints of blood on the wall and warning sign. And inside the laboratory, things were much worse. Glass covered the floor, crunching as she stepped inside. Nearly every vial, flask and test tube had been broken, and her papers, most of which were blood splattered, lay in disarray all over the place.

The cage was where it always was. Right in the centre of the room, the door wide open. They'd learned from past experiments that it needed to be bolted down. The animals could easily topple it over. That could lead to an escape. That had been her worst nightmare. And now it happened.

She sighed as she stepped forward to the cage. For some reason, she found herself staring at the identification plate on the door. Subject 1717-85H. The digits represented the number assigned to Project Saevio, 1717, plus the year and a letter representing the specimen number. This was the eighth chimp.

In the early days, she used to give them names. Nothing silly like Bobo or Coco, but something less clinical that described their appearance or behaviour, such as Grey Chin or Smiler. She stopped doing that by the time the fourth chimp died.

At the start of the project, she knew what they were trying to do, or thought she did. Now, she wasn't so sure. Things had changed. Dr Cunningham had become more secretive, less willing to explain what they were doing. It was Shannon's job to monitor the animal's behaviour. Note any oddities. And the behaviour of each specimen was getting odder and odder. Yet when Shannon questioned her, Cunningham would refuse to answer. 'You do your job,' she would insist. 'And I'll do mine.'

After looking around at the disorder and chaos for a few minutes, Shannon turned to leave, only to see a figure in the doorway.

'What are you doing, Dr Long?' Cunningham said, her voice was as cold and sterile as the laboratory.

'I ... just wanted to see it for myself.'

'You shouldn't be in here,' Cunningham said.

Shannon looked back at the cage and the blood covered laboratory. 'There was something wrong with it, wasn't there?'

Cunningham stepped forward and tilted her head back. 'I have no idea what you are talking about.' She then gestured to the door.

Shannon took one last look at the carnage then stepped outside. 'We both know that is not true. You need to them know what they're dealing with.'

Cunningham puckered her lips and her eyes buzzed behind her glasses. 'I will tell them what they need to know. Nothing more.'

'It could pose a risk to people.'

'Nobody needs to know anything!' Cunningham insisted. She leaned close, her mouth inches from Shannon who could smell the coffee on her breath. 'And if you say anything, you know what will happen?'

She leaned her head back and studied Shannon carefully, her eyes peering over her glasses like a woman trying to thread a needle. 'There are few opportunities in research these days. You wouldn't want to ruin your career before it has barely started.'

After a long pause, she added, 'The best thing you can do, Dr Long, is keep quiet. Take some time off until things have calmed down. When we get a new specimen, we can then continue where we left off.'

Shannon didn't say anything. She just nodded and walked back down the corridor.

'Good, girl, I knew you'd understand.'

The estate house in Monymusk, a mile or so south from Paradise Woods, had all the grandeur of a gothic castle. Tall conifers and towering pines enclosed the grounds and long drive, while the house, with its rotund and pointed tower and numerous spire-like chimneys, looked almost Slavic, especially against the backdrop of the dark morning sky where the sun was creating streaks as it began to rise.

Jennings let out an impressed, 'Wow' under his breath as he pulled up outside the front. Yet Anderson was less enthusiastic.

Despite the journey taking less than five minutes, he'd fallen asleep again, resulting in Jennings having to jab him in the ribs as they crunched up the gravel drive behind Ferguson's police car. 'We're here.'

After coughing himself awake and relighting the extinguished cigarette in his lips, he got out, exercised his neck, then looked up at the building and exclaimed, 'Bloody hell, it's Castle Dracula.'

'Nice place, eh?' Ferguson said, scampering over after slamming his car door shut, which gained the attention of a gardener who was on his hands and knees tending the flowerbeds surrounding the well-trimmed lawn.

'Yes, impressive,' agreed Jennings.

'We're here to find the gamekeeper, not write an article for Country Life,' grumbled Anderson, locking eyes on the gardener, who had stood up and was scratching his head at the sight of the early morning visitors.

Anderson turned back to the other two. 'Well, what are you waiting for? Go wake up his lairdship before this bloody chimp ends up in Glasgow.'

'It'd fit right in there,' Ferguson said under his breath, causing Anderson to unleash a volley of expletives.

'Watch it,' Jennings whispered, as he and Ferguson walked up the stone step to the door. 'He's touchy about his native land.'

They pulled the door chain and waited. And waited. And waited.

'Nobody home, guv,' Ferguson shouted back, spotting the gardener amble over to Anderson, who was decorating the gravel drive with tar-coloured phlegm.

'Can I help you chaps?' Jennings heard the gardener say, while wiping the sweat from his brow.

'Yes, you can wake up the lazy, privileged, in-bred sod that lives here,' Anderson said.

The gardener straightened. 'You mean Mr Gough?'

Jennings then heard Ferguson swear under his breath before cantering over to the exchange. 'Inspector!'

Anderson ignored him and instead continued to berate the gardener. 'Yes, the bloody laird, who do you think I'm talking about? And hurry up about it, Worzel. I ain't got all day.'

'Sir,' said Ferguson. 'This is his lairdship. Sir Henry Gough. Sorry, Sir Henry, didn't realise it was you.'

'Evidently,' Gough said, eyes fixed on Anderson, who didn't at all seem disconcerted by his faux pas. 'And how can I help you ... gentlemen?'

'We're sorry to bother you at such an early hour,' Ferguson said, his voice laced with reverence. 'But we are looking for Mr Brophy.'

'Old Jim? Have you tried his cottage?' Gough pointed down a small track cutting its way through the trees.

'Not yet, sir.'

'Well, if he's not there, he could be anywhere. He has hides all over the estate. Is it important?'

'Yes, sir,' Jennings said.

Gough frowned and his hunkered eyebrows suggested he wanted to know more.

'There has been an incident at the research centre in Paradise Woods,' Ferguson said.

'What sort of incident?' the laird asked.

'Somebody broke in last night,' continued Ferguson. 'They let out one of the research animals.'

'A chimpanzee,' added Jennings.

Gough's eyebrows rose up his head. 'A chimpanzee?'

'Aye, and a bloody dangerous one at that,' Anderson said.

'We're hoping Brophy may be able to help us track it down,' said Ferguson.

Gough blew out his cheeks. 'Well, nobody knows these parts better than he does. As I said, you best try his cottage. But if he's not there, you may have to wait until opening time. He'll be in the Gough Arms by then if I know old Jim.'

Anderson's face lit up on the mention of the pub.

'Thank you, sir,' Ferguson said. 'And you may want to avoid going for any walks on the estate until we track this creature down. It has already killed two people.'

'My word. Who?'

'We think they were from the animal rights camp.'

Gough shook his head. 'Well, if I can be of anymore assistance you know where to find me.'

'Thank you, sir,' Ferguson said. 'That's much appreciated.'

Chapter Seven

Roger woke up shivering. The ground sheet and nylon sleeping bag were no match for the morning's cold dew. He snuggled up next to the warmth of Liz's body as she gently snored next to him. He needed a pee, but he was too cold to venture outside. Oh, why did he suggest camping in the Cairngorms in October? While the walks had been nice, and spending the week alone with Liz with nobody around to bother them had been wonderful, but boy was it cold.

They'd been together for six months now, yet they struggled to get any quality time together. They both still lived with their parents. Roger's mum and dad were liberal enough to let them share a bed at the weekends, but he had three brothers and two sisters, so they got very little privacy. And staying at her place was out of the question. Her parents were devout Catholics so would never permit them to share a room.

That's why he planned this trip. A chance to spend some real time together. Neither of them had much money. They both worked, he at a record shop in the centre of Liverpool, she at a hairdressers in Birkenhead, but neither took home more than a hundred pounds a week.

But camping was cheap. If only he'd planned it a bit better. They came with nothing more than a few spare clothes, his guitar and the camping equipment. He now wished he had brought a duvet, or something more substantial than the skinny sleeping bags.

Liz hadn't complained, though. Even when the Metro broke down just passed the Lake District. Roger managed to get it going again, but wasn't sure if it would make the journey home. But he'd worry about that when the time came. He was going to make the most of the next few days, no matter how cold it was.

However, he could no longer ignore his burgeoning bladder, so he unzipped the sleeping bag to go relieve himself, but before he could undo the tent flap, he heard a rustle outside. Then shadow flitted across the tent.

Strange, they weren't at an official campsite. Roger had wanted to keep away from other people, so they'd camped wild in the woods. Middle of nowhere. So who was outside?

He slipped out of the sleeping bag, struggled into his thick sweater, undid the tent flap and poked his head outside.

'Hello?'

While dim under the canopy of pines and poplars, and with the sun only just breaching the horizon, Roger could still see nobody was about. He listened carefully, but heard nothing. Everything was still, tranquil, quiet.

Must have been a deer, he thought, having seen several roe and red deer as he and Liz trekked through the moorlands and woodlands over the past few days. He never tired of seeing the illusive animals. He knew they were quick, one moment they were there, the next gone. But if one had just scampered past the tent, there was no sign of it now.

He slipped out of the tent, jogged over to the nearest tree and let out a large sigh of relief as his bladder deflated. He then scuttled back to the tent, rubbing his hands together and blowing raspberries from the cold. He looked forward to getting back into the sleeping bag and snuggling up next to Liz.

But when he poked his head back in the tent he froze halfway. Something was stroking Liz's face as she slept. Something hairy. Something big.

It took him several moments to realise what the creature was, but before he could wonder what on earth a chimpanzee was doing in the Cairngorms, let alone sitting in his tent, the animal had stopped stroking Liz. It now sat staring at him. Rapid puffs of breath came out of its half-open mouth, where two sets of large canines protruded over it lips.

Then it lunged.

The chimp's banshee-like shriek easily overpowered Roger's screams as did the animal's strength. It ripped and tore into Roger's face and arms and battered his body with its powerful arms, breaking ribs and puncturing his lungs. Yet after the assault, when Roger lay twitching and quiet, blood gushing from his throat, the chimp fell silent. Yet Roger could still hear screaming. Female screams. Screams that would continue for as long as Roger remained alive, which wasn't very long.

Helen hadn't slept. How could she? The events of the night kept replaying in her mind like a horror film caught in a loop. A continual tinnitus of screams echoed in her ears.

After she and Sarah ran from the research centre, Helen had wanted to go back. She'd argued that perhaps the boys were still alive. Sarah had dismissed her, insisting both were gone. Dead. She'd been cold about it. Resolute. Said that they'd just end up risking their own lives or being caught.

Deep down Helen knew she was right. But she wanted to do something, anything. She'd even suggested going straight to the police. But Sarah wouldn't have that either. She was convinced they'd be blamed for the deaths. Breaking and entering had just become manslaughter.

Yet Helen knew they couldn't keep it quiet forever. How long would it be before the police pieced everything together? Realised who else was there. And while Jason had kept their plans secret, even from the other PAAR members, it wouldn't be long before people started asking questions. Jason was PAAR's unofficial leader after all and would soon be missed.

This became evident as soon as Helen ventured from her tent that morning, shaken, dazed and confused.

Scamp caught sight of her and waved her over. He was a scruffy, dread-locked thirty-something that had never held down a job and described himself as a 'professional activist'. He wasn't too bright, and bordered on the simple, but the other members treated him like the camp mascot, although Jason would never have involved him in anything like last night's excursion.

'Have you heard?' Scamp said, running up to her. 'The police are all over the village. Apparently, there was a break-in at Paradise Woods last night and somebody let out the animals.' His buckled front teeth hung over his lower lip as he grinned.

'Err ... really?' Helen said, trying hard to suppress the tears that had been flowing all night.

'Ere, are you all right? Your eyes are red.'

'It's hay fever, Scamp. So, what's this about a break-in?'

He glanced about, as if ensuring nobody was overhearing. 'It was Jason,' he whispered. 'Him and Philip. They must have sneaked out last night when we all went to bed. Neither of them has come back yet. I've just checked their tent. It's empty. I bet they're hiding out in the woods, waiting for it all to die down.'

Helen didn't say anything. Couldn't. She just offered Scamp a thin-lipped smile, while he grinned then punched the air, ecstatic at what he thought as a major coup for the movement. He then ran off, presumably to spread the word among the other camp members, although judging by some of the huddled whispers and sly glances, most already knew. They were probably thinking Helen knew much more than they did, as she had become part of Jason's inner circle.

How long would it be before they heard about what happened to Jason and Philip? How long would it be before people pointed fingers at her and Sarah?

Sarah!

Helen had not seen her since they arrived back in the night. She had refused to listen to Helen's pleas to go to the police, hand themselves in. Admittedly, Helen was a little hysterical. She'd have to listen to her now. And if she wouldn't, Helen would make her.

She skirted around the camp, avoiding the other protestors as they chatted, prepared breakfast and had their bucket washes. Helen didn't want to speak to anyone. She felt too fragile. One wrong word and she'd burst into tears, and no doubt, spill everything.

The flap to Sarah's tent was still closed, so Helen whispered through the fabric to her. 'Sarah!'

She heard movement from inside. A gentle rustling of a nylon sleeping bag, but no reply.

'Sarah, it's me.'

'Go away!' Sarah's voice was raspy and hoarse.

'We need to talk.'

'Leave me alone.'

Helen started to feel angry. How dare she? Sarah wasn't the only one entitled to self-pity. They had both been there, both seen their friends die in horrendous circumstances. 'I'm coming in.'

She pulled at the zip to the tent flap and poked her head inside, but she felt a hand on her head pushing her back.

'Hey!'

'I said stay out.' While hoarse and raspy, Sarah's voice sounded menacing, angry.

'I'm not going to leave this,' Helen said. 'We need to talk about what happened. And what we are going to do.'

Silence.

Reluctantly, Helen trudged back to her tent. Sarah was just upset, perhaps even traumatised. She understood that. But she meant what she said. She would not let it rest and would try again, but she'd give her some space to calm down. She just hoped the police didn't turn up in the meantime.

Chapter Eight

With whitewashed walls, picket fence and leaded windows, Brophy's cottage must have once been a decent little house. Yet it obviously hadn't seen a lick of paint in years, the grass at front swayed at hip height, several of the windows were cracked, and dead rabbits, a pheasant and several small birds Jennings didn't recognise hung under the porch like a collection of macabre wind chimes. While a Land Rover with more dead animals attached to it was parked alongside the house.

'I've got a feeling we're in the right place,' Anderson said, ducking under a brace of rabbits. He nodded to Ferguson. 'You best knock. I know what you country folk are like—you possess more shotguns than you do brain cells.'

Ferguson rolled his eyes, yet when he banged on the front door, the old man appearing with a shotgun pointing at them did little to disprove Anderson's prejudice.

All three policemen jumped back.

Old man Brophy was certainly old. He could have been anywhere between seventy and a hundred. Despite the shotgun, he looked quite frail and infirm. He had a stoop and wore a pair of holey trousers that looked like he'd borrowed them from a Glaswegian tramp and a string vest that showed off skinny arms where loose folds of skin hung where his triceps should be. Yet his face was grim and determined with skin like old leather and covered in grey bristle. And if he had any teeth, none were visible when he opened his mouth.

'What do ye want?' he demanded to know, slapping a pair of gummy chops together. The old man's eyes then widened slightly on sight of Ferguson. 'A'ken ye!'

'Sorry to disturb you, Mr Brophy,' Ferguson said, 'but his lairdship told us you were here. We were hoping you could help us.'

Brophy frowned, adding more wrinkles to the corrugated face. 'I *disnae* see how.'

'You're the local gillie, are you not?' Anderson asked.

'That I am,' Brophy replied. 'And who you be?'

'These gentlemen are from Special Branch,' Ferguson informed him. 'We have a serious matter on our hands. Perhaps you could lower your gun, Mr Brophy.'

The old man studied both Anderson and Jennings with one grey, bushy eyebrow raised. He then lowered the shotgun and cleared his throat with a deep sniff. 'Ye best come inside, then.'

The cottage was dark, musty and as rustic as was possible. A simple oaken table, unpolished and covered in clutter sat in the middle of the room, dishes sat piled high around a grotty little sink area out the back, where more wildlife hung around the back door, from the rafters and above the cupboards.

'Housekeeper having a day off, is she?' Anderson said, ducking under a hare hanging from the ceiling.

'*Disnae* get many visitors,' Brophy said, placing the shotgun on the parlour table, taking a seat and stuffing a bulldog pipe full of tobacco.

'Strange that,' muttered Anderson. 'You seem such a welcoming soul.'

'So what is this all about?' Brophy asked, striking a match and setting light to his pipe.

Ferguson gestured if he could take a seat and the old man answered with a blink.

The PC sat and explained everything.

The old man's face didn't flinch when Ferguson told him about the escaped chimp from Paradise Woods. He just sat puffing on his pipe. When the young PC had finished, Brophy removed it from his lips and said, 'I still *disnae* see what you want from me.'

Ferguson coughed and glanced at Anderson and Jennings then back at the old man. 'We were hoping you could help us track it.'

The old man's face creased up a little. 'I *disnae* know much about chimpanzees.'

'Yes, but we were led to believe you know the countryside around here better than anyone,' Jennings said.

Brophy shrugged. 'Aye, but I take folk out to find stags, ne'er stalked a monkey afore.'

'Monkey, stag, what's the bloody difference?' Anderson snapped.

Jennings was about to explain the obvious anatomical differences, but thought better of it. One thing he'd learned about the inspector, was when he was in a foul mood, which was most of the time, it was best to keep it shut.

'Your assistance could help save lives,' Ferguson said, diplomatically. 'And we'd really appreciate it.'

Brophy shoved the pipe back in his mouth and sucked hard as he thought. 'I'd need permission from his lairdship.'

'Don't worry about that,' Ferguson said. 'We've already spoken to Sir Henry.'

Brophy sniffed. 'So, when do ye want to go out and look for this wee critter then?'

'As soon as possible,' Ferguson said.

'So get your shit together and get cracking,' Anderson added.

Brophy looked down at Anderson's feet. 'Ye'll need better footwear than that.'

'I ain't bloody coming,' Anderson said, glancing at his watch. 'I've got better things to do. Pub'll be open in a couple of hours.'

'We ... er ... we were hoping you could stalk this animal alone,' Ferguson said.

Brophy shook his head, slowly. 'Ye can ne'er go stalking on your own. Not safe. Besides, I'll need a pair of young eyes with me.' He tapped his temples. 'Peepers are nay as good as they used to be.'

'For the love of ...' Anderson looked at Ferguson. 'Right, you'll have to go with him.'

Ferguson shook his head. 'Sorry, guv, but the superintendent will want me back at Monymusk. We're short-handed as it is, and with this ape on the loose, not to mention those protestors he wants to question, I doubt he can spare me.'

Anderson smiled at Jennings then said to Ferguson, 'Lend him your radio.' Ferguson unclipped it from his lapel and removed the battery pack and handed it all Jennings.

Jennings frowned and did a double take, first looking at Brophy then at Anderson, and then back to the old man. 'Shouldn't you come, guv? You are senior officer.'

Anderson blew out his cheeks. 'Let me think. An afternoon in the pub waiting for Phelps to ID those two dead fellas, or spending a day thrashing around the bush with someone that looks like he had a bit part in *Deliverance*. Let me see ...'

He then slapped Jennings on the back. 'I'll be in the Gough Arms. Let me know how you get on.' He then winked at Ferguson. 'You can give me a lift to the village.'

'Yes, guv.' Ferguson got up from the table and filed out after Anderson, leaving Jennings alone with the toothless old man grinning at him and looking a lot less frail and a lot less infirm than he did before.

Chapter Nine

Jennings stumbled and tripped and swore and crashed through the undergrowth like a drunken elephant. Brophy, the old gillie, a rifle strapped to his back, a shotgun broken open across his arm, crumpled his face at him. 'I *disnae* know much about chimpanzees, but if the wee critter has got ears, we havney chance of seeing it with all the noise yer making.'

The early part of their hunt had been fine. Brophy took them down the neatly cut tracks that criss-crossed the woods. But after crossing a small suspension bridge that spanned the River Don, the going had been tougher. This was the wild forest, Brophy had explained, as opposed to the cultivated part of the laird's estate that ramblers, hikers and people on their morning walks more commonly used.

Jennings' jacket snagged on a branch. He tugged it free, causing it to tear. Damn, he only had one decent suit. 'Stalking bloody apes through woods is not in the police training manual. Why don't you go on alone? You'll have more chance of bagging this thing without me stumbling about behind you.'

Brophy sniffed and reached into his pocket for his pipe, and deftly, using one hand, packed in some tobacco. 'Aye, maybe I would, maybe I wouldn't, but it *isnae* me that wants to find it.'

They'd been at it hours. Jennings had driven them back to Paradise Woods in the anticipation Brophy could find some tracks or spores or anything they could use to follow the chimp's escape from the facility.

Yet the old-timer didn't even look around. Instead, he just ambled over to the surrounding woods, leaving Jennings to follow.

While there was no doubt the old gillie knew the terrain like the back of his hand, Jennings had his doubts as to whether he could help them find a chimpanzee among the thousands of square acres of forest, glen, mountain and valley. Concerns he voiced.

'Are you sure it could have gone this way?' he asked, once Brophy had his pipe lit and they continued their walk through the woods.

'No.' He then stopped and pointed to the south. 'But the village is south. *Isnae* much forest t' north. I *disnae* know much about chimps, but I know enough to know they like trees.'

Made sense, thought Jennings. 'But what about the east and west?' In fact, as he surveyed the mountains in the distance he realised that they could search for a year and never find the damned thing. 'He could have headed to the hills.'

'Aye, could have. Might be a bit cold for the wee critter, though.'

Jennings still wasn't convinced the old man knew what he was doing. Sure, he was probably the world's best at stalking deer, but to find an exotic animal like a chimp, surely they needed expert help. He didn't know from whom, perhaps somebody from a zoo, but anything had to be better than shambling through the wood with an ageing gillie in the hope they came across the elusive animal. He had tried to radio his concerns to Anderson, but nobody at the station's control room could find him, although Jennings knew full well where the inspector would be—in the damned pub getting half-cut, while Jennings was trekking through these wretched woods.

They knocked on Shannon's door at quarter to eleven. She'd been home for several hours, work having all but stopped at Paradise Woods, and since Cunningham had basically suspended her for the foreseeable future, Shannon was taking stock of her life when the doorbell went.

This wasn't how she had planned her career to go.

Primatology was a niche field, especially in Scotland. Her hope had been to get a job at one of the universities, working as a researcher and spending her days at a zoo studying animal behaviour.

Sadly, there were more primatologists than there were posts. Indeed, they probably outnumbered the number of primates in Scotland. So getting any type of job after her doctorate proved near impossible. Until Dr Cunningham and Paradise Woods came along.

Shannon never got into the field of ape studies to watch them in cramped cages while scientists pumped them full of drugs, but it was a job in her field, and for that, she felt grateful.

It was difficult at times. Especially as part of the work involved putting the animals to sleep and conducting autopsies once they had served their purpose. She cried the first time. And the second. Now she was hardened to it. Perhaps too hardened. Because something about Paradise Woods alarmed her, yet she was trying not to acknowledge it.

Whoever was banging on the door wasn't going away so she opened it. Two police officers, one a clean-shaven twenty-something, the other older, less well-groomed, stood with the noonday sun behind their backs, forcing Shannon to shield her eyes as they addressed her.

'Sorry to disturb you, ma'am,' said the young officer. 'I'm PC Ferguson, this is my colleague PC Ramsey. You may not have heard, but there was an incident over at the medical facility in Paradise Woods last night. We're just going door to door to warn local people that there may be a wild animal on the loose.'

'I know all about it, Constable,' Shannon said, seeing no point in lying or being evasive. 'I work at the centre.'

'Oh, I see,' Ferguson said, he shrugged, and still gave her the same spiel he gave everyone. 'I'm just warning people to keep their windows and doors closed. Just in case the monkey comes this way.'

'It's a chimpanzee,' Shannon said, 'but I don't think it will venture too near the village. They're naturally shy animals.'

'Better to be safe than sorry, miss ...?'

'It's Doctor. Doctor Shannon Long.'

The constable's eyebrows rose slightly. She could tell he was either impressed, or shocked that a young woman could hold such a title; it may have been 1985, but sexism was still rife. 'May I ask what it is that you do at Paradise Woods?'

Shannon raised her head suspiciously. 'Do you want to know what I do or what the centre does?'

Ferguson smiled and bobbed up and down on his heels. 'I'm well aware of the sensitive nature of your work, ma'am ... I mean, Doctor. I was more enquiring to your expertise.'

'My doctorate is in primatology.'

Ferguson frowned, his raised eyebrows indicated he would need more of an explanation.

'I study apes and monkeys, Constable.'

Ferguson glanced at his colleague. 'In that case, would you mind if I pass your details on to my Superintendent. You may prove to be quite useful. We have men out looking for this animal at the moment, but as you may appreciate, the Cairngorms is a large area, and finding this wee critter may prove to be quite difficult.'

Damn, thought Shannon. This was the last thing she needed, and would certainly be the last thing Cunningham would want of her. She was meant to be keeping her head down. But she couldn't lie to the police, not directly, so she smiled and nodded. 'Of course. I'll be happy to help.'

She then closed the door, resting her back against it. A long second passed before she heard the two policemen's footsteps disappear down her path. She then slumped to the ground and sobbed into her hands.

Chapter Ten

As the morning slipped into afternoon, the footslog started to take its toll on Jennings. He was huffing and puffing and gasping for breath, his legs aching, feet burning, yet Brophy continued his hike through the forest as if they were going for a Sunday morning stroll. Jennings couldn't see one bead of sweat on the old man's brow and his stride never slowed. No matter whether they were climbing a hill, traversing a fallen log or jumping a stream, he was a lithe and agile as a young deer.

They finally stopped for a rest just after two o'clock, according to Jennings' watch. He slumped on to a bank, removed his shoes, while Brophy sat next to him, repacked his pipe, and took a slug from a hip flask before offering it Jennings.

The whisky burned as it trickled down Jennings' throat, but he welcomed it since the only refreshment he'd had all morning was a few slugs of water from the old man's water bottle and a bite of a rather rank scotch egg that constituted Brophy's lunch.

Jennings took off his sock, winced at the sight of the blisters on his heel. 'I think we should head back and try again tomorrow. Give us chance to come up with a plan of action and for me to find some decent footwear.'

Brophy didn't seem to be listening. His eyes were transfixed on the sky and a group of crows, which cawed and screeched as they circled.

He stood.

'What's the matter?' Jennings asked, as the old-timer headed towards the direction of the crows, leaving Jennings to hurriedly replace his shoes before following. This resulted in him tripping, covering himself in dirt and leaf litter, before getting back to his feet and shuffling after the old man.

With his eyes fixed on the sky, and seemingly negotiating the brambles, thistles, tree roots and other obstacles by magic, the old-timer headed into a clearing, where several startled crows took to the air when the two men broke cover.

Fluttering in the gentle afternoon breeze, Jennings saw a bright orange tent.

Nothing unusual, he thought. Wild camping was common in this part of the world, yet the way Brophy snapped his shotgun closed and held it out in front of him as he approached the temporary campsite showed he didn't share Jennings' indifference.

The old man kept glancing up at the circling crows while scouting around the tent. He then stopped at the entrance. Broke the shotgun open over his arm and looked grimly at Jennings, who hadn't moved.

'You might want to take a look at this,' he said.

Jennings approached, warily. All of a sudden he realised how eerily quiet it was in the woods, how remote, how lonely. He felt his heart quicken as he realised what had alarmed the old gillie and excited the crows.

Around the entrance, where the tent flap fluttered gently in the breeze, the ground was stained with blood. Tentatively, Jennings reached for the tent flap and opened it.

'Jesus Christ,' he said as he stared at the gruesome scene inside.

Red streaks plastered the entire interior of the tent. Most of the blood had dried and crusted in streaks where it had once dripped down the nylon, and in the middle of the cramped confines, two bodies, bathed in blood, faces a mess of missing skin and chunks of flesh and almost unrecognisable as human.

Jennings removed his head from the tent far quicker than he had inserted it and fumbled at the radio in his jacket pocket. 'Control. Control. Come in. This is Sergeant Jennings, Special Branch. Anyone copy?'

At first, nothing but a fizz and crackle, and then finally a fuzzy voice replied. 'Go ahead. Over.'

'Get me Superintendent Garrick. We've got two more.'

According to the landlord, a jovial, pot-bellied fellow, full of smiles and wisecracks, the Gough Arms was eponymously named after the laird's family, who had owned the big house north of the village of Monymusk for the last three-hundred and fifty years.

The aged pub, situated in the village square, was full of ancient oak furniture and even more ancient customers, most of whom had little else to do other than while away their days sipping malt at the antique bar and staring at the buxom blonde barmaid behind it.

'Terrible barmaid,' the landlord said in a whisper, as the busty woman spilt Anderson's malt and apologised with a giggle that caused her cleavage to wobble up and down and led to several of the old men at the bar to nearly choke on their whisky. 'But she has her benefits.'

'Aye, I can see that,' Anderson said, who was doing his own share of leering. He'd booked two rooms at the Arms, his experience telling him they were here for the duration on this one. At least until they'd caught that escaped chimp. But it was no hardship, not when he could fill his belly full of malt, paid for on expenses.

He whiled away a happy couple of hours, sipping whisky and watching the landlord flirt with the barmaid and drink his profits. Nice life if you can get it, thought Anderson, but realised the landlord had his own share of worries.

Well before two-thirty, a big woman appeared from a back room. Wearing leggings that made her thighs bulge like a bag of potatoes, she had a jowly face plastered in makeup that made her look like a blow-up doll inflated to bursting point.

She scowled at everyone around the bar as she strolled the length of it, as if walking down a police line-up, and then demanded everybody finish drinking and get out, despite there being fifteen minutes left until closing.

When Anderson protested, the landlord just shrugged. 'Sorry, pal,' he whispered. 'That's the wife. It's her name above the door. Best do as she says or I'll be for it. You can take it to your room, if you want, but she won't let me serve you another. Not until tonight.'

Anderson necked back his malt and slammed his glass down. 'Forget it. I'd better go see how the local plods are getting on anyway.'

'They still not found that gorilla that's on the loose, then?' the landlord asked, as Anderson got up to leave.

'Not yet,' Anderson said, before pulling open the pub door and muttering, 'I best go tell them it's behind your bar.'

Once outside, Anderson rolled a smoke and glanced around the village. Monymusk was a picturesque place, if you liked that sort of thing. Which he didn't. With its quaint village square, complete with war memorial, stone cottages and castled church tower, it must have made a nice place for tourists, but it was too dull for him. He'd grown up on the Gorbals, where a pub was on every corner, kids roamed the streets, and Saturday nights meant mayhem as the Celtic and Rangers fans ripped chunks out of each other. Life in Glasgow was never dull. He moved away to the Highlands over a decade ago and he often found himself missing it.

What was he talking about? Nobody in their right mind missed Glasgow, and he realised his melancholy was more than likely induced by the malt whisky in his belly. So he pulled his collar to shield from the wind and went to light the roll-up in his lips. But a screech of car tyres caused him to pause.

A panda car hurtled around the corner from the main road and skidded to a halt at the opposite side of the road. PC Ferguson's head appeared out of it. 'Inspector!' he shouted, waving furiously.

Anderson jogged across the square, ignoring the keep of the grass sign. 'Yeah, what do you want?'

'Superintendent Garrick told me to come get you.'

'What for?'

Ferguson's face stiffened. 'They've found two more, sir.'

'Two more what?'

'Bodies.'

Anderson tossed the cigarette from his lips and jumped into the passenger side. 'Go on then, put your foot down.'

Ferguson did as he was told, but a little more voraciously than Anderson expected. He either had spent his youth as a joy rider, or had been on some advanced driver training programme, because he threw the car around the country roads as if he were in the Monte Carlo Rally.

Consequently, it took less than a couple of minutes to cover the two or three miles to the country lane where several police cars and an ambulance were parked amid a congregation of uniforms. By this time the whisky in Anderson's gut was threatening to come back up the way it came in.

'Jesus Christ,' he said, stumbling from the car and resting his hand on the roof while taking deep, rapid breaths.

'You all right?' Ferguson asked, his eyebrows frowning.

'What were you trying to do, bloody kill us?' Anderson snapped, feeling his stomach settle a little. 'You almost had us in a ditch half a dozen times.'

Ferguson chuckled. 'Nah, I know these roads like the back of my hand.'

'Drive like that again with me in the car and you'll be getting the back of my bloody hand.'

'Ah, there you are,' Superintendent Garrick said, spotting them both and walking over, his cap in one hand, the other was greasing back his thinning hair. His face turned grim. 'We've got two more bodies, Inspector.'

'You almost had four on your hands, thanks to Ari bloody Vatanen here.' With a trembling hand, Anderson took out his tobacco and proceeded to roll a smoke. 'So what happened?'

'Two young campers. A girl and boy, or so your man Jennings reckons, although he says it is hard to tell.'

'You called Phelps?'

'He is on his way in now. In the chopper. Looks like we'll have to airlift the bodies out.' He pointed to the thick woodland lining the road. 'They're in clearing about a mile and a half in.'

'I don't suppose they bagged that bloody monkey, did they?'

'Afraid not. Jennings says there was no sign of it.'

'Where is he?'

'At the scene with that old gillie. I told him to wait until the chopper gets there.'

A young PC then trotted over and gestured for Garrick's attention.

'Sir, we've found an old Austin Metro parked up in a lay-by on the other side of the wood.'

Garrick squinted at him, unsure of the relevance.

'We think it could belong to the victims, sir.' The PC removed a notebook from his pocket and flipped through it. 'It's registered to a twenty-two-year-old from Liverpool.' He turned the page in his notebook. 'A Roger Taylor. Uniforms say there is a map of the area in the glove box. Paradise Woods is circled on it.'

Garrick nodded. 'Good work. But let's keep an open mind for the moment, before we go breaking some poor mother's heart.'

All eyes then looked up as the thunder of rotor blades above. 'Ah, that'll be Phelps. If you will excuse me, Inspector.'

Chapter Eleven

It was dark by the time they had airlifted the bodies out of the woods. The wind had picked up to a howl and rain blew sideways, drenching Anderson as he stood with Ferguson and Garrick waiting as the helicopter landed in a clearing near where the police cars were parked.

After watching the transfer of the two dead campers into an ambulance, Phelps, Jennings and the bewildered Brophy scuttled over.

'Looks the same as the others,' Phelps shouted, clutching his toupee to prevent the downdraft of the helicopter carrying it away. 'One IC male and IC female. Young, both of them. Terrible wounds, just like the two from the research centre.'

'Faces were missing,' Jennings added.

Anderson held up his hands. 'Spare me the details.'

Garrick rubbed his forehead, as if trying to iron the creases flat. 'I think we can all agree that this escaped animal now poses a serious risk to the general public. Our priority should be locating and destroying it as soon as possible.'

'I don't suppose you saw any sign of it on your travels?' Anderson asked, ducking slightly as the helicopter thundered overhead.

Jennings shook his head.

Anderson pinched his nose. 'Then it could be miles away by now.'

'No, sir,' Brophy interjected. 'It was there.'

Jennings looked at him like a startled deer. 'Where?'

'You saw it?' Garrick asked.

Brophy shook his head. 'No, I *disnae* laid eyes on it, but the critter was watching us. I could sense it.'

'All right, Obi Wan Kenobi,' Anderson said. 'Let's stick to what you saw, not what the bloody force was telling you.'

Garrick cleared his throat. 'Well, I suggest we conduct a thorough search. I'm going to call in reinforcements from Aberdeen.'

'Does that mean you *wisnae* be needing me?' Brophy asked, adjusting the gun on his back.

'We'll still need somebody that knows the land. So, if you don't mind, we'd appreciate your help again.'

He shrugged but looked neither keen nor perturbed.

'One thing is for certain,' Jennings said. 'This is no ordinary chimpanzee.'

Anderson squinted at him. 'What are you on about now?'

'Remember what Doctor Cunningham said? These animals are only aggressive when provoked.' He pointed back to the woods. 'Those kids were in their tent when it attacked them.'

Phelps wiped the drizzle off his glasses using his tie and nodded. 'It was certainly a frenzied assault. I'd never have thought a chimp could do such a thing. A gorilla perhaps, but not a chimpanzee, not if I hadn't seen it for myself.'

'Well, we're all guessing, aren't we?' Anderson said. 'None of us know a thing about bloody monkeys. Including how to find it. What we need is somebody who knows what we're dealing with.'

'I think I know just the person.' Everybody looked at Ferguson. 'I met a young woman when I was doing door-to-door this morning. She works at Paradise Woods. As a primatologist.'

Anderson shook his head. 'A what?'

'Expert on apes and monkeys,' Jennings said.

'Good, she can help clear up this bloody mess. Go get her.' He raised his collar to defend against the chastising wind. 'But let's continue this discussion somewhere warm, shall we?'

'Oh, before you all disappear,' Phelps said, 'we've managed to identify one of the bodies from the research centre.' He placed his medical bag down and rummaged around in his pockets, pulling free a slip of paper. 'We got lucky, his prints were on file.' He handed the paper to Garrick who turned away and peered at it using the headlights from one of the police cars.

'Confirms what we know,' he said, handing Ferguson the paper. 'One of the animal rights activists. After you've picked up that ape expert, you and me will go pay them a visit.' Garrick then turned back to Anderson. 'I'll get on the phone to Aberdeen and let you know how many men I can muster for the morning. Are you staying locally?'

'The Gough Arms,' Anderson said. 'Which is exactly where I'm going now.'

PC Ferguson stood at Shannon's door with rain dripping down his face. He wiped away the moisture, smiled and said, 'Sorry to disturb you again, ma'am ... I mean, Doctor, but there is an inspector from Special Branch who wants to speak to you.'

'What about?'

'I think he is hoping you can help us find this escaped animal.'

This was the last thing she wanted to do. The last thing Cunningham would want her to do. But PC Ferguson looked persistent and bounced on his heels, eyes wide, a broad smile on his face. Besides, refusal would be suspicious. Suspicion was something she needed to avoid more than anything else.

She nodded keenly. 'I'll just get my coat.'

She grabbed her Mackintosh from behind the door, screwed her shoes on to her feet and followed Ferguson out. However, instead of leading her to his car and taking her to the nearest police station, which she presumed was in Inverurie, he crossed the road and led her to the pub.

She'd never ventured into the Gough Arms. She preferred to keep to herself. It wasn't hard, even in such a small place like Monymusk. She worked long hours and most of her neighbours were elderly, so other than the odd good morning nod, nobody really bothered her. Besides, she'd not been there long, having moved from Aberdeen a few months before. The drive to Paradise Woods, down those twisty country roads, especially at night, was perilous, so renting the little cottage in the village made sense, at least until her research finished.

More than a few pairs of eyes followed her as she walked in behind Ferguson. The place smelled of stale beer, cigarette smoke and polish. Most of the people in there were old. A few young faces stood around the flashing lights of a fruit machine, and another, in a stained suit covered in mud with a small tear at the arm, sitting at a table next to a scruffy middle-aged man with a droop moustache and a roll-up cigarette in his mouth.

'Inspector, this is Doctor Shannon Long. Dr Long, Inspector Anderson and Detective Sergeant Jennings from Special Branch.'

The scruffy-looking man pulled free his cigarette and with two yellow fingers, indicated she should take a seat. 'I know you, don't I?' he said, as she sat down, his eyes squinting at her. 'You were with that hard-faced Cunny-what's-her-face this morning, weren't you?'

'You mean Doctor Cunningham?' Shannon said. 'Yes, I work with her.'

'You poor cow,' Anderson said, waving his glass at Ferguson. 'Get them in, will you?'

Ferguson raised the lapel on his uniform. 'I can't, not while I'm wearing this. The landlady is a stickler for the rules.'

'I'll go,' said Jennings, taking Anderson's glass before smiling at Shannon. 'Can I get you something, Doctor?'

'No, I'm fine, thank you.'

Anderson then looked up at PC Ferguson. 'Are you going to stand there all night like a hard-on or are you going to sit down?'

Ferguson shifted uncomfortably. 'No, sir. I'd better be going. The superintendent wants me to head up to the protest camp.'

Anderson wafted his hand to him. 'Well, go on then. Bugger off. You are making the place look untidy.'

Ferguson looked down at the inspector, eyebrows raised in incredulity, before nodding to Shannon. 'Nice to see you again, Doctor.'

She reciprocated his smile and the PC disappeared out of the pub, leaving Shannon alone with the unkempt detective who leered in an objectionable manner at her open blouse.

'I ... erm ... understand you wanted my help?' Shannon said, doing up her buttons. 'May I ask what about?'

'About that bloody ape, what do you think I want to talk about?' Anderson snapped, as Jennings returned with a pint and a glass of whisky.

Jennings sat down next to Shannon and smiled genially. 'You'll have to forgive the inspector. He didn't get enough beauty sleep last night.'

'Shut it, you!' Anderson snapped, before taking a deep mouthful of the liquor then fixing his eyes on Shannon. 'I don't suppose you've heard, but your monkey has attacked two more people.'

Shannon gasped. 'Are they badly hurt?'

'Nothing Lazarus couldn't overcome,' Anderson said, the glass to his lips.

She gaped at him. 'You mean they are dead?'

'Like a doornail. Or more accurately, like two people with their faces ripped off and throats torn out.' He leaned forward. She could smell the whisky and stale tobacco on his breath. 'What I want to know is what the bloody hell are we dealing with and how do we track it down?'

Shannon flustered a little, unsure how to answer. 'What ... what happened?'

'I thought that was pretty clear,' Anderson said, leaning back on his chair.

'They were camping in the woods,' Jennings explained. 'It seems it attacked them in their tent.'

Shannon could feel her eyes widen and mouth drop open, yet could do nothing about it. This confirmed her suspicions. The incident at the research centre, she could have put down 85H being confronted by two people it didn't recognise. Feeling threatened, it did what all wild animals would do in a similar situation. It lashed out. But this suggested something else. It couldn't have just been a tragic accident, even if the campers had startled it. But what could she say?

'This chimpanzee is a wild specimen,' she said, trying to convince herself more than the two detectives. 'It wasn't domestically bred.'

Anderson sniffed and took a deep inhalation of smoke, which he proceeded to blow in her direction across the table as he spoke. 'And I suppose whatever it was you were doing with it at that bloody facility hasn't riled it up at all.'

Shannon felt her face stiffen and stuck to the line Cunningham had enforced in her that morning. 'We are a medical research facility. I can assure you, that animal has not endured any suffering.'

'Weren't too keen to stick around, though, was it?' Anderson said, draining his whisky glass. 'Took the faces off two kids in its eagerness to get out of your laboratory.'

'As I've already explained to you, it is a wild animal, Inspector.'

'This is getting us nowhere,' Jennings said, smiling at her.

She felt sorry for him. She'd worked with apes most of her adult life, but even the most feral of them wasn't as uncultivated as this inspector.

'What we really need to know is how we can track it down,' Jennings added.

'In the wild, chimps are normally territorial, but since it is in a strange place, and more than likely a little confused, its behaviour could be unpredictable.'

'We figured that out for ourselves,' Anderson said.

'Doctor Cunningham said chimps are only aggressive when provoked,' Jennings said. 'If that is true, why do you think it attacked those campers?'

Shannon had her suspicions, but she couldn't voice them. Instead, she shook her head. 'As I said, they are normally territorial. It is a male, so it is probably trying to establish itself in its new surroundings. It possibly saw those two people as a potential threat to its dominance...'

'So you think it will stay where it is?' Jennings asked.

She nodded. 'Most likely, yes. But their territories can be varied and quite large. Anything from a couple of miles to several hundred. It will stay in wooded areas, though. Chimps rarely venture out from the safety of the forest.'

Anderson looked at Jennings. 'How big is that wood?'

Jennings shrugged. 'Not sure. We seemed to walk for bloody miles this morning, but I daresay it is no more than four or five miles from end to end.'

'Doesn't the river run through the middle of it?' Shannon asked, remembering one summer afternoon when she'd gone for a walk there waiting for some test results to come in. It was pretty enough, but she'd never been that much of an outdoors person, so had only been once.

'Yes, that's right,' Jennings said.

'Well, rivers tend to act like natural boundaries for chimps. They don't like water much and it'll probably keep away from the footpaths and bridges to avoid people. So, it is probably in the same area where the attack took place.'

'That helps,' Jennings said. 'Cuts the area we have to search.'

'Yes, but they can be pretty elusive when they want to be,' Shannon said. 'If they don't want to be found, you are going to have a hell of a job spotting it.'

Anderson pinched his eyes and exhaled deeply, his breath reeking of whisky. 'What do we need to do to find it?'

Shannon leaned back, partly to think, partly to avoid the man's halitosis. 'You'll need somebody that knows the area well, especially the types of trees, food sources, that sort of thing.'

Anderson turned to the bar, where an old man, a brace of rabbits hanging on his belt, stood sipping whisky. 'We've got that covered. What else do we need?'

'You need me, Inspector.'

Chapter Twelve

The police arrived at the protest camp just after ten. Most of the activists were by the fire, strumming guitars, singing, passing joints back and forth. Most. Not all.

Helen spent all day in her tent, only venturing out to speak to Sarah. Or trying to. Sarah refused to see anyone, including Helen, no matter how much she pleaded. But now she'd have to speak to her. Now that the police were here.

Scamp had informed her of their unwanted visitors by thrusting his head into Helen's tent and saying excitedly, 'The filth are here. Quick.'

She didn't want to go. She wanted to pull the sleeping bag over her head until she woke from this nightmare, but she knew she couldn't. As a former law student, she was the camp's unofficial legal advisor. They'd all expect her to be there when the police started their heavy-handed tactics and made their threats. So, after taking a deep breath and grabbing her anorak, she followed Scamp to the perimeter of the protest camp where two police officers stood in confrontation with the activists who had formed an angry circle, shouting and jeering and pointing their fingers.

'What's going on?' Helen said, as she barged her way through the throng to the front.

One of the policemen, a senior and high-ranking officer judging by the pips on his collar, glanced at his younger, less superior colleague before lifting his head back and saying, 'And who might you be?'

'Helen Tanner?' she said, her voice struggling to be heard over the jeers from the other protestors. She gestured for her friends to calm and quieten down. 'What can we do for you?'

'I'm Superintendent Garrick, this is PC Ferguson. We'd like to talk to you all about what happened last night.'

She glanced at the other activists, their faces eager for her to do her thing. Normally, she relished antagonising the police. Not today. 'We've no idea what you are talking about.'

'So you are not aware that two of your ...' Garrick glanced at the mob before him, '... friends broke into the research centre in Paradise Woods last night and released one of their specimens. A dangerous specimen at that.'

'News to us,' Helen lied.

'Heroes,' somebody shouted out. Helen presumed it was Scamp as Garrick's eyes fixed on him.

'It cost them their lives,' Garrick said, causing the crowd to silence. Gasps and a muted whispers sounded from the crowd, then a gentle clamouring followed by tears and shouts of disbelief. Scamp looked at Helen, his eyes as wide as golf balls.

'Are you telling us that some members of our organisation have been killed?' Helen asked, as the clamour behind became louder and more hysterical.

Garrick tried to silence them with a raised hand, but it did little to reduce the cacophony. 'I'm afraid so. We have identified one of your ... friends.' Garrick clicked his fingers to Ferguson, who produced a notebook.

'Jason Kavanagh, sir,' Ferguson said.

'But we do need your help to identify the other deceased person,' Garrick continued.

Helen knew Jason and Philip were dead, so hearing it from the police wasn't a shock, yet she knew she had to feign ignorance, lest she raised suspicions. 'Jason is dead?'

'I'm afraid so, miss,' Garrick said. 'Perhaps you knew what he was up to last night?'

She shook her head rapidly then glanced at her fellow protestors. 'No, none of us did.'

'Really?' Garrick said. One eyebrow rose. 'I find that hard to believe especially as the evidence suggests there were more than two people involved in the break-in last night.'

A few people around her gasped.

'Obviously your friend Jason did not return last night. Neither did the other victim. So if you wouldn't mind letting me know who is missing from your ... group, I have relatives and family to inform.'

A few people began muttering Philip's name, and Helen knew she would have to tell the Superintendent who he was. She bowed her head. 'Philip is missing too.'

Ferguson had a pen hovering above his notebook. 'Philip who, miss?'

Helen suddenly realised she didn't know his surname. In fact, she doubted she knew anybody's surname for that matter. She realised she didn't really know any of the protestors. It all seemed so alien to her now. What was she doing here? None of it seemed important or worthwhile anymore.

'His name was Philip Daniels,' a voice from the crowd said. It was Rachel. Young, pretty and normally quiet, tears streamed down her cheeks. Helen realised why. She'd seen her and Philip come out of his tent together. Poor girl. But she wasn't the only one to lose somebody.

'I appreciate this must come as a shock to you all,' Garrick said, his voice sounding genuine and sympathetic. 'And I understand your strong feelings to what goes on at the research centre, but I'm sure you must all now realise how foolish and dangerous those actions were last night, and not just for your two friends.'

Helen looked askance at him, wondering what he meant. She soon found out.

'Two other people were found dead this afternoon,' Garrick said. 'We believe the animal released last night was to blame.'

Helen found herself trembling. What had they done? She remembered Jason's screams, the panic in his face as the chimp mauled at him, and the ferociousness of the attack. If this policeman was to be believed, two other people had suffered a similar fate. Two more lives snubbed out. And she was partly to blame. Garrick was right. It was foolish. Dangerous.

'So, we'd like to know who else was there last night?' Garrick added.

Helen wanted to say something, raise her hand, admit everything, but whether it was fear, panic, guilt, she found herself frozen to the spot.

'Okay, now listen to me.' Garrick's tone had gone from empathy to authority. 'I need to know exactly what happened last night. Four people are dead. Do you all understand that?'

He looked at the activists, all of whom stood still, silent, eyes lowered, like naughty school kids in the headmaster's office.

'We can either do this the hard way—I can arrest you all and charge you with perverting the course of justice,' Garrick said. 'Or whoever was there last night can come forward and explain to me exactly what happened.'

Nobody spoke, nobody moved.

A long second followed then Garrick said, 'I'll give you all until tomorrow morning to think about it.' He then waved his hand to Ferguson. 'And to ensure none of you decide to do anything silly, such as disappear overnight, PC Ferguson here will take all your names and home addresses. Do you understand?'

A muted confirmation followed.

'Oh, Jerry,' Barbara said as she squirmed on top of him and undid his trousers.

Jerry reached for the handle to tilt the front seat backwards to give her more room. He was well aware he had a bit of a gut on him. A consequence of owning a pub. Not that he owned it. It wasn't *her* name above the door. That wife of his.

His marriage had been stale for years, not that it had ever been what he would have described as passionate. But he loved running his own pub, and a loveless marriage was a price worth paying. Besides, since he'd hired Barbara as barmaid, his love life had improved dramatically.

Of course, he feared his wife finding out about his illicit nightly meetings with the staff, which was why he bought the dog. The Gough Arms needed a guard dog, he told his wife, but in reality he needed an excuse to go out every night.

The dog did bring its own problems, though.

'Can't you stop it from yapping?' Barbara complained, as Jerry pawed at her top, trying to unclip her bra. 'It's putting me off.'

He'd put the dog outside, trapping its leash in the door to prevent it running away, but the damned mutt wanted attention.

'Just ignore it,' Jerry said, his concentration absorbed by the sheer complexity of her bra clasp. 'Let's not waste time. I'll have to be back at the pub in ten minutes.'

'How can I ignore it?' Barbara said, glaring at the animal through the window. 'I can see it staring at me.'

Jerry sighed and, releasing the lace lattice behind her back, he opened the door. 'Go on, go for a run,' he said, shooing the dog to the trees.

Yapping as it went, the dog scampered off into the woods. They'd parked in their usual spot by the river, and Jerry knew Benji would soon run back again once called. It was a soft mutt, and he spoiled it. Like Jerry, it knew when it was on to a good thing.

'Peace at last,' Barbara said, as Jerry slammed the door shut again.

'Right, where was I?' he said, returning to the unfathomable puzzle of her bra strap.

Chapter Thirteen

As with all the others, Helen gave her details to the police, Sarah's too, explaining that she was unwell. Even now, with the police there, Sarah didn't leave her tent. PC Ferguson seemed nice enough, for a copper, and Helen wanted to confess all to him, but knew she couldn't, now without speaking to Sarah first.

If only she would speak to her.

She'd have to now that the police were involved. And if she wouldn't, Helen would make her. She tramped to Sarah's tent and told her, not asked, that she was coming in.

'Go away!' Sarah shouted, as Helen thrust her head into the tent.

The first thing that struck her was the smell, a putrid stench, a bit like chicken that had been left out of the refrigerator too long. It almost made her gag. She then saw Sarah's face. It was ashen grey, the eyes bleary and bloodshot. Blotches covered her cheeks and neck.

'Are you all right?' Helen asked, her anger replaced by concern.

'Go away,' Sarah snapped, turning over and showing Helen her back.

Helen ventured further into the tent, the pungent smell strengthened. 'We need to talk, Sarah. About last night. The police have been here.'

'I'm not well. Go away.' She waved Helen away, revealing her bare arm.

Helen grabbed it. 'Oh my God!'

The bite she suffered during the night had festered. Yellow pus oozed out and the source of the horrible smell became clear.

'Sarah, it has gone septic. You need to see a doctor.'

'Leave me,' Sarah said, retracting her arm. 'I said go away!'

Her voice rasped as she spoke and her breath smelled almost as bad as her arm.

'At least let me clean it.' Helen reached for her arm again, but Sarah lashed out pushing Helen backwards and she half-spilled out the tent.

Then Sarah went crazy.

She threw herself at Helen, hands around her throat, teeth bared and snarling at her. Helen struggled, kicked and tried to prise Sarah's hands free, but she was strong. Really strong. Helen couldn't even scream. Sarah's hands were too tight around her throat. But as Helen's strength ebbed away, another pair of hands appeared in her peripheral vision, grabbing Sarah and pulling at her arms.

In the dim light and in her state of breathlessness and confusion, it took a while for Helen to see her saviour. Then she made out the unlikely figure of Scamp and felt Sarah's grip ease from her throat.

Then Sarah launched herself at Scamp.

'Hey!' he shrieked as he tumbled to the ground. The short, stout girl, her pale blue pyjamas shimmering in the moonlight, straddled him and beat at his chest as if he were a kettledrum while Helen lay gasping, biting at the air to replenish her lungs.

Then Scamp screamed.

In the corner of her eye, Helen saw Sarah lean forward, clamp his cheek between her teeth and tear off a chunk as if biting into a rump steak.

Helen rolled to her feet, head glancing left, right, looking for anything with which to hit Sarah. All she could find was an old metal bucket, which they used for their morning ablutions. It was half full, making it heavy, so when she swung it, Sarah, who had blood trickling down her chin, fell from Scamp as if she were a bar skittle.

Scamp lay holding his face, squirming, crying while Sarah rolled to her feet, wiped the gore from her mouth with the back of her hand, and then after glaring at Helen for a long second, charged off into the night, screaming dementedly as she went.

'Jesus Christ, Jesus Christ,' Scamp screamed, clutching his face as Helen went to help. 'What just happened?'

Helen glanced over to the field and the distant tree line where Sarah's silhouette disappeared. 'I don't know,' she said. 'I don't know.'

Jerry sat panting as he zipped himself up and Barbara slumped into the passenger seat and slipped her knickers back on.

'We'll have to head back,' he said, glancing at his watch. '*She'll* be wondering where I am.'

Barbara pulled a face. 'When are you going to tell her about us, Jerry?'

Never was the real answer. Barbara was a great roll in the hay, but she was not worth losing a pub over. 'It's difficult, Babs, you know that.'

'I want more than just these quickies,' Barbara said.

'I know, I know.' He put her arm around her and kissed her cheek, but she turned her face.

'You best go get your dog.'

Jerry grumbled and opened the car door.

Outside was dark, but not pitch black. The headlights from the car and the full moon above his head enabled him to see the woodland clear enough. He cupped his hands around his mouth and called for the dog. 'Benji! Benji! Here, boy!'

Several seconds passed. Nothing.

Strange. Normally the mutt would come bounding up to him the moment he called. 'Benji, where are you, boy?'

He heard rustling ahead. Something was there, moving, so Jerry approached. It got darker as he breached the undergrowth, so Jerry took the lighter from his pocket, lit it, and using it as a torch held it into the darkness.

He then spotted the dog, lying down in the leaf litter.

'Benji, what are you doing?'

The dog didn't move.

Jerry squatted, grabbing the leash still connected to the dog's collar. 'Benji, get up, c'mon, laddie.'

The dog's head lolled back as he pulled the leash. Jerry lowered the lighter, which had started to get hot and burn his fingers, but he endured it for long enough to see the blood over the animal's muzzle.

'Jesus Christ,' Jerry said, as his fingers could take the hot lighter no longer. He let it go out and squinted as he lifted the animal's head in the darkness. As soon as he touched Benji, he knew the dog was dead. The head was limp, the body still, lifeless.

Then he heard the rustling again and something moved in his peripheral vision. Jerry lit the lighter again.

There.

Something flitted in front of him. Something fast. Something big.

He stepped forward, his arm outstretched to illuminate as much as he could.

The faint flicker from his lighter rested on a face.

A non-human face.

A face with large canine teeth and wide staring eyes.

It charged.

Despite his size, the animal easily knocked Jerry to the ground as it shrieked a high-pitched wail. It scratched and bit at Jerry's arm as he tried to fend the animal off. It was incredibly strong, yet Jerry wasn't going to let a damned monkey get the better of him. Using his foot as a lever, he kicked and pushed the animal off before scrambling to his feet and limping back to the car.

'What's going on?' Barbara asked as he jumped into the driver's seat and slammed the door shut. 'I heard noises.'

'It's that bloody escaped ape,' Jerry said, as the animal broke cover from the tree line and jumped on to the bonnet of the car, its arms raised, its chest protruding forward.

Barbara screamed.

The chimp screamed.

Jerry screamed.

He then turned on the ignition, slammed the gearstick into reverse and floored the accelerator, causing the chimp to somersault backwards as the car backed out of the lay-by.

As soon as he was clear, Jerry put the car into first gear and sped off back towards the village, slowing only when he felt certain the animal was a long way back.

'My God, you are bleeding,' Barbara said, as Jerry stared hard into the rear-view mirror.

'Bastard thing killed Benji,' Jerry said.

'We've got to report this.'

Jerry reached into the glove box and grabbed the cloth he used to demist the windows and wrapped it around his arm. 'We'll do no such thing. How do we explain what we were doing out here? The two of us! *She'll* find out.'

'But what if it attacks somebody else?'

He shook his head. 'I can't risk it. Anyway, I spoke to that inspector. He said they've arranged a hunting party to go look for it in the morning. The bloody thing will get what it deserves, you mark my words.'

Chapter Fourteen

Two police vans full of armed officers pulled into the village square at six o'clock in the morning before the sun had breached the horizon. Garrick was there, barking orders and looking as if he'd had a good eight hours sleep, his uniform neat and tidy.

The same couldn't say the same about Anderson, who was keeled over with a finger on one of his nostrils and blowing snot on to the pavement. He had dark rings around his eyes, greying stumble around his face and his skin was pale.

Jennings wasn't surprised.

The amount the inspector drank the night before was enough to inebriate a rugby team. By last orders, Anderson was encouraging the rest of the pub to join in with his rendition of *I Can't Get No Satisfaction,* much to the amusement of the pub's patrons and to the horror of PC Ferguson, who had poked his head around the door to check the landlord was closing up.

How Anderson got away with it, Jennings would never know. During their short acquaintance, he spent most his time either boozing in a pub somewhere or sleeping it off at his desk back in Inverness.

Still, he was the boss, and after standing around in the morning cold for ten minutes, Anderson called them all together once old Brophy turned up in his battered and rusting old Land Rover. The old gillie looked like an old poacher—trousers tucked into long rubber boots, deerstalker on his head, his pipe protruding from his mouth.

Doctor Shannon was there too, stepping from her front door in jeans and bleached white trainers.

'Right, so what's the plan?' Anderson asked, licking closed a cigarette.

Garrick looked at Shannon. 'Since you are our resident expert, what do you suggest?'

Shannon looked at Garrick, looked at Anderson and looked at Brophy then back at all the armed police officers milling around the square.

'Chimps don't like noise,' she said. 'I suggest you split your men into two teams. One to flush it out, the other to take care of it when it breaks cover.'

'Bit like shooting grouse,' old Brophy said, smiling.

Anderson sniffed loudly and swallowed whatever blocked his throat. 'Yes, but a grouse won't bite your bloody face off.' He then looked at Garrick. 'Have you got a map of the place?'

Garrick waved his fingers in the air, grabbing Ferguson's attention who was chatting to a gaggle of armed officers and was seemingly enamoured by their weapons. 'Get me a map of Paradise Woods.'

They waited for the young constable to jog to his car, scramble around in a glove box then trot over with what looked like a tourist information map. 'Best we have, sir.'

Garrick frowned at it, but spread it open on the bonnet of his car for all to see. 'I take it this is where we found that couple yesterday?' he said, tapping the map.

Jennings looked at Brophy, who nodded. 'Aye, poor wee bastards.'

'And the river cuts the woods in half here,' he said, following the blue line on the map.

'Then I think it will remain in this area,' Shannon said, tapping the map. 'The river will act as a natural boundary.'

Garrick looked back at the officers. 'Okay, we have a dozen men. I suggest we set up a team of six marksmen on the bridge here.' He tapped the map before looking at Brophy. 'You lead the rest of the officers through the woods to drive it out.' He looked at Anderson. 'I think you should go with them. I'll supervise on the bridge.'

'How about you go bloody trudging through the woods, while I wait on the bridge,' Anderson said.

'May I remind you I am a superintendent,' Garrick said.

'Which probably means you couldn't supervise an arse-wiping contest,' Anderson snapped. 'And may I remind you, this is a Special Branch operation?'

If there was one thing Jennings had learned about Anderson, it was that you didn't pull rank on him. Garrick's nose twitched uncomfortably, but Anderson was right, no matter what his rank, this was a Special Branch matter so Garrick had to follow orders.

'You go with him,' Anderson said, gesturing to Jennings. 'Make sure none of his lot get all trigger-happy and shoot some poor bastard taking his dog for a walk.'

Jennings sighed. 'Yes, guv.'

'What happens if I get a clear shot?' Brophy asked.

'Then shoot it,' Anderson said. 'But make sure you are nowhere near the bridge.'

Brophy nodded.

'What about me?' Shannon said.

Anderson looked her up and down, his face showing disdain at her jeans and trainers. 'You ain't coming, love. I don't want any civvies knocking about. You can wait here. If we need you, somebody will come and get you.' He twitched his head to Ferguson. 'Go get her a radio.'

'Hold on, I'm the only one that knows anything about this animal. I should be there. It might react badly,' she protested.

'Of course it will bloody react badly. We're going to shoot it, not serve it with a warrant. And the last thing we want is a bloody woman running round the woods.' He then sniffed at Garrick. 'There's enough tits about as it is.'

She scowled, Garrick scowled, Ferguson sniggered.

'We all ready then?' Anderson asked.

'I'll have to change first,' Garrick said, disappearing to his car and grumbling under his breath.

'Well, hurry up about it,' Anderson shouted. 'I want that chimp dead by opening time.'

The wound on Scamp's cheek looked angry when Helen went to see him in the morning. It hadn't scabbed over. He was running a fever and sweat covered his brow.

'Scamp, you need to see a doctor,' Helen said, changing the makeshift bandage she'd applied after the attack. Sarah had still not returned. Nobody had seen her, although everybody had heard about what she did. Helen couldn't understand it. Sarah was a pacifist, for heaven's sake, and she loved Scamp. They all did.

He didn't look well, but he wouldn't seek help.

'I'm not going to the hospital,' he said, almost deliriously. 'I don't want to get Sarah into trouble.

'I think it's infected,' Helen said. 'You need some antibiotics.'

He shook his head. He was barely conscious and his head lolled left and right. She didn't care what he said. She didn't care what trouble it would cause Sarah, cause all of them, she was getting help. And she was going to tell the police everything.

Something wasn't right.

They needed help.

Chapter Fifteen

He may have been a scruffy old codger, but Brophy knew his business. As the team of armed officers arrived at the far side of the woods, Garrick had tried barking orders at them to split them into teams of two, but Brophy shook his head.

'That *isnae* the way to do it,' he said, unloading stuff from the back of his old Land Rover. Jennings noticed it wasn't taxed and had two bald tyres, but he didn't say anything.

'What's all this?' Garrick asked, looking down at the pots and pans and dustbin lids and other junk Brophy had brought with him.

'Need something to scare the critter with,' Brophy replied.

'Haven't you got anything more sophisticated, like an air horn?'

'Works for game, *disnae* see why it won't work for a chimpanzee.'

'Old ways are often the best,' Jennings said, who stood with the six armed officers who were readying their weapons. They looked confused, as the old gillie handed out the bric-a-brac.

'Guv,' said a stout officer with a walrus moustache, 'we cannot carry all this as well as our rifles.'

'You *disnae* need you guns,' Brophy said. 'Be best if you leave them here.'

The officers all looked at Garrick with horror on their faces. 'I'm not sure venturing into the woods unarmed is a good idea,' Garrick said.

'You wisnae be unarmed. I have my rifle,' Brophy said, tapping the gun slung on his shoulder.

Garrick didn't look convinced and neither did his men. 'I think it might be best if they keep their firearms.' He turned to the armed officers. 'Make sure your safeties are on.'

The looks several of them gave him suggested he was telling grandma to suck eggs, but they slung their rifles over their backs and grabbed hold of the various pots, pans and other tin ware that Brophy handed out.

They looked a sight that was for sure, Jennings thought, with pots and pans and other kitchen paraphernalia in their hands and rifles on their backs. He understood why they were reluctant to leave their guns behind. He felt the same way and had taken his own service pistol from the car and checked the mechanism carefully before slipping it into a holster under his arm. He had only recently passed his firearms exam and never shot the thing outside a range, and he didn't think he'd need it, not with Brophy and all the uniforms with their rifles, but he felt a lot better with it on. After all, he'd seen firsthand what that animal could do. Twice. And he valued his facial features too much to take any chances.

Once Brophy had handed out his kitchen utensils, he gestured for everybody to spread out. Each man stood a good fifty paces from the next. Brophy in the middle, Jennings one side of him, Garrick the other, while the rest were in a line that must have stretched a quarter of a mile.

After a good ten minutes of gestures, shouts and radio messages to get everybody in position, Garrick raised his arm, paused and lowered it like a bowler sending a slow delivery.

The gesture was then repeated down the line.

And they moved into the trees.

'They're on their way,' Anderson said, after Garrick's voice crackled on the radio and told them they had moved out. 'Hope you lot know how to use those bloody things!'

The six firearms officers fiddling with the rifles on the bridge grunted, mumbled and rolled their eyes at one another.

'This has got bloody disaster written all over it,' Anderson muttered.

'I'm sure it'll be all right,' Ferguson said, his eyes focussed on the tree line.

Anderson snorted a laugh. 'You've not been in the job long, have you, sonny?'

'Five years.'

'Yeah, well if you'd been on as many *shouts* when there have been guns involved as I have, you'll soon change your mind. Look at 'em.' He nodded to the firearms officers. I've got haemorrhoids older than that lot. Half of 'em ain't started shaving, and yet some berk in Aberdeen has gone and give 'em rifles. Mark my words—if somebody doesn't get their arse blown off today, I'm a monkey's uncle.'

'Don't you mean chimpanzee's uncle,' Ferguson said, grinning, but Anderson ignored him and continued his rant.

'That's why I'm stood on this bridge and not rambling around in those bloody woods. If anyone is going to get a bollock shot off this afternoon, it ain't going to be me. And if you've got any sense, you'll keep your head down too.'

'Actually, if it is all right with you, I was going to go back to the village to see if Doctor Long has any more ideas. Just in case things don't work out.'

Anderson cocked an eyebrow at him. 'Were you now? And I know exactly what ideas you had in mind.' Anderson chuckled. 'Well, if you want to go and show a piece of fluff your truncheon, don't let me stop you. I'm sure we can manage without you.'

Chapter Sixteen

The house in Monymusk had been in Henry Gough's family for centuries. He had paintings in the drawing room of nearly all his ancestors who owned and ran the estate before him, yet despite this grand lineage, Henry was broke. Skint. Virtually penniless. Most people assumed he was rich. After all, he did live in an old manor house, but that didn't mean he was rolling in it. In fact, nothing could be further from the truth. His ancestors had not all been prudent with money, and along with death taxes, his ancestral wealth amounted to just the land and property.

With farm rents dropping dramatically in recent years, all the money that came into the estate went straight back out again—the upkeep of the house alone cost more than most the farmer's in the area made in a year, and he was struggling to keep the place going. He couldn't even afford to hire a gardener anymore, which was why he spent most mornings tending the lawns and flowerbeds outside the house himself.

He had to keep it neat and tidy. He relied heavily on tourists in the summer. The couple of pounds they spent to look round the house and go for walks on the estate went a long way in keeping the lights on. Yet it was not enough. It was never enough.

He stood up from the Clematis he was pruning and arched his back and flexed his hand. The damned pruning shears were sticking. Something else that needed replacing. It was relentless.

As he stood resting, he noticed a figure ambling up the drive. No, not ambling. Shambling. Staggering like a drunk. When the figure closed, he noticed she was wearing pyjamas. At least he thought it was a she. With the short hair, he found it hard to tell. But whoever it was, they had clearly been drinking or smoking something, or both.

'Can I help you?' he asked, as the strange figure closed. She didn't answer, just staggered closer and closer to him, walking through his flowerbeds and on to the lawn.

'I say, what do you want?' Gough said, his arms akimbo.

His words had no effect. She didn't even look but kept her eyes, which looked lifeless and sallow, fixed on the ground. Whatever she had taken obviously didn't agree with her, because she didn't look well. Her skin was the colour of putty, blotches covered her face and she had dirt and leaves all over her pyjamas, as if she'd spent the night in the woods.

Her stagger then turned into a sort of jog, then into a run.

Then she raised her arms, spread her fingers like a sparrowhawk about to attack a small bird in flight, and sprinted at him.

She was on him before Gough had time to react, digging her fingernails into his face, causing him to scream, causing him to topple backwards with the girl writhing on top of him.

Panting and gurgling, she tore her nails into his face. Her breath stank something rotten. Gough screamed as one of her fingers gouged into his eye, and then he screamed again as she sunk her teeth into his neck.

Despite her small stature, she was strong, and he couldn't lever her grip from his face or throw her off.

But he still had the pruning shears on his hand.

She bit his neck again. A spasm of pain erupted from his throat and he felt the warmth of blood gush down his neck.

So he lashed at her with the shears.

The first strike had little effect. Nor did the second. But he struck at her repeatedly, the shears squelching every time they punctured the flesh around her face and neck.

He must have hit her six or seven times, before he felt her grip loosen and he was able to shift her weight from on top of him. He threw her off and scrawled away, his vision nothing but a blur, his voice unable to call for help.

He clutched his throat to try to stem the bleeding but the blood gushed through his fingers. He tried to stand, but collapsed face first into the lawn.

The line of police all banging pots, pans and other kitchen implements moved slowly through the woods. Very slowly. The trees, bushes and sheer size of the forest that needed surveying required them all to take small steps, their eyes scanning left and right as they went.

Birds fluttered from trees and unseen animals rustled through the undergrowth to get away from the cacophony. At one point, a small herd of deer burst from the bushes and cantered away, causing several of the officers to reach for their rifles, but they soon relaxed.

Despite the din, it felt eerie and quiet to Jennings, especially when the officers next to him momentarily disappeared behind the bushes and bracken. Occasionally, Brophy would halt them, raising his hand, a motion repeated by everybody down the line. The old gillie would then listen carefully, before relaxing and gesturing for them all to continue.

This went on for nearly two hours.

Until they saw it.

As expected, Brophy spotted it first. He raised his hand, and the line came to a stop. Nobody suspected anything different to all the other times the old gillie had stopped them.

Until he unslung the rifle from his back.

All eyes followed Brophy's gaze, as the old man aimed his rifle at a group of poplar trees. At first, Jennings saw nothing, just the varied colours of autumn leaves. Then something moved in the branches. Something dark and agile.

The officers beside him dropped their cooking pots and removed the rifles from their back, but Garrick raised his hands, ordering everybody to keep still and keep calm.

Jennings felt the hairs on his neck bristle as his eyes went from the swinging form high up in the canopy, to old Brophy, his gun wavering left and right as he tried to line up the sights.

He fired.

He may have been a crack shot at bagging deer and grouse, but as the noise from the rifle echoed around the woods, causing even more birds to flutter from the trees, nothing fell from the tree other than a few leaves and twigs.

'You missed,' Garrick shouted.

Jennings could no longer see the ape. Some of the branches above their heads rustled. Rifles trained left and right to the canopy above their heads.

Some of the officers farther down the line had begun jogging towards where they thought the action was. 'Where is it?' somebody shouted.

'There,' cried somebody else.

They followed the reverberating ring of another shot as one of the officers spotted it, and the little tranquil wood in the middle of the Cairngorms erupted into something resembling the Battle of the Bulge.

Everybody armed with a rifle let fly with round after round into the trees. Leaves, twigs, branches, even dead birds, fell from the trees, and even Jennings had pulled out his gun and knocked off a couple of rounds at nothing in particular, until Garrick screamed loud enough to be heard above the gunfire.

'Cease fire! Cease fire! For the love of God, hold your fire!'

The shots petered out, leaving the smell of cordite hanging in the air, and far fewer leaves hanging on the trees.

'Did anybody hit it?' somebody asked.

Brophy stepped forward in the direction of where the majority of shots were fired.

'Anything?' Garrick shouted, stepping forward and standing on tiptoes to peer over a clump of bushes between him and the gillie.

Brophy turned around and shook his head, just as something burst from the undergrowth at Garrick's feet and leapt at the superintendent.

After a long second, both Brophy and Jennings ran to help as Garrick screamed and writhed on the ground, trying to fend the creature off. Jennings had his pistol at arm's length, but there was no way of letting off a shot without hitting Garrick.

Then Brophy let off a shot into the air.

And it worked.

The creature bolted back into the undergrowth, the bushes rustling as it made its escape farther into the woods, while Jennings ran up to the stricken policeman.

It didn't look too bad. Garrick's shirt was ripped, his jacket dishevelled, and he had a small gash across his cheek. The only significant wound was on his hand, which he must have used to deflect the chimp's assault but even that didn't look as if it needed stitches.

The radio lay at his feet, and as all the armed officers cantered up to help, Jennings picked it up. 'Are you there, guv?'

The radio crackled and fizzed then Anderson's Glaswegian drawl came through on the other end. 'What the bloody hell is going on? It sounds like World War Two in there.'

'Never mind that,' Jennings said, his eyes fixed in the direction the ape had bolted. 'It is heading your way.'

Chapter Seventeen

Ferguson parked outside Shannon's house and rapped gently on the door. A moment later, it partially opened and Shannon's face appeared. Her eyebrows rose on sight of him. 'Yes?'

'Sorry to disturb you, I just thought I'd let you know the search is underway.'

She glanced at her watch. 'And?'

Ferguson suddenly felt like an idiot. What was he doing here? As if somebody as smart and erudite as Dr Long would be interested in a rural flatfoot like himself.

'I ... er ... also wanted to thank you for your help. I know it may not seem like it but we all appreciate what you have done.'

'Really? Does that include that Inspector Anderson?'

Ferguson frowned and bowed his head slightly. 'Sorry about him. Coppers like that still think it is the 1970s. I just wanted to make sure you didn't think we were all like that.'

'I don't,' she said, sharply. Then just as Ferguson resigned himself to walking away, her face softened slightly. 'Sorry,' she said. 'You must think I'm being a really hard-faced bitch.'

'No, of course not.'

Her eyebrows rose again.

'Well, maybe just a little bit. But you have good reason.'

'It's no excuse. I guess it's been a long couple of days.'

'No need to apologise. I understand.' A long, awkward second of silence followed before Ferguson tapped his radio and added, 'As soon as I hear anything else, I'll let you know.'

She nodded, but also opened the door wider. 'Unless you have something else on, why not come in and wait? I've just put the kettle on.'

Ferguson felt his face contort in an uncontrolled grin. 'That'll be great, thanks.'

She stepped aside to let him in then led him down the hall, gesturing to the front room. 'Go make yourself comfortable. Do you take sugar?'

'Two, thank you,' he said stepping into the living room. It was quiet sparse. Beside the sofa and chair, both of which must have come with the property, as they were old, worn and floral, the room contained just a TV, a bookcase loaded with academic texts, and a table covered in papers and a *Tandy* computer.

'So how long have you been in the force?' Shannon shouted from the kitchen, as Jennings fingered the keyboard on the computer, causing the green screen monitor to spring into life.

He stepped away quickly, thrusting his hands at his side. 'About five years, give or take.'

'Did you always want to be a policeman?' she asked, above the sound of cups being stirred.

'Pretty much, yes. It was either that or farming. There's not much else in the way of career opportunities round here.'

'But Aberdeen is not that far away,' she said, walking in with two steaming mugs of tea.

'I guess not,' he said, as she handed him a mug. 'But I've spent my whole life here. To us country bumpkins, Aberdeen seems as exotic and faraway as the Caribbean.'

She smiled, her bookish and serious features melted away to reveal a pretty and girlish face. Another long, awkward pause followed, which was broken by banging on the door. Quite aggressive and determined banging.

'Who the hell is that?' Shannon said, handing Ferguson her mug before marching to the door.

He heard a brief conversation and another female voice, and then Shannon reappeared. 'It's a young girl,' she said. 'Wants to speak to you.'

'Me?'

Shannon shrugged. 'She asked if there was a policeman here.'

He handed Shannon both the mugs and stepped out of the front room.

A young girl stood at the door, dressed in a scruffy, woollen sweater, jeans that looked like bleach had been spilt all over them and a pair of cheap, muddied trainers. Ferguson recognised her as one of the hippy activists he remembered seeing at the protest camp the previous evening.

'Can I help you?' he said, returning his voice to the more authoritative tone he used at work.

'We need your help,' the young girl said, before speaking at machine gun speed. 'It's my friends—one of them has gone missing—another is hurt—sick—she attacked him—went mad—I think it has something to do with the chimp—because it was us—we were there the other night—at Paradise Woods—we didn't mean for this to happen—I'm really sorry.' She then burst into tears.

'Whoa, slow down, I didn't get a word of that. Are you telling me you were involved in the break-in at Paradise Woods?'

The girl nodded, her face red, tears streaming down her cheeks. 'We only wanted to free the animals. We didn't want anybody to get hurt. But Sarah has gone mad. She attacked Scamp, and now she's missing.'

'Who? What? Can we start again?' Ferguson glanced behind at Shannon who was standing behind him. She shrugged, indicating she had no idea what the girl was babbling on about either.

Ferguson turned back to the young girl. 'Now, what is your name?'

She wiped her eyes and snorted back her tears. 'Helen. Helen Tanner.'

'Well, Helen Tanner, this better not be some sort of prank. You mentioned a missing girl.' He removed his notebook from his pocket and opened it. 'Who is she?'

'Sarah. Sarah Nesbitt. She ran off in the middle of the night. After you were there.'

Ferguson made a note of her name. 'And what was she wearing?'

'Her pyjamas.'

He then looked up. 'Where they blue by any chance?'

Helen's face went still. 'Yes, how do you know?'

'Because I think I've just seen her on my way down here.' He'd seen this girl staggering down the lane after leaving the woods. He was going to stop and question her, but walking down the lane in nothing but your jim-jams was hardly a crime, no matter how weird it was, and he figured she was from the hippy camp, so had become accustomed to their weird antics. Most of them spent all day smoking pot, so he wasn't surprised at the sight and presumed she was stoned off her face.

'So, you see,' continued Ferguson, 'she's not missing at all. Now what's this about you being involved in the break-in?'

Helen ignored the question. 'Where was she?'

Ferguson frowned. 'Walking towards the laird's house, why?'

'Because she's gone mad, berserk. It was the chimp. She was bitten by it. I think it might have had rabies or something. Now Scamp is ill. That's why we need help.'

Ferguson turned around to Shannon. Her face had turned tight and grim. 'You had better go,' she said.

Chapter Eighteen

After Anderson had heard the shots and was told the animal was heading his way, he told Jennings to stay where he was. He knew what was going to happen. It was inevitable. And he was proved right.

The tree line in front of the bridge now resembled a butcher's shop window. The firearms officers had bagged three deer, birds of innumerable species, and even somebody's house cat. In fact, as soon as something moved in the trees, somebody let off a round, no matter how much Anderson shouted and screamed and told them to hold fire until they could identify what they were shooting at.

If Jennings, the old gamekeeper, Garrick or one of the armed bobbies poked their heads through the trees, he was certain somebody would shoot it off. Dead civilians were bad enough. But a dead copper! They'd crucify him for that.

He only hoped no ramblers or hikers were in the woods. The entire area had been signposted, warning civilians away, but this was Scotland. Sticking up a 'keep out' sign only encouraged people to disobey it. You couldn't order a Scot not to do something. William Wallace was testament to that.

After barking loud enough to get the firearms officers to cease fire, he ordered them to space out, to ensure they had the entire tree line beyond the river covered.

'But for Christ's sake, don't shoot unless you are sure it is that ape. You are not in the bloody *A-Team*.'

Feeling his ulcer boring a hole in his stomach, he reached into his pocket for a his pills and swallowed two down dry, while keeping his eyes glued to the trees for sign of their quarry.

A minute passed, which turned into two, then into three, and finally after five minutes of patient waiting, Anderson stepped ahead of one of the firearms officers and gestured for the man to lower his weapon. He wanted a closer look.

'Fire that thing while I'm in front of you and I'll shove it up your arse,' Anderson said, as he stepped closer to the trees and peered into the woods.

As forests went, it wasn't dense or impenetrable. More the sort of place you'd take your dog for a piss on a Sunday morning. Several paths cut their way through the trees, which were spaced a good distance apart. Being autumn, the leaf cover was sparse and naked branches covered most of the trees, meaning there were few places for a chimp to hide. Yet he couldn't see any sign of it.

He raised the radio to his lips. 'You sure it is heading this way?'

The radio crackled for a second then he heard Jennings' voice. 'Definitely, guv. We've pulled back into a small gully so should be safe from any fire your end, but Brophy's gone to look, so you best watch out for him.'

Anderson stared through the trees, the radio still at his mouth. 'Well, stay frosty. There's a chance it might have doubled back. I can see no sign of it—'

Something caught his eye.

He craned his neck left and right to try to get a better look. Was it the breeze moving that bush or something else?

The defiant scream, like a high-pitched siren, and the charging black mass shooting from the undergrowth told him exactly what it was.

'It's coming!' he hollered, as he turned round and sprinted back towards the bridge.

He could hear the animal's footsteps closing, as well as its ear-piercing shriek getting louder. He glanced back and screamed at the sight right on his heels.

'Shoot it. Shoot the bloody thing!' he shouted.

The police officers wavered, unable to get a clear shot, and when Anderson reached the narrow suspension bridge, he glanced back once more, screamed again at the sight of the hairy animal scrabbling behind him on all fours, then he tripped, ending flat on his face.

He quickly turned on to his back as the animal bore down him.

Then it stopped, rose up on two legs and raised its arms like King Kong under attack from the biplanes.

'Help!' Anderson screamed, as he cowered behind his hands as the chimp leapt at him, its mouth open and revealing its large, dagger-like canines.

Then a shot rang out.

The animal slumped on to the bridge next to him, lifeless and still.

Anderson sat up.

The firearms officers glanced at each other, all of them shrugging.

Then Anderson saw his saviour.

In the trees and heading towards them, a scruffy figure that looked like *Grisly Adams* following a starvation diet.

Brophy, smoke billowing from his rifle.

Anderson stood up, looked down at the dead chimp. Blood pooled around it. Then he looked up at Brophy, now slinging his rifle on his back. 'I owe you a drink,' Anderson said. 'And by God, I'm going to go get one myself while I'm at it.'

Chapter Nineteen

Anderson looked relieved when they loaded the dead chimp into the back of a police van in the lay-by just outside the woods. His hand trembled as he raised one of his roll-ups to his lips, and despite the cold breeze, a thin layer of sweat shimmered on his brow.

'You glad it's over, guv?' Jennings asked.

'You could say that,' Anderson replied, his eyes fixed on the van as an officer slammed the door shut.

'Didn't go too badly, all things considering,' Jennings said, clicking the safety catch on his pistol.

'Glad you think so.' Anderson said, taking another shaky puff from his roll-up. 'And go tell that to Garrick.' He jabbed his cigarette over to where an ambulance driver was bandaging the superintendent's hand.

'He'll be all right,' Jennings said. 'Just a couple of scratches.' He then nodded to Brophy as the gillie loaded two dead deer into the back of his Land Rover. 'Looks like he's done all right out of it. I bet there'll be venison on the menu at the Gough Arms tonight. Shame we'll have to make a move.'

'Shame! I nearly had my face ripped off by a deranged monkey. I'll be glad to see the back of this piss hole. I tell you what, though. I'm going nowhere until I've had a drink.' He checked his watch then slapped Jennings on the back. 'Hurry up. I don't want that fat witch behind the bar shutting up shop before I've calmed my nerves.'

Ferguson sniffed a laugh, just as a young constable came jogging up to them. 'Which one of you is Anderson?' he asked, slightly breathless.

'Who's asking?' Anderson said, flicking his fag end into the breeze.

The constable held up a radio. 'I've just had PC Ferguson on. He says you need to get up to the laird's house, straightaway.'

'I'll do no bloody such thing. I'm going to the pub.'

The constable glanced behind nervously. 'You don't understand, sir. They've found two more bodies.'

Anderson looked at Jennings, and then both looked at Garrick, who, seeing their faces, marched over.

'What is it?' he asked, rubbing the bandage on his hand.

'Looks like the little bastard managed to kill two more people before we bagged it,' Anderson said, glaring at the van as it drove off.

Anderson was standing with Jennings and a couple of police officers when Phelp's marched up the laird's drive past the two ambulances and four police cars. The pathologist had a grim look on his face, which went grimmer on sight of the two bodies on the lawn.

'So it's ruddy true, then?' Phelps said, putting down his medical bag and glancing up at the dark clouds gathering above their heads. 'It's killed two more?'

'We're not sure,' Anderson said, staring at the bodies. 'It doesn't look quite right to me.'

Phelps frowned and looked askance at him, before picking up his bag. 'How do you mean?'

Anderson gestured for the mawkish police to step back to give the pathologist room. 'Take a look.'

They'd all been making assumptions and estimations as to what had happened. None of them could work it out.

The two bodies lay as Ferguson had discovered them. The laird, Henry Gough, face down, blood soaking the grass around his neck. The girl, face up, a similar pool of blood around her.

Yet she didn't look right.

If Anderson didn't know better, he'd have said she'd been dead for more than a week, judging by the skin colour and general sight of decaying flesh on her arms and neck.

But that didn't make sense.

Neither did the injuries.

Gough's were consistent with a chimp attack: huge bite marks on the face and neck, one having torn out his windpipe. Yet the girl had been stabbed. Multiple times. And Gough's hand contained a pair of bloodied pruning scissors.

Was it murder?

So far, the only theory that made any sense was that Gough had killed the girl before being attacked by the chimp, but that didn't account for the poor state of her body.

'Perhaps he killed her a few days earlier and was in the process of burying her when the ape attacked,' Jennings said, as Phelps studied the two bodies.

'What? In his front lawn?' Anderson said. 'Are you bloody mad? Anybody could have seen him.'

'Maybe he was dragging her into the woods.'

Anderson shook his head and pointed to the glistening red patch around her head. 'What about the blood. That looks fresh to me.'

Phelps stood up after his preliminary examination, shook his head and scratched at his chin.

'What's up?' Anderson asked, as the pathologist's face creased up in confusion.

'Well, at first glance, I'd say the girl's been dead a week. Perhaps longer, judging by the decomposition on her body.' He scratched the top of his head, causing his toupee to slide about slightly. 'But you're right, Inspector, that doesn't fit with the blood.'

Phelps then crouched at the laird's body, now on his back, and removed his pen, using it to probe around the man's neck. 'This wasn't your chimp.'

Anderson and Jennings glanced at each other. 'Then who was it?' Anderson asked.

'Teeth marks are human,' he said, prodding at the wounds.

'Are you sure?' Anderson asked.

Phelps looked up, his eyebrows raised. 'I've become a bit of an expert in identifying primate bite marks of late. And these aren't it. Human definitely.' He looked over at the girl's body. 'I'll take some casts, but judging by the size, I reckon they're hers.'

'But how can that be?' Jennings asked. 'If she's been dead a week.' He nodded to Gough's body. 'We saw him ourselves yesterday, so he must have been killed since then.'

'Oh, I agree, A couple of hours ago, I'd say, judging by the bleeding and lividity,' Phelps said.

'Liver what?' Anderson asked.

'Livor mortis. When the blood stops flowing and starts to clot. It's only just started, so I'd say he's been dead two hours. Three at the most.'

'Then how could she have killed him?' Jennings asked.

Phelps shrugged, puffed out his cheeks and squatted next to the body. He probed around the girl's neck with his *Biro* then lifted one of the girl's arms.

'This definitely looks like decay,' he said, waving the arm at Anderson and Jennings, causing the inspector to shirk back, his stomach gurgling in contempt at the sight. 'It's as if she'd been dead a week or more. Let me take her temperature. That might give us a better idea.'

He opened his bag and took out a thermometer. Expecting him to insert it into the girl's mouth, or under her armpit, Anderson almost puked when Phelps pulled down the girl's pale blue pyjamas—something else that was odd about the picture—and shoved the glass temperature gauge up her backside.

'Oh, you dirty bastard,' he squealed.

Phelps frowned at him. 'Sorry, but it is the only way to check.'

After a moment, he retracted the thermometer, studied it, shook it and shoved it in his top pocket without even cleaning it. He then stood up, his face still crumpled. 'Dead two hours according to her body temperature.'

'What about the state of her?' Anderson asked.

Phelps shrugged. 'No idea. Could be some form of necrosis, I suppose.'

'What's that?' Jennings asked.

'Premature cell death. Happens in severe cases of frostbite, or with gangrenous injuries, that sort of thing. I'll know more when I've cut her up.'

'When will that be?' Anderson asked.

Phelps sighed. 'As you may be aware, I'm a little backed up at the moment. Haven't even started on those two campers yet. Could be tomorrow, could be the day after. Unless you unearth more ruddy work for me in the meantime.'

He nodded to the two paramedics standing by the ambulance. 'Go on, load them up.'

'So, it looks like she attacked him, and he used those shears to fend her off. Then they both died from their injuries,' Jennings said.

'Well, that makes more sense than your other bloody theory,' Anderson said. 'We best tell Garrick. Where is he?'

'Inside,' Jennings said. 'Comforting Lady Gough.'

'Bloody typical. First murder this village had probably had in recorded history and the regional commander can't be arsed.'

'Apparently, he and the laird go back a few years. Knew each other from school. I must admit, though, the super was acting a bit odd earlier.'

'Public schoolboys are all odd,' Anderson said, taking out his tobacco. 'An adolescence full of masturbation and canings will do that for you.'

'Ferguson is in their too,' Jennings added, 'along with a friend of the dead girl.'

'Then she's got some questions to answer.'

Chapter Twenty

When somebody knocked the door, Shannon thought it would be PC Ferguson again. It wasn't. It was the last person she wanted to see.

Dr Cunningham didn't wait for Shannon to invite her inside, not that she would have. Instead, she barged straight passed and into the living room, her humourless face curling up at the quaint furniture and ageing décor.

'I understand you have been busy, Doctor Long,' she said, once Shannon followed her in.

Shannon eyed Cunningham suspiciously. 'How do you mean?'

'Helping the police with their hunt for 85H.' Cunningham took a seat and crossed her legs with contempt, as if somehow Shannon's furniture was dirty.

'How did you know about that?'

'I saw you. Last night. You went into the pub where that atrocious inspector is staying.'

Shannon suddenly felt uneasy. 'Have you been spying on me?'

Cunningham glared at Shannon, her eyes unblinking. 'You better have not said anything.'

'Say anything? How can I? I don't know anything, do I?'

Cunningham leaned her head back, her teeth gnawing at her lips. 'You may know more than you think. But I must remind you, Dr Long, you signed a confidentiality agreement. Breaking it would be terminal for your career.'

'Don't you think I don't know that?' Shannon snapped, trying to show Cunningham she was neither scared of her or her threats. Which was a lie.

Cunningham sniffed contemptuously and locked eyes on Shannon who turned her back, turning to the window to gaze outside and break Cunningham's stare. 'I heard a girl tell the police one of her friends was bitten by 85H,' she said. 'She thinks her friend has rabies.'

Cunningham snorted. 'Rabies. Nonsense.'

'Then what is it?' Shannon asked, rounding on Cunningham.

Cunningham stood and placed her hands on Shannon's upper arms, not grabbing them hard, but it was menacing enough. 'Nothing that concerns you. You just keep quiet.'

'It has killed more people!'

Cunningham tightened her grip. 'You know nothing about it, Dr Long.' She shook Shannon. 'Nothing! Do you understand?'

'They'll find out, sooner or later. That inspector may come across as an oaf, but he's sharper than you think.'

'That's why I want you to demand the animal's body once they have caught it.'

'Me!'

'Why not? It's our property. Our specimen.'

'But surely it would be better coming from you? You are head of the research centre.'

Cunningham shook her head slowly and grinned. It looked more like a snarl than a smile. 'I'm not the one that's cosied up to the police, am I?'

'What if they want to do an autopsy? After what this girl has said, that inspector is bound to want to know what was wrong with 85H.'

'What's he going to do? Ask the pathologist to cut up a chimp?'

Shannon shook her head and shrugged. 'They might get a vet in. Or an expert of some sort.'

'You are an expert. That's why you should ask for the body. Who is better qualified to do an autopsy on that animal than you?'

'What if they won't hand it over? What if they don't trust me?'

Cunningham lifted a loose lock of Shannon's hair and returned it over her ear. 'Then you had better make sure they trust you, hadn't you?'

Jennings was no expert, but he knew enough to know Gough's house was in dire need of repair. Cracks and chips covered the oak panels lining the walls. Where there were rugs, they were moth bitten. The floorboards were loose and creaked underfoot. It was also draughty and cold, smelled of damp, and unlike other country estate houses, contained very few antiques or valuables.

They found Constable Ferguson in what Jennings presumed was a drawing room. He looked uncomfortable, standing by the patio doors, hands behind his back, unsure where to put himself. On the sofa, a scruffy-looking young girl sat consoling an even scruffier ageing woman wearing a thick woollen jumper and bed socks. The girl had her arm around the woman's shoulders as she shook and trembled with sobs.

Like the rest of the house, it needed redecorating, but it did feel a little warmer thanks to the portable electric fire whirring away at the sobbing woman's feet.

The crying woman, who Jennings presumed was Mrs Gough, stopped her sobs for a moment, raised her head, revealing makeup streaking down her cheeks, and said, 'Do ... do you know what happened yet?'

'Not yet,' Jennings said. 'We're still piecing it all together.

'I take it you knew the dead girl?' Anderson said to the girl on the sofa, his tone indelicate.

The girl nodded. She looked frightened, confused, but then Anderson could frighten and confuse anyone.

'Her name's Helen Tanner,' Ferguson said.

Anderson stared at her, his nose twitching as he took in the uncombed hair and tie-dyed T-shirt peeping through the holes in her sweater. He then looked back at Ferguson. 'Well, Helen Tanner. Has anyone interviewed you yet?'

She shook her head, her eyes now wide with fear.

'The superintendent said he wanted to do it,' Ferguson said. 'But I'm not quite sure what he's doing.'

'Where is he?' Anderson asked.

'He's in Sir Henry's study,' Ferguson said, raising his helmet to the door, which he clutched under his arm like a rugby player holding a ball.

Mrs Gough looked up, her lip trembling. 'It is at the other end of the house, next to the back stairs.'

'Thank you, ma'am,' Jennings said, sympathetically as he could. 'And we are sorry for your loss.'

Anderson leaned towards the girl. 'You'd better not go anywhere, lassie. I want to speak to you.' He then gestured for Jennings to follow him and they tramped back through the house, a chorus of squeaks and groans from the floorboards accompanying every step.

Study was far too grandiose a word to describe the room in which they found Garrick. More like a utility room office containing a desk littered with papers. The damp smelled worse here and much of the wallpaper had peeled and begun rolling itself back up, while several metal buckets dinged every second or so on the floor as droplets of water dripped from the ceiling.

Garrick stood at the window, overlooking the rear of the estate, one hand virulently scratching at the bandage.

'You any idea what happened yet?' he asked, not turning round but evidently hearing their footsteps on the creaky floorboards.

'Working on it,' Anderson said, rifling through the papers on the desk. Jennings noted the words 'final demand' written across the top of most of them.

'The theory we are working on is that the girl attacked the laird and he stabbed her with his pruning shears to defend himself,' Jennings said.

Garrick turned around. Red circles ringed his eyes, like a man who'd been up all night. His hand still scratched at his bandage. 'Theory! What about the chimp?'

'Sounds like the ape has a foolproof alibi, if Phelps is right about the time of deaths,' Anderson said. 'Although he's been wrong before. We'll know for certain after the post-mortem.'

Garrick shook his head. 'And no clues on the motive?'

'Not yet, but we think the girl in there knows something,' Jennings said. 'Have you cautioned her? Or do you want us to interview her?

Garrick's jaw was clenched. 'I'll get the bitch to talk.'

Jennings looked at Anderson. Up to now, the superintendent had been as professional as they come—a typical straight-backed high-ranker, a by-the-book superintendent. He was now beginning to sound like Anderson.

'I understand Sir Henry was a friend of yours,' Jennings said.

'Yes, he was. I've just had to tell his son his father's dead.'

'Perhaps it'll be a good idea if you leave the investigation to us, then,' Anderson said.

He glowered at them, his jaw working away as if trying to grind his teeth into powder. 'You! I wouldn't trust you to investigate a lost puppy. You've got that escaped animal, so Special Branch is done here. This is my region, Inspector, and as soon as you leave it the better.' He sounded aggressive and followed his words with a thousand yard stare.

'With respect, we are still investigating the break-in at the research centre,' Jennings said, diplomatically. 'We have to speak to that girl in there, anyway.'

Garrick turned back to the window. 'I said leave her to me. We'll see what she has to say after a sleepless night in the cells at Inverurie.' His head then twisted to one side and his voice suddenly changed from wrath and vengeance to a high-pitched squeal. 'Oh, look! A red squirrel.'

Anderson glanced at Jennings, who must have had the same look of bewilderment on his face because they both shrugged, before backing out of the room and closing the door behind them, quietly.

'What the bloody hell has got into him?' Anderson whispered as they walked back to the drawing room.

'Must be grief,' Jennings said. 'Perhaps he and the laird were closer than we thought.'

'Aye, probably buggered each other senseless at that posh school of theirs. He's right about one thing, though.'

'Oh, what's that?'

Anderson stopped outside the drawing room, his hand resting on the doorknob. 'As soon as we are out of this place, the better. My guts are telling me something ain't right about all this.'

'You sure it's not just your ulcer?'

'Just shut up and go get that girl. I'll speak to her outside. I don't think it'd do the merry widow much good to hear what she's got to say.'

'Crikey, I never had you down as the caring type.'

'Hey,' Anderson snapped, looking round for somewhere to extinguish the cigarette that had been burning in his finger the past couple of minutes. 'I have a mother too.' Not finding anywhere for his fag butt, Anderson then marched to the main door.

'I'll send her my sympathies,' muttered Jennings.

Chapter Twenty-One

Helen followed Jennings out of the house. The bodies had gone, leaving just a couple of nasty stains on the lawn, and most of the police had left too, leaving just a couple of constables standing guard at the bottom of the long, winding drive, their feet stamping up and down to keep warm.

It was cold, the afternoon sun was dying above the trees and bringing with it a cold wind that created small tornadoes of swirling leaves on the lawn, where the disagreeable, middle-aged detective stood smoking what she at first thought was a joint, but realised was just a roll-up.

'You wanted to see me?' she said, as Jennings ushered her on to the lawn.

The inspector turned round. He looked typical for a copper with his long, drooping moustache, hair that needed cutting, stained shirt and dishevelled jacket. He could have been anywhere from forty-five to late fifties, had a creased face that carried a permanent pained expression, and bloodshot eyes that narrowed as he turned round and studied her.

'Just tell Inspector Anderson everything you told PC Ferguson,' Jennings said.

'I'm not sure where to start,' she said.

'How about at the bloody beginning,' Anderson snapped. 'And be quick about it. The pub's open and I don't want to spend my evening chatting to some loopy hippy.'

His rancour took her aback, and she realised just how much trouble she was in. She looked to Jennings who gave her a half-smile and prompted her with a nod.

'I was there the other night,' she said, head bowed to demonstrate her contrition. She knew they could lock her up for what she was about to say.

'Where?' Anderson asked, flicking his fag end into the breeze.

'The animal testing place at Paradise Woods.'

Anderson stepped close. 'So you let that monkey out?'

She didn't say anything, just kept her head bowed.

'The one that killed two of your friends and those two kids in the woods.' He leaned closer and bobbed his head low, so his face was under hers. She could smell the remnants of his cigarette as he spoke. 'It ripped their bloody faces off like it was peeling a banana.'

She burst into tears.

Breaking into Paradise Woods seemed a good idea at the time. A worthy cause. But now that Jason and Philip were dead, and Sarah and those two people in the woods, not to mention the man whose lawn on which she now stood, the foolishness hit home, bluntly and brutally.

'Guv, go easy, she just lost her pal,' Jennings said, causing the inspector to step back a bit.

'Pal! You mean the one that has just tore a chunk out of an old man's throat so he bled to death on his own lawn?'

Helen thrust her face into her hands. Anderson didn't speak until her eyes emerged from behind her fingers. 'Was she with you when you let out the chimp?' His voice was softer, but hardly welcoming.

Helen nodded, tears dripping from her eyes. She wiped them away. 'We just wanted to stop them torturing the animals.'

'Great bloody job you did,' Anderson said. 'All those rabbits you released were ripped apart by the guard dogs and the monkey has been shot. Is that why your pal killed the laird? Was she upset about his grouse shoots and deer stalking? Is that it? Did she decide to put an end to his bloodlust by ripping his throat out?'

'No! ... I mean, I don't know.' Helen shook her head. It didn't make sense, none of it did. Something was wrong. Very wrong. 'Sarah wasn't herself. She hadn't been since the break-in. I think it has something to do with the chimp bite.'

Anderson frowned. 'What bite?'

'During the break-in, when we were leaving. The chimp attacked us. It killed Jason and Philip, and Sarah was bitten. Since then, she wasn't the same.'

'How do you mean?' Jennings asked.

Sarah shrugged. 'She was withdrawn, aggressive. Then last night, after you lot turned up, she went berserk. She attacked me, and when Scamp pulled her off, she attacked him. She bit a lump out of his cheek. Now he is feeling sick, the way she did. I think it might be rabies or something.'

'And who is this Scamp?' Anderson asked.

'Somebody else from the camp.'

'Was he there during the break-in?' Jennings asked, taking notes.

Helen shook her head. 'No. It was just the four of us, but I'm worried for him. Whatever sent Sarah mad, I think has infected him too.'

'What about you?' Jennings asked. 'You said this Sarah friend attacked you.'

Helen rolled up her sleeves and showed her bare arms. There were no scratches or cuts on them. 'She didn't scratch or bite me. But Scamp is in a bad way. He needs medical help.'

Jennings looked at Anderson. 'Could it be possible?' he said, his face showing alarm. 'Rabies, in Scotland!'

Anderson didn't say anything, just stared at the house. Jennings followed his gaze. 'And if it was the chimp that was infected—'

'Let's not jump to conclusions,' Anderson said, lowering his eyes to Helen. 'You can come with us. There is somebody I want you to see.'

'What about Scamp?' Helen protested.

'We'll sort your friend out later, but first, I want to know what we're dealing with.'

Shannon stepped back in surprise when she opened the door and saw Inspector Anderson, his sidekick Jennings, and the young girl who'd turned up a few hours earlier.

'How did it go?' she asked, as Anderson stood puffing on his cigarette on her doorstep. 'Did you find it?'

'Found it, caught it, killed it,' he said, flicking his roll-up to the ground. 'But so are two other people.'

She stepped further back from the door, her hand automatically rising to her mouth. 'It's attacked two more people?'

'Your monkey hasn't, no.' Anderson looked round to the girl. 'But she seems to think it might have had something to do with it.'

Shannon shook her head. 'I don't understand.'

Anderson stepped inside and leaned towards her. 'What exactly was wrong with that animal?'

His face was close, his eyes glaring into hers, his smoky breath making her wince. Her head shook rapidly. 'I don't know what you mean.'

Anderson pushed passed her, gesturing for his sergeant and the young girl to follow. Jennings offered Shannon a smile as he ushered the young girl into the front room leaving Shannon to shut the door behind them.

'Do you mind telling me what all this is about?' she asked, marching in behind them. The inspector was pulling books from the bookshelf, reading the spines, and then putting them back horizontally.

He turned round. 'I was about to ask you the same bloody question.' He held up a book on chimp anatomy. 'Your ape was wild wasn't it?'

Shannon nodded. 'Yes, captured in the Congo.'

Usually apes came from captive breeding programs, but Dr Cunningham insisted they obtain an animal that had minimal exposure to human pathogens. At the time, Shannon didn't know why. Now she was starting to understand.

'So there's a chance it has rabies then?'

Shannon shook her head and acted as innocent as she could. 'No, of course not. We tested for that. Why, what's happened?'

'Perhaps you should tell her,' Anderson said to the girl now sitting on Shannon's sofa next to Jennings. She looked confused, upset and frightened.

'Go ahead,' Anderson said, pressing the girl to speak. 'She was your friend, wasn't she?'

The girl glanced at Shannon, looked back at Jennings, who prompted her with his eyebrows, and then looked back to Shannon. After a long second of silence, she said, 'Her name was Sarah.'

Her lip trembled when she spoke, so ignoring Anderson's glare, Shannon walked over to the arm of the chair and sat next to the girl. 'And you are?'

'Helen. Helen Tanner.' She looked up at Shannon. 'They tell me you work at the research centre.'

Shannon nodded. 'Yes, I'm a primatologist.'

Helen's nose flared and her eyes narrowed. She no longer looked frightened or confused, but angry. 'So you torture chimps?'

Shannon frowned and shuffled away slightly. 'Of course not. I study them.'

'In a cage, where it hasn't got room to move.'

Shannon stood up. 'I'm not going to be lectured by you,' she snapped.

'All right, all right,' Anderson said. 'Can we leave the bitchiness aside for a moment and get to the point?'

'Which is?' Shannon asked, returning Helen's thousand-yard stare.

'Her friend was bitten by the chimp,' Jennings said.

'How? When?' Shannon asked.

'When we broke into your laboratory the other night,' Helen said, defiantly.

'So it was you that let it out. Do you have any idea what you have done?' Shannon was shouting now, her finger wagging at the young girl.

Helen stood up, her own finger waving. ‘We did it to save the animals from your sick experiments!’

‘For crying out loud,’ Anderson shouted, his fingers pinching the bridge of his nose. ‘Will you both bloody shut up!’

Shannon and Helen stared at each other for a moment, neither wanting to break their gaze. Then Jennings said, ‘Tell Dr Long about your friend.’

Helen, her eyes still fixed on Shannon, sat down. ‘She became ill after the chimp bit her. The wound became septic. It stank. And she started acting strange.’

‘What do you mean strange?’ Shannon kept her voice calm, but inside her chest, her heart was beating like a war drum.

Helen shrugged. ‘Just strange. She attacked me and Scamp then ran off.’

‘Where is she now?’ Shannon asked.

‘Aberdeen mortuary,’ Anderson replied, bluntly. ‘Along with the laird from the big house. She killed him. Ripped his windpipe out.’

Shannon sat, aware her hands were trembling.

‘I’m worried about Scamp,’ Helen added. ‘Sarah bit him. He was feeling sick last time I saw him. I’m worried the same thing is going to happen to him.’

‘Where is he?’ Shannon asked.

‘Back at the camp.’

Shannon stood, her eyes fixing on Anderson. ‘I need to see him.’

‘Why, what’s wrong with him?’ Jennings asked.

Shannon shook her head. ‘I don’t know, not until I see him.’

Chapter Twenty-Two

It was dark by the time they arrived at the PAAR camp. The campsite was on the edge of the woods, about a mile from the research centre. As Jennings drove them to the expanse of grass where all the tents and placards and banners fluttered in the nightly breeze, Helen knew something was wrong. She could see the silhouettes of her friends standing around one of the tents. Normally at this time, they'd be huddled around the fire, drinking, smoking, eating. Yet it looked like some sort of meeting was going on.

Jennings parked and he, Anderson, Shannon and Helen got out, just as Graham, one of the activists, jogged over.

'Helen, where have you been?' Graham asked. He was young and normally quiet and less vitriolic compared to Philip and Jason, but she guessed since they were gone, he'd been elevated to spokesman for the group.

'Something terrible has happened,' she said, trying to contain herself while she broke the news about Sarah.

However, Graham misinterpreted, evidently thinking she sensed the unease in the camp. 'Yes, it's Scamp.'

'Scamp!' she looked round to Jennings, Shannon and the inspector.

Graham placed a hand on her shoulder and lowered his head, keeping his eyes fixed on hers. 'I know you were close, so I don't know how to say it, but he's dead, Helen.'

She realised the rest of the protestors were congregating around Scamp's tent. She pushed Graham aside and ran over, barging her way through the crowd. Several of the activists gave her sympathetic smiles and somebody passed her a torch.

She scrabbled on the ground and raised the flap to Scamp's tent. A malodorous, fetid smell wafted out. She coughed. Then under her torchlight, she saw him. He was sat up, his face grey, gaunt, lifeless. The wound on his cheek had gone yellow.

A pair of hands pulled her out the tent, and she found herself, along with the other activists, being pushed aside by Jennings, as Anderson and Shannon made their way through the small crowd.

Jennings raised his hand, gesturing for Helen to stand still. He then took her torch, crouched down and shuffled into the tent.

He returned a moment later, a handkerchief around his mouth. 'He's definitely dead, guv.'

Shannon snatched the torch from Jennings, pushed him aside and ventured into the tent, returning a few moments later, her head shaking. She looked white, frightened.

Anderson stared hard at her. 'Isn't it about time you told us what is going on?'

Jennings pointed to the tent. 'Is it rabies? 'If it is, we need to warn Garrick. He was scratched by that chimp.'

Shannon shook her head. 'I don't know, honestly.' She looked at Anderson with a hard, unyielding stare. 'The chimp. Where is it now?'

Anderson shrugged. 'No idea.'

'I need to see the body.'

He lifted his head back and stared down his nose at her, his fingers stroking his moustache. 'What for?'

'An autopsy. It is the only way to be sure.'

She hesitated, looked at Anderson, at Helen, at the crowd of activists shaking their heads with mournful looks on their face, but before she could speak, flashing blue lights caught everybody's attention.

A car door slammed shut, and the form of PC Ferguson appeared in the gloom as he approached the tents. 'There you are,' he said, his eyes fixed on Helen. 'I've orders to take you in.' He then looked at Anderson. 'You haven't seen the superintendent by any chance, have you?'

Anderson frowned. 'Garrick?'

'Aye,' Ferguson said.

'No,' Jennings said, looking back at Scamp's tent. 'But we need to speak to him.'

'He's gone missing,' Ferguson said.

'What do you mean, missing?' Anderson asked.

Ferguson, glancing at all the protestors, shook his head. 'We were at the house and he told me to wait for the laird's son.' He then looked at Helen. 'He then ordered me to take *her* to the station at Inverurie before saying he was going for a walk, to clear his head. I've not seen him since.' He looked at the protestors again. 'So, what is going on here?'

Anderson puffed out his cheeks. 'Call Phelps. I want to get a proper doctor's opinion before we jump to conclusions.' He then glowered at Shannon. 'If you can't tell me what's going on, perhaps he can.'

Phelps arrived just before ten. He looked as tired as Anderson felt. He trotted from his car, the medical bag causing his shoulder to sag, the long hours causing the bags around his eyes to do the same. 'This is getting beyond a ruddy joke, Inspector,' he said, as Anderson welcomed him with a less than cheery wave. 'What are you trying to do to me? I'm not on piece work, you know.'

Anderson shook his head. 'Do you think I want to be standing in a bloody field full of hippies when the pub is open?'

'So, what is it this time?' Phelps said, removing his glasses and giving them a wipe with his tie.

'We were hoping you can tell us.' Anderson pointed to the tent where they found the dead protestor. 'He's in there.'

The protestors had been moved away. Ferguson was watching over everybody to ensure nobody disappeared, including Shannon, who sat huddled with Helen and the other activists.

Jennings was with them too, but he trotted over as Phelps made his way to the tent where they had found Scamp's body.

'There's talk among the hippies about abandoning the camp,' Jennings said, his arm wrapped around his jacket to keep out the breeze.

'Nobody's going anywhere,' Anderson snapped. 'Not until I know what the bloody hell is going on. They could all be infected with whatever it is.'

'Do you think it's rabies?'

Anderson shook his head. 'I've no idea. But I reckon she knows more than she's letting on.' He nodded at Shannon.

'What makes you say that?'

'You're getting married soon, aren't you, laddie?'

Ferguson frowned. 'Yes, in a couple of months.'

'Then you'll want to learn to spot it when a woman is pulling the wool over your eyes.' He then looked at Ferguson. 'Go tell him to get hold of that armed unit that was down here this morning. Find out what they've done with that dead monkey. See if you can get it brought back here.'

'Yes, guv.'

'If she wants to do an autopsy then let's let her,' Anderson continued. 'The sooner we get some bloody answers the better.'

As Jennings walked up to Ferguson to relay Anderson's orders, Phelps came staggering over. 'Is this some sort of ruddy joke.'

His face was red and creased with wrinkles.

'What you on about?' Anderson asked.

'Where is it?' Phelps asked.

'Where's what?'

'The ruddy body you called me out to examine.'

Anderson glanced at him then at the tent. 'It's in there.' He nodded to the pathologist's glasses hanging around his neck. 'Why don't you put them on and look.'

Phelps cocked his head to the side. 'I can assure you, Inspector, there is not a body in that tent.'

'Were you looking in the right one?' Anderson pointed at it.

'I'm not stupid, man,' Phelps snapped, as Jennings came back over.

'What's up?' he asked.

'Go and show Mr Magoo here the body.'

Jennings frowned. 'Guv?'

'Just do it,' Anderson snapped, watching the two men amble back to the tent.

After opening the tent flap and poking his head inside, Jennings emerged, his face wide with confusion. 'It's gone,' he shouted.

Anderson jogged over, dropped to his knees and looked inside. Sure enough, other than a sleeping bag and a fetid stench, the tent was empty.

'Will somebody mind telling me what the hell is going on?' Phelps asked sharply.

Anderson looked at Jennings, looked at Phelps, and then looked around the entire camp. 'I wished I bloody knew.'

It was nearly last orders when Ferguson walked into the pub, which resulted in anxious glances at watches and muted whispers. But he wasn't there to check on licensing hours.

After a quick look left and right, he spotted Anderson and Jennings, removed his helmet and walked over.

'I've asked control to send a car to the camp during the night,' he said, placing his helmet on the table. 'It's about the best I can do.'

'No, the best you can do is to bloody nick 'em all,' Anderson said, behind a fug of blue smoke.

'On what charge?' Ferguson protested.

'He's right, guv,' Jennings said, a glass of cola at his lips. 'We can't prove any of them moved that body, and I don't see how they could have, not without us seeing them.'

Anderson screwed out his cigarette and immediately rolled up another. 'Somebody's playing silly beggars, I can tell you that. Phelps was fuming. Poor bastard. He's not been out of his shoes for two days.' He licked his roll-up closed then pointed it at

Ferguson. 'What about that Tanner girl? You taken her to the station like Garrick asked?'

Ferguson shook his head. 'I thought it best if we keep her in the village until we know what's going on. Dr Long has said she can stay on her sofa.'

Anderson's eyes widened. 'The hippy animal rights protestor with the vivisection queen. Are you bloody mad? Hasn't there been enough bodies over the last few days?'

'I'm sure they'll be all right,' Jennings said. 'Any news on Garrick?'

Ferguson puffed out his cheeks. 'Nope, nobody's seen him since he left the laird's house. I've checked everywhere.'

Anderson and Jennings swapped glances.

'Oh.' Ferguson removed his notebook. 'I've also tracked down that chimp's carcass. Somebody is bringing it over first thing tomorrow. Where do you want it?'

Anderson waved his fag at the window. 'Go speak to Dr Frankenstein over the road. She wants to do an autopsy.'

'I'll go see her now and ask her.'

'Yes, you might just catch her in her nightie, you dirty sod.' Anderson laughed as Ferguson felt his face flush.

'Do ... er ... you want to do a search for that kid's body in the morning. It can't have gone far?'

Anderson nodded slightly. 'Aye, I suppose so. Get some flatfoots to have a look for it. Ask them to rough up those protestors while you are at it—find out who's playing games.'

The pub then silenced. They looked round to see the landlady of the pub stagger from behind the bar with a suitcase in her hand. Her face was stern and rigid and she sported a shining, black eye. She gave the blonde barmaid a deathly look, and then dragged her suitcase to the door and left the pub, leaving muted whispers and chatter behind her.

The stout publican was in the doorway behind the bar, watching his wife leave. He didn't say anything, just turned around and walked back up the stairs.

Anderson checked his watch. 'I wonder if he'll be up for a lock-in.'

Chapter Twenty-Three

Anderson staggered down the stairs at nine o'clock. Jennings had been occupying the pub's only bathroom for the last twenty minutes and Anderson needed a pee. Badly. So had come to use the pub toilet.

The bar was a mess. None of the glasses had been cleared from the previous night or any of the ashtrays emptied. God only knew where the landlord was. Probably still celebrating his freedom, thought Anderson, as he staggered across the pub to the gents.

He unzipped himself at the urinal, relieved himself, and staggered back out, stopping at the table he'd been sitting at until the early hours that morning. He picked up a half-smoked roll-up resting on the ashtray, shoved it in his mouth and lit it. Then he wavered at the door leading back upstairs and glanced across the bar and the optics.

It was early, even for him, but he had a hangover. A bad one. Nothing like hair of the dog to sort that out, he thought, glancing through the backroom door to ensure the landlord wasn't coming down the stairs.

He lifted the bar hatch, grabbed a glass from the counter, flicked the remnants of whatever was in it to the floor, wiped the inside clean with his shirt tail and poured himself a glass.

As he raised it to his lips, he became aware of a crunching sound beneath his feet. Lifting his foot, he looked down and saw broken glass on the floor. Then he saw spots of blood, then pools of it, and finally, the blonde barmaid lying lifeless at the far end of the bar.

'Jesus H Christ.' Anderson placed the glass down and tentatively walked over. Turning the woman over, he gagged. Her face was missing a nose and her windpipe looked like a burst hose.

'What's up, guv?'

Anderson jumped, yelped and turned round to see Jennings, towelling his hair dry. The sergeant squinted at the woman on the floor. 'What the hell's happened?'

Anderson shook his head. 'I'm buggered if I know, but Phelps is going to go bloody spare.'

He rummaged in his pocket for his pills. The sight of the dead woman had triggered off his ulcer, which was threatening to burn a hole in his belly. He pointed to the bar phone. 'Call Ferguson. Tell him to get the troops down here, now.'

Jennings lifted the receiver then held up a loose wire. 'Out of order! Looks like somebody has pulled it out of the wall.' He pointed to the dead woman. 'Perhaps she was trying to call for help.'

'There were two bloody coppers upstairs,' Anderson said.

'To be fair, guv, with the amount you supped last night, I doubt you'd have heard her if she was murdered at the foot of your bed.'

Anderson scowled. 'And what about you?'

'Once I'm asleep, I'm as good as dead.' He approached warily, his face scrunching up at the sight. 'Poor cow. Do you think the landlord did that? He was the only other person in here last night.' He then glanced left and right. 'Where is he?'

'God knows. Just go see if Ferguson is in the village. He's probably hanging around that bird's house over the road.'

Jennings nodded, and still carrying his towel, dashed out of the pub.

Despite his burning guts, Anderson needed that drink, so he picked up his glass and winced as it trickled down his throat. Then he heard a door open.

Expecting it to be Jennings, he only glanced round, but then his head did a double take when he saw the landlord shambling out of the ladies. The man wore barely any clothes, just underpants and a string vest covered in blood. His grey pallor, blank eyes and blotches covering his skin gave him the appearance of a bloated waxwork held too close to the fire. He stopped in the middle of the pub, his eyes fixed on empty space. Then his head turned, slowly, his unblinking eyes glaring at Anderson standing with a glass of Scotch to his lips.

Anderson lowered the glass.

The landlord rushed the bar.

Despite being close to twenty stone and with a gut hanging beneath his vest, the middle-aged publican, with his teeth bared and fingers outstretched, vaulted the bar like a steeplechase runner.

Fortunately, he didn't land like an athlete and toppled over, smashing glasses and causing several of the optics to fall from their holders and shatter on the floor.

It gave Anderson, the whisky glass still in his hand and fag end still burning in his mouth, enough time to back away.

But he was cornered.

As the large man got to his feet, making a snarling noise like a dog with something stuck in its throat, Anderson found himself almost standing on top of the dead barmaid, just as the landlord rushed him again.

With nothing else to hand, Anderson hurled the whisky glass at the demented man. It struck him square in the face, smashing on impact, yet it did little to halt the publican's assault.

Within seconds, Anderson found himself on top of the barmaid and sandwiched by twenty stone of country-inn publican, while glasses and full bottles of spirits cascaded on top of them.

The landlord had his hands around Anderson's throat and his mouth snapped and bit at the air inches from his face. Anderson thrust his fingers in the large man's eyes. Yet he didn't squeal, didn't yelp and his bulk didn't budge, nor did the grip around Anderson's throat.

Feeling consciousness slipping away, Anderson scrabbled around on the floor among the broken glass and spilt ashtrays and grabbed something hard and heavy. A bottle.

It smashed on the side of the landlord's head, knocking him off, but not out. Anderson got to his feet and clambered over the bar, but he felt a hand grab his trouser leg. Turning around he kicked the landlord square in the face, his foot making a squelch as it landed. Blood and mucus went flying, as did the landlord, who smashed against the row of optics on the back of the bar.

But even that didn't stop him.

He climbed over the bar, glass sticking out of the back of his neck, spirits dripping down his face, and again launched himself at Anderson as the inspector scrambled for the door.

As he felt the landlord's hands grab his shoulders, Anderson turned and pushed the man's head back as his open mouth tried to bite a chunk out of his throat. He stank, badly. Even the drenching of whisky and vodka did little to mask the pungent, fetid smell emanating from the publican's mouth.

The whisky and vodka dripping off the man did give Anderson an idea, though. As the landlord's mouth neared his windpipe, Anderson reached into his pocket for his lighter and flicked it on, igniting the publican as if he were a gas lamp.

The landlord released his grip and staggered back just as flames caught light to Anderson's sleeve. He threw himself to the floor, rolling and patting at his arm until it went out.

He sat up and saw the landlord staggering about, as a blue, almost invisible flicker of burning alcohol engulfed his face and body. He didn't scream or try to extinguish the flames in anyway but he fell against the wall, causing one of the curtains to catch fire. He took a step forward. Then another. Stood for a long second. Then, with the ceiling above his head turning brown with smoke and fire creeping up the wall behind him, he crumpled to his knees then slumped face first to the floor, as if he were a marionette that had had its strings cut.

By the time Anderson got to his feet, the fire had become an inferno. Flames licked along the walls, ceiling and ran along the spilt spirits on the bar as if they were a line of gunpowder.

The smoke stung his eyes and for a moment, disorientation caused him to stagger left, right, trying to establish the way out.

With his jacket over his mouth and face, Anderson tried to make it to the door, but the intense heat from the fire around the entrance caused him to retreat.

Coughing and staggering he headed back to the backroom door by the bar, but the fire there was raging even more ferociously, with many of the spirit bottles exploding, causing glass shrapnel to ping around the pub.

Staggering this way and that, Anderson felt his head go light as the oxygen in the room depleted, and just when he thought it was all over for him, a shaft of light cut through the smoke and the bar door splintered open. In the doorway, two figures, one with a small fire extinguisher who doused some of the fire around the entrance, but had little effect on the raging inferno inside the pub. But it was enough for Anderson to stagger to cool fresh air racing in and feeding the fire.

He stumbled, tripped, but a pair of hands grabbed him around the shoulders and dragged him outside.

He fell to the ground, coughing and biting at the gloriously fresh air. When he turned over, he saw Jennings and Ferguson, the constable still holding the small fire extinguisher in his hand, most likely taken from his police car. Two figures stood behind them: Dr Long and the hippy girl Helen.

'What the hell happened?' Jennings screamed, as Anderson got to his feet and everybody backed away from the inferno.

'I found the bloody landlord, that's what,' Anderson snapped.

'Have you called the fire brigade?' Ferguson shouted over to Shannon, who nodded.

'Going to be too late to save the place,' Jennings said, as he and Ferguson helped Anderson stagger farther from the burning building.

'What happened, guv?' Jennings asked, as Anderson slumped on the grass square in the centre of the village. He still had the half-smoked nub end in his mouth. It had gone out, so he relit it.

‘I wish I bloody knew,’ Anderson said, taking a deep, well-deserved drag of his cigarette before coughing up a lump of tar the size of a golf ball, which caused him to throw the nub end away. ‘He just went bloody berserk.’

Chapter Twenty-Four

Jennings had been right, by the time they heard the wailing of a fire engine, the pub was just a charred shell and two of the connecting cottages had caught light too. Around the village, everybody was out of their homes, many in just their nightclothes. Ferguson, keeping everybody back, shook his head as the fire engine pulled into the village square.

'Superintendent Garrick isn't going to like this,' he said, as Anderson and Jennings helped urge the locals to keep their distance. The threat of arrest and a hail of expletives from Anderson succeeded where Ferguson's diplomacy failed.

'Has Garrick turned up, then?' Jennings asked, once the villagers had trudged to the other side of the village green to watch the fire brigade do their thing.

'As a matter of fact, no,' Ferguson said. 'No sign of him, and he's not the only one that's disappeared.'

Anderson and Jennings swapped glanced. 'What do you mean?' Jennings asked.

'I asked one of our patrols to check on the protest camp in the night, like I said I would,' Ferguson said.

Anderson frowned. 'And?'

'They've gone. All of them.'

Anderson shook his head. 'I knew they'd do a runner.'

'I'm not sure that they have,' Ferguson said, removing his helmet and wiping some of the soot from his forehead. He found a handkerchief and finished the job. 'The tents are still there, and according to our lads, there are signs of a disturbance.'

'What sort of disturbance?' Anderson asked, as Ferguson handed him his hankie so he could wipe his own face.

Ferguson shook his head. 'Not sure, but they said some of the tents were ripped. Looked like there was some sort of ruckus. I was going to go back up this morning to get a look for myself. But I came down here to tell Dr Long they're bringing that chimp up to the research centre this morning.'

He looked at the pub, where smoke was now billowing out of roof. 'Then this happened.'

Anderson looked at Shannon's house, where the doctor stood with the young girl Helen in the doorway. 'Now that she's got her monkey back, maybe I'll get me some answers. Like what the hell is happening in this place.' Anderson then looked at Jennings. 'You and I'll take her on our way to that campsite. I want to see what's gone on.'

'What about the young girl?' Jennings asked. 'Shall I bring her along too?'

'What do you mean, bring the girl? This is a police investigation, not an episode of Scooby bloody Doo.'

'Yes, guv, but she might be able to shed light on what happened up at the camp. They were her friends, after all. Besides, without Dr Long keeping an eye on her, she might do a runner too.'

Anderson grunted and huffed. 'Okay, but she's your responsibility. I'm not paid to babysit.' He then looked at the burning pub. 'Damned shame. That was a nice boozer. Watching a pub like that burn down is like seeing your missus give birth. You know they'll fix her up, but you also know it'll never be the same again.'

It was as if nothing had happened. All the mess, bloodstains and markings left by the police had been cleared away. The laboratory was like it had been before the incident, albeit quieter with no chimp in the room. No live chimp. The dead one lay on the dissection table in a police body bag.

Dr Cunningham wasn't in yet. She normally arrived after eleven, which gave Shannon close to an hour to get the autopsy done. While her employer had insisted she obtain the specimen from the police, Shannon knew Cunningham would not want her examining the animal. She might learn something. Something she knew Cunningham was desperately trying to keep hidden.

In fact, Shannon felt apprehensive as she unzipped the body bag. Part of her didn't want to know what was going on. It frightened her.

As she pulled back the plastic bag and revealed the specimen, she knew instantly something was amiss. Apart from the smell, which even for a dead animal was overpowering—it reeked as if dead weeks, not a little over a day—it looked in a state of advanced decomposition. The skin on its face and under its arms was putrid, and when she pressed the flesh with her latex gloves, her fingers sunk into the body cavity as if the animal were made of putty.

She reached for her scalpel and cut a Y-incision into the animal's chest, before peeling back the skin. Then using the bone saw, she opened up the ribs. And gasped.

Shannon had lost count of the number of animals she had dissected. Early on in her career, she hated doing it. She never got into primatology to cut up dead animals, but it was part of her work—to understand the anatomy. Yet she'd never seen anything like this.

The organs had turned black and putrefied. Except the heart. That looked normal, but was covered in a fine yellow film. She stepped back from the table. *How on earth could the animal have survived for so long, let alone have killed several people with an internal anatomy like this?*

'Astonishing, isn't it?' said a familiar yet chilling voice.

Shannon turned to see Cunningham in the doorway.

'This doesn't look like any of the others,' she said, turning back to the chimp. Every animal that she had dissected at Paradise Woods looked normal. This one was anything but. 'What did you do to it?'

'Shouldn't that be we?' Cunningham said, stepping close and peering into the animal's body cavity. 'You are part of the programme too, remember?'

'You hired me to observe their behaviour, and that's what I've been doing. You never told me what it is you've been pumping into them.'

Cunningham smiled and peered at the animal's putrefied organs. 'It's incredible, isn't it? How a complex organism can sustain itself with virtually no functioning organs. And you should see the brain.' She tapped the dead animal's skull. 'It'll look like Swiss cheese by now.'

'What have you done?' Shannon asked, backing up, trying to put as much space between her and Cunningham as possible.

'What I was asked to do,' Cunningham said.

'What is it? What have you infected it with?'

'It's Latin, you know,' Cunningham said. 'Saevio. It means fury. Rather apt, wouldn't you say?'

'What is it?'

Cunningham smiled. 'So naive. That's what made me hire you in the first place. You were so eager, so willing to please, I knew you wouldn't ask too many questions and would keep your mouth shut.'

'You are not going to be able to keep this quiet,' Shannon said. 'This infection could spread. Is spreading. The police ... they are asking too many questions. They'll want to know what I've found out.'

Cunningham nodded to the specimen. 'You'll tell them nothing. We'll place the specimen in the incinerator. And that will be an end to it.'

'What about the people already infected?'

Cunningham shrugged. 'Every great scientific discovery has its victims.'

Shannon removed her gloves with a snap, and placed them on the dissection table next to the scalpel and bone saw. 'Do you honestly think I'm not going to say anything?'

She went to walk past Cunningham, but the doctor sidestepped, blocking her way. 'I can't let you do that, Dr Long.'

'You can't stop me,' Shannon said, trying to push Cunningham out the way.

Cunningham resisted her. 'I can and I will.'

Shannon went to push her out the way again, but for an older woman Cunningham was quick. She grabbed Shannon's hair and twisted it, pulling her backwards. Cunningham then dragged her backwards towards the vivisection table. Shannon heard the distinctive scrape of a metal object then saw a scalpel blade glinting under the fluorescent lights before her eyes.

'No ... please,' Shannon pleaded, her hands trying to prise Cunningham's grip from her hair.

'Sorry, Dr Long, but I need to be assured of your silence.'

Cunningham lowered the scalpel blade towards Shannon's throat. Shannon screamed, and releasing Cunningham's hand holding her hair, grabbed the one holding the blade and pushed it aside.

Instead of plunging into Shannon's throat, the scalpel struck Cunningham's hand. She squealed, released Shannon's hair and staggered back, clutching her hand. 'What have you done? What have you done?' Her face was taut as she stared at the wound.

And seeing her chance, Shannon shoved Cunningham backwards and ran.

Chapter Twenty-Five

Ferguson had been right. The campsite was deserted. The tents were still there, and the protestor's detritus: stoves, clothing, placards, banners, but there were no signs of any people.

'Looks like they left in a hurry,' Jennings said, slamming the car door shut and wrapping his jacket tight around his midriff.

'Maybe it's giro day,' Anderson said, getting out before leaning into the car and jabbing a cigarette towards Helen in the back seat. 'You stay there, unless we need you.'

He slammed the door and joined Jennings as he traipsed towards the tents.

The camp looked as it did the day before, when they found what they thought was a dead body. Now Anderson wasn't so certain. If the kid had been dead, somebody had moved the body, but he couldn't figure out how, not with him and Jennings there. He looked into the same tent and shook his head. It stank like a Glasgow halfway house. 'Are you sure he was dead?'

'I ain't stupid, guv,' Jennings said, as Anderson pulled his head back out. 'I know a corpse when I see it.'

'Oh, I forgot. You've got a degree, haven't you?'

Jennings crumpled his face at the obvious sarcasm.

'Well, it couldn't have just got up and walked out. Somebody must have moved it.'

Jennings shrugged. 'I don't see how, guv. One of us would have seen something. And that doesn't explain where everybody else has gone.'

They checked some of the other tents. A few were ripped and had half collapsed, but they didn't see anything untoward until Jennings called spotted something on the ground. 'Guv, look!'

Anderson trotted over and Jennings pointed near one of the tents. 'That looks like blood.'

With is joints cracking, Anderson dropped on to his knee and peered at the ground. 'Aye, could be.'

'And look,' said Jennings pointing further up the grassy field. 'There's more here. Somebody might be injured. Whoever it was, it looks as if they headed into the woods.'

Both men stared at the tree line, then both yelped and jumped at the sound of Helen's voice. 'Did you find anything?'

'Bloody hell, girl, I told you to wait in the car,' Anderson said, clutching his chest.

'Sorry, I got bored—what you looking at?' She then noticed the blood at Jennings' feet. 'Is that ...'

'Calm down,' Jennings said. 'We don't know what's happened, but it looks like some of your friends headed into the woods.'

'Then what are we waiting for?' she said, marching off towards the trees.

'Oi, where the bloody hell are you going?' Anderson said, jogging up to Helen and grabbing her arm. 'You can wait here.'

'On my own!' She appealed to Jennings with wide, doe eyes.

'She's got a point, guv. With everything that's been happening around here, it might be best if we stick together. If something happened while we were away ...'

Anderson rubbed his temples. He had a headache coming on. Having been nearly murdered that morning as well as nearly being broiled alive wasn't doing his constitution any good. He needed a drink to calm his nerves, but with the pub out of action, he wasn't going to get one anytime soon. He didn't even know where they were going to stay that night.

'All right, all right,' he said. 'But don't go running off. This ain't a bloody girl guides' picnic.'

Jennings glanced nervously at the woods then leaned in close. 'Shall I get my piece out of the car?'

'Your piece! You ain't Dirty Harry. It's a bloody gun not a piece, and you can leave it where it is. After that farce in the woods yesterday, the last thing I need is you running around with a loaded shooter.' He slapped Jennings on the back. 'Just get your radio and keep an eye on her.'

By the time the fire brigade finished, there was not much left of the Gough Arms. The building was intact, but inside was just a mess of black sludge and smoking timber. Damned shame. The place had stood there for centuries. He was certain somebody would rebuild it—it was listed after all—but in his crude way, Anderson was right. It'd never be the same again.

The crime unit had turned up, nearly a dozen other constables, along with Phelps, the pathologist. Not that there was much for him to do. The fire brigade brought out the two bodies and Phelps said they were so badly burned, it'd be like doing an autopsy on two lumps of coal. This caused him to mutter something along the lines of Inspector Anderson being the angel of death, which amused Ferguson, until he saw the bodies for himself as they bagged them up and loaded them into an ambulance.

He'd seen death before, mainly in road traffic collisions. But the events of the last few days around the village were something else. And the unexplained deaths weren't the only that bothered him. Garrick was still missing, and this was causing a stir among the force. The superintendent's wife had called numerous times, wanting to know the whereabouts of her husband. Nobody had seen or heard from him in nearly 24 hours.

And other people were asking questions too. The local press had heard about the laird's death, and it wouldn't be long before the nationals got wind that something was going on. Then there were the locals. People who lived in small villages such as Monymusk were used to knowing everything and anything, and murder was something that would keep tongues wagging for decades. They'd all congregated around the village square and murmured and chatted as they watched what was going on.

Ferguson had known these people all his life and he'd never seen them so afraid. They weren't stupid and knew something ominous was occurring in their erstwhile tranquil village. There had been more suspicious deaths in the area that week than the entire county would see in a year. People were puzzled, frightened and concerned.

He doubted Monymusk would ever be the same again. Nor would he be. He may have only been a rural beat bobby, but he knew enough to know something sinister was going on.

His morose lifted slightly when he saw a familiar figure jogging down the road. It was Shannon, her long ponytail swinging behind as she jogged towards him. He then realised something wasn't quite right. She kept glancing back down the road behind her and when she saw him, her ambling jog turned into a staggering sprint and she fell.

Ferguson sprinted up. 'Are you okay?'

Despite the cold air, sweat streamed down her face and she had a desperate look on her face, fear gripped her eyes.

'Is there something wrong?' he asked. She tried to speak but just lay breathless and panting. 'Doctor, quick,' Ferguson shouted to Phelps as he stood chatting to the fireman outside the pub.

Phelps' face tightened on sight of the woman swooning in Ferguson's arms. 'What on earth is it now?'

He jogged up, dropped his medical bag on the floor, removed his stethoscope and slipped it in Shannon's blouse. 'Her heart sounds like a ruddy race horse's.' He then placed his hand on her forehead and probed around her eyes. 'What on earth have you been doing, my dear?'

Shannon pointed a shaky hand back down the road and tried to speak.

'Shh ... shh,' Phelps said, before looking at Ferguson. 'Best find a place where she can lie down.'

'She only lives over the road,' Ferguson said, gesturing for one of the constables outside the pub.

The constable scurried over and helped Phelps and Ferguson carry Shannon across the square to her cottage. Ferguson rummaged in her pocket for her keys, opened the door, and the three men carried her to the front room, where they lowered her on to the sofa.

She tried to sit up, but Phelps gently urged her back down. 'I think you need to rest. You look exhausted.'

'You don't understand,' she said, panting and breathless. 'Dr Cunningham ... She ...'

'She what?' Ferguson asked.

'She ... tried to kill me.'

Ferguson looked at Phelps then at the constable next to him. 'Have you run all the way back from Paradise Woods?'

Shannon nodded. Her face looked strained, desperate and agitated. She tried to sit up again and fought against Phelps, Ferguson and the constable as they held her still. 'I need to speak to the inspector.'

'It can wait,' Ferguson said. 'Just try to get your breath back and rest a while.'

Phelps rummaged around in his bag and pulled out a syringe.

'What you doing?' Shannon asked, beating at Ferguson and the constable's hands.

'Just a mild sedative to calm you down and give you a chance to recover.'

'No!' she screamed. 'I need to warn everyone.'

'That can wait,' Ferguson said, holding her arm still while Phelps administered the drug.

Almost instantly, she calmed down, allowing the three men to release her. 'No wonder she's exhausted if she ran from Paradise Woods,' Ferguson said. 'It's over five miles.'

'Do you think there's any truth in what she said?' Phelps asked.

He puffed put his cheeks. 'No idea, but something's scared her witless.'

'You best get hold of Anderson then,' Phelps said.

'I intend to.'

Chapter Twenty-Six

The mid-afternoon sun disappeared behind the canopy as they entered the woods. Anderson, Jennings and Helen stood among the trees and looked around for any signs of the missing protestors. They saw nothing but fallen leaves, branches and the odd squirrel.

'Waste of bloody time,' Anderson said. 'They'll all be in Aberdeen by now, if they've any sense.'

Jennings pocket crackled into life and he halted and raised his hand for silence as he strained to listen with the device at his ear. 'What's that ... She said what? We're on our way.'

He pocketed the radio. 'That was Ferguson. Apparently, Dr Long has arrived back in the village in a right state. Says that Dr Cunningham tried to kill her.'

'Probably just hysterical,' Anderson said. 'But we might as well go talk to her, we're achieving bugger all out here.'

'But what about Scamp?' Helen said. 'You need to find him.'

'I don't need to do anything,' Anderson snapped. 'Besides, your *friends* have probably buried the poor sod somewhere. No doubt trying to pull a fast one by hiding evidence.'

'Why would anybody want to cover that up? They already know about Sarah. It doesn't make sense.'

'When have bloody hippies like you ever made sense? Too much pot and sex has addled your brains. Anyway, we ain't going to find anything just ambling around like a bunch of wandering Jews. We'll have to get the sniffer dogs out here.'

'I wouldn't be so sure,' Jennings said, his eyes focussed on something beneath a hedge. He walked over, crouched down, and then stood, examining something in his hands.

'What you got there?' Anderson asked, prompting Jennings to turn round. It was a cap. A peaked cap. A black peaked cap with a checked stripe around it.

'It must be Garrick's,' Jennings said, glancing around as if looking for the superintendent.

He handed the cap to Anderson who wiped clean the polished insignia belonging to Aberdeenshire police on the front. Anderson then looked at his fingers. Blood.

'Look!' Helen shrieked, rather loudly as her words echoed around the woods and scared a few nesting grouse into the air.

She pointed to the ground at more blood. And lots of it. Anderson and Jennings exchanged nervous glances as they saw more splattered on the pale bark of a tree, and red stains on the leaf litter that formed a meandering path through a clump of bushes. Bushes that began to rustle.

The three of them backed up, Anderson holding his breath, which he released in an audible gasp as the old gillie Brophy broke cover and stepped into a shaft of sunlight breaking through the canopy overhead.

He looked as shocked to see them as they were to see him.

'You!' he said, his shotgun extended before him. His eyes flickered from Jennings to Anderson to Helen.

'Jesus, you old git. You scared the crap out of us,' Anderson said.

'I heard voices,' Brophy said, glancing back through the undergrowth. His face looked grave, concerned. 'I think you better come and see this.'

'See what?' Anderson asked.

Brophy slowly lowered his gun. 'You best see it for yourself.'

He turned and made his way back through the leaves and branches behind him and the others followed.

They broke cover in a small, dark clearing where tall poplars prevented any shafts of light from penetrating the foliage above. Brophy pointed to a dark shadow beneath one of the trees. 'It's over there.'

After exchanging glances, and telling Helen to stay put, Anderson and Jennings trudged over to the tree, where the dark shadow became clearer in form.

'Jesus,' Jennings said, his voice hushed. 'Do you think it's the dead kid?'

Anderson, staring at the corpse and trying hard not to vomit at the sight of the gouged out eyes and mutilated face, shook his head. 'I doubt it. Not unless he's grown tits in the night.' He pointed to the ripped and torn sweater where a lace bra peeked through the wool.

'Then who is it?'

'That's Rachel!' Helen screamed.

'Get her away,' Anderson ordered.

A noise in the distance, perhaps a voice, perhaps nothing more than the local wildlife, caught their attention.

'What the hell is going on,' Jennings said, both his voice and face showed his alarm. 'It's like the Village of the Bloody Damned out here.'

'I think it best if we get out of here,' Anderson said. He turned to Brophy. The old man's face still looked grim. 'If I were you, I'd piss off back to your hunt and barricade the doors until we know what's going on and can get some support up here.'

Brophy offered a toothless grin and patted his shotgun. 'You nae need to worry about me.'

While drowsy from the mild sedative Phelps had given her, Shannon was alert enough to sit up when Anderson, Jennings and Helen arrived at the house. Ferguson was still there, sat on the edge of her sofa, but Phelps had gone. Undoubtedly, he was the busiest man in Scotland at the moment. How many people had died so far? She couldn't count. The sedatives made everything cloudy. But one thing was crystal. All of it was down to what Cunningham was doing at Paradise Woods.

Shannon knew she bore her own responsibility too. She'd known something was not right for months now. But she'd been so desperate for work, it wasn't hard to avoid asking those awkward questions niggling at the back of her mind.

'Right,' Anderson said, after a muted discussion with Ferguson. 'I want to know everything that you know, and I want to know it now.'

'Go easy on her,' Ferguson said. 'She's had a terrible shock.'

'Ain't we bloody all? I've just seen another poor sod missing half their face. Not to mention that I've been nearly mauled by a rampaging ape, had a deranged publican try to throttle me, been half-burned alive and seen more dead bodies this week than a mortician at the Somme.'

He stepped close to Shannon and leaned over her. 'Now, if you don't mind, pretty please with a cherry on top, what the pissing hell is going on?'

Shannon told him about Cunningham. About how she attacked her. About how Cunningham was trying to cover up Project Saevio. About the chimp and what she found during its autopsy.

'So what is this disease?' Jennings asked, after she relayed her tale.

Shannon shook her head. 'A virus of some sort. It seems to attack both the nervous system and the organs, turning its victims into mindless ...'

'Zombies?' Jennings said.

She had to admit, it sounded far-fetched. She had a hard time believing it herself.

'Why would somebody develop something like that?' Ferguson asked. 'It doesn't make sense.'

Shannon bowed her head. 'Paradise Woods is government-funded. When I started, I thought we were developing vaccines, but then all sorts of people kept turning up. Government types, and everything was meant to be ultra secret. Even I didn't know what Project Saevio was about. But I do now. I think it is some sort of biological weapon.'

Anderson stroked his moustache and rubbed his brow, with his eyebrows half way up his forehead. 'Let me get this straight. You've been working on some sort of germ warfare weapon that kills people, but only after turning them into murderous zombies. And when you figured this out, Cunningham tried to kill you.'

She nodded.

Anderson looked at Ferguson. 'What exactly was it that Phelps injected into her, LS-bloody-D?'

'I believe her,' Ferguson said, offering Shannon a thin-lipped smile.

'That's because you are trying to get into her knickers all week,' Anderson snapped. 'You'd believe it if she said there were fairies at the bottom of the garden.' He looked back at Shannon and cocked a sarcastic eyebrow. 'There aren't, are there, love?'

'How else do you explain what's been going on?' she said, aware her head was clearing as the effects of the sedative wore off.

'She has a point, guv,' Jennings said. 'I'm struggling with it all myself but at least it's an explanation.'

'And what would you have me do?' Anderson said, to nobody in particular.

'We could bring in Cunningham for a start,' Ferguson said.

'On what grounds, releasing the next best thing to anthrax in the middle of the Cairngorms?' He nodded at Shannon. 'Just on her say so? The procurator fiscal would laugh his bollocks off.'

'Cunningham did assault her,' Jennings reminded him. 'That's enough to bring her in, surely. At least we'll have the chance to interview her. We could demand some answers. You never know, she may admit everything.'

Anderson frowned at him. 'And why the bloody hell would she do that?'

Jennings shrugged. 'I dunno. Guilt perhaps.'

'You really know bugger all about women.' Anderson rubbed his head, then looked at Jennings and Ferguson in turn. 'Okay, we'll go see her, but if this turns into a cock and bull story.' He glared at Shannon. 'I'll have her for wasting police time.'

'I think I should stay here with Dr Long. Somebody needs to keep an eye on her,' Ferguson said.

Anderson's eyes widened. 'And you think that somebody should be you?' He placed an arm around Ferguson's shoulder. 'It might be an idea if you stopped thinking about your dick for one second, laddie, and let's start focussing on the job in hand.'

He pointed at Helen. 'Little Miss Save-The-Whale can keep an eye on Dr Long.' He scowled at Helen and Shannon. 'Neither of you go anywhere. Not until I get back. You understand?'

Both shook their heads obediently.

Chapter Twenty-Seven

They drove to Paradise Woods in Ferguson's police car. Consequently, the security guards lifted the barrier on sight of it. The three policemen then got out and marched into the research facility.

Somebody in a white coat was standing by a coffee machine in the reception area, and without breaking his stride, Anderson barked at him. 'Dr Cunningham. Where is she?'

The man wavered for a second but pointed down a corridor. 'Not sure. You can try her office. To the right. Second door on the left.'

Without thanking him, Anderson followed the directions to a pinewood door with a small plaque emblazoned with Cunningham's name and her abbreviated credentials. He didn't knock, just walked in.

A man was sitting behind Cunningham's desk. Wearing an expensive suit, neatly trimmed hair parted on one side, a cigarette in a holder held between long fingers, and sporting a sanctimonious expression on his face that would have earned a punch in any Glaswegian pub, Anderson recognised the man straightaway.

He looked up and smiled at the visitors. 'Ah, if it isn't Inspector Anderson,' the man said in his slow, condescending Home Counties accent. 'How splendid to see you, old boy.'

'Who is that?' Jennings said.

'James Bond's effeminate older brother,' Anderson said, glaring at the smug face smiling at him. 'I thought all this had a bad smell about it, and now I see why.'

The man smiled and looked at Jennings who had a confused, gormless expression on his face, mouth open, eyebrows melding together.

'I see you have a new partner,' the Englishman said. 'Try not to get this one killed. You are getting a terrible reputation up at the Home Office.'

'Where is Cunningham?' Anderson asked.

The Englishman shrugged. 'Your guess is as good as mine, old boy. Damned filly seems to have disappeared. They're like that, these academic types. As soon as things get a little dicey, they abscond. My third wife was just the same.'

He cocked his head to the side to get a look at Ferguson standing behind them both. Then he returned his attention to Anderson. 'I suggest you ask your two chums to go for a little walk. You and I need to have words.'

Anderson looked at Jennings and twitched his head to the door. 'Go wait in the car.'

He waited until they both left the room and heard it shut before saying, 'So it's true then?'

The Englishman placed the cigarette holder between his lips, inhaled and let the smoke gently seep from the corner of his mouth. 'Truth is often subjective, my dear inspector. I thought you'd have learnt that by now.'

'I tell you what ain't subjective,' Anderson said. 'The dead bodies piling up at Aberdeen mortuary.'

The man chuckled gently behind his cigarette holder. 'That is where you are wrong, Inspector. Death is very much a point of conjecture.'

Anderson could feel one of his headaches coming on. 'How about translating that from posh bollocks into plain English?'

The man laughed. 'As forthright as ever, I see.' He stood, turned to the window and prised open the slats in the blind before letting out a satisfied hum on sight of the local scenery.

Without turning round, he said, 'How much do you know?'

'Enough,' Anderson replied. 'That Cunningham has been playing Dr Frankenstein with something that makes AIDS look like the common cold.'

The Englishman turned round, smiled and nodded. 'You are referring to Project Saevio. And no, Dr Cunningham is just the latest in a long line of researchers we and our friends over the Atlantic have employed to help develop this pathogen.'

'What is it then, this Project Sarajevo?'

'Saevio,' the Englishman said. 'It is our latest tool for playing the great game.' He sat back down and gestured for Anderson to take a seat opposite, which he did.

After placing his cigarette holder on to an ashtray, the Englishman clasped his long fingers together and sat forward. 'Have you ever wondered what the inevitable conflict with the Soviets will be like? What the consequences will be?'

Anderson shrugged. He'd not given it much thought, although he had seen *Threads* on the BBC a few weeks earlier, which had scared the crap out of him. 'I thought we'd all get three minutes to bend over and kiss our arses goodbye and that'd be that.'

The man smiled. 'Contrary to popular belief, any conflict between us and the Soviets won't be solved by who has the most nuclear weapons in their arsenal. You can never totally wipe out an entire country. There will be survivors. Armies are as much a requirement of modern warfare as they always were, to mop up on the battlefields of the future, to take physical control of locations. Sadly, we are rather lacking in that department. An invading Soviet force will outnumber our own chaps by five to one, and we can't rely on our transatlantic friends; they'll have their own problems to deal with.'

'Is this going somewhere?' Anderson asked.

'Saevio,' the man said. 'Imagine a pathogen that does the mopping up for you. Of course, both sides have been developing weapons for germ warfare for some time. But the problem with most of them up to now is that they are too damned effective.'

'Say again?'

The man picked up his cigarette holder and refilled it from a silver case that he kept tucked in his inside pocket. He offered Anderson one, who declined and pulled out his *Golden Virginia.*

'You see,' said the man, letting out a lungful of aromatic and expensive smelling tobacco. 'Germs such as anthrax kill far too quickly, which means there is little time for infection to spread to pandemic proportions. Additionally, these germs linger in the environment making it uninhabitable, often for many years.'

He leaned forward, a smile lit up on his aquiline features. 'Now imagine a pathogen that not only took its time to kill its victims, and in the process, encouraged them to infect others. That's what Saevio does, it turns them violent and unpredictable.'

He leaned back again. 'It is the ultimate in germ warfare. Its victims become completely taken over by it. Their minds blank with nothing more than a desire to attack others. It really is a marvel of biology.'

He lifted up a folder on the desk. 'According to our research on mice, the effect on the victim's body is also incredible, with necrosis of the flesh often giving the appearance of the person being dead. Yet they are quite alive.' He smiled, as if somehow what he said deserved congratulations. 'Up to now, we used mice to develop the virus, but the damned bug refused to jump species. Thanks to Cunningham and her work with chimps, we now have a fully working, albeit primitive, strain.'

'You seem to be forgetting something,' Anderson said, flicking ash on the floor.

'And what's that?'

'This is the bloody Scottish countryside, not post-apocalypse Vladivostok. And your bloody perfect weapon could end up wiping out half of Scotland. Christ man, what were you thinking?'

The Englishman raised his palms upwards, conceding Anderson's point. 'That's why we chose this area for our research. It's isolated, sparsely populated, and away from any major conurbation in case of ... little accidents like this.'

'Little accidents!' Anderson jabbed his roll-up towards the window. 'Aberdeen is only twenty bloody miles away. That's two-hundred thousand people.'

The Englishman patted the air as if trying to slow an advancing vehicle. 'Calm down. That's why I'm here, to contain our little problem.'

'Oh, well. Now I feel a whole lot better. Lord-bloody-Fauntleroy is on hand to sort things out. I'd really like to hear how you are going to clear up this bloody mess.'

'Really, Inspector. Ye of little faith. Everything is already in motion. We have a company from the Gordon Highlanders en route as we speak. We are going to evacuate the local populace and place a temporary exclusion zone around the area. Nobody in, nobody out.'

'And what are you going to say to people when they ask why they should leave the comfort of their nice warm houses? That you have accidently unleashed a biblical plague in the area? People tend to take exception to such things.'

The man stuck out his lower lip. 'I've concocted a little story about radon gas. The mention of radioactivity gets most people all in a tizzy. The locals shouldn't be a problem.'

'Shouldn't be a problem! This is the Cairngorms not Detroit. Dead bodies tend to get talked about around here. And we've had more than half a dozen in the last couple of days. One of them was the owner of the local boozer. How you going to keep that quiet?'

The Englishman sighed. 'Inspector, please. The great British public are many things, but they do not lack patriotism. Even you Scots. The mere mention of the Official Secrets Act, and perhaps a small cheque from the Home Office, should keep people quiet. Besides, who's going to believe the ramblings of a few country bumpkins? After all, it does sound a little far-fetched, wouldn't you agree?'

Anderson realised his roll-up had burned to his fingers so he dropped it on the floor and stamped it out. 'And the press? The local rag is already asking questions.'

'D-notices are already in place. There isn't an editor in the country that will print a word of what's gone on up here.' He leaned forward and winked. 'We've told them it has something to do with the IRA. The Irish have their uses sometimes.'

'And what about those infected?' Anderson glanced behind, out of instinct to ensure nobody was listening. 'We've got a missing police superintendent for starters.'

The Englishman flashed his teeth in a grimace and sucked air thorough his teeth. 'I'm afraid this is where things get a bit murky.'

'This is where it gets murky!' Anderson shook his head in disbelief and noticed the Englishman's eyes had narrowed and his lips had disappeared from his smile. 'What do you mean by murky?'

The man lifted up a few sheets of papers from the folder. 'According to Cunningham's notes, Saevio has a relatively quick incubation time—usually about twelve hours. But those infected can last for up to a week before succumbing to the infection.'

'During which time they are going around killing people,' Anderson added.

'Quite. But eventually they will die. So, I'm afraid we are going to have to wait it out until those carrying the disease succumb before removing the exclusion zone.'

'And what happens if they don't want to stick around?'

The Englishman adjusted the knot of his tie and coughed gently. 'We've given instruction for the Highlanders to shoot on sight anybody that approaches the exclusion zone.'

'And what happens if you miss a few folk during the evacuation? These parts are full of hikers and ramblers, not to mention all the farmers.'

The Englishman shrugged. 'Then, let's hope they stay put until all this blows over.'

Anderson sighed and rubbed his head. How could something like this happen? As if the country didn't have enough to worry about, what with the Irish blowing up pubs, the Soviets threatening Armageddon and the bloody Tory party selling off British Industry as if it were a closing down sale. Now the posh idiots in charge were using Scotland as a testing ground for some Cold War pox.

He then noticed the Englishman's features still had that false look of contrition on it. 'There's something else, isn't there?'

The Englishman grinned apologetically. 'I'm afraid those that have had any sort of exposure to the disease need to be quarantined. That includes those who work here and anybody that have come into contact with those protestors who broke in and started this damned outbreak in the first place.'

'Quarantined!'

The Englishman nodded. 'They'll need to stay in the exclusion zone until we are sure they are not infected.'

Anderson felt uneasy by the stare the Englishman gave him.

'I'm afraid that means you too, Inspector.'

'You what!' spluttered Anderson. 'You mean I've got to stay here? For how long?'

'A week, no longer. Just until it has all blown over and we're sure you are in the clear.'

'How infectious is this bloody disease?'

The Englishman stood up and looked thorough the blind again. 'I'm sure you have nothing to worry about. The research is in its earliest phases. We hope to develop it so that it can become virulent when airborne, but as it is, only those who have come into contact with bodily fluids are at risk.'

'Bodily fluids?'

'Blood, saliva, that sort of thing. But to be sure, we'll need you to stay put for a little while. Just a few days or so. Think of it as a little holiday.'

'If I wanted a bloody holiday, I'd have packed my swimming trunks. Besides, I prefer Torremolinos. Call me fussy, but I prefer holiday destinations absent of marauding zombies.'

'Oh, Inspector, you do exaggerate. Anyway, there are people who'd kill for a few days in such nice scenery.'

'It's the folk running around this nice bloody scenery doing the killing that worry me.'

Chapter Twenty-Eight

Anderson and Jennings watched the last army truck leave the village, the inhabitants of Monymusk sat in the back minus Shannon, Helen and Ferguson who had stepped out of Shannon's cottage to watch the exodus.

'So, that's it then,' Jennings said. 'We're on our own.'

Ferguson had his radio clamped to his ear and was nodding as he listened to the instructions coming through on the other end.

'The army has set up roadblocks off the A96 north of Paradise Woods and south where the Don meets the B993,' he said. 'That means we are in the middle of about fifty square miles. I suggest we hunker down together. Safety in numbers and all that.'

A click of metal caused Anderson to look down at Jennings' hands. He had his gun out and was checking the mechanism. 'Yeah, Pistol Pete here will keep us all safe.'

'Would you rather I left it in the car?' Jennings snapped. The sergeant's temper was a little frayed, but that was understandable. He had young fiancé waiting for him back in Inverness. And while Anderson had nothing other than a freezer full of ready meals to go home to, without a pub in the village, things looked grim.

'You can all stay at mine,' Shannon said, 'I only have one spare room, so some of you will have to sleep on the floor.'

'I can do better than that,' Ferguson said. 'One of my lads went to see Lady Gough when they evacuated her. She's gone to stay with her son, but has given us permission to use the house if wanted. She says there's plenty of food in the freezer and there's enough space to accommodate all of us—it has twelve bedrooms.'

Jennings looked at Anderson. 'What do you think, guv?'

'A haunted bloody house? I'd rather sleep in the car,' Anderson said.

'Well, you're in charge,' Ferguson said. 'But Sir Henry used to like a tipple, so I bet there's plenty of Scotch in the house.'

Anderson flicked the cigarette he'd been smoking into the wind. 'Then what we waiting for. I've always fancied being a laird.'

The old house was eerie, especially when night fell and Helen, sat in the laird's front room with the others, knew they were the only people for miles. The only *normal* people.

Nobody had fully explained to her what was going on, but she had been told enough. There was some sort of outbreak, a disease caused by the chimp, and all her friends at the protest camp were possibly infected. She could be too. They all could, which was why everybody kept giving each other suspicious glances as they pretended to be calm.

Ferguson and Shannon played gin rummy, Jennings paced up and down checking the patio doors and every window to ensure they were locked, and Anderson sat sprawled on an ageing Chesterfield, a glass of the laird's whisky in one hand and a cigar the size of a carrot in the other.

Helen stared out the patio doors into the darkness. The silhouetted tree line of Paradise Woods was visible in the distance. The trees swayed and shapes shifted in the darkness. They were out there somewhere, Graham and the others, roaming the countryside in some sort of stupefying trance, while the infection slowly killed them.

'Isn't there anything we can do for them?' she asked, breaking the silence of the room.

Shannon looked up from the fan of cards in her hands. 'For whom?'

Helen stared back out into the darkness. 'Those with the infection. Letting them die out there, alone, it's inhumane.'

'Oh, here we go,' said Anderson, his voice slightly slurred from the amount of whisky he'd consumed. 'The trouble with people like you is, you're always looking to save something. Rights for women, rights for animals, rights for gays, now you want rights for bloody murderous zombies. If you're so bloody keen to help them, why not pop outside with a glass of milk and a biscuit, see what thanks you get.'

'Go easy on her, guv,' Jennings said, checking the patio doors for the umpteenth time. 'They're her friends, remember?'

'It's not those out there she needs to worry about,' Anderson said. 'Who's to say one of *us* hasn't contracted that bloody disease. If I were you, love, I'd be more concerned with the people in this room rather than your former friends.'

'You really haven't got a streak of decency in you, have you?' Shannon snapped.

'Hey, hang on. It wasn't me that let that bastard ape out. It is her fault we're in this bloody mess in the first place. And yours come to think of it. You and that bloody Cunningham.'

'What you did in that place was evil, criminal, inhumane,' Helen said, rounding on Shannon.

Shannon flopped her cards on to the table and stood up. 'Hey, I was just sticking up for you. And I had no idea what

Cunningham was doing. I was just there to monitor the animal's behaviour.'

Ferguson stood up and moved between them, arms apart as if breaking up a brawl. 'Everyone, please. I know we're all a little anxious about what's going on, but fighting among ourselves isn't going to help anyone. Look, it has been a long day and I'm sure everybody's tired, so I suggest we all turn in for the night.'

'Everywhere's secure,' Jennings said. 'But I suggest we take turns to keep watch. I'll do the first shift.' He pulled his gun out of his pocket and placed it on the table where Shannon and Ferguson's cards lay. 'Do you want to do the next, guv?'

'Don't you worry about me,' Anderson said, taking his jacket from the back of the Chesterfield, lying down and covering his torso with it, all without spilling a drop of the whisky in his hand or removing the cigar clenched in his teeth. 'I'll have my eyes open all night.'

Jennings sighed and looked at Ferguson. 'I'll come and wake you in about four hours.'

Ferguson nodded then gestured to the main hall with his hand. 'After you, ladies.'

'Night, night,' Anderson hollered after them. 'Don't let the disease-ridden zombies bite.'

They ignored him. Helen and Shannon followed Ferguson into the main hall, the floorboards creaking as they walked, then up the impressive staircase to the upstairs landing. It reminded Helen of an old hotel, as it consisted of a long corridor, lined with doors on both sides. While a few paintings hung on the walls, the carpet was worn, it smelled damp and musty, and the floor creaked even louder up there than it did downstairs.

'I'll take the room on the end,' Ferguson said pointing down the landing. 'You take whatever rooms you like. The bathroom is the second door on the right.'

Ferguson opened his door and bid the pair goodnight and disappeared into the room at the end.

Helen and Shannon stood for a long second and swapped steely stares, then they both gave a cold, 'goodnight,' before disappearing into doors on opposite sides of the landing.

Helen found herself in a large but cold room. She could see her breath as she breathed out. The whole houses seemed to be heated by antiquated radiators that provided plenty of clanging and rattling but very little warmth.

The room faced the front of the house. Through the large bedroom window, she saw the same silhouetted tree line as downstairs. She kept imagining Graham and the others staring at her from the undergrowth, their eyes just like Sarah's—lifeless, dead, bestial.

Was it true that they were really lost? Did nothing remain of the people that once inhabited the bodies now addled by infection? She struggled to believe they couldn't be helped. Even after Sarah's attack on her, she felt that deep inside, her friend was still there, trapped, overpowered by the terrible disease that robbed her of her senses. She knew nothing of medicine, but surely, some antidote or vaccine or antibiotic might work.

She shuddered. The sense of being watched seemed overwhelming. So she drew the old, musty curtains, kicked off her shoes and climbed into bed, leaving her clothes and the light on.

Chapter Twenty-Nine

Creaking floorboards on the landing and the sound of men whispering awoke Helen. Although, she wasn't sure she'd slept at all. It certainly didn't feel like it. She recognised the voices of Jennings and Ferguson and presumed they were swapping shifts. After listening to the creak of floorboards move to the staircase, she pulled the blankets around her tighter and tried to go back to sleep.

It wasn't happening.

The room was too cold and she was too awake. She also felt uneasy. Not frightened. The strange thing was that she did not feel scared. Odd for somebody that could never sit through a horror film. Yet they were all facing something that made even the worst *video nasty* pale in comparison and while it all unnerved her, it didn't terrify her.

Didn't mean she could sleep, though.

She got out of bed, keeping the blankets wrapped around her. The laird must have been a penny pincher because she checked the radiator and it was cold to the touch.

She needed a brew. That was the answer. Not only would it warm her up, but it'd also settle her nerves. The power of hot tea could never be underestimated in her opinion.

Keeping the blankets around her, she crept from the bedroom and made her way downstairs. The creaking floorboards cut through the silence of the house and caused Ferguson to step from the front room to see what was coming down.

'Oh, it's you,' he said. 'What's the matter, couldn't sleep?'

She shook her head. 'Thought I'd make a cup of tea. Do you want one?'

He smiled. 'Lovely, thanks.'

'What about the inspector?'

Ferguson opened the door a little wider and the sound of loud, boorish snores filtered out of the room. 'I think he's fine.'

She chuckled, and dragging the blankets behind her, made her way to the kitchen on the opposite side of the main hall.

The house was even colder here. Bare flagstones covered the kitchen, and since she still had no shoes on, she pranced around on the balls of her feet as she filled the kettle and turned on the gas stove.

The stove backed up against a window looking out into the laird's back garden. With the light on in the kitchen, she saw nothing but blackness.

Until a face appeared.

She screamed, and dropping the blanket, dashed out of the kitchen to the main hall.

Ferguson had sprinted out of the front room to meet her, Jennings' gun in his hand. 'What's the matter?'

'There's someone outside.'

Ferguson scurried past her to the kitchen, switching off the light. 'Where?'

Helen pointed, her hand shaking. 'It was there.'

Ferguson looked left and right through the window. 'I can't see anything.'

Footsteps sounded on the stairs and Shannon and Jennings appeared a moment later. Both fully dressed, albeit absent of shoes.

'What's going on?' Jennings asked. 'I was just nodding off when I heard a scream.'

'She said she saw somebody outside,' Ferguson said, brandishing the gun around dangerously. Jennings took it from him and looked through the window. 'I can't see anyone. What exactly did you see?'

'A face. At the window. It was horrible. Grotesque. It was one of them, I'm sure of it.'

Helen was shaking, and she looked at everyone in turn, eventually locking eyes on Shannon, who placed a sympathetic arm around her shoulder and shook her gently. 'Shhh, whatever it was, it has gone now.'

'What the hell is going on?' Anderson's voice startled everybody and they spun round to see him staggering out of the sitting room, his shirt untucked, his hair awry.

'There might be someone outside,' Jennings said, backing from the kitchen, his gun raised like some cop from an American film. 'Everybody, wait here.'

He then dashed around the house, turning out lights and peering through windows. 'No sign of anyone,' he said, returning to the main hall where everyone stood huddled together.

'Pah, she's probably seeing things,' Anderson said, yawning.

Then the front door rattled.

Everybody turned towards it, eyes wide, necks extended, like a gang of meerkats hearing a predator.

The door handle moved.

'There's somebody there!' shrieked Helen.

Jennings stepped forward, gun extended in one hand, arm holding everyone back with the other.

Then the door burst open and everybody screamed.

Anderson had no idea how Jennings managed not to open fire when the Brophy burst into the main hall. Despite the relief that it was only the old gillie, his appearance caused Anderson no end of discomfiture. If it weren't for his dodgy prostate, he would have wet himself on the spot.

'What ye all doing here?' Brophy asked, after Anderson had finished a tirade of expletives. The old man wore boots, carried a shotgun across his arm and had a wax jacket over what looked like his pyjamas.

'Never mind that, what the bloody hell are you doing, creeping around in the middle of the night?' Anderson snapped. 'These poor lassies nearly wet themselves.'

'I saw the lights on, and as her ladyship *isnae* here, I thought I'd see what's going on.'

'Were you at the back window a minute ago?' Jennings asked, holstering his gun.

'Aye, *wisnae* sure the house hadn't been burgled. When I saw yon lassie in the kitchen, I thought I'd see what she was doing.'

'How did you get in?' Anderson asked, scowling at Jennings. 'I thought you'd checked the door was locked.'

'I did,' protested Jennings.

'His lairdship keeps a key under the mat,' Brophy said, dangling a large key on a piece of string.

'Jesus Christ.' Anderson gripped his forehead. 'Lock the bloody door for God's sake.'

'Will someone tell me what is going on?' Brophy said, bewilderment across his face.

'Sergeant,' Anderson said. 'Fill him in. I'm going for a bloody drink to calm my nerves.'

The old gillie was completely unaware of the situation. Being in the middle of nowhere, the authorities had missed his cottage. So Jennings, Ferguson and Shannon had to explain about the outbreak, how the village and surrounding area had been cordoned off and most of the inhabitants evacuated.

To Shannon's surprise, he took the news calmly enough. He didn't even ask any questions. She half-assumed he wasn't quite grasping what was going on, although he protested a bit when Jennings insisted he stay at the house with the rest of them.

'Safety in numbers,' Jennings said. 'Besides, I'm really not sure you understand the gravity of the situation we are in. Those people infected are extremely dangerous.'

'Aye,' said Anderson. 'Will rip your throat out as good as look at you.'

'They also pose a serious risk of infection,' Shannon added, soberly.

'You *disnae* have to worry about me,' said the old-timer patting his gun. 'I can look after myself.'

'Nobody is doubting that,' Ferguson said. 'But if it is all the same with you, it is best if we stay all together until this thing blows over.'

He grumbled a bit, but after Anderson gave him a glass of the laird's malt and told him to, 'Sit the bloody hell down and shut the bloody hell up,' all was settled, and the others decided to get some sleep, except Jennings, who seemed reluctant to hand his gun back over to Ferguson, so said he'd stay downstairs.

Ferguson, Helen and Shannon ascended the creaky stairs back to bed, but on reaching the landing, Helen halted Shannon, gently grasping her arm once Ferguson disappeared into his room.

'I'm sorry,' she said.

She looked still shaken from her fright.

'About what?' Shannon asked.

'Giving you a hard time about Paradise Woods. I know none of this is your fault. It's my fault, and I'm sorry for putting you in danger.'

Moisture glistened in her eyes and Shannon could see she was being earnest. 'What's done is done. The important thing now is we all keep our heads and stick together.'

Helen smiled thinly and nodded, but when Shannon turned round to go into her room, she tugged at her arm again. 'Can I stay with you tonight?' Her eyes were wide and her bottom lip trembled slightly.

Shannon wasn't that much older than Helen was, but as they stood there on the landing, she realised beneath all that bluff and anger about animal rights, there was really just a frightened little girl.

'Sure,' Shannon said, widening the door for her. 'As long as you promise not to snore.'

Chapter Thirty

Helen and Shannon descended the stairs in the morning to the smell of bacon wafting through the house. Helen had been a vegetarian for five years now, and while she'd never have admitted it, she found the smell irresistible.

Jennings was in the kitchen, an apron around his waist, frying pan in his hand. 'Good morning, girls. Full Scottish?'

'Just toast for me, thanks,' Helen said.

'Any coffee?' Shannon asked.

Jennings nodded to a full pot on the stove. Shannon picked it up and waved it at Helen. 'Yes, please. Where are the others?'

'Front room,' Jennings said. 'Go through, I'll bring your toast when it's done.'

'Thanks,' they said in tandem.

The front room had taken on a distinctive manly smell—sweat, aftershave, stale smoke and alcohol, the latter two emanating mainly from Anderson. He sat on the sofa, same shirt on, hair awry, greying bristle sprouting on his chin, fag end clamped in his teeth, Brophy sat at the table, still in his wax jacket, while Ferguson stood at the patio doors, staring at a bright but cold-looking morning.

'Good morning,' Shannon said, cheerily.

Ferguson turned and smiled, Brophy muttered something about the day being half over, while Anderson made a groaning, gurgling noise.

They fell into an awkward silence until Jennings came in with plates of food, handing a full Scottish breakfast to Brophy, a couple of plates of toast to Shannon and Helen, and a bacon sandwich to Ferguson.

'You sure you don't want anything, guv?' he asked Anderson.

The inspector shook his head, removed a bottle of pills from his pocket and rattled it. 'Got my breakfast here.'

'If anybody wants any more, there's plenty left,' Jennings said, tucking into a sandwich.

'You'll make a lovely wife someday,' Anderson said.

Jennings flashed him a sarcastic grin and other than the sounds of mouths slapping together as they all ate, the room fell silent, until Helen asked, 'So what we all going to do today?'

'The weather looks to have cleared,' Ferguson said, finishing his sandwich while staring at the fresh, bright morning. 'Shame we can't go outside. But there are some board games in my room. They might while away a few hours.'

'God, kill me now,' Anderson said.

'C'mon, guv,' said Jennings. 'Nobody wants to be here. We might as well make the best of it.'

'I intend to,' Anderson said, reaching for a half-drunk bottle of Scotch on the coffee table.

'Bit early, ain't it, guv?' Jennings said, shaking his head.

'As I said, you'll make a bloody good wife, what with your nagging.'

'Hold on!' Ferguson stared hard through the patio doors. 'There's somebody coming up the drive.'

Everybody bolted from their seats and massed around. 'Who is it?' Jennings said, to nobody in particular.

'Well, I doubt it's the Avon woman,' Anderson said, peering through the glass.

They all watched the figure approach, the sounds of their rapid breaths the only noise. Then Ferguson said, 'It's one of them, isn't it? Look at the way he's staggering.'

'Aye, he *disnae* look well,' Brophy said, picking up his shotgun from next to his seat.

Jennings also picked up his gun, and they all watched as the shambling figure staggered up the drive and on to the lawn and stopped. It stood swaying slightly, head twitching, and then Helen realised who it was. She recognised the clothes.

'That's Graham!'

'Who?' Shannon asked.

'From the camp. I've known him years.'

'What's he doing?' Ferguson asked.

'Who the bloody hell knows,' Anderson said. 'Probably looking for someone to mutilate.'

'What shall we do?' Helen said. 'We can't just leave him out there.'

'There's nothing we can do.' Shannon placed an arm on Helen's shoulder.

'Perhaps I should go out and put him out of his misery?' Jennings said.

'He's not a wild dog!' snapped Helen. 'What gives you the right to kill him? He's still a human being!'

Shannon gave her another friendly squeeze. 'He's no longer the person you once knew.'

'Besides,' Ferguson said, 'you don't know how many more are out there. I suggest we step back and not draw attention to ourselves. Perhaps he'll go away.'

Jennings jiggled the key sticking out one of the patio doors to ensure it was locked, then said, 'I'm going to check the downstairs doors and windows again,' before marching out of the front room.

'The rest of you, do as the constable says,' Anderson said, staring at the figure on the lawn. 'Let's keep back.'

They all did as he suggested and moved away from the patio doors. Except Helen.

She refused to believe there was nothing they could do. That Graham was beyond help. That despite the infection, he wasn't in there somewhere trying to get out.

So tentatively, she reached for the key, unlocked the patio door and ran on to the lawn towards him.

Shrieks and cries erupted behind her, telling her to come back, but she didn't listen. She jogged closer, until Graham saw her. His head rose slowly. He looked awful. His face was ashen, with red and black blotches covering his skin. His arms drooped at his side and swung lifeless as he took a step towards her.

She held out her hands. 'Graham, it's me, Helen.'

He took another shambling step, his eyes staring blankly at her.

'I know you can hear me. I want to help you.'

He didn't respond, just took another shambling step in her direction and sort of gurgled.

'Graham, it's me.'

He stopped and his head twisted to one side as he fixed his vague, lifeless eyes on her. Then the dead arms rose up, he opened his mouth, baring his teeth and made a kind of hissing scream.

Then charged towards her.

Helen screamed. A loud bang sounded behind her, and then the back of Graham's head erupted like a party popper and he slumped to the ground.

Shrieking and screaming, Helen turned to see Brophy, smoking shotgun at his shoulder, and Ferguson running towards her. She turned back to the ghastly sight on the lawn. Graham lay with blood pouring from his head.

'Get back to the house,' Anderson shouted, from the patio doors, his finger pointing down the drive. 'There's more of them.'

At the bottom of the laird's drive, another figure staggered towards them. Then from the right, another broke cover from the undergrowth. And yet another from the other side of the lawn. Most she recognised from the protest camp. But she didn't stay long enough to have a good look because despite her legs not wanting to move, Ferguson grabbed her and pulled her back to the house.

'Quick, shut the doors,' Anderson yelled as Helen, Ferguson tumbled into the room.

'Brophy is still outside,' Ferguson yelled.

And then Helen heard another shotgun blast, and then a scream from outside. And found herself buried on Shannon's shoulder while sobbing uncontrollably.

Chapter Thirty-One

'They've got Brophy!' Ferguson screamed, as Anderson locked the front door and saw two figures pounce on the old gillie. Their shabby dress indicated they were from the animal rights camp, but the way they tore into the poor old gamekeeper suggested they were no longer vegetarian.

By the time Jennings ran into the room with his gun, it was all over for the old man. He laid twitching on the lawn, the two dead protestors before him that he'd shot, another two tearing into his body as if he were an all-you-can-eat buffet.

Another shambling figure suddenly appeared at the patio doors.

'Barricade the door,' Anderson shouted.

Ferguson and Jennings grabbed hold of the ancient sofa and pushed it up towards the patio doors, while Anderson tipped over the coffee table and threw it on top.

'I don't think that's going to hold them,' Jennings yelled as one of the figures banged against the glass.

He was right. It took seconds before the glass smashed and one of the bedraggled figures had its arm through, its fingers spread as it reached and clawed at those inside, blood gushing from wounds in its arms.

Jennings fired. Once. Twice. Three times. But it wasn't until the fourth round did the figure slump to the ground. The rest had gone. Even the ones on the lawn had vanished, leaving Brophy, or what was left of him, in a puddle of blood.

'They're going round the back,' Jennings shouted, as breaking glass sounded from the behind the house. He scampered out the room.

'Get her upstairs,' Anderson said to Shannon.

Helen was still hysterical, and Shannon had to half carry her into the main hall and up the stairs.

'Lock yourselves in one of the rooms,' Ferguson said. 'And don't open the door.'

Three shots sounded from the backdoor next to the kitchen and Anderson and Ferguson ran through the main hall to see Jennings shooting through the glass. Several arms clutched at him. 'I think I've killed another one, but I've only got a couple of shots left.'

'There must be some shotguns or something in this bloody house,' Anderson said to Ferguson. 'Go find them.'

The constable ran into the laird's study, returned a moment later shaking his head then tried the next door, which must have been a laundry room as it contained nothing but linen piled in baskets. 'I'll check upstairs.'

'Well, hurry up about it,' Anderson ordered, as Jennings let off two more shots.

'I can't hold them much longer,' Jennings shouted, letting off another round, and then his gun clicked empty.

He looked back at Anderson, his eyes bulging wide, then the door splintered and two pairs of arms devoured him like the tentacles of a giant octopus.

Jennings screamed and Anderson ran to help, but as the sergeant disappeared, another figure appeared in the doorway.

This one was bigger than those they'd seen on the lawn. Taller. Broad shouldered. And he had set back eyes and a face, which despite being covered in what looked like the pox, Anderson recognised.

Garrick.

The superintendent glared at Anderson though vague and bloodshot eyes, pupils mere pinpoints. He made a guttural, growling noise, like somebody about to throw up, and then he stepped forward, slowly and steadily. Anderson took a step back. And another. And a third. Then he ran for the stairs, bounding up them two at a time until he collided with Ferguson on his way down.

'Get back up,' Anderson shouted. Ferguson's eyes bulged and his face went taut on sight of Garrick like a man straining for the toilet. He froze, staring, until Anderson slapped him around the head and dragged him up the stairs.

'He's coming,' Ferguson shouted, as Garrick appeared at the top of the stairs and lumbered towards them.

The two men backed up as the large figure plodded down the landing, his throat making those guttural noises.

Then he charged with his arms outstretched and his hands ready to tear into the two men.

Ferguson and Anderson, almost tripping over each other, ran down the landing. The door at the end was closed, and when they fell against it, heads glancing behind as the lumbering figure looming up behind them, they realised it was locked too.

Anderson rattled the lock, turned, screamed, and just when Garrick was within a few strides away, the door flew open and Anderson and Ferguson fell into the room, while Shannon slammed the heavy, oak door behind them, locked it and jammed a chair underneath the handle.

'That's not going to hold him,' Anderson said, as the door bounced in its frame, causing Helen to scream.

The door may have been oak and heavy, but the frame wasn't, and each time Garrick threw his body against it, it creaked and cracked. Anderson pressed himself against it, as did Ferguson, who had a truncheon in his hand.

'What the bloody hell you going to do with that?' Anderson said. 'Give him an enema? We need firearms, not a police issue dildo.'

'I've checked every room,' Ferguson said. 'There's nothing up here.'

The door thudded again, and both men struggled to keep their bodies pressed against it.

'We're going to have to do something soon,' shouted Ferguson.

Shannon ran over to the window, opened it and thrust her head outside. 'There's none of them down there,' she shouted back.

'We could try to run to Brophy's place,' Ferguson said, as another thud sounded on the woodwork behind them. 'He's bound to have another shotgun or two.'

Helen joined Shannon at the window and peered down. 'It's a long way down.'

Shannon pointed to the unmade bed. 'Grab me the sheets.'

'Hurry!' Anderson said, as Garrick bashed into the door again, causing the wood around the frame to crack and splinter.

As Anderson and Ferguson pushed all their weight against the door to prevent Garrick from bursting through, Shannon hastily tied a couple of knots in the sheet and secured it to the ancient radiator beneath the window.

'Help them!' Anderson said to Ferguson.

The young constable dashed to the window, looked out and then clambered down the makeshift rope.

'Hurry,' he hissed.

'Yes, bloody hurry,' Anderson said as Garrick thumped against the door again, breaking the lock and pushing the chair back several inches. Anderson knew one more barge and he'd be through, yet Shannon was only just clambering on to the windowsill.

With a crash, the door flew open, sending Anderson reeling across the room.

'Get the hell out,' he shouted to Helen, who was standing watching Shannon climb down the sheet, while Anderson lay looking up at the diseased Garrick.

The former superintendent stood in the doorway for a moment, Anderson lying before him, helpless. Yet he obviously found the petite frame of Helen more appetising because he charged towards her, growling like a dog as he lunged.

Helen screamed as Garrick grabbed hold of her arm as she tried to back out the window.

Mouth open, he slowly pulled it towards her, but Anderson was on his feet. He charged at Garrick and shoulder barged him against the wall before he could take a chunk out of her. As she clambered on to the windowsill, Garrick glared at Anderson.

The superintendent's mouth opened, revealing teeth filled with detritus. Then he surged towards Anderson with his arms out.

He grabbed Anderson around the throat, lifted him up and charged across the room, slamming the helpless inspector against the wardrobe on the far wall, expelling the air out of Anderson's lungs.

Lifting Anderson up by the throat, Garrick cocked his head to one side as he studied him, then opened his mouth to take a bite.

Anderson shoved both his fingers in Garrick's eyes, causing the grip on his throat to loosen. Throwing his head forward, he brought it down on Garrick's face. He heard a squish and crack and Garrick went barrelling over the bed. Anderson bolted to the window and jumped on to the sill, grabbed hold of the sheet, but before he could make his way out, Garrick grabbed his ankle.

He dragged Anderson's leg towards his mouth, intent on taking a bite. With his free foot, Anderson kicked, catching Garrick in the face and sending him barrelling back over the bed and Anderson barrelling out the window.

Chapter Thirty-Two

He landed on his feet, but the snap in his ankle was almost as loud as his scream and Anderson lay on the ground, swearing and screaming.

Ferguson, Shannon and Helen ran over. 'Shhh,' Ferguson said.

'Don't bloody shush me,' Anderson said. 'My leg ... it's bloody broken.' He gritted his teeth from the throbbing pain shooting up his leg, while above, the face of Garrick appeared at the window glaring down at them.

'We better get going,' Ferguson said.

'He can't walk,' Shannon said, peering down at Anderson's leg. 'Just lie still. We need to set it. Look round for something to make a splint.'

'No time,' Ferguson squealed as two figures shambled around the corner of the house. 'Grab him.'

Ferguson and Shannon scooped Anderson off the ground, their arms under his, as he screamed and cursed from the pain engulfing his leg.

'Hurry, they're coming,' Helen shouted, as they dragged Anderson away from the house.

Every time his foot caught the ground, fiery pain caused him to scream and they barely made it a few yards, before he insisted they stop.

'It's no good,' Helen shouted, they're coming.'

'We can't leave him,' Ferguson said, glancing behind. Despite the shooting pain, Anderson stole a look too. Garrick was there, behind two of the former protestors, all three limping towards them. Not fast, but faster than Anderson could go. The sight was enough to spur him on, though.

'No, you're not bloody going to leave me,' he snorted, trying to hobble under his own steam away from their pursuers. His efforts paid him in agonising pain and he fell.

Shannon and Ferguson scooped him up but Helen started walking back to the house.

'Just keep going,' she said. 'I'll see if I can draw them away.'

'Don't be stupid.' Ferguson pointed down the path. 'The cottage is just down here.'

'Just go,' Helen shouted, waving them away. 'I'll be all right.' She then jogged towards the three infected figures.

'Helen, no!' pleaded Shannon.

It was no good. The young girl had sprinted away, and urging Shannon onwards, Ferguson helped Anderson up and they half-carried him down the track.

The pain was intolerable. His leg felt as if it had been doused in acid. By the time Brophy's cottage appeared at the bottom of a small rise, the game still hanging around his front door and his Land Rover parked alongside the house, Anderson was barely conscious, but he heard Ferguson say, 'Let's put him in the Land Rover. We can get away in that.'

'Where to?' Shannon replied. 'If we go near the road blocks, we're as good as dead. We've nowhere to run to.'

'We can at least get back to the village. Put some space between us and them,' Ferguson insisted

'Not without Helen, we're not,' Shannon said, resolutely. 'We wait here until she gets back.'

Anderson then passed out.

The infection may have taken away their personalities but it hadn't robbed them of all their faculties. When Helen ran back up to distract them and allow the others to escape, she could tell the infected were thinking. The tall one in the police uniform glanced at Anderson, Ferguson and Shannon then back at Helen, and then back at the others again.

At first, she thought her plan wouldn't work, but whatever was left of their minds must have decided her proximity made her an easier target, and they began their pursuit, arms stretched, running headlong toward her.

She recognised two of them. One was Rachel. But she put their names and faces to the back of her mind. They were no longer people, her experience with Graham on the lawn had shown her that.

Helen was no athlete or sprinter, but her pursuer's addled minds and bodies meant they stumbled and staggered as they charged after her, making it easy for her to stay ahead. She made sure not to charge too far ahead. She didn't want them doubling back until she felt certain Anderson, Shannon and Ferguson had made it to the relative safety of Brophy's cottage.

A meadow led from the path, with a small wooded area behind. Helen figured if she led them into the trees, they might get lost. They may have shown some intelligence, but she guessed they'd be easy to fool.

And she wasn't wrong.

As soon as she broke the tree line and glanced behind, she saw one of her former protestor friends walk from tree to tree, as if unsure how to negotiate them. It stopped, cocked its head one side and walked into the trunk, bouncing off with a bewildered look on its decaying face.

Only when the other two barged past did it continue its pursuit, with Helen shouting and taunting them to ensure they continued after her.

She dashed through the trees, stealing the odd glance behind her, until she lost sight of them. After stopping and catching her breath, she decided to double back and find her way to the cottage to meet the others. After climbing a gentle rise, the trees thinned, and she judged that the lane running from the estate would be just beyond the last of them.

Skirting around the edge of the wooded area, to avoid coming into contact with the three infected, she made her way down the rise towards where she thought the track would be.

She'd been right, after clearing a few bushes, she saw it beyond a large, thick oak tree. After glancing behind, just to be sure, she jogged towards the path, but skidded to a halt when a tall figure in a police uniform appeared from behind the tree.

She gasped but didn't scream, not until he lunged at her with his mouth open, teeth bared, a gurgling howl coming from his throat.

Brophy hadn't locked his cottage before venturing over to the laird's house, but Ferguson did, as well as bolting it. He also bolted the back door leading off from the small kitchen. He then helped Shannon lay Anderson on the parlour table. The room contained little else: no TV, no sofa, only hunting gear, hanging game animals and a musty stench.

A cabinet at the far wall contained Brophy's guns. Ferguson pulled out a second a shotgun, a hunting rifle and several boxes of cartridges and ammunition. He loaded them before placing them against the wall, near the door.

Meanwhile, Shannon ripped open the lower half of Anderson's trouser leg. She sucked in her breath. It didn't look good. The bone was protruding through his skin. As she touched his leg, Anderson came to, screamed, half sat up, and then collapsed back on to the table.

'This might be useful,' Ferguson said, picking up an odd-looking walking stick. The end tapered to a near point and a handle that folded out into a sort of seat. She presumed you could stick it in the ground and sit down. Must have been ideal for stalking deer. Useless for making a splint.

'He won't be able to move unless I reset his leg,' she said, as Anderson's head lolled left and right. 'Look round for anything we can use as a dressing. Check the bathroom. See if there is a first aid kit.'

Ferguson placed the walking stick against the table and disappeared. Shannon followed his footsteps as the constable rummaged around up the stairs. A few moments later, he reappeared. 'Nothing in the bathroom.'

Shannon looked around the parlour. 'See if you can break that chair,' she said. 'I might be able to use one of the legs as a splint.' As Ferguson did as she asked, Shannon pulled off her shirt and ripped it into strips.

'You're going to have to hold him down,' she said, wearing nothing but her bra.

Ferguson stared at her, his mouth open.

'Now!' she said, snapping him from his daydream.

He pinned Anderson's shoulders to the table, but the inspector opened his eyes. 'Wait ...' he croaked. 'Is there any booze in the house?'

Ferguson looked around the parlour. A couple of whisky miniatures sat on a dresser. He grabbed them, opened them up and one by one, tipped them into Anderson's mouth while supporting the man's neck.

'You might want to bite down on this,' Shannon said, picking up a wooden spoon left lying by the sink.

Anderson nodded. Whisky dripped down his chin. His eyes were wide. Frightened. But he did as he was told, biting down on the spoon.

Shannon then went to work.

Held down by Ferguson, Anderson's body squirmed and his teeth clenched tight on the wooden spoon as she pulled at his leg. Then it clicked into place. His eyes bulged from their sockets, he muffled a scream, and then he slumped out cold.

'He needs stitches,' Shannon said, as she applied the dressings and splint. 'And antibiotics. This wound will fester without them. And he'll need some painkillers when he comes round. Strong ones.'

'Where we going to get all that?' Ferguson said. 'The nearest pharmacy is outside the road blocks.'

Wiping sweat from her forehead, she stepped away from the table. She had done all she could. 'We have some at the research centre. I'll be able to make a proper splint there too.'

Ferguson was about to say something, but the front door rattled, as if somebody was pushing against it.

He snatched up the shotgun and approached.

'It's me,' hissed a voice through the woodwork. It was Helen. 'I think I've lost them.'

Ferguson and Shannon exhaled loudly before letting her in.

Chapter Thirty-Three

'He's coming round,' Anderson heard a voice say.

His eyes flickered open and he saw three blurry figures looking down at him. The pain in his leg had eased. Rather than fiery agony, it was now a dull, relentless throb. Until he tried to sit up, and then it stabbed at him.

'Lie still,' Shannon said. 'You need to rest as much as you can.'

'How long have I been ...' His voice cracked as he spoke. An odd-looking walking stick lay by his side and he felt a cold draft on his leg. Looking down he saw his trousers ripped off at the knee and a hastily made splint bandaged to his leg.

'Most the day,' Ferguson said. 'You had us worried.'

'Didn't know you cared.' Anderson coughed. He needed a cigarette. His hands patted at his jacket and he pulled out his tobacco. He then remembered what happened to Jennings and he uttered his name, mournfully.

'Here, let me,' Helen said, taking the *Golden Virginia*. 'I'm really sorry about your friend. He seemed like a nice guy.'

'He was,' Anderson said as she rolled him a smoke.

Jennings was a good, clean cut and decent cop. He didn't deserve what happened to him. Anderson could only imagine what it would be like to be ripped apart by those diseased and cannibalistic creatures.

Helen placed the cigarette in his mouth and rummaged around in his pocket for his lighter. 'What happened to you,' he asked, noticing her sweater was ripped.

'I caught it on a tree when I was running away from those ... those—what exactly are they?' She appealed to Shannon and Ferguson.

'Zombies,' Ferguson said. 'Like in that film ... Night of the Living—what's it.'

Shannon scowled at him. 'They are nothing of the sort. They have contracted a degenerative disease. A virus. They are not the walking dead.'

'They seem to be working together?' Ferguson said. 'How is that possible?'

Shannon shrugged. 'I don't know. Maybe it is part of the disease's design. We are dealing with a man-made biological organism, after all.'

'Whatever they are, there's no sign of them.' Ferguson said, peering out the window. The light was fading outside.

'So, what are going to do? Just wait it out here?' Helen asked.

'What else can we do?' Ferguson said. 'We're trapped in the area, remember? Why don't you go and put the kettle on.' He pointed at the kitchenette leading from the parlour. 'I'm sure we could all do with a cuppa.'

Helen filled the kettle in the kitchen then returned a moment later. 'Can I borrow this?' she asked, removing Anderson's lighter from the parlour table. 'Need it for the gas.'

He nodded and waved her away, wincing as his leg throbbed. Shannon removed the cigarette from his mouth and looked down at him, pulling his eyelid wide and peering at his pupil. Her face was taut, serious. 'I need to get to Paradise Woods and get some medical supplies.'

'We'll all go,' Ferguson said. 'I'm sure the keys to the Land Rover will be around here somewhere.'

'He can't be moved,' Shannon said, peering at Anderson's leg.

'I'm not dead yet,' Anderson snapped.

'You're not going on your own,' Ferguson added. He started rummaging around in the parlour, until something rustled outside.

'What was that?' Helen asked, returning from the kitchenette.

Ferguson scooped up his shotgun and glanced left and right at the window. 'Might have been the wind, or a wild animal or something.'

His words did little to comfort any of them. Ferguson checked the front door. It was thick and heavy and the bolts were of a decent size. Even so, he glanced at the stricken Anderson on the parlour table.

'Sorry about this, Inspector.' He grabbed the edge of the table and gestured for Helen to help. The pair slid the table against the door.

'What the bloody hell am I, a human barricade?' Anderson shouted as the table hit the door, inches from his feet.

'Shhh,' Ferguson said, returning to the window.

Nobody spoke. Everybody listened.

'There,' Shannon whispered. 'Did you hear that?'

Something else rustled.

Anderson saw Ferguson pick up a hunting rifle propped against the wall. The constable loaded it and handed the gun to Shannon.

'I can't use that thing,' she whispered.

'Just hold it hard at your shoulder and reload by pulling the bolt back,' Ferguson said, shoving the rifle at Shannon.

Then they all listened intently.

Until the kettle whistled unceremoniously from the kitchen. All their heads shot in its direction and the sounds outside became more animated.

'It's them,' Helen said, fear causing her voice to squeak.

A loud thump at the door jolted the parlour table.

Anderson screamed.

He screamed again as it thumped again.

Ferguson aimed his shotgun at the front door and waved the others back. 'Keep away from it,' he whispered.

'What about me?' Anderson said, squirming beneath the barrel of Ferguson's raised gun and staring at the door at his feet. He scrambled back slightly, and saw Shannon pointing the rifle dangerously in his direction. 'Watch what the bloody hell you are doing with that thing!'

She lowered the gun, and everybody froze.

Other than the whistling kettle in the kitchen, all was silent.

They stood, breaths held, watching the door.

Nothing.

Seconds past.

Then a minute.

'I think they've gone,' Helen whispered.

The three figures above Anderson leaned towards the door as they listened for activity outside.

They heard nothing.

Until the back door imploded.

Chapter Thirty-Four

Garrick was the first to burst in. He lumbered into the kitchen and wavered, his head slowly surveying the inside of Brophy's cottage until he spotted the four people in the parlour. Then two others appeared shortly after.

A deafening bang followed as Ferguson let off a shot, followed by another. One of the infected fell backwards against the stove, a large hole in his chest, while smoke from the shotgun cartridges filled the room with a thick fug.

Through it, Garrick and the other infected protestor, a girl, continued their shambling advance towards Shannon and the other, unperturbed by the gunfire.

'The rifle, quick,' Ferguson said.

Shannon fumbled it as she passed it to him, and it fell, while Garrick and the protestor advanced.

'Do something,' Anderson yelled, helpless on the table.

'Wait!' shouted Helen as Ferguson scooped up the rifle. 'Don't fire. I smell gas.'

She was right. A shotgun pellet must have pierced the gas pipe at the stove because the unmistakable smell of it cut through the acrid stench of gunpowder.

'The table, move it,' Ferguson yelled, throwing the rifle at the two advancing beings. He and Shannon slid the table back and fumbled at the bolts on the door.

Then Anderson screamed.

Shannon looked back to see Garrick tugging on Anderson's bad leg, pulling him off the table.

Helen, standing motionless, horrified, awoke from her terror and scooped up the walking stick on the table. She smashed it against Garrick's head. The superintendent's skull cracked. He released Anderson and staggered back in to the infected girl.

'Quickly,' Helen shouted, passing Anderson the walking stick and helping him haul himself off the table.

The smell of gas had intensified. The pipe must have been broken clean through because the room was filling up, and Shannon felt her head spin and go light.

She and Ferguson, both coughing and gagging from the smell, opened the door causing the cold air to rush in, replacing the butane in her lungs. It banged against the table but was open enough that Ferguson could squeeze through. She turned, grabbed Anderson's shoulders and dragged him through the gap in the door.

'Helen, come on,' she shouted, once Anderson was clear.

Helen froze for a moment as Garrick and the protestor eyed her through the now clearing gun smoke and approached.

'Helen!' Shannon repeated. 'Quickly.'

Helen looked at her for a moment then down at her arm, unrolled her sleeve, and revealed a red, inflamed wound. A bite.

Shannon gasped. 'Helen ... please, you might be all right.'

Helen shook her head slowly and took Anderson's lighter out of her pocket.

'No, Helen, don't!' Shannon screamed.

But Helen didn't move, she just stood there until Garrick and the protestor reached out and grabbed her. 'Shannon, go!' she screamed.

They were her last words.

Despite Shannon's protests, Ferguson grabbed hold of her and pulled her away with Anderson, who hobbled from the cottage using the walking stick and swore and cursed with every step.

They were at the Land Rover when the cottage exploded.

Shannon laid motionless, ears ringing. The blast had knocked her to the ground, sucked the breath out of her lungs and scorched the back of her neck. Yet she was alive. So was Ferguson because as debris and burning detritus rained down on them and the Land Rover he rolled to her feet.

Anderson was ominously still.

'Is he alive?' Ferguson asked, after helping Shannon to her feet. At least that what was she thought he had said. She could barely hear above the tinnitus caused by the blast.

Shannon probed at the unconscious inspector. He was breathing, but it was laboured. 'Yes, but we need to get to Paradise Woods, and soon.'

She looked back at the cottage. There wasn't much left. More rubble than building. Flames flickered on the smouldering pile of bricks and thatch and timber. And buried underneath all of it. Helen.

As if reading her thoughts, Ferguson placed a hand on her shoulder and gave it a gentle squeeze. 'She wouldn't have felt anything,' she heard him say. The ringing in her ears blocked out the rest of his words. It didn't matter. Platitudes wouldn't bring her back.

Shannon burst into tears.

Ferguson held her close and she sobbed, but she soon pushed him away. 'We need to go,' she said, looking down at Anderson. 'He'll not make it else.'

Ferguson nodded and helped haul him up by propping his head under Anderson's shoulder. Shannon pulled at one of the backdoors. It was unlocked. The pair slid Anderson in the back seat and Ferguson placed his walking stick in after him.

The Land Rover was parked facing the cottage so Shannon opened the passenger door to get in, Ferguson stopped her, turned her around and held her at arm's length. 'It's over,' he said. 'We're going to be okay.'

She smiled, then realised he had spoken too soon.

A movement in the rubble, some bricks and timber moved. Then a figure stood. A tall figure. Blackened and bloody. An arm missing. Yet it emerged from the wreck of Brophy's cottage as if unharmed.

'Garrick!' Ferguson either whispered the word or Shannon's hearing was still dulled, but she reacted as if he'd bellowed it in her ear.

'He's coming,' she screamed as Garrick trudged out of the smouldering ruins and limped towards them.

She jumped slid over to the driver's side while Ferguson piled in the passenger door behind her, locking it shut as Garrick shambled towards them.

The keys weren't in the ignition or in the side of the door or under the sun visor. As she scrambled around looking for them, Garrick appeared at the passenger door and slapped his only hand against the window.

'Out the way,' Ferguson yelled, pushing Shannon back in her seat and lying across her lap.

'Quickly!' she said, as Garrick slapped the glass again, harder, his disfigured face leering at them.

Ferguson pulled out the ignition cylinder and yanked wires free, twisting them together, seemingly randomly, hoping to hotwire the old vehicle.

'I think you had it then,' Shannon said, as the oil and battery light flickered on the dash. 'Go back.'

Garrick slapped the glass again, repeatedly, each strike louder and harder than the one before, until the glass finally shattered, peppering Shannon in small fragments. She screamed, which caused her ears to pop, and screamed again, when Garrick thrust his hand into the Land Rover.

'I think I've got it,' Ferguson said. The ignition lights flickered on, then off, then on again, then the starter motor sounded.

'Go,' Ferguson shouted, as Garrick's outstretched hand pawed at his thigh.

With a grind of metal against metal, Shannon put the Land Rover in reverse. Garrick's hand disappeared from the cabin as they backed away to the track.

She struggled to get the Land Rover into first gear, hearing nothing but grinding metal as she shoved the lever forward.

'He's coming,' Ferguson yelled, as Garrick lumbered towards them.

As he arrived on the track and shambled towards them, Shannon felt the satisfying clunk of two cogs meshing. Garrick was right in front of them, his one arm outstretched.

'This is for Helen,' Shannon said, lifting the clutch and flooring the accelerator.

When the Land Rover hit him, Garrick got caught in the bull bar at the front. He pawed at the bonnet as Shannon shoved the gear lever into second. The jolt freed him and he slipped free.

A bounce under both axles told her that he'd not be a problem anymore.

Ferguson flicked the headlights on, and Shannon found third, and they drove steadily but quickly away.

Chapter Thirty-Five

Anderson stirred and realised he was being dragged out of a vehicle. He felt deathly. Hot, cold, shaky. His ears rang and his leg no longer pounded but felt numb. He knew that wasn't a good sign.

'Here, grab this,' he heard Shannon say. He felt the handle of the walking stick being thrust in his hand.

'Where are we?' he asked, his vision a blur.

'Paradise Woods. The research centre,' Ferguson's voice said. He then felt the constable prop his head under his arms.

'I'll go open up,' Shannon said. 'Bring him in. Lie him in the couch in reception and I'll get the medical supplies.'

It took a long time to hobble the few yards from the Land Rover to the front door, and just as long to make the four or five yards to the sofa in reception.

The fluorescent lights burned Anderson's eyes, so he squinted to shield them.

'What happened?' he asked, as Ferguson lowered him to the sofa, propping the walking stick against the wall.

'It's over,' he said. 'They're all dead.'

Anderson's vision was blurry, but he knew there was only one Ferguson with him. 'The ... girl?'

Ferguson breathed deep. 'She saved us all. Now lie still. Dr Long will be along to sort you out. You'll be right as rain before you know it.'

'I couldn't half do with a fag,' Anderson said.

'Tough,' Ferguson said.

Anderson didn't know how long passed as he seemed to slip in and out of consciousness, but soon a blurred figure appeared over Ferguson's shoulder.

He presumed it was Shannon with the medical supplies.

He was wrong.

He heard a scream, and opened his eyes wider, his vision clear enough to see somebody's jaws clamped around Ferguson's throat. Anderson couldn't move and watched as blood gushed from Ferguson, the young constable's leg twitched as teeth bit through nerves, sinew and arteries. Then Ferguson stopped squirming and he slumped to the floor.

His assailant straightened and looked down at Anderson.

Cunningham.

Blood covered her face. Vacant eyes stared from deep sockets. Hissing and gurgling came from her throat. Then she lunged at him. Her nails like talons as they bore down on his face.

But they never reached him.

Cunningham suddenly stood rod straight, arched her back, and made a nasty, gurgling sound.

Something protruded from her chest. A spike of some sort.

She slumped to the ground. Anderson's walking stick jutted out her back like a corner flag on a football pitch. Anderson looked up and smiled at the sight of Shannon Long.

Then blackness.

Anderson awoke in a morphinic haze. He didn't know where he was and it took him a while to comprehend his surroundings. The room danced around him. His head spun. He knew by the flock wallpaper and the fact he was on a sofa he wasn't in a hospital. The room looked vaguely familiar, as did the person entering it.

'Oh, you're awake.' Shannon peered into his eyes and gave a couple of satisfied grunts. She then shoved a thermometer into his mouth. A moment later, she took it out, studied it and nodded approvingly as she shook it. 'Your fever's gone,' she said.

Anderson tried to sit up. A tugging on his arm and a stiffness in his leg prevented it.

'Might as well disconnect this,' Shannon said, sliding out a cannular drip from his arm. 'How's the leg?'

Anderson looked down to see his leg in a cast resting on two cushions. 'It itches.'

'That's a good sign. Means it is on the mend. I half-feared you might lose it.'

Under the blanket he realised he wore nothing but his vest and boxer shorts. He pulled the blanket coyly over his chest. 'How long have we been here?'

'Four days,' she said, moving to the curtain. She pulled it open. 'Everybody's back. I guess that means it's all over.'

He sat up. He could hear activity outside. Brophy's walking stick was beside the bed. He reached for it.

'Hey, lie still,' Shannon said.

He pushed her aside. 'I've spent enough time on my back,' he snapped.

She scowled but helped him up. As he stood, he winced as the blood rushed down his leg causing it to throb, but he ignored it and with Shannon's help hobbled to the window.

Under a bright autumnal morning, people milled about the square outside. A van and a group of workmen stood around the

Gough Arms erecting ladders and carrying building supplies into the burned building. The local people had gathered in groups to watch, chatting, laughing, relieved to be home.

'Look at them. Oblivious,' Anderson said.

'I guess we're the only two people who really know what's gone on here,' Shannon said, her voice croaked a little.

'I take it Ferguson didn't ...'

She shook her head solemnly.

Anderson stared back out the window. 'It's as if nothing has happened.'

A voice sounded behind them. It was English and familiar. 'That's because nothing did happen.'

Anderson turned to see the man with the cigarette holder smiling at them. 'Who the hell let you in?' Anderson said.

The man smiled. 'Nice to see you on your feet and in good humour.'

Anderson glared at him. 'You're lucky I'm half-cut with morphine otherwise I'd bloody brain you.' He raised his walking stick and nearly toppled over.

'Steady,' Shannon said, helping Anderson back to the sofa.

The Englishman waved his cigarette holder. 'There's no need to be like that, old boy. I came to say thank you.'

'For what?' snapped Anderson. 'Covering your arse? Or covering up this fiasco?'

'Both,' the man said, no longer smiling. 'And for what it's worth, I'm sorry. You'll be pleased to know Project Saevio has been cancelled. This incident has led to a complete rethink on biological programmes.'

'Doesn't bring back Jennings or the others, does it?' Anderson said.

The man offered a thin smile. 'I'm sorry about your partner, truly I am. But it is all over now, and for that, we have you to thank. Both of you.' He smiled at Shannon. 'Now Paradise Woods has been closed, you'll be wanting employment. I'm sure we can arrange something in your field.' He handed her a business card. 'Just call me. It's the least we can do.'

'No, the least you can do is piss off and crawl back under that stone you came from,' Anderson snapped.

The man shrugged. 'I take it you don't want a lift back to Inverness then? I thought you'd be keen to leave this place.'

'I'd rather crawl,' Anderson said.

The man shrugged and turned to leave.

'Wait,' Anderson said. 'You can at least give me one of your fags before you go.'

The End

By the Same Author

Murder Laid Bare

A Hope and Carver Mystery

When a body is discovered on a nudist beach, the struggling seaside resort of Milhaven is thrust into the media spotlight. Fortunately, Inspector Hope has just arrived at the sleepy coastal town, much to the annoyance of brassy Detective Sergeant Elaine Carver.

Forced to work together, the temperamental Carver and rather prudish Hope delve into the dead man's past and uncover a darker side to the goings on at the seemingly innocent nudist resort.

Both Hope and Carver are themselves hiding dark secrets and have far more in common than they think. The investigation soon leads them on a path of self-discovery where they have to face their inner demons as they uncover the seedier side to middle class suburbia.

Death of an Angel

A Hope and Carver Mystery

When Milhaven's annual biker event culminates in a shooting, Hope and Carver are called to investigate. But with Carver struggling to juggle work with her personal life, and the pair facing nothing but a wall of silence, even she doubts that they can get a result this time.

As the collateral damage from the shooting escalates, and biker gangs clash in the once peaceful seaside resort, a taskforce prepares to take over the investigation, leaving Hope and Carver under pressure to find the culprit. But even if they can solve the case, Carver realizes it could all be too late for Milhaven, which may never be the same again.

ROGUES

They say elephants never forget...

Mercenary Frank Humbolt takes on one last job: to capture a rebel leader deep in the heart of Africa. Only he hasn't anticipated the local wildlife.

A group of rogue elephants, seemingly angered by years of poaching, are wreaking revenge and bringing wanton destruction to the region. Humbolt and his team soon find themselves hunted by both men and beasts.

To get out alive, Humbolt has to rely on a young zoologist for help, while the fate of an entire nation hinges on his very survival.

About The Author

Robert Forrester is a writer and journalist based in Birmingham, United Kingdom. He is the author of the Inspector Anderson Mysteries, Hope and Carver Mystereies and the thriller Rogues.

15145187R00361

Printed in Great Britain
by Amazon.co.uk, Ltd.,
Marston Gate.